TH'
B'

EASTSIDE

A NOVEL

EASTSIDE

A NOVEL

CALEB ALEXANDER

SBI

STREBOR BOOKS

NEW YORK LONDON TORONTO SYDNEY

Strebor Books
P.O. Box 6505
Largo, MD 20792
http://www.streborbooks.com

This book is a work of fiction. Names, characters, places and incidents are products of
the author's imagination or are used fictitiously. Any resemblance to actual events or
locales or persons, living or dead, is entirely coincidental.

ISBN-13 978-1-59309-120-0
ISBN-10   1-59309-120-6
LCCN 2007923506

First Strebor Books trade paperback edition July 2007

Cover design: www.mariondesigns.com

10 9 8 7 6 5 4 3 2 1

Manufactured in the United States of America

For information regarding special discounts for bulk purchases,
please contact Simon & Schuster Special Sales at 1-800-456-6798
or business@simonandschuster.com

This novel is dedicated to the Mothers
and to the Survivors

IN MEMORY OF
CHAD L. DAVIS
A righteous soldier, who lost his life
in an unrighteous war.

ACKNOWLEDGMENTS

First and foremost I want to thank the Almighty Creator. It would take an entire novel for me to list all of the blessings that have been bestowed upon me. I know that it was during some of the darkest moments of my life, that He carried me. I am a living witness to His kindness, forgiveness, charity, and compassion. He's real, and His mercy and greatness is bottomless.

I want to thank my brother Theron, for giving me my imagination. He helped to develop and foster my creativity. He has an imagination and wit that is uncanny. If he ever picks up a pen and starts writing, the world is in for a treat. I want to thank my grandmother, Lillie. There are no words that could even begin to convey my feelings there. She is my heart. I want to acknowledge my wife, Jennifer; my sons, Curtis and Caleb; and my daughter, Cheyenne. My mother, Gwen; and my dad, Charles.

I want to say thank you to Zane, and Charmaine, and to the best agent in the world, Tracy Sherrod. Big ups to Keith Saunders for the cover design. Thanks to Shayla Cobb for her typing skills.

Shout out to: Stacey Wynn, Cornell Cleaver, Syidah Shaheed, Omar, Maleek, Momma Robinson, Big Lou (Sheffield), Greg Palmer, Wayman Goodley, Bart, Twin, Fresh Reggie (Williams), Magic, Stag, Unc, Tuck, Tyrus Foster, Charles Deese, Mo-Mo (Elmo Johnson), JP (James Peters), Terance Spellmon, Quentin Henry, Wynell, Stephen, Theron Duncan, Edward Brown, Timmy, Skibo (Dashawn Batts), Chrissy Barefield, Baby Ray Mathis, Dimebox, Charlie Hustle, Buggy (Albert Gistard), Shawn Butler, Smoke (Keith Theus), Ron Johnson, Ced Quigley, JR, Keith Franklin, Black, Jesse Brooks, Fred and Sharonda Carter, Tyshea Wagner,

Julon, Jarveon, Low Life (Stacey Robinson), Nick Clay, Nikki Smith, Monekka Smith, Jo Ann Smith, Dwayne Pleasant, Ernie and Valerie LaCour, Mike LaCour , Brian Green, JV Green, Can't Get Right, Kenneth Macracken, Shawn Macracken, Staci Denise, Erin, Polly, Cibon, Greg, El ijah, Kennedy, Arboni, Janice, Devean, Kelvin, Michelle Monciaviaz, Nicole Hood, Teke Beck, Jason, Pat, Joe Linton, Quick (Terry Williams), Grave Digger (Donnell), Billy Pen, Anthony Frisco, Tony and Olga Owens, Dana, Deon, Ronnie, Marcus, Thomas, Lisa, Mildred, Betty, Matthew, Bubba, Marshall Simmons, Rene Simmons, Tony, Daphane, Briana, Ebony, Belinda, Avante, Amaya, Audrey, Darlene, Jimmy, Keanna, Deandre, Jennae, Juwan, Gail, Rodney, Ivory, Sylvia, Uncle Jerry, Aunt Libby, Aunt Joyce, Cookie, Pam, Uncle Richard, Uncle Thomas, Uncle Billy, Aunt Fanny, Thad, Comfort, Big Cibon, Trisha, Anna, Gloria, the Smith Family, the Spellmon Family, the Williams Family, the Lacour Family, the Washington Family, the Small Family, the Luna Family, the Gafford Family, the Small Family, the Stephens Family, the Hearn Family, the James Family, the Bailey Family, the Sheffield Family, the Dawson Family, the Childs Family, the Huff Family, the Owens Family, the Shaheed Family, the Moorman Family, the Zumalt Family, the Hernandez Family, the Gordon Family, the Capprietta Family.

Those of you who I forgot to mention, it was not on purpose. Please forgive me. I owe so much to so many, and I sincerely thank you all for being there for me all of these years

FOREWORD

This is the book *Eastside*. It is an extremely accurate and violent portrayal of inner-city life, particularly the gang warfare that accompanies it. *This book is not for the faint of heart.*

I chose to set this book in the Eastside of San Antonio, Texas, for several reasons. One, San Antonio typifies the average American city; and two, I am intimately familiar with the city.

The characters in the book run the gamut. They are varied and rich, as this is a character-oriented book. The language is graphic, and there is a lot of slang. These are necessary in order for me to properly convey the feelings of the characters, and to instill a genuine feeling of authenticity within the book.

When you read this book, do not do so from a purely entertainment aspect, but also view it as an informational tool. Let it be your window into another world, a world that is still very much in existence today, although this book is set in the early nineties.

In the end, I hope that you are left shocked. I hope that this book shocks you into picking up the telephone, calling your local Big Brother or Big Sister program, and volunteering.

The story is about two years in the life of a young man named Travon. It is about the things he endures, the people he meets, the family that supports him, and the obstacle he must overcome on his journey toward manhood. There are Travons in every major city in America, as well as Cooneys, Little Fades, Dejuans, Mrs. Davises, Tamikas, and Shielas.

The characters you will come to know in this book will touch on every emotion. You will laugh with them, you will cry with them, you will cheer, you will hate, and you will love. Some who you thought were good, will ultimately show themselves to be evil, while those thought to be evil incarnate will ultimately find redemption for themselves and others. However, none of the characters in this book are innocent, as they are all human, and subject to all the fallibilities and frailties that their humanity entails. A common theme prevalent throughout this book is the wrong execution of the right idea. As we all know, the road to hell is paved with good intentions.

I wish that I could tell you to enjoy your reading, but deep down, I do not want you to. I want you to be confused, and upset, and disturbed once the last page has been turned. I want you to question what was said, what was not done, and in the end, ask what *needs* to be done.

I thank you sincerely for your time and patience, and for your support. And now, I would like to welcome you to the...

Eastside.

The San Antonio Police Department recorded 1,262
drive-by shootings in 1993. It was the first year that the
department began compiling the statistics. It was also the year
that San Antonio officially became known as the capital
of the drive-by shooting.

Those of us who lived on the city's eastside at the time,
know that 1992 and 1991 were even worse.

"The responsibility of a writer is to excavate the experience of the people who produced him."
— *James Baldwin*

CHAPTER ONE

Travon smacked his lips. "Man, you're stupid."

"Why?" Justin asked, shifting his gaze toward Travon. "Just because your brother got killed don't mean I will. Besides, it's for the hood."

Travon exhaled, and lowered his head. "I told my brother that he was stupid too, and now he's dead."

The boys continued around the side of the old red-brick school building toward the back. Staring at the ground, Justin haphazardly kicked at gravel spread along the ground beneath his feet.

"Yeah, Tre, but at least Too-Low went out like a soldier," he replied.

They were headed behind the middle school to a pair of old wooden green bleachers that sat across the well-worn football field. They could see the others standing just in front of the peeling bleachers waiting for them. Travon shifted his gaze from the waiting boys back to Justin. He started to speak, but Justin interrupted him.

"Tre, what's up with you?" Justin asked. "You ain't got no love for the hood? Your brother was down; he was a straight-up G. Don't you wanna be like that? Making everybody bar you and catch out when you step on the scene?"

Travon stared at Justin in silence. His silence seemed to only anger his friend more.

"I know that you're still trippin' over your brother getting killed, but he'd want you to ride for the hood!" Justin shouted. "He'd want you to be down!"

Travon halted in mid-step, and stared at Justin coldly. "How do you figure that?"

Like a precious family heirloom, Travon considered his brother, his brother's thoughts and wishes, as well as his memory, to be sacred. They were his and his alone.

Justin paused to formulate his reply, but one of the waiting boys shouted. "Y'all lil' niggaz hurry the fuck up! We ain't got all muthafuckin' day!"

Now filled with even more nervous anxiety, Travon and Justin quickly ended their conversation and hurriedly approached the waiting group. A tall, slender, shirtless boy stepped to the forefront. His torso was heavily illustrated with various tattoos and brandings, while his body was draped in gold jewelry, glimmering brilliantly in the bright South Texas sun.

"So, y'all lil' niggaz wanna get down, huh?" the shirtless boy asked.

Another boy anxiously stepped forward. "Say, Dejuan, let me put 'em on the hood!"

Dejuan, the first boy, folded his arms and nodded.

Travon walked his eyes across all of the boys present. There were six of them, all adorned with large expensive gold necklaces, watches, bracelets, and earrings, and all of them had gold caps covering their teeth. They were members of the notorious Wheatley Courts Gangsters, or WCGs for short. The WCGs were one of the most violent drug gangs in the State of Texas. Their ruthlessness and brutality was legendary.

Travon nervously examined the boys one by one. Those who were not shirtless were clad in burnt-orange University of Texas T-shirts. Burnt orange was the gang's colors, and the University of Texas symbol was their adopted motif. It stood for the location of their home, the Wheatley Courts. It was their municipality, their ruthless domain, their merciless world. It was a place where their will was law, and where all those who disobeyed were sentenced to death.

The Wheatley Courts was a low-income housing project where drugs and violence were the rule, and not the exception. It was also a place where many more than just a few of its occupants had made millions in their professions as street pharmacists. Perhaps worst of all, the Courts were home to the WCGs, a gang of ballers, and stone-cold murderers.

Travon shifted his gaze to his left; Justin had begun to remove his T-shirt. He looked back at the group of boys, to find that several of them were removing their shirts and jewelry as well. The festivities were about to begin.

"Let me whip these lil' niggaz onto the hood!" Tech Nine asked Dejuan again.

Without waiting for a response, Tech Nine walked away from the group and onto the football field, where he was quickly joined by Quentin, Lil C, and T-Stew. Once out on the field, the boys turned and waited for Justin.

Hesitantly, Justin made his way to where Tech Nine was waiting patiently and cracking his knuckles. Once Justin came within striking distance, Tech Nine swung wildly at him. The blow slammed into Justin's face.

"Muthafucka!" Justin shouted. He quickly charged Tech Nine and tackled him. Both boys hit the ground hard.

Lil C approached from the side and kicked Justin in his ribs. Justin cried out and rolled over onto his side. Justin tried to lift himself from off the ground, only to be met by a fist from Quentin. Justin grabbed his bloody nose.

"Wheatley Courts Gangstas, you punk-ass bitch!" Tech Nine shouted, as he charged Justin. "This is WCG, nigga!"

Lil C delivered a kick to Justin's back, just as Quentin swung at Justin again.

"Get that muthafucka!" Dejuan shouted from the sidelines.

Justin was able to roll away from Tech Nine's lunge, but had to take another blow from Quentin. He was able to make it to his feet just in time to receive another punch from Lil C. Although tired and out of breath, Justin was able to sustain the blow and remain standing.

"WCG for life!" Quentin shouted, advancing again.

Lil C swung at Justin again and missed. Justin, however, was unable to dodge a kick from Tech Nine. It landed directly in his groin.

Justin stumbled back, and Tech Nine kicked again, this time missing Justin and striking Lil C.

"My bad, man!" Tech Nine shouted. "I was trying to kick that little muthafucka!"

"Shit! Aw, fuck!" Lil C slowly descended to the ground while clutching his groin.

This brief intermission gave Justin time to recover and go on the offensive. He quickly dropped to one knee and punched Quentin in his groin, just as Quentin was about to swing at him.

"Aaaaaargh, shit! Punk muthafucka!" Quentin fell to the ground clutching his crotch.

Tech Nine maneuvered behind Justin, and threw a hard punch to the back of his head.

"Yeah, muthafucka, this is Wheatley Courts on mines!" Tech Nine shouted.

Justin rose, stumbled forward, and tripped over Quentin's leg. Tired, he hit the ground hard; this time, he could not find the energy to get back up. Tech Nine hurriedly approached and began kicking.

Justin, unable to move, curled into a ball and waited for the pain to be over.

"Punk muthafucka, fight back!" Tech Nine continued to kick brutally. He kicked Justin until he became tired, and retreated to where the others were standing.

Dejuan turned to Tech Nine. "Do you think that's enough?" he asked laughingly.

Tech Nine, sweating profusely, swallowed hard before answering. "I think he can get down. I think he's got enough nuts." He shifted his eyes to Travon. "You lucky I'm tired today, but tomorrow, I'm going to enjoy putting hands on you."

Travon's heart slowed to a semi-normal pace once he realized that they would not be jumping on him today. He quickly walked to where Justin was lying curled in a ball on the ground. Travon dropped down to his knees beside his friend.

"Justin, are you all right?" Travon asked.

No answer.

"Justin." Travon grabbed Justin's shoulder and shook it gently. "Justin."

"Yeah, I'm cool," Justin answered weakly.

"Leave him alone, he's all right!" shouted Lil C, who was slowly rising to his feet again.

Tech Nine shifted his eyes toward his friend. "Say, C, are you all right?"

"Yeah, muthafucka," Lil C answered. "Just watch where in the fuck you kicking next time."

Justin slowly uncurled, and pain shot through his body as he tried to brace himself to stand. Travon helped his friend off the ground.

"Yeah, you WCG now, baby!" T-Stew shouted.

Quentin, Tech Nine, T-Stew, and Dejuan quickly surrounded Justin.

"You WCG for life now, baby!" exclaimed Dejuan.

"Gimme some love, homie!" Tech Nine shouted.

"It's all about that WCG!" Justin declared weakly.

"Yeah!" T-Stew shouted. He extended his right arm into the air and made a *W* by crossing his two middle fingers. Doing the same with his left arm, he cupped his hand and formed the letter *C*.

"Wheatley Courts, baby!" Lil C shouted, as he and Justin embraced.

"Wheatley Courts!" T-Stew repeated, maneuvering into position for his embrace.

Dejuan swaggered away from the group, over to a pile of T-shirts lying on the ground. He lifted up a burnt-orange University of Texas T-shirt and examined it. On the front of the shirt rested a large white *T*. On the back of the shirt, printed in Old English script were the words *Wheatley Courts for Life*. Dejuan turned and walked back to where the boys were waiting, and Travon watched in fear, disbelief, and a slight bit of jealous envy as Justin was given Dejuan's very own Texas T-shirt to put on.

CHAPTER TWO

Weeks Later

Tonight, like every other night since his brother's death, Travon dreamt of him. Sweating profusely in the blistering South Texas heat, he tossed and turned as his last conversation with his brother was replayed inside his head.

"How do you like these Jordans, Tre?" Too-Low asked.

"They're pretty clean." Travon nodded. "Are you gonna let me sport 'em?"

Too-Low smiled at his younger brother. "I gotta stay on the cuts all night, 'cause tomorrow's the first. If I make enough ends, I'll take you to the mall and get you some."

"Cool!"

"So, how are your grades in school?" Too-Low asked.

"They're all right."

"All right? They need to be better than just all right." Too-Low leaned forward and jabbed his finger into Travon's chest. "You better not be fuckin' up in school!"

"I'm not." Travon frowned. "My grades are okay."

"I'll tell you what," Too-Low told him. "I'll spring for some fresh gear for school this fall, if you do well the rest of this year."

"Put me down, and I can buy my own shit," Travon replied.

Too-Low slapped Travon across the back of his head.

"Fuck!" Travon shot a venomous glance toward his bother. "What the hell was that for?"

Too-Low jabbed his finger into his younger brother's face. "Tre, if I catch you anywhere near this shit, I'ma put a foot in your ass! Do you hear me?"

"You're doing it, so why can't I?" Travon replied. "You won't even let me get down with the hood! That shit ain't fair, Too-Low!"

Too-Low kicked a crushed beer can that was lying on the ground near his foot, sending it tumbling noisily across the roughly paved street.

"Fuck this shit, Tre!" Too-Low shouted, once he had turned back toward his brother. "I'm doing this shit so you don't have to! And I already made it clear to everybody that I'll kill anybody who puts you on the hood, and everybody who was there watching!"

"Everybody else is down!" Travon protested.

"Tre, you better not ever join a gang, or pick up any kind of dope. Do you hear me?"

Travon shifted his eyes away from his brother, to a distant spot down the dark and empty street.

Too-Low grabbed Tre by his arm and shook him violently. "I said do you hear me?"

"Yeah, yeah, I hear you!" Travon yanked his arm away from his brother and again stared down the dark, trash-strewn street. All of his friends were joining, and it wasn't fair that he wasn't allowed to. All the girls in school were falling all over the guys who had joined. He would almost kill to be able to wear burnt orange to school.

"This shit is dangerous," Too-Low added. "The first chance I get, I'm getting us the hell outta these fuckin' courts!" When he saw the moisture welling in his younger brother's eyes, Too-Low decided that he had been a little too harsh. He decided to make up for it.

"Here." He reached beneath his burnt-orange University of Texas T-shirt and pulled out his nine-millimeter Beretta handgun. He handed the cold, steel, death black weapon to Travon. "Take this home and put it under my mattress. Go straight home with it, Tre. And don't be fuckin' 'round with it either."

Travon lifted the weapon into the air and examined it. After a few seconds, he turned back toward his brother. "You ain't gonna need this tonight?"

Too-Low shook his head. "No. Lil Anthony, Pop, and Tech Nine are on their way. We all gonna stay down tonight. I know that them fools is strapped, so I don't need to be. 'Sides, if one time runs up on us tonight, I ain't trying to catch a pistol case."

Travon slid the gun into his pants and pulled his shirt down over it. Too-Low reached into his pants pocket and pulled out a wad of rolled-up bills. He counted out fifteen hundred dollars and handed it to Travon.

"Tonight, when Momma goes to sleep, put four hundred dollars in her purse. Don't let her catch you. If she asks you in the morning where it came from, just tell her that you don't know. You can keep a hundred for yourself, so that leaves a thousand. Put the G under my mattress, along with the strap."

"All right, Too-Low, thanks!" Travon extended his fist and gave his brother some dap. "Good looking."

Too-Low roughly rubbed his hand over his brother's head, messing up his waves. Travon smiled, ducked away, and turned and headed for home. Of course on the way to his apartment, he would have to stop by Justin's and show off his brother's gun.

Once out of his brother's sight, Travon turned and made a beeline for Justin's apartment. He cut across the alley, then through the playground, taking the shortcut to his friend's apartment. He could faintly make out the sound of deep bass notes resonating from a stereo system. The notes grew progressively louder until finally a dark blue Hyundai came into view and passed by on the street just in front of him, silencing its stereo system. Travon watched from the shadows as the car slowed and turned the corner. Moments later he heard the sound of semi-automatic weapon fire crashing through the midnight silence, and quickly decided that he had better head for home.

Once safely inside his apartment, Travon did as his brother had instructed, and then retired to his bedroom. After awhile, he heard a knock at the front door, which was followed by his mother's screams.

Travon bolted up from his bed. His bare chest heaved up and down, his breathing was hard and labored. Travon wiped away the heavy beads of perspiration from his face, and then tried to focus his eyes. A slow glance around his balmy dark room quickly confirmed what he had suspected. He had, once again, suffered a nightmare.

Seven a.m.

"Tre! Tre!" his mother called out to him. "Travon! It's time to get up and get ready for school, boy!"

"Shit!" Travon swore under his breath and rubbed his eyes as he slowly pulled himself out of bed, then staggered to his bathroom. After washing his face, brushing his teeth, and taking a piss, he headed back into his bedroom. He had just begun to put his clothes on when his mother appeared at his door.

"Travon, I got breakfast waiting downstairs."

"Momma, what are you doing at home this morning?" Travon asked, rubbing the top of his head.

"I had to change jobs, baby. The company I was working for only want to do home health care now, so they need people with cars. I have to work in a nursing home for right now, at least until I can get us a car. And the only positions the nursing home had open were night ones, so I work at night now," she explained.

Travon stretched his arms and yawned. "Oh, I was just wondering what you were still doing home at this time, that's all."

His mother smiled. "You're not afraid to stay at home by yourself at night, are you?"

Travon frowned. "Naw, I ain't scared a nothing."

Elmira rolled her eyes toward the ceiling and crossed her arms. "All right, bad ass. You just better have your butt in the house by ten o'clock."

Travon dropped his shirt. "What?"

She uncrossed her arms. "You heard me."

"I can't even sit on the porch?" he asked.

Elmira stepped into the bedroom and caressed her son's chin. "Tre, you know what happened to your brother. So just bear with me for a little while, okay?"

Travon shifted his gaze to the floor and nodded. He could never forget what happened to his brother. He could never forget the night that his life changed forever.

"Okay," he said softly.

Elmira turned and started for the door. "Now come on downstairs and eat you some breakfast." Quickly, she whirled back toward her son. "Speaking of food, I haven't seen Justin in a few weeks. Where is he?"

"Well, he um, he got himself some new friends."

Elmira tilted her head to the side. "Tre, look at me, and don't lie to me. You and Justin were as thick as thieves, and now he don't even come around anymore?" She placed her hand upon her hip. "What happened?"

"Uh, nothing, Momma. We just don't kick it that much anymore."

"I was born at night, but not last night," Elmira replied. "Justin done joined that damn gang, ain't he?"

Travon's gaze fell away from his mother. "Well, I guess. I don't know, Momma."

"Tre, baby, just stay away from them and find you some new friends. Baby, just as soon as things get better, we'll get the hell outta this place. It's just gonna take some time."

Elmira lifted her hand and pointed out the window. "I don't want those people's welfare or food stamps. I have to do it without those things, so it will take us just a little bit longer to save. But we will get outta here, baby. One day, we will get the hell outta this place!"

With his gaze still focused on the floor, Travon nodded. "Yes, ma'am."

CHAPTER THREE

Martin Luther King, Jr. High School

The hallway was crowded with students changing classes, while faculty and staff stood vigilant to make sure that they did so in an orderly manner. Travon stood at his locker.

Today Tamika was wearing her cheerleading outfit. It gripped her body snugly, displaying her shapely young figure. She leaned against a nearby locker, with a flirtatious smile spread across her caramel-colored face.

"Hey, Tre," she called out seductively. "What have you been up to?"

Travon returned her pearlescent smile. "Nothin,' what's been up with you?"

Tamika shrugged and tilted her head slightly to one side, causing her hair to fall over her shoulder. "Nothing, just chilling and working."

Travon's eyes flew open wide. "Tamika, you got a job?"

Her smile widened, displaying her deep dimples. "Yeah. Why you acting like you're so surprised?"

Travon shook his head. "I can't see you working anywhere."

Tamika flung her hair back over her shoulder and lifted an inquisitive eyebrow. "What do you mean by that?"

"Shit, girl. You're just too fine to be doing any kind of work. You're supposed to just ride around and look pretty."

Together they laughed.

Tamika raked her fingers through the loose black hair at the end of her ponytail and smiled at Tre again. "So, you think I look good?"

Travon bit down on his bottom lip and nodded. "Yeah, I think you look real good. That ass is fat, girl!"

Tamika laughed and glanced over her shoulder, down toward her posterior. "How do you know? You ain't never seen it."

Travon walked his eyes down her body, stopping at her wide hips. "I can't help but see it. I mean, the way it's sticking out from underneath that skirt."

"I'm talking about naked. Until you see it naked, don't comment on it."

"When can I see it naked?"

"Whenever you want to." Tamika smiled, turned, and sashayed away.

Travon stood at his locker enjoying the view, as Tamika strutted down the hallway. His undressing of her with his eyes was disturbed by someone shouting behind him.

"*GANGSTERS!* Wheatley Courts in the muthafuckin' hiz-house!"

"Shit," Travon turned and mumbled under his breath.

Draped in thick gold jewelry, and clad in Texas T-shirts and tan Dickey pants that were hanging well below their waistlines, Baby T, Jay Rock, Lil G, Dre, and Justin were heading in his direction. Justin's tall Afro was now braided to the back in long, thick cornrows, and his mouth was filled with gold teeth.

Travon smiled. "What's up, Justin?"

"What's up, youngsta?" Justin replied with a smile. The other boys that were with him snickered and laughed. "Oh yeah, the name is Lil Texas now."

"What?" Tre asked in a voice that was a little too loud for everyone's comfort. What in the hell was going on with Justin, he wondered. Whatever it was, he knew that he would have to get him away from the other boys to find out.

"Say, Justin." Tre nodded toward a less crowded area down the hall, away from the other boys. "Let me holler at you for a minute."

Justin folded his arms and tilted his head to one side. "Holler."

They stood staring at one another for several moments, before Travon smiled to break the tension.

"I meant, in private."

"Yeah, whatever," Justin replied. "And like I said, the name's Lil Texas."

Travon and Justin turned and slowly walked away from the group of boys and began to make strained conversation.

"So, why haven't you been by the house to holler at me lately?" Travon asked.

Justin rubbed his fingers over his thick gold watch. "I've been clocking dollars. You know I gots to get mines."

Travon smiled and nodded. "Yeah? So, what's with all of the jewelry? And what's up with all a this Lil Texas stuff?"

Justin frowned. "What do you mean by that, Travon?"

"I just wanted to know what you've been up to, that's all, Justin," Travon replied.

Justin stopped and turned to face his old friend. "Look, Tre. You know where I've been, and what I've been doing. If you want to kick it, stop being a pussy and get put on the hood." Jabbing his index finger into Travon's chest, he continued. "Your brother was down, he was a muthafuckin' soldier! It kind of makes me think that you were adopted. What you need to do is take your nuts outta your mommy's purse and get down for yours!"

He shook his head in disgust. "I thought you were down, but I see that I was wrong. You need to stop acting like such a punk-ass bitch!"

"Fuck you!" Travon shouted.

"Naw, nigga, fuck you!" Justin shouted, balling his hands into tight fists. "It's Wheatley Courts on mines, what's up?"

The boys squared off. A teacher, the vice principal, and a custodian quickly pulled them apart.

Justin struggled to break free. "You don't want to be down with the hood, then get the fuck outta the hood!"

"I don't get down with bitch-ass niggaz!" Travon shouted. "And I don't get down with bitch sets!"

Justin was quickly whisked off into the principal's office, while Travon was taken into the vice principal's office. The vice principal stormed in behind him, slamming his office door.

"Sit down, Mr. Robinson!" Mr. Reed bellowed. He seated himself behind his desk and scowled.

Travon dropped into a large overstuffed chair opposite the vice principal's. Mr. Reed was an ex-football coach, and had the build of the professional football player he used to be. His cheap, dark brown suit was pulled tightly around his bulging chest and massive arms.

"Now, Tre, what's all this about?" Reed interlaced his fingers and placed his hands on his wooden desk. "I thought that you and Justin were the best of friends?"

Travon shook his head. "It ain't nothing, Mr. Reed. We just exchanged a few words, that's all. Everything's cool."

Reed leaned forward in his chair. "It sure didn't sound like nothing. Do I need to suspend you two for a while, so that you can both cool down?" He lifted a questioning eyebrow toward Travon. "Talk to me, Tre. You're a good student; this is not like you."

Travon shook his head. "Naw, it's cool. It's over with, trust me."

Reed leaned back in his gigantic leather chair, playing the role of a vice principal. He lifted his hand to his face and embedded his fingers deeply into his jowls, as if he were pondering the fate of the free world. After a few moments of gazing steadily at Travon, he nodded.

"Okay, I'll take your word for it. I'll let this one slide, because no punches were thrown, and because you are a pretty good student. Just make sure that it doesn't happen again."

Travon nodded. "Yes, sir." He stood to leave.

"Travon, I'm proud of you, son," Reed told him. "It takes a strong man to stand alone, and stand up for what he believes in."

The office door slowly opened and the principal stepped inside. Reed stared at his boss, who in turn gave a slight nod. Reed turned back to Travon and nodded at the office door.

"Get outta here, son."

A wide, unintentional smile spread across Travon's face. "Yes, sir. And thanks, Mr. Reed."

The vice principal nodded again and Travon bounded out of the office.

The principal smiled at his vice principal. "I don't get down with bitch sets?"

"First time I heard that one," Reed told him with a smile.

They shared a long laugh.

Three Forty-Five p.m.

Travon was walking home from school lost in his thoughts, when the minivan pulled up beside him. For several moments the van drove alongside him, steadily keeping pace with his slow steps.

Travon squinted and strained to peer inside of the van, past its dark tinted windows. He could barely make out the occupants. Behind the steering wheel sat Lil C, while Quentin was in the front passenger seat. They were both from The Courts, and were old friends of his brother, which gave rise to the hope that they would offer him a ride home.

The minivan was a Dodge Caravan to be exact. But its factory paint job had been ditched, instead it had been coated several times with a silver metallic paint. The wheels were chrome-plated Dayton Wire Wheels, enshrouded in extremely low-profile tires. The bass from the van's custom stereo system seemed to be vibrating the pavement beneath them. Travon could see several television screens hanging from the roof of the interior.

Slowly, the side door of the van slid open, and out leapt Lil Texas, Dre, Tech Nine, and Lil G. Travon knew that they meant trouble, so he increased his pace.

Lil Texas ran up behind Travon and shoved him. Travon stumbled forward several steps before turning around and facing him.

"What the fuck's up with that shit?"

Lil Texas raised his arms into the air. "What's up with that shit you was talking at school? Say it now. Call my set a bitch set now, muthafucka!"

Travon shook his head and begin to walk away. "Fuck you, Justin."

Lil Texas swung at Travon but missed. Travon had been expecting it.

"Kick his ass, Lil Texas!" Quentin shouted, exiting the van.

Lil Texas charged Travon and the two boys locked arms. They began to wrestle for dear life, with neither boy wanting to fall or let go. Tech Nine snuck up behind Travon and dropped down onto his hands and knees. Lil Texas moved Travon back; he tripped over Tech Nine, and all three boys hit the ground hard.

Travon managed to get his right hand free and throw a wild punch. His punch landed not on Lil Texas, his intended target, but on Tech Nine.

"Fuck!" Tech Nine grabbed his right eye and rolled away. He stood and immediately tried to reenter the fray, but was grabbed by Quentin.

"Whip his ass, Lil Texas!" Lil G shouted.

Travon managed to climb on top of Justin, and began to punch him hard in his face. This was a battle he desperately wanted to win. He wanted to beat some sense back into his friend.

"Wheatley Courts for life!" Dre shouted.

This rallying cry was followed by several more from some of the other boys. Travon understood what they meant, so he began hitting Justin harder and more solidly.

At this singular moment in his life, Travon hated Justin more than anything. He hated him for placing him in this situation. He hated Justin for his betrayal of their friendship. But more than anything, he now hated Justin because it was his fault that Travon was now about to become another statistic.

Like wolves upon a fallen deer, the boys descended upon Travon and began to beat him brutally. With fists and feet striking him from every direction, Travon could do nothing more than curl up into a tight ball and wait to die.

The boys continued to kick Travon brutally. They kicked him until he could not feel his leg any longer. They kicked him until he could no longer feel their blows. They kicked him until he could no longer feel any sort of pain.

Living in the Courts and knowing what would come next, Travon simply lay on the ground and waited for the gunshot that would end his young life. The sharpness of the report momentarily brought him back into a state of semi-consciousness, but he could not feel where the bullet had struck him. In truth, he no longer cared. He simply wanted it to be over. Blackness engulfed Travon's mind, and he drifted off into a deep, calming sleep.

❖❖❖

"I don't give a fuck what he said; this is Too-Low's brother!" Dejuan shouted, pointing toward Travon's curled-up form. "This is my mutha-fuckin' dead homie's little brother! Quentin, if you want to kill him, then I suggest that you kill me first! Other than that, I suggest you put away that strap, get the fuck back in the van, and get the hell outta here!"

Quentin and Tech Nine, who both had their weapons drawn, slowly placed them back inside their waistbands and pulled their Texas shirts down over them. They, along with the rest of the boys, hesitantly piled back inside the minivan and then slowly drove away.

Once the van had turned the corner and driven out of sight, Dejuan placed his weapon back inside his pants and pulled his shirt down as well. He turned to the passengers sitting inside his large white Mercedes, and waved for them to join him.

"T-Stew, Anthony, help me put him in the car," Dejuan told them.

T-Stew and Anthony exited the Mercedes S600 and walked to where Dejuan was standing. T-Stew bent down and in a single motion scooped Travon up into his massive arms.

"Say, lil homie, are you all right?" T-Stew asked Travon.

Travon could not answer.

Anthony peered over T-Stew's shoulder, and rested his hand gently on Travon's shoulder. "Shit, lil man, just hang on."

T-Stew gently placed Travon on the backseat, then he and Anthony piled back inside themselves. Anthony shook his head as he glanced at Travon, who was lying against the rear passenger window.

"Tech and Quentin was gonna smoke this lil dude, can you believe that shit?" Anthony asked.

Driving, Dejuan glanced back over his shoulder at Travon. "Man, I don't know what's wrong with them." He smacked his lips and shook his head slowly. "They are the homies, but man, they be trippin' sometimes."

CHAPTER FOUR

Brooke Army Medical Center
Fort Sam Houston Army Post

Three Days Later

"Mrs. Robinson?"

"Yes, Dr. Bailey?" Elmira Robinson rose from her chair in the hospital waiting room, along with Vera and Regina, two of her sisters.

"I thought that you would like to know that I just came from Travon's room and he's awake now."

"Awake!" Elmira exclaimed. "We just stepped out about twenty minutes ago!"

Dr. Bailey smiled his signature sunshine smile and extended his hands in a calming motion. "Well, that's how these things work. He's asking for you and Too-Low."

Elmira lifted her petite hands to her face and began sobbing. "Too-Low was his brother, my other son. He was killed a few months ago."

Dr. Bailey nodded his head solemnly. "I know, I remember you and your sisters. I worked ER that night." He clasped Elmira's hands gently. "How have you been?"

Elmira shook her head slightly. "Trying to make it, Doctor, but it's so hard. It's just so hard."

She began crying heavily again. Vera and Regina began to comfort their sister. Regina wrapped her arms around Elmira and pulled her close.

"Elmira, girl, Tre is gonna be okay," Vera told her. "I done told you that the Lord don't put no more on you, than you can bear."

Elmira shook her head. "I know, girl. I know." She shifted her gaze toward the doctor. "Thank you again, Dr. Bailey. Thank you."

Slowly, the sisters filtered out of the waiting room, and made their way down the hospital's halls toward Travon's room. They stood at the door for several moments gathering themselves, clearing away their tears. They did not want Travon to know that they had been crying.

Elmira lifted her hand to the white hospital door and slowly pushed it open. Travon reclined on his hospital bed, with a bandage wrapped around his head. He was awake.

Upon seeing his mother and aunts, Travon smiled. "I'm hungry and thirsty," he told them, swallowing hard.

Elmira laughed and began sobbing. Vera did the same. Both sisters rushed to Travon's bedside, leaned over the bed's metal railing, and embraced him tightly.

"Travon, I'm gonna kill you when you get home," Elmira told him. "You scared the shit out of me!"

Regina, who had stayed at the door, now walked to his bed and hugged her nephew tightly for several moments, before releasing him, leaning back, and staring at him.

"If something would have happened to you, I don't know what I would have done!" Regina told him. "Boy, are you trying to give me gray hair?"

The four of them shared a laugh. Their revelry was interrupted by a nurse entering into the room.

"The doctor wanted me to let you know that it'll still be a while before we can release him. He wants to keep Travon here for at least a few more days for testing and evaluation." She removed Travon's medical chart from the end of his hospital bed, examining it silently for several moments. "The tests we've run so far have all come back good."

The nurse flipped several pages of Travon's medical chart. "No broken bones, no brain damage or expected memory loss, so all of that is good."

Travon shifted in his bed so that he could get a good look at the nurse.

She looked like one of his aunts. In fact, his mother, and his Aunt Vera were identical twins. The nurse reminded him more of his Aunt Chicken, though. Her long silky hair and shapely figure, as well as her high-yellow complexion, high cheekbones, and slanted eyes, made her the mirror image of his aunt. All the nurse needed was that wide, perky little Robinson nose, and she could have easily passed for a long-lost aunt.

"Say, Nurse Lady, where did I get shot at?" Travon asked.

"Shot?" Vera, Regina, and Elmira cried out in unison.

"Well, Mr. Robinson, my name is Virginia. You may call me Nurse Virginia, or even just Nurse. But I will not answer to, Nurse Lady."

Vera and Elmira threw their heads back in laughter.

"By the way, Mr. Robinson, you did not get shot," Nurse Virginia told him. "You almost had your brains beat out of you, but you did not get shot."

Vera clasped her hands together. "Thank you, Lord!"

The nurse made some notations on Travon's medical chart, replaced it at the foot of his hospital bed, and exited the room. Regina turned to her sisters.

"El, girl, I got to get home and get some dinner started. You call me as soon as you get home." She hugged her sister tightly. Then she leaned over the bed railing and hugged Travon. "You stay your ass out of trouble, you hear me?"

Travon nodded.

Regina strolled out of the room and stopped in the hall just in front of the door. She turned back toward her sisters. "I'll see y'all later."

"All right, girl," Elmira replied. "I'll call you as soon as I get home. Thank you so much, Gina."

Regina placed her hands on her hips. "Now, El! You know that if anything happens to any one of these kids, I'm there!" Regina waved her hand through the air, dismissing her sister. "So you can go on with all of that 'thank you' stuff."

"I know, girl." Elmira nodded. "I'll call you."

"I'll call you tonight too!" Vera shouted. She and Elmira turned and continued their visit with a bandaged and bruised Travon.

❖❖❖

As the sisters walked through the hospital lobby after visiting hours, Elmira gently clasped Vera's elbow.

"Vera, there's something that I want to ask you."

Vera lifted an eyebrow. "What's the matter, El?"

"Now, I got this new job. Girl, I'm barely in the door. I can't take off and spend the time with Tre that he is gonna need. But what I'm really concerned about is his being there at night all by himself." Elmira clasped her sister's arms, and gave them a slight squeeze. "Vera, what if they try to get after him again? I'm scared." Elmira lifted her hands to her face and began sobbing.

Vera grabbed her sister's hands and caressed them gently. "I can look in after Tre, or he can come and stay with me. You know I'd love to take him, and I have plenty of room."

"That's what I'm asking, Vera. Please take my baby." Elmira began crying heavily. "I don't want them to get my baby. He's all I got left now."

Vera pulled her sister close, and they embraced each other tightly. "Elmira, you know that I would do anything for you. Anything!"

"Thank you, V. Thank you!" Elmira released her sister, lifted her wrinkled hand to her face and wiped away the tears that were cascading down her soft, buttery cheeks. "I'll tell him when he gets ready to get out. I want him to go straight to your house from the hospital. I don't want him back in those damn Courts for one minute!"

Vera placed her arm around her sister's shoulders and they started for her car. "Come on, girl. I'll take you home and help you pack his stuff."

❖❖❖

On the way home from the hospital, Elmira and Vera drove through The Courts, and as usual, there were several large groups of boys hanging out in the streets. Elmira's eyes locked on to one particular group, and she began to tap her sister's arm.

"Stop the car, V!"

Vera turned and stared at her sister. "What?"

"Girl, stop the damn car!" Elmira shouted.

Vera pulled over to the side of the road, and watched in shock as her sister leapt from the vehicle and charged toward a group of boys standing on a nearby corner.

As she approached them, Elmira was greeted with several indistinguishable "Hello, Mrs. Robinsons." The group that she had singled out included Tech Nine, Snuff Dog, T-Stew, Baby T, J Roc, and Lil Texas. Elmira steadied her legs, dug in her heels, and cleared her throat in such a way as to make sure that all of the boys could hear her. She then placed one hand on her hip and pointed a work-weary, wrinkled finger at the boys.

"Let me tell you all something," she told them. "I welcomed all of you into my home. You were all friends of my son, Too-Low. I never judged you, or asked what any of you were doing. I tried to be a mother to you all. I knew the kind of shit you boys were into, and at first I didn't want Too-Low around any of you. But you were his friends, and I had to let my baby grow up and make his own choices. He chose to be friends with you, so I accepted it, and I accepted all of you. I know that you all loved Too-Low, and that he loved all of you. I let him become a part of you and this life that you live."

Elmira spat her words out at the group of boys like they were poison. "I gave you Too-Low, but I'll be God damned if I let you have Travon! Leave my son alone! If you ever cared anything about Too-Low, anything for him, please leave his brother alone! You asked me at Too-Low's funeral if there was anything you could do for me. Well, yes, there is! Please leave my other child alone! My son Too-Low was down for this hood, as you call it. He was a soldier, as you say. He died right here in this hood, loving this hood, and loving all of you!"

She pointed to a patch of green grass near a stop sign. "He died right there on that corner, and his blood is forever in the grass. I gave you one; now please let me have my other son. Please…"

Elmira lifted her hands to her face and began crying heavily. Vera, now out of the car and standing just behind her sister, wrapped her arms around her and slowly guided her back to the car.

Elmira looked over her shoulder toward the silent crowd of boys. "Please…"

Vera opened the passenger side door and helped her sister inside. Then she walked around to the driver's side and climbed inside, and they slowly drove away.

CHAPTER FIVE

Aunt Vera's House
The Denver Heights

Four Days Later

Travon bounded down the stairs and into the living room, where his cousins LaTonya, Marcus, and Darius were seated.

"Aunt V, me and Marcus are gonna go to the store, and then to the park and kick it for a while."

Darius turned off the television and stood. "Hold up, T. I'm going with y'all."

Aunt Vera walked into the living room from the kitchen, where the boys were about to go out of the front door. "Y'all be back before it gets dark. Darius, you're just trying to get out of here because it's your turn to wash dishes. I ain't crazy."

Darius shook his head. "Naw, Momma, I did 'em last night. It's LaTonya's turn to do 'em tonight."

LaTonya lowered her book, placing it on the coffee table. "Boy, that's just 'cause I paid you to do 'em for me. Last night was my night, tonight is your night, so you can stop trying to run game!"

Darius balled his hands into tight fists and frowned. "Girl, what I tell you about using that word around me? It's Be-cause, not that ol' crab shit! Don't make me put hands on you!"

LaTonya rolled her neck as she answered him. "You do that, and that'll be the last time you put hands on anybody!"

Darius walked quickly to where his sister was seated, scooped her up into his arms, and then lifted her high into the air. She screamed.

"Quit playing!" LaTonya thrust forward her hands and clasped her brother's neck so that he would not drop her. "Momma, look at Darius!"

Vera, who had seated herself on the sofa and started to watch television, shifted her gaze toward her children. "Boy, put your sister down, and watch your damn mouth too!"

Darius placed LaTonya back onto solid ground, and then walked to his mother and gave her a kiss on her cheek. "We'll be back in a little while."

"The dishes will be waiting for you too," Vera said calmly. Travon, Marcus, and Darius walked out of the front door, down the front porch steps, and started down the walkway. Their trip was cut short when Vera peered out the front door.

"Tre, come here real quick, baby," she called.

"What's up, Aunt V?" Travon asked.

Vera extended her right hand and caressed the front of Travon's shirt. "You can't wear that shirt out here, baby."

Darius turned and examined Travon's shirt. "Oh, shit! I forgot what he was wearing!"

Vera stepped aside, allowing the boys to walk back into the house. Travon inquisitively shifted his gaze from one person to the next.

"What's wrong with what I'm wearing?" he asked, tugging at the front of his shirt. "It's my North Carolina jersey. I'm just representing for my boy Mike."

Vera smiled and nodded. "It's a nice shirt, baby. But things are little bit different out here than in the Courts." Different, but not a hell of a lot better, she told herself. She turned to Marcus. "Go and get Tre one of your shirts to put on."

Marcus quickly disappeared up the stairs, only to return moments later with a red-and- black Chicago Bulls T-shirt. He tossed the shirt to Travon. Vera smiled sadly at her nephew, then strolled into the kitchen with her head down.

"Hurry up and change so we can bail," Marcus told Travon.

Travon pulled off his North Carolina jersey and tossed it onto the couch. He quickly put on the red-and-black shirt, and then examined his cousins. For the first time, he noticed that Marcus, Darius, and LaTonya were all wearing different variations of Chicago Bulls shirts. He then recalled how his Aunt Vera had changed into a Forty-Niners jersey just to go to the neighborhood grocery store.

"Let's bail," Darius told them.

The three boys headed out of the door and quickly made their way up the street. Travon was no stranger to his Aunt Vera's house, or neighborhood for that matter, but now he noticed things that he had never paid attention to before.

Red graffiti was spray painted on all of the buildings, the street signs, and in the middle of the streets as well. Silently, Travon began to read the graffiti on some of the abandoned houses in the neighborhood: *DHE, DHM, DHT, DHB, DLB, MCs, PURO OCHO, PIRU, BOUNTY HUNTERS, WSV, WSB, LSB, STIX, SLB, SLP, BGF, TREES, UNLV, RCGs, RCT, KP, BTP, BCGs, SGs, BRIMS, THE JUNGLE, OPE.* But the marking he saw the most was BSV. It was the tag of the notorious Blood Stone Villains. Unbeknownst to him or his mother, Travon had moved into the epicenter of violence.

Though the neighborhood was officially the Denver Heights on real estate maps, it was more commonly known as *The Jungle*. The Jungle was base camp to every Blood gang in South Central Texas, whether they had their own neighborhoods or not. The Jungle was their assembly area, safe haven, drug and weapon depot, their *dope spot*, their home, their *holy land*, and a lot of times, their war zone.

Travon pointed at one of the houses. "What does all of that mean?"

Darius exhaled loudly. He had known that he would eventually have to explain to Travon the way things worked, but he hadn't expected the moment to arrive so soon.

"Everything with a D in front of it is from the Denver Heights. The DHGs are the Denver Heights Gangsters, DHM stands for Denver Heights Mafia, and DHT is Denver Heights Texas; that's where we are."

"If you see somebody wearing a red Texas Tech jersey, especially the ones with the big double *T*s on the front, it means that they are from Denver Heights Texas," Marcus added. "The DLBs are the Denver Lane Bloods, and the DHBs are the Denver Heights Bloods. LSB stands for Lime Street Bloods, BTP stands for Big Time Players, and BCG stands for Blood Crazy Gangstas. You will rarely see them crazy muthafuckas out here in the Heights. They keep their crazy asses on the Westside, where they belong."

"The Stix is the name of those projects over by where Aunt Chicken's house is," Darius continued. "That's where the Stix and Treetop Bloods come from. The UNLV stands for Untouchable New Lite Village, and it also means Untouchable Niggaz Livin' Violently."

"The RCGs are from the Rigsby Courts, and SB stands for Second Baptist," Marcus explained. "That's those projects over there off of East Houston Street. The SLBs are the Skyline Bloods, and KP stands for Kirby Posse. BGF stands for Black Guerilla Family. Those dudes are from Converse, Universal City, Schertz, Selma, Cibolo, Windcrest, and Kirby, Texas."

"The Puro Ochos and the MCs, which stands for Midnight Colors, are Mexican Bloods from out here in the Heights," Darius told him. "The LCGs are the Lincoln Court Gangstas, and the WSBs are the West Side Bloods, and the WSV are the West Side Villains. Those are all of the Blood sets that we allow out here in the hood."

"But we really don't fuck with the BCGs, or the RCGs," Marcus added. "Tre, you're gonna have to learn all of this stuff, now that you are living out here."

"The Jungle is where we are now, it's where we live," Darius explained. "It's The Heights and the hood right across East Houston Street. It goes all the way past OPE, which is Olive Park East, another Blood hood."

"Camelot is another major Blood hood out on the Northeast side," Marcus added. "Camelot, The Heights, and Rigsby Courts are all the big Blood spots that are competing to be *The* main Blood hood."

"Camelot, Converse, Kirby, Universal City, Seguin, Shertz, Selma, The Glens, and Sunrise all ride together, and they all call Camelot and Camelot

Two their home," Darius told him. "They are deeper than a muthafucka, really about half our strength. Now, BSV is a little bit harder to explain. It's *The* set. Sometimes, it's like everybody put together. All of the Bloods who I just told you about, plus a whole lot of others."

"But, BSV is also its own set," Marcus added. "Like us, we're BSVs through and through. The muthafuckin" real McCoys."

"Shit," Travon muttered, as he contemplated the numbers.

The boys turned the corner onto Palmetto Street, and continued on their journey to the neighborhood store.

"It must be a million of y'all," Travon told Darius.

Then they heard the music. The thumping bass notes grew progressively louder as the boys approached the next street. A street named Cactus. A street that was the hub of the neighborhood's activity. The words to *Piru Love* emanated throughout the neighborhood.

"How far is the park from here?" Travon asked.

"Not that far," Marcus told him. "It's about a mile down the road. It's the hood park. You know where Pitman Sullivan Park is, Tre."

Still confused, Tre shook his head.

Darius pointed. "Right there where they have 'Take Pride in the East Side,' and the Martin Luther King celebration after the MLK March."

Travon shook his head again.

Marcus smacked his lips and folded his arms. "Right there where they have Midnight Basketball."

"Oh," Travon nodded. He remembered those games. The last one he had gone to had been with his brother.

The boys approached Cactus Street, and Travon was totally unprepared for what he saw. As they passed the corner house and Travon was able to look down the street toward the music, he stopped cold. There appeared to be a wall of red.

"Oh, fuck," slipped out of his mouth.

Red T-shirts, bandannas, shorts, shoes, shirts, pants, berets, cars, hats, graffiti, and what appeared to be at least one hundred people were scattered up and down the street. A boy wearing a red baseball cap turned backward, cupped his hands around his mouth, and called to them. Another boy waved his hands, beckoning for them to come over.

"What's up, Blood?" Darius shouted as they started toward the massive conglomeration of red.

Travon watched silently as his cousin pulled a red bandanna from his back pocket and allowed it to hang freely.

"It's all about that BSV!" Darius shouted. He twisted his fingers into a gang sign. He placed the gang sign over his heart.

Travon turned toward Marcus, who was spelling out the word *Blood* across his chest.

"You know it!" replied the boy with the red hat.

Marcus, Darius, and Travon approached one of the groups. Smiling broadly, Darius glided up to a tall, lanky boy who wore his hair in a gigantic Afro.

"Say, Fro Dog, I can hear your shit all the way down Palmetto!" Darius told him.

"When did you get your shit out?" Marcus asked.

Fro Dog walked to his vehicle and stood proudly in front of it. Darius, Marcus, and Travon followed closely behind. Fro Dog turned toward Darius and crossed his arms.

"Check it out, Blood," he said.

Darius walked slowly around the perimeter of the car, examining it carefully. Fro Dog turned his attention to a group of girls seated on the hood of his freshly painted car.

"Y'all hoes wanna get the fuck up off my shit?" he asked them.

"Fuck you, nigga, I aint no ho!" one of the girls protested.

Fro Dog placed his hand over his stomach and bowed. "Oh, I'm sorry. Y'all tricks get y'all asses off my shit!"

Laughter broke out amongst the crowd of boys.

"Fuck you, you black bastard!" another girl told him. "If I'm a trick, then yo woman's a trick! And the next time that nappy-headed bitch calls, I'ma tell her that you fuckin" Wanda!"

The girls slid off the car and walked into the yard.

"You do, and I'ma put some hot lead in yo ass!" Fro Dog told her. He shifted his gaze to a boy seated in the driver's seat of his car. "Say, Lil Fade, hit the switches."

An albino with cold, penetrating, pale blue eyes leaned forward and flicked one of the numerous switches that were scattered across the car's chrome-and-leather dashboard. The red convertible '64 Chevrolet Impala's front end leapt up off the ground. The albino's hat flew off, and a monstrous, sandy-colored Afro popped out.

Travon began to examine Lil Fade. There was something about him that made goose bumps appear on Travon's arm. Lil Fade was grotesquely pale, with numerous tattoos on the parts of his skin that were exposed. His crystal blue, almost white eyes made it seem as though he was looking through you instead of at you. Travon was scared of Lil Fade.

Another switch was hit, and the rear end of the car bounced up. Lil Fade flicked another switch, and the right side of the car dropped down. Another, and the left side plopped down.

"That shit is hitting!" one of the boys shouted.

Marcus turned and shifted his gaze toward the boy. "Say, Lil Bling, when are you getting your shit out?"

"Them muthafuckin' Mexicans be bullshittin'!" Lil Bling told him.

It was easy for Travon to see why they called him Lil Bling. Every tooth inside of his mouth, top and bottom, was capped in gold. It was a perfect match for his golden skin and jewelry-adorned body.

"I went down there to check on my shit today," Lil Bling continued. "And them muthafuckas was talkin' about another two weeks!"

He searched the crowd for several moments, until he located the person he was looking for. "Say, Tevin, pretend like you a muthafuckin' quarterback and pass the muthafuckin' forty."

Tevin, a six-foot-six, three-hundred-pound mass of dirt and filth wearing a red T-shirt that was two sizes too small, extended his arm and passed Lil Bling the beer that he had been sipping on.

Travon turned away from them and began to examine Fro Dog's car. The automobile was absolutely gorgeous. It was covered with multiple layers of red-candy paint, with tens of millions of sparkling red flakes throughout. The paint reminded Travon of a brand-new bowling ball that had just been polished with oil. The interior of the vehicle was covered in white leather, with red leather piping and blood-red carpeting. The car's front grill, bumpers, rims, mirrors, and trim pieces consisted of highly polished chrome. The car was truly a rolling work of art.

"My shit is gonna be like this," Lil Bling announced, pointing at Fro Dog's car. "Except my car is burgundy, with gold rims, grill, and trim."

"Say, Marcus. Where was y'all headed?" asked another one of the boys.

"To the hood store."

"Is that y'all kinfolk from The Courts that y'all said was gonna be staying with y'all?" the boy asked.

Marcus nodded.

The boy walked to where Travon was standing, and extended his hand. "Say, lil homie, my name is Big Pimpin."

Travon extended his hand, and he and Big Pimpin tapped each other's fist. "I'm Travon, but everybody calls me Tre."

"Rewind the B-side!" Lil Bling shouted to Lil Fade.

Big Pimpin reached into his pants pocket and pulled out a wad of rolled-up bills. He peeled off a twenty and handed it to Travon. "Bring me back a forty-ounce of Red Bull and a forty-ounce bottle of O.E. You can get you whatever you want, for going to the store for me."

"Say, Big Simple, I mean, Big Pimpin," Lil Bling called out to him. "Get me a bottle of M.D. and some bigga-rettes."

"Nigga, fuck you!" Big Pimpin told him. He turned back toward Travon. "Get a bottle of Mad Dog and a pack of Kools."

Travon nodded, and then stuffed the twenty-dollar bill into his front pocket. He and Marcus turned, and started back down the street, continuing on their journey to the neighborhood store. Once they had reached a point where he was sure that they could not be overheard, Marcus turned to his cousin and nudged him in the side.

"So, Tre, do you think that you are gonna like it out here?"

"I think I'll be aight. It seems like everything out here is pretty cool. Everybody is real laid-back." Travon lifted his head toward the sky and took in the last warming rays of the lazily retreating sun. He turned to his cousin and nodded. "Yeah, I think I'm really gonna like it."

CHAPTER SIX

The Hood Store

Travon grabbed two Red Bulls and walked to the checkout counter. He sat the beers down on top of the counter, and then walked to the wine freezer, where he grabbed a bottle of MD 20/20. He returned to the counter with the bottle of wine.

"ID, kid?" a lady of Asian descent asked him. She spied Marcus ambling toward the counter through the corner of her eye. "Are you with him?" she asked Travon.

Travon nodded. "Yeah."

She proceeded to ring up the items.

"Add two packs of Kools to that also," Travon told her.

The petite Asian clerk reached into the overheard cigarette dispenser, where she pulled down two packs of cigarettes. Marcus stepped up to the counter.

"Hello, Marcus," the clerk greeted him. "How's your mother doing?"

"She's all right, Mrs. C," Marcus answered. "How about you, how are you doing?"

"Oh, I've been doing pretty good," she told him. "Just arguing with that damn insurance company again. Have you seen Lil Fade today?"

"They're all at Big Pimpin's house right now."

"Is that where you're headed?"

"Yes, ma'am," Marcus nodded.

"Good. Then you can give him a message for me. Tell Lil Fade that my husband said that he has some new AKs in. I think he said that he had three of them. Well, anyway, tell him that Mr. C said that he will make him a good deal if he gets all three of them right now."

Travon's mouth fell open.

Outside, a blue-and-white San Antonio Police Department patrol car pulled in front of the store. Mrs. Chang spied the patrol car out of the corner of her eye.

"Hurry up, give me your shit!" she said, thrusting her tiny, pale hands out toward them.

Marcus pulled a Glock model twenty-three, forty caliber, semiautomatic handgun from his waistband, and handed it to Mrs. Chang. Travon was paralyzed from shock and fear. Mrs. Chang quickly hid the weapon beneath the counter, and placed the beer and cigarettes that the boys were buying on the floor behind the counter. The cops walked in.

"Ching, chong, chang, separate mines from yours, Ms. Thang," said one of the officers.

Mrs. Chang opened the cash register and gave him a wad of money. The second officer approached Travon and Marcus.

"What's up, Lil Marcus?" The officer nodded. "What have you been up to? I see that you're still slobbing. You know that you shouldn't be hanging around those pussy-ass Bloods."

Marcus frowned. He balled his hand into a tight fist, and blood rushed to his face.

"Them Crips over in the East Terrace say that they got all the juice," the officer continued. "They say that they got it going on, and that y'all Slobs ain't shit."

"Fuck them punk-ass Crabs!" Marcus shouted.

Travon's eyes flew wide, and his heart began to drum rapidly. He had never heard anyone talk to a police officer like that. He had heard people talk bad about them after the cops had left the scene, of course, but not actually curse them to their face.

The officer shook his head. "Now, Marcus, why you gonna talk that way about my homies? You know we boys in blue all stick together. Now I'm gonna have to shake you down too."

With a wide grin, the officer began searching Marcus. His partner walked over to Travon and did the same. When they finished, the officer had taken a total of one hundred and twenty-nine dollars off the boys.

"Lunch money, huh, partner?" asked the second officer.

"Yep, and a little bit of beer money to go with it!"

The patrol officers shared a hearty laugh.

Travon examined the officers' name tags. Cooney and Preto.

Cooney was the tall pale one with sky-blue eyes, and chocolate brown hair. Preto was the short, stocky one with green eyes, tanned skin, and black hair in a crewcut. Cooney stepped in closer to Travon.

"What's your name, nigger?"

Travon frowned, hesitated, and then stammered out his name. "Travon."

"Travon what?"

"Travon Robinson."

The officer turned to his partner and began snapping his fingers. "Robinson, Robinson, Robinson, hmmm. Seems like I know a Davon Robinson."

Travon noticed the sparkle in Cooney's eyes, and became hesitant to answer.

"Well, fuck face?" Cooney demanded.

"He was my brother," Travon whispered.

"You gotta be shittin' me!" Cooney shouted. He jabbed his finger into Travon's chest. "You're Too-Low's little brother?"

Travon looked down and nodded.

The look of astonishment on Cooney's face quickly turned to one of anger. "What the fuck are you doing hangin' out with this fuckin' slob?" he asked, pointing at Marcus.

"He's my cousin!" Marcus shouted.

Cooney nodded. "Oh, that explains it! He's slumming with the fucked-up side of the family."

Preto laughed.

"Look here, Travon. Wait, what's your nickname?" Cooney asked.

Travon shrugged. "Just Tre."

Cooney stared at Marcus. "Y'all can't even give the kid a decent nickname?" Cooney turned toward his partner and shook his head. "That's why I hate Slobs."

The officers shared another laugh.

"Look here, Tre. Let me give you some advice. Go back to The Courts, and make you some money. Slobs are fuckin' poor. You are too good for them. Go back to The Courts right now, and I won't tell the homies in the hood that you got Slobs in your family. Okay?"

Travon stared at him coldly.

"We got to add this one to the gang file as a Blood, but possibly a WCG," Preto told his partner.

"Hopefully, we'll add him as a WCG in the future. I need a new truck." Cooney laughed, and turned toward Travon with a feigned look of care and concern. "Say, Tre. Work with me on this, and go back to The Courts. I'll go easy on you; I'll even put you on a flexible payment plan."

Cooney and Preto laughed heartily, as they adjusted their gun belts and strolled out of the store. Travon, Marcus, and Mrs. Chang stood silently, in bitter, seething rage, until the officers climbed into their vehicle and pulled away.

"Fuckin' bastards!" Mrs. Chang shouted. "Here, take your beer, and here." She handed the bag to Travon and the gun to Marcus. "Don't forget to tell Lil Fade what I said about the guns. I think that he said that they were fully automatic, or that he was going to convert them to full auto. I forget which one it was, but either way, they'll be just like he likes them. Don't worry about paying me for the beer and cigarettes; I know those bastards took your money."

Marcus slid the gun inside of his waistband, and grabbed the bag of beer from Travon. "All right, thanks, Mrs. C."

"Later, Blood," said a smiling Mrs. Chang, as the boys left the store.

Tre and Marcus headed down Palmetto, back toward Cactus Street. They were only a few blocks away from the store when a large white, late-model Mercedes pulled up alongside of them. Marcus quickly reached for his gun. Travon placed his hand over Marcus's to stay him.

"It's cool." Travon nodded. "Trust me, it's okay."

The tinted window on the driver's side slid down, and Dejuan stuck his head out of the car. His gold teeth were glistening brilliantly in the bright

South Texas sun, while his long, curly, rubber-band-sectioned hair blew gently in the mellow breeze.

"What's up, Lil Tre?" Dejuan asked.

"Shit, nothing much." Travon shrugged. "Just been chilling out here with my kinfolk."

Dejuan smiled. "I see that you're doing better."

A big, dark, muscular guy leaned forward in the passenger seat, and offered Travon a smile. "How you feelin'?"

Travon recognized him instantly: Big Mike, a member of thenotorious East Terrace Gangstas, or ETGs for short. What Denver Heights was to the Bloods, East Terrace was to the Crips.

When Marcus also recognized Big Mike, his hand began to twitch.

"Shit, I'm all healed up," Travon told them. "Thanks for helping me out that day, Dejuan. I would probably be dead right now, if it wasn't for you."

"Shit, man, you're my homie's little brother. Plus, your brother was like my brother. He saved my ass a few times." Dejuan paused, and then shook his head. "Damn, lil homie. I didn't want you to move out of the hood. Man, that shit was all fucked up. Them niggaz be trippin' too much. We at war with them fools right now."

"What?" Travon shouted. The news had taken him by surprise.

The opportunity was just too good for Marcus to pass up. He leaned forward and stared at Dejuan.

"I thought that all of y'all was Wheatley Courts, and that y'all stick together like family?" Marcus shifted his gaze toward Big Mike. "I'm glad that Bloods don't kill each other like that."

Dejuan ignored Marcus, keeping his attention on Travon. "Shit, the hood is divided, and we takin' it to each other right now. Ain't nobody makin' no money or nothing."

"What did y'all get into it for?" Travon asked.

"Shit, you ain't heard?" Dejuan asked incredulously. "Them fools killed T-Stew."

"What?" Travon asked in shock. "Who?"

"Man, Quentin, Tech Nine, Lil Texas, and Dupriest," Dejuan told him.

"They say that Quentin shot him, but Lil Texas and Dupriest finished him off. That boy had twenty-nine holes in him, from four different guns. That shit pissed me off. And it was all behind a bitch too. T-Stew was supposedly fuckin' Quentin's baby's momma. Me, Act One, Baby T, Lil C, and PayDay, T-Stew's brother, is taking it to them niggaz. Shit, really, everybody in the Courts done chose sides. Last night, Dre shot Heavy G in the neck. They don't know if that fool gone live or not."

"What?" Travon repeated.

"Fuck!" slipped from Marcus's mouth.

Travon shook his head. "Man, y'all niggaz is crazy. I'm glad that I got the fuck outta there."

"Niggaz is getting shot every day in the Courts, or by the Courts. That shit is hectic." Dejuan turned to Big Mike and smiled, and then turned back to Travon. "Anyway, trick that shit. How you living? I got something for you."

He reached beneath the seat and pulled out a small paper sack. When Marcus saw what it was, he released the grip on his weapon.

"Here, it's five OZs in here, just for you." Dejuan handed Travon the paper bag. "When you get through with it, call me. My number's inside the bag also. Just bring me back two Gs, lil homie."

The power window on the big German sedan glided back up, and the Mercedes slowly eased off.

Later That Evening

Travon was lying in bed when someone knocked on the door.

"Come in," Travon called without looking up from his book.

Darius entered, followed by Marcus.

"What's up?" Travon asked. He closed his book, and sat up.

"Nothin.' " Darius shook his head nonchalantly. "Just came to holler at you about a few things."

Travon became suspicious. "What?"

Darius bit down on his bottom lip. "Well, Marcus told me about what happened today. About y'all hollerin' at Dejuan. He said that Dejuan put you down with some yea-yo."

Travon nodded. "Yeah, but I don't know if I'm gonna do it. I ain't made up my mind yet."

Darius sat on the edge of the bed. "Say, T. You're my cousin, and I'm a look out for you, always. Let me let you in on a few things. First, Dejuan is a user. That's all he does is use people. He used Too-Low, and now he's trying to use you. I used to tell Too-Low all the time, to quit fuckin' with them niggaz. Think about it, Tre. How many people do you know that ride around with bags of dope with their cell phone numbers in them, ready to be passed out? Dejuan was looking for you. He don't care about you, he don't care about nobody but Dejuan, and how much money you can make him. It's all about money to them dudes. They whole clique is all about makin' money, and their only loyalty is to the dollar."

Pointing toward the window, Darius continued, "They are at war with each other in the Courts. Can't nobody sell shit, because one-time is all over the place, because of the bodies. Geekers and niggaz is afraid to go out there and buy anything, so Dejuan ain't makin' no money. His boys can't sell his shit out in the Courts for him, and they damn sure can't come out here, or go in the Terrace, so he finds you. Don't be stupid, Tre. Dejuan doesn't really give a fuck about you. That muthafucka is just trying to move his dope. Game peeps game. He's probably also tryin' to pull you into his clique, because right about now, I imagine he's in desperate need for a new triggaman."

Darius rose from the bed and faced his cousin. "That's what Too-Low was for him. So who better to replace Too-Low than his little brother? Your brother put in all the work for them niggaz, while they got rich." Darius shook his head and looked down. "I loved my cousin to death, but he wasn't exactly the brightest thing in the world. Did Too-Low ever tell you about some of the things he did? Do you remember the time that all of those Colombians got killed in that motel on Austin Highway?"

Travon tilted his head to the side and frowned. "Yeah?"

"Well, Dejuan set that up, and Too-Low did the killin'. They won for six keys and sixty Gs. How do you think Dejuan came up? Off of your brother. People were scared of Dejuan, because they was scared of Too-Low. Without Too-Low, Tech Nine, Quentin, and Dupriest, WCG ain't shit!"

Travon swallowed hard to try and clear away the lump that had formed in his throat, as he digested what Darius had just told him about his brother. His stomach began to churn; deep down, he wondered whether all the rumors that he had heard about his brother just might have been true.

Too-Low, the person he had looked up to, and loved more than life itself, might have been a stone-cold fuckin'g murderer. His brother, the person who took care of him, helped raise him, and made sure that he always did well in school, might have been a monster. It was too much for him to even begin to digest.

"Say, y'all, I'm a think about this shit, and I'll let you know what's up tomorrow," Travon told them.

Marcus noticed the look on Travon's face and realized he hadn't known about the things Too-Low had done. Darius, who had been too busy talking, had missed it.

"All right, kinfolk. But if you need me to, I'll show you the game," Darius replied. "I'll teach you how to cook it, cut it up, and sell it. I'll even stay down with you while you get your feet wet. We gotta get you a strap too. Remind me tomorrow."

Travon nodded. "Later," he told them, swallowing hard again, and forcing a smile across his face.

"Later," Marcus replied.

"Later," Darius said.

They walked out, closing the door behind them. Just as quickly as it had closed, the bedroom door reopened, and Darius stuck his head back through the door.

"Tre, you not paying that muthafucka back shit, either. Not one fuckin' dime!" Darius shook his head and smiled. "Old Dejuan is just gonna have to charge them Os to the game."

CHAPTER SEVEN

Travon tossed and turned in bed as he dreamt of his brother. Too-Low's words barraged him, bits and pieces of their last conversation replayed inside of his head.

"Tre, you better not ever join a gang."

"I do this shit so that you don't have to!"

"If I ever catch you with any kind of dope, I'm a put a foot in your ass!"

"Do you hear me, Tre?"

"Tre!"

"Tre!"

"Take this money and put it in Momma's purse."

"Put the rest under my mattress."

"Mattress, mattress, mattress."

Travon bolted up from his sleep. "Mattress," he muttered to himself. Slowly, his thoughts became cohesive, and he remembered his last conversation with Darius: "We got to get you a strap."

Travon smiled to himself. "I already got a strap," he declared to the moonlit shadows dancing across his bedroom walls. "I got my brother's."

Sleep did not come easy the rest of the night.

Eight-Thirty a.m.

Travon was dressed and heading out the back door. Vera appeared at the kitchen door.

"Travon, where do you think you're going?" she asked him.

"I'll be right back, Aunt V," Travon lied. "I've gotta run around the corner real quick."

Travon hurried out and jumped on his bike. He'd made it into the front yard when he suddenly remembered something. He dropped the bike on the ground, bolted back inside the house, and ran upstairs to his room.

"Where is it?" he asked no one in particular, frantically rummaging through his closet. He pulled several items from the closet before pausing for a moment to gather his thoughts. Then it came to him.

"I know where you are!" Travon fell to his knees, reached beneath his bed, and pulled out his old backpack. Now that he had found what he was looking for, it took him only seconds to bolt from his room, down the stairs, and out the front door. Without looking back, he mounted his bicycle with a running start, and was off.

The trip to his mother's apartment in the Courts took only twenty-five minutes. He had pedaled fast, and traffic had been agreeable today. Travon carefully laid his mountain bike on the ground in front of his mother's apartment, and cautiously surveyed the area to make sure that no one was watching him. Once he was certain that no one was, he searched the door sill for the key that his mother kept there. It was gone.

Travon lifted the cheap, tattered, woven straw welcome mat; the key was not there either. This left him with only one other option. It was the option that he had wished to avoid, but no longer could. He walked to the window where his brother's room used to be, and stared up at it. It was a room he had not been inside since the day his brother died.

Travon shrugged, sighed, uttered a quick prayer, and began to climb the large oak tree that stood just in front of his brother's window. It was a climb that he and Too-Low had made many a time, when their mother had restricted them from going outside to hang out with their friends. His heart wished that he could be climbing the tree for such a reason today.

Once Travon reached the point on the tree that roughly ran parallel to his brother's window, he uttered another quick prayer, and then reached over and gave the shut window a tug. It slid open.

"Yes!" he exclaimed, climbing through the old metal-framed window.

Inside, Travon examined his surroundings. His mother, who was not yet ready to let go of her oldest son, had touched nothing.

He walked softly to the dresser, where a stereo sat collecting dust. There was a shirt lying on top of the stereo, crumpled, waiting to be re-worn or washed. Travon lifted the shirt to his nose and inhaled deeply. He could still smell the faint scent of his brother on the T-shirt. It brought tears to his eyes.

Travon reverently sat the shirt back on top of the stereo, and walked to his brother's bed, where he lifted up the top mattress. Lying exactly where he left it so many months ago was his brother's gun. Next to it was one thousand dollars.

"Yes!" he exclaimed again. He had forgotten all about the money. He grabbed both.

Travon next turned his attention to his brother's closet. First he searched his brother's clothing, which hung neatly on hangers, never to be worn again. Nothing. His attention was then drawn to Too-Low's neatly arranged pairs of shoes.

Travon stuck his hand inside them, checking each carefully. The first and second shoes were empty. The third shoe, however, yielded treasure. Travon's hand would not go all the way into the tennis shoe, so he banged it against the floor to dislodge whatever was inside. A wad of rolled-up bills slid to the rear of the shoe. A smile slowly crept across Travon's face.

Travon grabbed the next shoe and repeated the procedure. The next three pairs of shoes yielded an equally handsome sum. The fourth pair yielded a treasure of a different sort. There was one quarter of a kilogram of cocaine in each shoe.

Meticulously, Travon continued to check the rest of Too-Low's shoes, but nothing else was to be found. He gathered up his newfound treasure and placed it into his backpack, along with the handgun and the other money. He then rearranged the closet, putting everything back the way it was prior to his arrival. When this was done, he walked to his brother's bed, and seated himself upon the edge of it. His lack of sleep, the early morning hour, and his fast-paced bike pedaling to get there, all took their toll on him. Content with the success of his mission, he lay back on his brother's bed and fell sound asleep.

Two-Thirty P.M.

Travon awoke suddenly. The unfamiliarity of his surroundings caused his heart to beat rapidly at first, and then he remembered where he was. Travon shifted his gaze top the clock on the stereo, but it was an hour behind. His brother had not been alive to spring forward.

Travon quickly deduced the correct time; it was late in the afternoon, and he had slept way too long. He rose from the comfort of his brother's bed, straightened it back up, and that was when the thought hit him. Travon immediately dropped to his knees and began searching beneath the bed.

There were several boxes. Some were large, some were not. All were covered with a thin film of dust from neglect. Travon pulled the boxes out one by one, and then opened them in the same fashion.

Inside the first box were several photo albums and loose pictures. Pictures of his brother and people from the neighborhood. Some were dead; many were in prison, others were just long gone. Many were pictures of women, and there were quite a few pictures of people who were still in the Courts. Travon tossed the photos back, and then turned his attention to the next box. More pictures, and lots of obituaries of Too-Low's lost friends. Travon closed the two boxes and slid them back underneath the bed. He then pulled close another box and opened it.

Inside were two guns, and lots of ammunition. Travon pulled one of the weapons from the box, turned it on its side, and read the print stamped into it. The weapon was an Israeli Military Industries' Desert Eagle. It was a very large and extremely heavy handgun; the caliber on the weapon read fifty magnum, and its color was a cold, empty, death black. Travon tossed it onto the bed and grabbed the second weapon.

This one read Israeli Military Industries also. It was an Uzi semiautomatic pistol, nine-millimeter; like the other weapon, it too was a cold, dull black. He tossed this one onto the bed as well, and slid the large box to the side.

The next box contained a portion of Too-Low's comic book collection. The idea of his brother collecting comic books made Travon smile. He could imagine his brother looking down on him from above and going ballistic because he was messing around in his comic books. He would give anything to have his brother be able to yell at him again.

Travon reverently placed the comic books back in their box and slid the box back beneath the bed. He opened the next box. More comics. Travon closed it, slid it back underneath the bed, and grabbed the last box. This one was extremely long; he had to pull the box all the way out from beneath the bed. Travon tilted the long box slightly upward, and found himself staring down into the barrel of a rifle.

"Fuck!" he exclaimed. "My brother was planning to take on an entire army."

He reached down into the box and felt a second weapon. Carefully, he pulled both of them out. The second weapon was short and stubby, with an odd shape. The weapon had a large, round cylinder in the center of it, and the cylinder itself contained several large chambers. It looked very much like a gigantic revolver, with two large handles at the bottom. The weapon also had a short folding stock at the rear and a long black nylon strap at the top, for ease of carrying. Travon turned the weapon on its side and read the stampings:

12 GAUGE STRYKER 12 ARMSCOR REPUBLIC OF SOUTH AFRICA

Travon, not being very familiar with weapons, did not understand that he was holding what was more commonly known as a Street Sweeper.

He placed the weapon back in the box, and lifted the other, longer one. It was an assault rifle. This one read, *.308 GALIL, ISRAELI MILITARY INDUSTRIES.* Travon took the rifle and attempted to slide it back, but it would not go all the way. Something was impeding its progress.

Travon made several attempts to replace the weapon, all to no avail. Finally, he lifted the box and tilted it forward. Out slid the Street Sweeper and three live hand grenades.

"Oh, fuck!" he yelled, once he realized what the objects were. His heart skipped a beat, but then began to make up for it by pounding hard and fast inside his chest.

Travon lifted the rifle, and placed it back inside the box. He followed the rifle with the Street Sweeper, and finally but very carefully, with the hand grenades. He slid the box back underneath the bed, and then removed several packs of ammunition from one of the previous boxes. He placed the ammunition into his backpack, along with the two guns he had tossed onto the bed. Travon then turned his attention to his brother's chest of drawers.

Rummaging around, he found Too-Low's jewelry, wallet, and pagers amongst the clothing. He stuck these items in his backpack as well, and then grabbed Too-Low's T-shirt. It was getting late, and he had to hurry up and get back to Aunt V's house, or else she'd be worried. Travon examined the bedroom, and then straightened out whatever needed to be straightened. Once satisfied that the room looked undisturbed, he climbed out of the window, closed it, and then made his descent from the tree.

On the ground, Travon shrugged off the backpack and sat it on the ground. He opened the pack, and removed from it his brother's Beretta pistol. He stuck the handgun inside his waistband and pulled his shirt down over it to conceal it. Although he would be pedaling as fast as he could out of the Courts, it was no longer morning, and the guys he wanted to avoid would definitely be awake now. It was definitely better to be safe than sorry. Especially when sorry meant death.

Travon lifted his backpack, tossed it onto his shoulders, and mounted his bicycle with a running start. It was a long way back to the Heights, and Aunt Vera was probably already sending out Darius and Marcus to look for him. Plus, he *had* told her that he was only going around the corner real quick. Damn! He had already caused his aunts and his mother enough worry.

Travon turned the corner at full speed and slammed into a group of boys walking through the Courts. He and several of the boys tumbled to the ground.

"Watch where in the fuck you're going!" one of them shouted.

Travon peered up from the ground. Lil Texas was standing over him with a widening smile.

"Well, well, well, what the fuck do we have here?" Lil Texas asked, as the smile stretched even further across his face.

"Looks like another victim," Tech Nine answered.

"There is a God," added Quentin.

CHAPTER EIGHT

Lil Texas kicked Travon in his chest. "You little punk-ass bitch!"

Travon cried out in pain and grabbed his chest.

Quentin threw a right punch, striking Travon across his left eye. "Yeah, bitch! What's up now? Dejuan can't save your ass now, can he?"

Travon's mind flashed. He thought of the pain from the first beating, the stay in the hospital, the move to the Heights, his mother's fear, and his dead brother. He quickly came to a conclusion. Not again. It was not going to happen again.

Travon quickly reached beneath his shirt and pulled out the Beretta.

"Look out, he's strapped!" Lil Texas yelled.

The boys began to flee.

POP, POP, POP, POP, POP, POP, POP.

The earsplitting sound of gunfire filled the air.

Travon jumped to his feet and ran in the opposite direction of the boys, while continuing to fire his weapon at them. He heard them returning fire, but was several blocks away, before he realized that his gun was empty, and that he was still pulling the trigger.

CLICK, CLICK, CLICK, CLICK, CLICK.

"Shit!" Travon tucked the empty weapon into his waistband, pulled his shirt down over it, and continued to flee.

Back in the Courts, Quentin was lying on the ground cursing. Blood was oozing from his stomach.

"That lil nigga shot me!" he moaned, clutching his stomach. "I can't believe it, I'm shot!"

"Fuck!" yelled Lil Texas, who was pacing back and forth near Quentin.

"Just hang on, man. It's gonna be all right," said a nervous Tech Nine, who was kneeling over Quentin. "Just hang on."

"Fuck! Oh, fuck! Oh, shit!" Lil Texas had stopped pacing and was now tapping frantically on Tech Nine's shoulder.

"What?" Tech Nine shouted angrily.

Lil Texas pointed. Tech Nine turned his head in that direction, then instantly leaped to his feet.

"Fuck! Oh, shit! Oh, shit!" Tech Nine began shouting.

The little girl who had been swinging in the playground from which they had just come was now lying on the ground. The empty swing was swaying with the gentle breeze just above her twisted form. Soon, a mother's scream pierced the air, and sounded as though it could be heard around the world. The child would swing no more.

Travon gasped for air; his chest and lungs were burning, but he was now well over two miles away from the Courts. He felt as though he were about to collapse. Then he heard the siren.

Travon looked over his shoulder and saw a police car just behind him. He tried to flee, but the police car simply angled in front of him, cutting him off. The passenger-side door flew open; Travon slammed into it and fell backward, crashing down into the ground hard. When he opened his eyes again, Officers Cooney and Preto were standing over him.

"You just couldn't do what I asked?" Cooney told him. "Not only did you not get down with the Courts, you went out there and shot the place up!" He bent over, grabbed Travon by his arms, and lifted him up. "Come here, you little shit!" He slammed Travon against the scorching hood of the police car and handcuffed him.

Preto took Travon's backpack and tossed it into the front seat. Together, the officers searched Travon, removed the Beretta, and then placed Travon in the backseat of the patrol car. Quickly, they each walked to their respective sides of the car, climbed inside, and drove away.

"You dumb fuck!" Cooney shouted from the driver's seat. "What in the hell did you think you are doing?"

Travon remained silent.

"You know what, Travon, you're making me feel really stupid. I don't like to feel stupid, especially if it's because of a nigger! I know how to pick them, Tre. My partner says that you are a lost cause, but I know that you can't be. I was right about Too-Low, and I know that I'm right about your black ass. But you're making it kind of hard for me, you dumb, stupid, fuck!" Cooney banged on his steering wheel. "Why should I give you another chance, huh?"

Travon remained silent.

"Do you know that your ass is all over the radio?" asked Cooney. "Three down, suspect fleeing on foot, black T-shirt, black knapsack. How fuckin' hard do you think it is to spot your little black ass, running through the middle of the street?"

Preto, who was rummaging through Travon's backpack, turned to his partner. "Look at what we found here!" He turned back toward Travon. "This will not only get us promoted, but it'll get your little black ass twenty to thirty years in the Feds. But only after you come back to life, because Texas is gonna fry your black, gangbanger, dope-dealing ass for that little girl you popped!"

Travon sat up. "What the fuck are you talking about? I ain't shoot no little girl!"

"Oh, that's right, you probably don't know," said Cooney. "Well, some young nigger girl got popped during your little Wild West shoot-out."

"Fuck!" Travon kicked at the partition separating him from the officers.

Cooney and Preto exchanged knowing glances and slight smiles. They knew that they had him. Preto's instincts had been correct. Travon was not like the others; he wasn't a hard-core gang member yet. So he would not want to go to prison. Travon was now firmly inside their pockets. He would sell drugs for them, inform on others for them, kill for them, and do whatever else it was that they asked him to. No, change that. He would do whatever they *told* him to. It was too good of an opportunity to pass up. Cooney and Preto looked at each other and decided instantly that there was no way on God's green earth that this meal ticket was going to rot in prison. Especially when it could be out on the streets making them rich.

"Look here, Travon. I don't give a fuck about the little coon you popped," Cooney told him. "She was probably gonna be just another loose jungle bunny, collecting welfare and food stamps, and living in the projects. Hell, you just saved a lot of decent, hardworking folks some tax dollars. So look here, boy, this is what we're gonna do. We're gonna take half of this here money, as sort of a down payment; kinda like good-faith money. Our little arrangement is gonna cost you a thousand dollars a month for the next three months. Then it's gonna cost you two thousand dollars for the next three months after that. Then it goes up to three thousand, and finally, it jumps to five. You let us know what your Slob-ass homeboys are up to, you buy straps from us, and you throw us a good bust every once in a while. In exchange, you don't go to prison today. Do you understand what I'm saying, boy?"

Travon hesitated for a moment, and then nodded. "Yeah."

"Good," said Cooney. He turned to Preto. "How much is there?"

"Eleven thousand dollars, half a bird, and three straps."

"Fuck! I'm almost tempted to turn you in and make lieutenant," Cooney told Travon. He shifted his gaze back to his partner. "Give Sambo back five G's, the half bird, and the straps. He needs to come up so that he can make his monthly payments."

Preto shrugged. "Okay, Sarge." Preto lifted the nine-millimeter Beretta into the air. "Hey, do you remember this?"

Cooney glanced at the Beretta and laughed. "I sure do."

"So, you found your brother's guns, huh?" Preto asked Travon.

"How do you figure that those are my brother's guns?" Travon replied, trying to be cool.

"Because I'm the one who sold them to him, you little shit!" Cooney shouted.

"That's the one he used in that big shoot-out at the park last year, isn't it?" Preto asked.

Cooney stared at the gun again and then nodded. "Yeah, now that you mention it, I think that was the one."

Preto whistled. "Boy, that Too-Low sure could shoot!"

"And make a shit load of money too!"

Both officers shared a hearty laugh.

"I sure miss ol' Too-Low," Preto told Travon. "The Courts died down a little bit after he got killed."

"Yeah, too bad them Crips killed him," added Cooney. "He was one mean nigger."

"But ol' Tre here is gonna take his place." Preto smiled, and looked back at Travon. "Ain't that right, boy?"

Travon nodded. His thoughts were elsewhere. His thoughts were on Cooney's last comment. *The Crips had killed his brother.*

For several long months, dozens of potential suspects had passed through his head. He had surmised that it had been someone affiliated with one of the local Crip gangs; he had even gone so far as to narrow it down to some members of the East Terrace. But now, now he knew for sure.

Elmira had talked to several detectives, and had been assured numerous times that they were working diligently to solve the case. They had refused to give her any idea who they were investigating, or who they suspected. And yet, they knew. They all knew. And they had known it all along.

Travon's anger built up like a pressure cooker. The Crips had killed his brother. The thought of Dejuan riding around with Big Mike made Travon feel as though he wanted to explode. He felt betrayed; thoughts of vengeance and malice danced through his mind.

"I'ma kill his ass," Travon muttered.

"What was that?" Preto asked.

Travon shook his head and stared out of the window. "Nothing."

"Well, look here, this is how it's gonna go," Cooney explained. "If somebody starts cutting in on your profits, or getting in the way of your comin' up, let us know and we'll roll on 'em."

They pulled into the parking lot of Mrs. Chang's grocery store and stopped. Preto and Cooney climbed out of the vehicle, walked to the rear where Travon was seated, and pulled him forcefully out of the car. Preto shoved Travon, turning him around, and then slammed him against the trunk, where he proceeded to uncuff him. Cooney reached into the passenger side of the vehicle, grabbed the backpack; which was now six thousand dollars lighter, and slammed it into Travon's chest.

"How do I find you guys to pay you?" Travon asked.

"Don't worry, we'll find you," Cooney replied.

"What about my bike?" Travon asked. "It's in the Courts where the shooting happened. And what about the guys? Lil Texas, Quentin, Tech Nine, and all of them?"

"Don't worry, Tre. We'll take care of all of that," Preto told him with a smile. "Relax, we're partners now."

Cooney climbed back inside the squad car.

Preto gave Travon a wink, and opened the passenger side door. "Trust us."

"I ain't partners with no niggers," Cooney shouted at Preto as the latter climbed into the vehicle.

Travon could hear Cooney continuing to protest Preto's choice of words, as the squad car pulled away. Once the car was fully out of view, Travon staggered into the store.

"What's up, Mrs. Chang?" Travon asked, upon entering into the store.

"Oh, nothing," Mrs. Chang exhaled. "Just trying to assemble this damn camera."

"Why? What's up? Has somebody been fuckin'g with you?"

"Oh, no! Nobody's been fucking with me. Everybody knows that you boys would kill them." Mrs. Chang smiled. "No, it's for this damn insurance company. I'm trying to get my theft insurance down, so I have to put in this camera. They think that every store in a minority neighborhood has theft problems. For some reason, they have a problem believing that minorities can work and pay for what they want."

Travon laughed, then made the short trip to the cooler. He opened up a cool frosty bottle of Red Bull, and turned it up to his lips. The cold liquid felt rejuvenating to his tired, thirsty, and mentally exhausted body. He drank nearly half the bottle before venturing to the counter, paying for it, and then heading out for the trip to Aunt Vera's house.

Travon struggled down Pine Street, made the turn onto Palmetto, and was halfway down that street, when a small, two-door Hyundai passed him up, hit its brakes, and then slowly began to back up toward him. Too tired to run, duck, hide, or shoot, Travon simply kept walking forward to meet whatever destiny that fate had bequeathed him. He did not know much, but he did know one thing. If he was going to die, he was at least going to die with his thirst quenched. Travon lifted the beer bottle to his lips and drank heavily.

The window on the passenger side of the Hyundai rolled down slowly, and a familiar face came into view. It was Tamika.

"Tre! Tre!" She waved as she called to him.

The car pulled up beside Travon.

"What are you doing out here, girl?" Travon asked. He could not help the smile that spread across his face.

"Just cruising with my sister before I go to work," she answered.

"Where do you work at?" he asked. "You never told me."

She pointed. "Right up the street at Church's Chicken on New Braunsfels Road."

"You lying!" he said excitedly. The restaurant was just up the street from where he now lived. He could walk there.

She nodded. "For real! So, what are you doing out here?"

He leaned against the roof of the car and peered inside. "I stay out here now. I live with my aunt."

Her eyes flew open wide. "Oooh, for real? Then you can come to my job and kick it with me."

"Yeah, you know I'm down for that. Say, Tamika, you never gave me your phone number either."

"There are a lot of things that I ain't gave you, that I'm gonna give you."

"Girl, shut your hot tail up!" Varika, Tamika's sister, shouted from the driver's seat.

Tamika opened the glove box, grabbed a pen, and wrote her number down on a loose piece of paper. She handed the paper to Travon.

Travon examined the number and smiled. "I'm gonna call you tonight. What time do you get off?"

"At ten. But I won't get home until about ten thirty, so call me about eleven."

Travon nodded. "Okay."

"So, where are you going now?"

He stared down the street. It looked even longer now than it did five minutes ago. A bead of sweat rolled down his forehead. "To my aunt's house."

"Do you want a ride?" Tamika asked.

"Yeah." Travon backed away from the door, giving Tamika room to open it.

She climbed out of the tiny car, lifted the latch on the seat, and pulled it forward. Travon moved the seat belt out of the way and clumsily climbed into the backseat.

"Thanks," Travon said to Varika.

Tamika climbed back inside the car and closed the door.

"I'm gonna show you where I live now, so don't forget," Travon told Tamika. "You know, just in case you want to come and visit me late one night."

Travon and Tamika laughed, while Varika smiled and shook her head.

"Bust a left, then a right, and then go straight down until I tell you to stop," Travon told Varika.

Tamika turned toward Travon, and patted her sister on her shoulder. "Oh, Tre, this is my sister, Varika."

Travon nodded. "What's up, Varika?"

"Hi." Varika smiled at Travon through the rearview mirror and gave a slight wave. She was the mirror image of her younger sister.

"Tre, one day I'm going to kidnap you, and I'm going to hold you hostage for days," Tamika told him.

"You know that you don't have to kidnap me, I'll go anywhere with you, girl," Travon told Tamika. He turned and tapped Varika on her shoulder. "Right up here where this burgundy house is."

Varika pulled up to Aunt Vera's house. Tamika climbed out of the car and lifted the seat up so that Travon could climb out of the back.

"I see your work, kinfolk!" Darius shouted from the porch.

Tamika smiled, grabbed Travon's head, and then pulled him close and stuck her tongue in his mouth. Startled, Travon froze. He had kissed girls in the Courts before, but none as pretty, or forward, as Tamika. He had had a crush on her since kindergarten. And now they were kissing.

Tamika slowly pulled her lips away from Travon's, quickly climbed back inside of the car, and ordered her sister to drive away quickly. Travon could hear them giggling as he stood near the curb in a trance-like state, watching as the car rounded the corner and disappeared.

A familiar voice called out from the porch. "What's up, Blood?"

It was a voice Travon knew all too well; a voice that brought goose bumps and raised the hairs on his arms. "Shit," he whispered, as he turned toward the porch. He hadn't noticed his Aunt Chicken's car in the drive-way. Now his cousin Capone walked out of the front door, followed by his other cousin, Romeo. Capone was one year older; Travon and Romeo were the same age.

"I hope they go home soon," Travon whispered beneath his breath.

"What's up, Tre?" Romeo asked.

"Nothin', kinfolk," Travon replied. He forced a smile and hugged Romeo. When finished, he turned and hugged Capone.

"You know we served them niggaz after we heard what they did to you," Capone told Travon.

"Oh, yeah?" Travon was surprised. Although knowing his cousins, he knew that he should not have been. They irritated him to death, but they also stuck together. Theirs was a close family. In his opinion, too close.

"Hell yeah, Blood!" Romeo shouted. "We took they motherfuckin' hats to 'em!"

Aunt Chicken walked out of the front door.

"Tre, baby, come and give your Aunt Chicken a hug," she told him, spreading her arms wide.

Travon dragged himself up the porch steps and embraced his aunt tightly.

After hugging him, she leaned back slightly and stared into his eyes. "Are you all right?"

Travon nodded. "Yeah, I'm okay."

"That's good. Now come on in here and call your mother. She's been worried sick about you. They been shootin' over in them damn Courts again." Chicken shook her head and frowned. "I don't know why Elmira insists on staying out there, when she can come and live with me, or Vera, or Gina, or a hundred other people. She's just so damn prideful and stubborn!"

She pounded her two tiny fists together. "Times like this, I just get mad at her!"

Travon walked inside, lifted the telephone, and dialed his mother's number.

CHAPTER NINE

"Hello?"

"Momma, it's me, Tre. What's up? Chicken said that you was worried about me."

"Oh, baby, I just wanted to hear your voice, and make sure that you was all right. V said that you left early this morning, and that she hadn't seen you since. Plus, Miss Martha told me that they had a great big old shoot-out over here earlier."

"Oh," Travon said, hesitating for several moments, before finally regaining his composure. "Naw, I'm doing fine. I just ran around the corner to kick it for a while."

"Well, they say that Quentin got shot in the stomach, and that Smoke got grazed in the head. The bad part is, Miss Elly's granddaughter got killed." Elmira sniffled, trying to hold back her tears. "I know what that woman is going through right now."

Travon could not speak.

"The police are saying that it was them Crip boys that did it, and that it was just a gang shooting. Them the same group a boys that they say shot your brother, and they ain't got them boys yet. They need to close that damn East Terrace down, and put all them boys in jail! Oooh, Tre, baby, it's on TV right now! Channel Five, hurry, baby!"

Travon lifted the remote and turned the television on. He quickly flipped to Channel Five News and turned up the volume.

The news showed footage of Quentin lying on a stretcher and throwing up gang signs as the paramedics loaded him into an ambulance. The news cameras then cut to Smoke One, who was seated on the curb, holding a large blood-stained bandage to his forehead.

"Another shooting on the city's Eastside occurred today," the anchorman announced to the audience. "This one happened in the city's Wheatley Courts housing projects. It left two wounded, and one child dead."

The camera cut to footage of a woman holding a little girl's limp body, while screaming hysterically.

"Tre," Elmira called to her son over the telephone. "Tre."

"Hold on, Momma, let me cut the TV down." Travon lifted the remote control and silenced the television. "Okay, I'm here."

"Boy, you say something when I'm talking to you," Elmira told him.

"Momma, the night Too-Low died, he told me to hold some money for him. I been holding it, but...Momma, I know that he would want you to have it. It's enough to buy you a car. You could work the day shift, and do home visits, and make enough money to get out of there. Momma, I could move back home and help out, and you wouldn't have to take the bus no more. We could probably be out of the Courts in a couple of months."

"Tre, honey, all this time you and your brother been sticking money in my purse, and pretending like I didn't know, what did you think that I was thinking? Did you think that I believed in the Good Fairy? Tre, I know that you mean well, but I don't want your brother's money. Buy you a car, buy you some school clothes, or take your Aunt Vera out to eat. Have fun with it, it's yours now."

"But, Momma! You could buy you a car, and you wouldn't have to ride the bus at night, and then have to wait all morning until they start running again!"

"It's dope money, Tre!" Elmira shouted. "It's poison! I don't want your brother's blood money. I have never complained about riding the bus, not once, have I, Tre?"

"But, Momma."

"Tre!" Elmira cut him off. "Do you know what I did with your brother's money?"

Travon remained silent.

"I saved it! I saved all of it, and I used it to bury him. I paid for his funeral with it. The same money that he got from putting people in the ground, I used to put him in the ground!" Elmira shouted. She began sobbing heavily. "I took his death money, and I paid it to the funeral home, and I buried my child! I buried my child," she repeated softly.

"I'm sorry, Momma," Travon whispered. "I'm sorry."

Elmira sniffled. "Don't be sorry, baby, just do something for yourself. That part of our lives is over now, Tre. Now go on with *your* life and do something for yourself. If you really want to help Momma, then go to school and graduate. Become a doctor, or a lawyer, or something. Make me proud."

"But I want to help you now."

"Baby, I know, and I love you for it. If you want to help that much, then go to school in the daytime, and get a job working after school. We'll open us an account together, and we'll both put money into it. We'll use it to buy a car, so I can work in the daytime and get my ass outta these Courts. Then you can come and live with me again. How does that sound?"

"It sounds good," Travon told her.

"All right, baby, I got to go and get ready for work. But I'll talk to you later."

"Okay."

"'Bye," Elmira whispered softly. "I love you, baby."

"Love you, too."

Travon placed the telephone receiver down into its base. With his thoughts still on the conversation with his mother, he rose from the living room couch and slowly walked to the front door. He stood silently, peering out of the dark screen door, not ready to be seen or partake in the conversation between his Aunt Chicken and the others, who were now seated around the front porch.

"Anybody ever tell you that you are finer than a motherfucka, Mrs. C?" Lil Fade asked.

"Boy, go on!" Chicken replied. "I'm old enough to be your mother."

"Say, they don't make women like you no more, Mrs. C," Lil Bling told her. He lifted his bottle of beer to his lips and took a long swig from it. "You can cook, you clean, you work, you stay in shape, and you down."

"What, you think that just because I got kids, I'm supposed to be an old fogey? I know what's up." Chicken smiled, and walked to where Big Pimpin was standing. He had both hands hidden behind his back. Chicken wrapped both arms around him, as if she were about to give him a seductive embrace, and then stepped back, holding the joint that he had been trying to hide. Holding it in the air like a cigarette, she turned and sashayed away from him, switching her curvaceous hips. On the way back to her spot on the porch, she lifted the joint to her full red lips and drew from it.

"Momma!" Romeo called out to her. "What are you doing smoking weed?"

"I smoke weed all the time. Or at least whenever I can steal it from your brother's hiding spot in the backyard."

Capone's cheeks flushed red with embarrassment, and he quickly shifted his gaze to the ground.

"Haaa, Mrs. C is down, boy!" Lil Fade shouted.

"Say, Mrs. C, I wish my moms was down like you," Lil Bling told her.

"Where is that little girl you was talking to?" Chicken asked. "What was her name? Niesha? I like her, she is so sweet, and cute too."

Lil Bling shook his head. "Man, she be trippin', Mrs. C. She don't want to give me none. She talkin' about wait until she thinks it's right."

Chicken leaned back against the porch banister. "Why should she? All those girls you be messin' with. Boy, what if you gave her something, or got her pregnant? You ain't got no job, no house, no nothing." Chicken pointed toward his thick gold herringbone necklace. "And that little hustle you got, it ain't gonna last too long."

Chicken waved her well-manicured hand at Lil Bling, dismissing him. "Boy, you crazy, that ought to be the one you want to keep. That tells you that she ain't no hot-tail little girl."

Lil Bling nodded. "Yeah, Mrs. C, I know you right. I'll just hang on to her, and dip with somebody else."

Chicken slapped him across his shoulder. "Boy, that ain't what I said!"

The boys gathered around the porch broke into laughter.

"Mrs. C got all the answers," Lil Fade declared.

Chicken puffed on the joint, and exhaled seductively into the air. "I'm thirty-six years old, with a nineteen-year-old daughter, an eighteen-year-old daughter, a seventeen-year-old son, and a sixteen-year-old son. Child, I do not have all of the answers. As you grow older, you'll make mistakes, but you'll learn from them."

Travon opened the front door and stepped out onto the porch. If his Aunt Chicken wanted to play the wise old sage, then he had a problem that he wanted to present to her.

"Aunt Chicken, Momma be trippin'," Travon announced. "I tried to give her some money that Too-Low left, but she won't take it. Can you talk to her for me?"

"Tre, baby, your momma is very proud, and very stubborn," Chicken told him. "She's been that way since we was little girls. If she don't want to take the money, ain't nothing I can say that will change her mind."

Travon shook his head and looked down.

"Tre, the only thing that I can tell you is to get a job and give her the money little by little, like you're getting it from your paycheck," Chicken added.

Travon lifted his head and smiled.

"El don't have to know how much you make, or where the money is really coming from, sweetie," Chicken continued. "Hell, you can just tell her that you got a job, and give it to her little by little."

Travon squinted and peered off into the distance. *Damn*, he thought, she really did have all the answers.

Lil Fade turned up the volume on the CD player, and Chicken quickly made her way onto the grass, where she began dancing.

"Say, Mrs. C," Lil Fade called out. "Anybody ever tell you that you look like Vanessa Williams' identical twin?"

"Child, Vanessa's titties and ass ain't as big as mines," Chicken replied.

"Momma! You need to cut that shit out!" Romeo yelled.

Chicken smiled devilishly. "It's the truth."

Travon seated himself on the porch banister and examined his Aunt

Chicken. Today, she was wearing tight-fitting, low-cut, faded blue jeans, red furry slippers, and a red half-shirt that exposed her tight, muscled midsection. Her sandy hair was pulled back into a long, silky ponytail, and her natural green eyes sparkled like emeralds every time the sun struck them. For the first time in his life, Travon realized just how beautiful his Aunt Chicken really was. And as she began dancing and moving around provocatively to the booty-shaking song that was playing on the radio, Travon came to one more conclusion. His Aunt Chicken really was fine as hell.

"Damn!" Lil Fade cried out, watching Chicken dance.

"Damn!" Big Pimpin agreed.

"Damn!" Lil Bling shook his head.

Travon saw a different side of his aunt that evening. It was a side that had always been there, but one that he had paid little attention to. She really was down, he thought. She was cool, understanding, and eternally youthful. She was someone he could trust, someone he could talk to, someone who would listen, and understand, and have his best interest at heart. A new level of respect was found that evening, as well as a new ally. Aunt Chicken was the shit.

CHAPTER TEN

In a House on Colorado Street

"Hand me the Pyrex," Darius told him.

Travon walked to the kitchen table, grabbed a long glass dish, and handed it to Darius. Darius took the dish, poured half a kilogram of cocaine into it, and then walked to the sink. He sat the Pyrex dish on the counter next to him, then opened a cupboard and removed a glass. He filled the glass with lukewarm water and then handed it to Travon, who was standing just behind him, watching his every move.

Darius grabbed the Pyrex dish from the counter and carried it to the kitchen table, where he sat it down. Travon followed with the glass of water and placed it next to the Pyrex dish.

"Open that box of baking soda on the counter, and bring it here," Darius commanded.

Travon did as he was told. Darius poured some onto a triple beam scale, which had also been sitting on the table. He turned to Travon.

"This is about how much baking soda you need for a half a key."

Travon nodded.

Darius lifted the Pyrex, and held it near the scale. He then gently raked the baking soda into the dish with the cocaine, whereupon he carefully stirred the mixture with his index finger.

"Tre, hand me that spatula."

Travon lifted a rubber spatula from off of the counter and placed it in his cousin's waiting hand. Darius sat the Pyrex dish on the table and carefully began to add water from the glass, all the while stirring gently with the spatula.

"Cut on the two burners on the left side," Darius ordered, pointing toward the stove.

He continued to nurse his mixture, stirring gently, and adding water when necessary. When finally his mixture reached the desired consistency, he carried the off-white, pasty substance to the stove, where he placed it on top of the two lit burners. He then turned and smiled at his cousin.

"I'm the best at this," Darius boasted.

On the stove, his pasty mixture began to melt into an oily, yellowish liquid, as he stirred with increasing speed.

"Tre, hand me that jar that I brought from the house," Darius ordered.

Travon lifted the jar into the air and examined it. "What is this shit?"

"That's how we win, boy!" Darius announced excitedly. "It's vitamin B-12. It blows up the dope, so you get more. It's like putting yeast in a biscuit. Don't worry, I'm gonna teach you how to win! If it's one thing your kinfolk is, it's a winner."

Darius poured some of the powdery substance into his oily mixture, and stirred until everything was blended perfectly. Then he turned off the burners on the stove.

"We gotta let it cool down now," he told Travon. "Then we'll cut it up, weigh it, and bag it."

One Hour Later

Travon and Darius removed the hardened substance from the stove, and placed it on a large plate that was sitting on the table. Also on the table was a scale, several other plates, a bag of razor blades, a box of sandwich bags, and a large plastic grocery sack. Darius removed one of the razor blades from the bag, and peeled off its protective paper cover.

"Now is the fun part," Darius announced.

Marcus breezed into the room carrying a large bucket, which he sat on the floor next to Darius.

"What's that for?" Travon asked, pointing at the bucket.

"It's acid," Marcus told him. "Just in case the task force tries to run in on us."

"Yeah." Darius nodded. "We can dump this shit in a hurry. This is about a life sentence in the Feds, and I ain't trying to give them hoes that long. I really ain't trying to give 'em nothing!"

Marcus left to resume his station at the living room window. Travon and Darius turned their attention back to the hard, brittle substance on the table.

The crack was sitting on a plate, in three large, thick, yellowish-white slabs. Darius took two slabs and put them on a separate plate, to get them out of the way. He then took his single-edge razor blade and began to cut on the third. Each cut with the tip of his blade made the substance snap precisely into several large pieces. He placed each piece on the scale, and then cut or added smaller pieces until the scale read twenty-eight grams.

"Tre, bag these up as I give them to you. Each one of the sandwich baggies will have an ounce in it."

Travon removed the pieces from the scale, placed them into a small plastic sandwich bag, and tied the bag up tightly. He then took a razor blade, peeled off its protective paper cover, and used it to cut off the excess plastic from each of the sandwich bags.

"It's still a little bit wet," Travon told Darius.

"I know it ain't all the way dry, that's why we're baggin' it now. We want to keep in as much of the moisture as possible, because that's part of how you win. If they weigh it, it'll come out to twenty-eight grams, because of the water. But it's not really twenty-eight grams of dope. Them fools is paying for the water too!" Darius howled a sinister laugh. "I'ma teach you all the tricks of the trade, so that you can come up."

Darius turned his attention to the table, where he counted out twenty-six ounces, each bagged separately. He lifted eight of them into the air.

"These are the overs, Tre," he announced. "I'ma give Marcus one for looking out, and I'm a take three for cooking. These twenty-two are yours. We gotta give the dope fiend all of the crumbs for letting us cook here." Darius pointed to a plate full of small white chips. "That's about a sixteenth right there. That ought to keep his ass happy."

Travon lifted the ounces up to the light and examined them. "What do you think I ought to charge for each one of these?"

Darius shrugged. "Shit, charge seven hundred to the homies, and seven fifty or eight to the rest of them niggaz. Ain't nothing out there right now but boo-boo, for four and five hundred."

Travon quickly calculated the figures inside of his head. Seven hundred dollars, multiplied by twenty-two, was fifteen thousand, four hundred dollars. Plus, another thirty-five hundred dollars for the ounces that Dejuan had given him, and the six thousand dollars in cash that he found in his brother's room, made twenty-four thousand, nine hundred dollars. It was a car and a down payment on a house for his mother. But, what if he didn't get rid of it in bulk? What if he broke the ounces down to twenty-dollar pieces, and sold those pieces himself? How much could he make then?

"D, how much do you think I could make if I cut these up, and sold them stone for stone?"

"Shit!" Darius recoiled. "Probably about two Gs apiece."

The mathematical side of Travon's brain shifted into overdrive once again. Two thousand dollars, multiplied by twenty-seven, was fifty-four thousand dollars, plus the six thousand dollars that he had from his brother made sixty thousand dollars.

"Fuck," Travon whispered. He could buy his mother a house in the Heights, probably one close to his Aunt Vera's, and he could move back home. But first, he would have to get a job, or at least make his mother think that he had a job. But where?

It was something that he would have to think about later. For now, there were other details to work out. Again, he turned to Darius.

"Say, D, how long do you think it would take for me to sell all of this shit rock for rock?"

"What? Stone for stone, are you crazy?" Darius shook his head. "The object of the game is to move that shit as fast as you can, and then re-up."

"Yeah, but from who?" Travon asked. "Do you think Dejuan will be kind enough to let me score from him after I just got him for five ounces?"

"Good point," Darius conceded. "But there are other niggaz you could score from. Shit, you could score from Big Pimpin, Lil Bling, or any one of the other homies who are up."

Travon shook his head. "I want to do this a different way. So how long do you think it'll take?"

"To move one zone, it'll probably take you about three days, because everybody out here is pumping. But on the first and fifteenth, shit, it be rolling! You could probably sell about an ounce a day from the thirteenth to the third, and from the fourteenth to the sixteenth."

"So, I could probably sell about ten a month?"

"Maybe." Darius shrugged. "But you gotta grind your ass off. Straight hustling, and no sleeping."

Travon shifted his gaze to the white clumps lying on the table. They held his future. They controlled his destiny. Again, he began to calculate.

In roughly four months he could have the money to move his mother out of the Courts, he thought. In four months, he could change his life dramatically.

"Tre, I know that you're not thinking what I think you are thinking."

Travon smiled. "Yep."

"Shit." Darius shook his head. "Well, if you are serious, I think I know a good spot in the hood that ain't hot. We could probably set it up, and eventually get it jumpin.'"

Travon nodded. "Cool, I'm down." He and Darius clasped each other's hand, and then hugged.

Marcus strolled into the room. "Y'all ain't done yet?" He stretched and yawned. "Y'all need to hurry the fuck up!"

Later That Evening

"Hello?"

"Momma, what are you doin'?" Travon asked.

"Nothing," Elmira replied. "How are you doing, baby?"

"I'm doin' good," Travon told her. "I even got some good news for you."

"Oh, really? I was just about to call you and share some good news with you."

"What?"

"Naw, you first, baby," Elmira told him. "What's your good news?"

"I got a job," Travon announced.

"Oh, baby, that's wonderful! I'm so proud of you! Where are you working at?"

"I'm working at the neighborhood grocery store. You know Mrs. Chang?"

"Oh, baby, that just made my day! That really is the icing on the cake. I knew that everything would start working out for us. You just have to keep the faith."

"What's your good news?" Travon asked.

"Well, remember that program that Chicken went through to become an RN?"

"Yeah?"

"Well, I just got my acceptance letter in the mail today! I'm going to be working and going to school at the Humana Women and Children's Hospital! It's right downtown on the bus line, and they are paying me to go to school and get my RN."

"That's good, Momma!"

"Guess what else? Part of the program is, I'm going to be working for them as a nurse's aide from six until three; then from four to seven, I'll be attending classes right there in the hospital!"

"Momma, I'm so happy for you!"

"Happy for me? You should be happy for us! It only takes two years, and then I'm finished. The only thing is, I'll have to work for them for another four years before I can get another job. But I don't mind, because they are gonna be paying me more than I'm making right now anyway. It pays thirteen dollars an hour, and once I finish school, it goes up to thirty dollars an hour! Momma is going to be able to save, and get us a car, and get the hell outta these Courts. I can't wait for you to come and stay with me again."

"It'll be sooner than you think," Travon muttered under his breath.

"What's that, baby?"

"Nothin', Momma."

CHAPTER ELEVEN

Weeks Later

"Tre, where are you and Tamika going tonight?" Aunt Vera shouted into the living room.

"We're goin' to the movies again," Travon answered from the front door, about to exit.

Aunt Vera strolled into the living room wiping her wet hands on the apron tied around her waist.

"Tre, are you and that girl getting serious?" Vera asked.

"Well, I don't know, Aunt V. We have been kickin' it pretty tough lately, now that I think about it." Travon peered off into space, and nodded. "She's pretty cool."

Vera's expression turned serious. "Tre, you just better be careful. You know that stuff is out there." She jabbed her finger into his chest. "Don't bring home nothing you ain't left with, and that includes a baby!"

The color bled from Travon's cheeks, and he shifted his gaze to the floor. "I won't, Aunt V."

"That's the same thing that Chicken's fast-tail gal said, and she done already made me a great-aunt at the age of thirty-eight."

Travon folded his arms and tilted his head to the side. "Thirty-nine."

Vera balled her hand into a tight fist and waved it at him. "Oh, you want to get fly out the mouth, huh? If I want to be thirty-eight in my own damn house, then I can be thirty-eight!"

Travon laughed, rushed to his aunt, and kissed her. "Thanks, Aunt V."

Vera lifted her hand to her face and touched the spot on her cheek where she had been kissed. "What was all that for? Am I going to die or something?" She waved toward the kitchen. "Hell, Darius just came into the kitchen and started washing the dishes for me, and it ain't even his night. Marcus is up in his room sleep, and LaTonya ain't going out tonight because she says that she has to study! Lord, what have you kids done?"

Travon laughed. "Nothing, Aunt V."

A car horn sounded.

"That's my ride," Travon said, opening the door.

"Tre, baby," Vera paused, and stared at Travon sadly. "Just be careful."

"I will, Aunt V," Travon whispered. "I promise." He bounded out of the front door and down the porch steps.

"Tre, before I forget," Vera called out to him. "I just want to let you know that when you get home, we are gonna talk about you climbing in the window at six o'clock this morning."

Travon smiled at his aunt. He hadn't realized that he had been caught.

Vera frowned. "Be back before two, or have a damn good excuse when you walk into this house!" The scowl left her face just as quickly as it had appeared. She lifted her arm and waved. "Have a good time."

Travon climbed into the vehicle, and immediately leaned forward and kissed Tamika passionately.

"Hey, baby." Tamika smiled.

Travon nodded. "Hey, what's up?"

"This." Tamika leaned over the seat and kissed him passionately. By the time she finished, she was breathing heavily; Travon found that he had stiffened considerably.

"Hey, y'all cut that out!" Varika told them. "My man ain't here with me, so I'm a cock block."

Travon smiled at Varika, and then began to examine his surroundings. They were in a different vehicle tonight, and it piqued his curiosity. Varika usually picked him up in her Hyundai, and he had never seen her drive this burgundy Camry before.

"What happened to the other car?" Travon asked.

"It's at home," Varika told him. "I just wanted to drive my Camry tonight."

"When did you get this one?" Travon asked.

"I been had it," Varika answered. "I just don't want to put a whole lot of miles on it."

Travon turned and stared out of the window. They were getting on the highway, which was normal, but they were heading in the wrong direction. He leaned forward and tapped Varika on her shoulder.

"Say, ain't you going in the wrong direction?"

Varika shook her head. "No. I forgot something at my apartment. It won't take long."

Travon shifted in his seat, trying to reassure himself by ensuring that his handgun was tucked securely in his waistband. After a few moments, he shifted again, this time discreetly moving his hand across the handle of the Beretta. Tamika could tell that he was uncomfortable.

"Tre, just chill and enjoy the ride," Tamika told him. She shifted her gaze to her sister, and offered a slight smile. Varika countered by giving Tamika a knowing wink. Travon caught it all.

Varika exited the highway after a while, and traveled two short blocks before turning into King's Row apartments.

Travon again shifted nervously in his seat. He knew the apartments. On the Northeast side of the city, they belonged to the Bloods who inhabited Sunrise and the Glens; two notoriously violent neighborhoods whose inhabitants had a reputation of defending what they considered to be their territory.

Varika pulled up to an apartment in the rear of the complex, parked, and handed Tamika a single key. Tamika leaned over the seat once again, and gave Travon a quick kiss on his cheek before exiting the vehicle and disappearing up a nearby staircase. Travon turned his attention to Varika.

"So, where your man at?"

"He's in the Army," Varika answered.

Travon nodded. "That's cool. I thought about joining when I finish high school."

"Why?" Varika laughed. "You can't rap, or play sports?"

Travon joined in the laughter. "Either rapping, playing sports, or the military."

"Seems like those are the only ways out of the hood," Varika said.

"You forgot one," Travon added.

Varika's laughter slowly morphed into an engaging smile. "What other way is there?"

"Death."

The smiles faded from both their faces as their thoughts drifted to long-lost friends and family members. The expressions on each of their faces revealed the buried but still painful scars within. Travon turned away, and peered out of the car window. He knew he had to change the subject.

"So, where is your man at now, and why you ain't with him?"

"He's in Georgia right now," Varika replied. "But in two months he's coming back, and then we're going to Hawaii."

"Hawaii!" Travon sat up, quickly becoming animated. "Shit, that's a mutherfuckin' win right there! Kicking it on the beach, watching the hoes walk by, waves crashing at your feet and shit. That shit is lovely."

Varika faced Travon, her right eyebrow raised. "Why we got to be hoes?"

"Not you, you know what I mean." A smile slowly crept across Travon's face. "Prostitutes."

Varika shook her head and rolled her eyes toward the roof of her car. "Yeah, right. Prostitutes."

Travon smiled again.

Varika turned toward her apartment. "Damn, what's taking this girl so long? Tre, could you go and tell that girl that I said hurry up."

Travon nodded, and slowly climbed out of the vehicle. He closed the car door, rested his hand on the handle of his gun, and made his way up the stairs to Varika's apartment. He could hear music playing inside, but the apartment was dark.

Travon pushed open the door and slowly stepped inside. There were lit candles on the dining room table, and the thick sweet smell of incense permeated the air. The darkness was unnerving to him, and the sound of the car horn only served to rattle his nerves even more.

Travon rushed to the living room window and peered outside; only to see Varika's car pulling away. A pair of soft hands reached around his head and covered his eyes. He smelled Tamika.

Travon smiled, grabbed her hands, pulled them to his lips, and began to kiss them gently.

"Remember when I saw you walking down the street in the Heights, and me and my sister gave you a ride?" Tamika asked.

Travon turned and faced her. The realization of her nakedness startled him more than the car horn had. His eyes flew wide and he gasped.

Tamika placed her hand beneath Travon's chin, and pulled his face close to hers. Their lips locked, and her tongue entered into his mouth, and soon, into his ear. She could feel him throbbing against her naked thigh.

"Tamika, what's up with the setup?" Travon asked softly. "We could have just went to a room like we been doing."

"Tre, I always wanted to steal you away," Tamika whispered. "It's my fantasy, so just play along."

They kissed again. Slowly, softly, at first, until their passion climbed to a fiery plateau. Breathing heavily, Tamika pulled away from Travon, and nodded toward her sister's bedroom. Her chest felt tight, and her breaths were heavy. She was ready.

"C'mon," she whispered, taking Travon's hand and kissing it softly. Slowly, she turned and walked into the bedroom.

Travon stood in the living room, watching her taut, tan body stroll down the hall. She was beautiful in the candlelight

Keith Sweat's "You May Be Young but You're Ready" began playing on the CD. The song made him shake his head and smile. Tamika had planned everything perfectly.

Travon entered the bedroom to find Tamika pulling the sheets down on the bed. He slowly began undressing.

"I wanted to do that," Tamika told him. She smacked her lips and pouted.

Travon walked to where Tamika was standing and stopped just in front of her. Tamika sat down on the bed and began to undo Travon's pants.

"Tre, don't laugh," she said, nervously. "But I want to try something."

A smile slowly crept across Travon's face. "Go ahead." He thought that he knew what she was going to do.

Tamika leaned forward, placed Travon's zipper between her lips, and unzipped his pants with her teeth. Travon laughed heartily, placed his hand over his private area, and stepped back. Tamika quickly joined in the laughter.

"Girl, you are silly," Travon told her.

Smiling, Tamika climbed into the bed and patted the spot next to her. Travon quickly dispensed with the remainder of his clothing, and then joined her.

Travon's tongue slowly glided down Tamika's neck, causing her to lift her head and moan softly. It felt good to her. She thought his warm tongue to be magical. He moved slowly up her neck, and then up to her earlobe, where he began to nibble softly.

"That tickles," Tamika whispered, as she wiggled away.

Travon's tongue glided slowly down her neck and onto her chest, where he began nibbling gently.

The sensation caused her to moan loudly. Travon moved from one breast to the other, engulfing her nipples, sucking, nibbling, and licking. Tamika could feel him throbbing against her leg. It made her yearn for him desperately.

"C'mon, Tre," she whispered.

Travon smiled at Tamika, and continued his journey south. His tongue glided over her stomach, worked its way around her navel, until finally, he reached his destination. Tamika moaned loudly, and placed her hand on the back of his neck. His tongue glided across her, and she spread her legs father apart. Travon lashed out with his tongue, stroking her deeper and deeper with each passing, each time evoking a louder and more passionate cry. Tamika gripped his head tightly with both of her hands, and began to rotate, squirm, and gasp for air. Finally, she reached the summit of her passion, arching her back and stiffening for several moments.

"See what you did?" she told him softly. "Boy, I could kill you."

Together, they laughed.

"Can I try something now?" Tamika asked.

Travon began his journey northward, licking and kissing Tamika all over her sweating body, until they were once again face-to-face.

"Lay back," she ordered.

Travon lay back onto the bed, and Tamika began to kiss his neck softly. Pecking lightly, she slowly descended, licking his chest, and stopping briefly at his navel. Travon grabbed her arms, halting her descent.

"You don't have to do this, just because I did it to you," he told her.

"I want to try it, Tre," she told him. "So just lay back."

Tamika continued to kiss Travon's lower body, until finally, he felt her around his manhood. His body shuddered, and he quickly grabbed her by her head.

"Oh, shit! Oh, Tamika!"

Tamika's tongue became playful around his privates. She tickled parts of him that he didn't know were sensitive. Soon, she engulfed him once more, and began to move in a rhythmic stroke that quickly had an effect on Travon. He had to grab her.

"Tamika, you'd better stop. Hold on, girl!"

Tamika laughed, and began to journey upward. When she reached his lips, they kissed passionately. Tamika straddled Travon, gently placed him inside of her, and began to move her body in a rhythmic, counterclockwise motion. He felt good to her, and she to him, grinding, thrusting, pumping, and moving their bodies in ways they had only recently discovered. Travon watched the moonlight creeping through the blinds dance across her glistening body, and was reminded of just how beautiful Tamika really was.

"Ooooh, Tre," Tamika moaned.

Travon slowly slid in and out of her. Their rhythm built, their moans increased, until finally they both reached a back-arching, climactic release that soothed them both. Exhausted, the two of them lay basking in the soft glow of the moonlight creeping through the blinds, blissfully unaware that they now had become three.

CHAPTER TWELVE

Weeks Later

"Yeah, just drop us off at the park; we can get a ride home," said Marcus.
Darius nodded. "All right, y'all lil niggaz get in."

Travon and Marcus quickly climbed into the backseat of Darius' 1990,
candy-apple-red Cadillac Fleetwood.

"Boy, D, you got this motherfucka looking lovely," Lil Fade told him.
"Red candy paint, red flakes, white crushed guts, gold and chrome Caddy
discs, vogues, gold cc grill, white rag, gold buttons, and a gold fifth! Shit,
all you need is some juice now!"

"Fuck juice!" Darius told him. "All that shit does is fuck up your ride.
You know what I'm saying, Blood?"

"Yo mothafuckin' ass done came up, Blood!" Lil Fade told him. "This
shit is lovely. Lovely!"

Darius turned the volume up on his car's stereo system, and the trunk
began to rattle from the heavy bass notes.

"You need to get that shit checked," Marcus shouted.

"Say, y'all niggaz is gonna have to show me y'all spot!" Lil Fade told them.
"Shit, I wanna come up too!"

Darius turned toward Lil Fade and smiled. "Yeah, whatever, man."

"Say, put in some mothafuckin' Scarface, man. Get that mothafuckin'
whack-ass shit outta here." Lil Fade ejected Darius' CD from the stereo,
rolled down his window, and tossed the CD out onto the road. "Put in some
mothafuckin' Texas shit. Some Scarface, UGK, Big Mike, Ghetto Boys,

PSK, Terrorist, or some 4 Deep. Don't be playing no bullshit when I'm rolling with you!"

"Nigga, fuck you!" Darius shouted. "If you don't like my mothafuckin' music, you can get your ass out and walk!"

"Say, Blood, who did your shit?" Marcus asked Lil Fade.

"I had that little hood rat Tawanna braid it for me last night," said Lil Fade.

"That shit is cleaner than a motherfucka," Marcus told him.

Lil Fade lowered the side sun visor and examined himself in the mirror. His hair had been sectioned off into lots of neat, orderly squares, with red rubber bands at the roots of each section. The hair itself spiraled down into long, silky, sandy-colored Shirley Temple curls.

Suddenly a police siren sounded behind them.

Darius peered into his rear view mirror, and spied the red-and-blue lights of a police car, signaling for him to pull over.

"Fuck!" Darius banged on his steering wheel, and then turned down the stereo. He turned to Lil Fade. "You dirty?"

Lil Fade shook his head. "No, for the first time in my life. I ain't never got pulled over before and not have to bail. This shit ought to be fun."

Darius threw his head back in laughter, and carefully pulled his car to the side of the road. The patrol car pulled up just behind them.

The officer seated on the passenger side walked to the rear passenger side of the Caddy, where he stood with his gloved hand resting on his service automatic. The driver approached Darius.

"I noticed that your music was kinda loud back there, that's why I pulled you over," the officer told Darius. "Can I see your driver's license, and proof of insurance?"

Darius pulled out his wallet and gave the Bexar County Sheriff's Deputy what he wanted. The deputy walked back to his patrol car, climbed inside, and began running a check on Darius.

"Shit, is that all they be wanting?" Lil Fade asked.

The boys shared a laugh.

"Say, D," Marcus called out. "Where in the hell did you get that fake-ass insurance from?"

Darius peered over his shoulder at Marcus. "Fuck you, nigga! My shit is real!"

An additional Bexar County Sheriff's Department patrol car arrived, and two more deputies climbed out and approached. The officer standing just behind the Cadillac held up four fingers. The new deputies nodded. One of them returned to their patrol car and immediately began to use the radio. The second continued on to Darius' car.

"Hi, how are you fellows today?" the deputy asked. "I'm Deputy Gomez, that gentleman behind the vehicle is Deputy Martinez, and his partner is Deputy Sergeant Fisk. My partner over there is Deputy Sergeant White. When Deputy Fisk stopped you, he kind of noticed that you guys were all wearing the same colors, and that your car stands out just a little. We've been having a lot of problems with gangs lately." Deputy Gomez held up his hands. "Now, I'm not saying that you guys are gang members, but we would like to identify you for future reference. That way, we can make sure that you are not mistaken for gang members by other deputies. It won't take long; we're just going to ask you some questions and have you do a few things for us. It's for your safety and ours, and it will make things go a whole lot faster for us."

Gomez looked up; White exited his patrol car and nodded. Gomez stepped back, and pulled open Darius' car door.

"I need for you to exit the vehicle for me, please," he told Darius and Marcus.

White walked to the passenger side of the vehicle, asking Lil Fade and Travon to exit the vehicle, one by one.

Gomez pointed to a spot in the grass next to the road. "Could you lie down here for me?" he asked Darius. Gomez turned to Marcus. "I need for you to get out and lie down over here in the grass next to your buddy."

Fisk exited his patrol car and briskly walked over to the others.

Gomez turned to his partner. "Could you bring those two over here for me, Sarge?"

White led Travon and Lil Fade to where Darius and Marcus were lying in the grass and motioned for them to join their buddies. Then each deputy searched one of the boys.

"Clear," White announced.

"Clear," Martinez followed.

"He's clear," Fisk told the others.

"Clear over here," Gomez declared. He clapped his hands together, to get the boys' attention. "Okay, good. Listen up, guys. The hard part is all over with, so you can sit up now. That way you don't have to be lying in all that itchy grass."

White patted Gomez on his back. "Good work, Gomez."

Fisk cleared his throat. "You boys have been cooperating nicely, and everything is going along smoothly. We need to ask you a favor now. Which one of you is Darius?"

"I am." Darius lifted his hand into the air.

"Can we have your permission to search your vehicle?" Fisk asked.

Darius shrugged. "I don't care."

"Just hurry the fuck up!" Lil Fade told them.

Fisk lifted a finger toward Lil Fade. "Don't start."

"Are we under arrest?" Lil Fade.

"Look, man, just be cool," Gomez told Lil Fade. "We've been cool with you, so just be cool with us. We haven't handcuffed you, stuck you in the back of a squad car, or anything."

Lil Fade smacked his lips and turned away.

Two Bexar County Sheriff's Department Ford Explorers and two all-white unmarked Crown Victorias with tinted windows pulled up. Out came a dog, a dog handler, two men in suits, and ten more deputies.

"Shit!" Lil Fade looked down and began shaking his head. "I knew I should have bailed."

"Who bagged?" one of the suited gentlemen asked Fisk.

"Me and Martinez, but Gomez got the lead, because he's got the rap."

The suited gentleman turned toward the other suit, and they began whispering. After several moments, they turned and approached a deputy with numerous stripes on his uniform. The three of them conversed in private for several moments, before turning and heading toward the boys.

The handler began running his dog through Darius' vehicle, and three of the uniformed deputies began to search the inside of the vehicle as well.

"I'm Special Agent Riley, and this is Special Agent Danforth, and we're part of the local Federal Gang Task Force," the suited agent informed Darius. "We're here to ask you boys some questions and get some general information from you. We'll need your name, date of birth, nicknames, street name, place of residency, the name of your gang, and we'll be checking for scars, birthmarks, tattoos, and things of that nature. We'll also need to know what that body art means, when you guys joined the gang, where the gang is located, and we'll also be taking your fingerprints as well."

"G.T.F. One, what is your location and status?" the dispatcher inquired over the crackling radio.

Special Agent Riley lifted his radio to his mouth. "Houston and Coliseum, over."

"G.T.F. One, PC Fifty-two has five possible pulled over at the Diamond Shamrock on W.W. White Road, just north of Interstate Thirty-five, what's your ETA, over?"

"Ahhh, negative on that ETA, Dispatch," Agent Riley replied. "We'll be about another thirty minutes on this one, over."

"Roger, G.T.F. One," Dispatch replied. "Will dispatch G.T.F. Four, out."

"We'll head over and assist Fifty-two until Four arrives," Fisk told the other deputies.

Deputy Dominguez, the one with all the stripes, nodded and patted Fisk on his shoulder. "Roger that, and good bag, guys. We got us two knowns here. I know Darius and Lil Fade already, so it's just a matter of adding the other two to the file. Good work."

Fisk and Martinez climbed inside of their patrol car, and slowly pulled away, quickly followed by White and Gomez. Deputy Dominguez turned toward the Federal Agents and waved for them to approach.

"Riley, could you and Danforth come over here for a minute," Dominguez said. The Federal Agents walked around the Cadillac and approached the waiting senior deputy. Dominguez gathered them close, wrapping his arms around them and enveloping them into a whispering huddle.

"I know two of the boys," he informed them. "They are definite BSV's, which is a well-known faction of the Bloods. The other two boys, we'll just have to tag and release, and then we're outta here. Judging by the dress, they are in all probability also affiliated with the Bloods, so this one looks like it'll be pretty easy."

"Good." Danforth nodded.

"Do we have complete files on the two knowns?" Riley asked.

"Yep. They've been banging for a long time. They should be in the high-level, active files."

Danforth shifted his gaze toward the boys. "Shit, we got us a couple of One Alphas here!"

"This ought to be exciting," Riley added.

Dominguez wanted to call them idiots, but professional courtesy prevented him from doing so.

"So, what's the plan?" Danforth asked. "Are we going to go with the good cop-bad cop routine?"

Dominguez squinted as he examined the agent. "So, did you attend Boston College on a scholarship?

Danforth shook his head. "No, my parents paid for it. Why?"

Dominguez shook his head. "No reason. Just wondering if my tax dollars paid for it. No need for any routine."

Deputy Dominguez was a plump, rough-and-tough, dark-skinned Hispanic who had worked the streets of San Antonio for more than twenty years. He knew the streets and the players like he knew the back of his hand. He was a veteran, and a professional.

"Lil Fade, stand up for me, and take your shirt off!" Dominguez barked. He waved his hand around like a conductor at a symphony as he gave his orders. "You too, Darius. And hurry it up; I don't wanna be here all day."

Dominguez shifted his eyes toward Travon and Marcus. "You two youngsters do the same."

Danforth and Riley stood just behind Dominguez, hanging on the veteran's every word.

"Turn around!" Dominguez told the boys. He approached Lil Fade.

"Shit!" Lil Fade smacked his lips, and reluctantly turned around.

Dominguez began to point at Lil Fade's heavily tattooed torso, as if he were a professor at a medical school. "See the red eyeball, with these red tattooed tears coming out of it? These stand for their fallen comrades."

The words tattooed above the red eyeball read: *Tattooed tears, for the homies that ain't here.*

Dominguez smiled pointing to an adjacent tattoo on Lil Fade's albino torso. "This blue eye, with these blue tattooed teardrops, stand for the murders that this kid has committed."

Danforth's and Riley's eyes walked down Lil Fade's back, as they counted teardrops. When finally they reached the bottom of the tattoo murder scorecard, they could do nothing more than gasp.

"Shit!" Danforth exclaimed. He'd counted nineteen blue ones, and thirteen red ones. "Why in the hell is this kid *not* behind bars?"

Dominguez smiled again. "There are a lot of reasons, one of which you just named. Our juvenile system sucks, and it is overwhelmed. We have no direct evidence on any of them, or almost no evidence. The witnesses won't testify, and the ones that do never show back up. They either get killed, their houses get shot up, or someone in their family gets killed, and they suddenly lose their memories. Some of the murders were done in Houston, Dallas, Austin, and other places. Some are still open murder cases. Besides, I'm Gang Unit, not Homicide, so you'll have to ask those guys."

"Nineteen murders and no evidence?" Riley shouted. "What the fuck's going on down here in Bubba Land?"

Travon swallowed hard when he heard the numbers, and his opinion of Lil Fade changed once again. He was now absolutely certain that Lil Fade was a psycho.

Lil Fade smiled at the conversation going on just behind him. He hadn't had his tattoos worked on in a while. He would have to add five more blue teardrops, and two more red ones.

Dominguez took exception to Riley's bubba remark. "Look, we do the best we can, with what we've got! We can't get sufficient Federal funding for our gang programs, because we're not busting big-time dope dealers and seizing tons of shit! Instead, we do the grunt work, and we get the crumbs. We make it safe for old ladies to sit on their porches at night, and not have to worry about drive-bys. We raid the crack houses, and the gang hangouts, and we get the fully automatic weapons off of the streets. We police the clubs, the movie theaters, and your got damned midnight basketball games, but when we request help, what do they send us? They send us you two, and six more like you! Boy, now we can surround the sixteen thousand gang members this city has! Agents Riley and Danforth, you are here to assist, observe, and learn, so please, observe!"

Dominguez turned and faced Lil Fade once again. "This is Lil Fade. He has been active since he was about eight years old. Turn around, Lil Fade!"

Lil Fade turned and smiled at the deputy.

Dominguez pointed at a tattoo on Lil Fade's chest and explained.

"This kid is a BSV. He's been shot eight times, and he's put his poor mother through hell. She's called the cops on him a couple of times. Said that she'd rather have him in jail, than dead. Real nice lady." Dominguez squinted and fixed his gaze on Lil Fade. "How many bullets do you still have inside of you?"

"Shit, about fourteen," Lil Fade answered.

Dominguez patted Lil Fade on his shoulder. "You're gonna die of lead poisoning, kid." Dominguez moved down the line to Darius. "Where y'all headed?"

"To Pletz Park," Darius answered.

Dominguez nodded. "Turn around, D."

Darius turned and faced the deputy.

"Any new tats?"

Darius shook his head. "No."

"Any trouble with the ETGs lately?" Dominguez asked.

Darius shrugged. "No, not really."

"Nothing you can't handle, huh?" Dominguez asked with a smile.

The boys laughed.

Dominguez pointed at Travon and Marcus. "So, what's the deal with the youngsters, Darius? I thought we talked about that. You guys, the ETGs and the WCGs said that you were gonna leave the kids alone. No new members."

"I ain't recruited nobody, and I ain't put nobody on the hood," Darius told him. He pointed toward Travon and Marcus. "That's my brother, and our cousin."

"Is that Lil Marcus over there? I didn't even recognize him."

"And even if somebody was to wanna get down for the hood, how could I stop them?" Darius added.

Dominguez turned toward the other deputies. "We got *three* knowns over here. The other is Lil Marcus."

A deputy approached, pointing at the boys. "We got all the info we need on these two, and I'm sure that we got all of Marcus's info, we just need to pull it up. That leaves us with just one unknown."

"Car's clean, Boss," another informed Dominguez. "Everything's okay, no tickets, no warrants, good insurance. We're all a go. K-9's heading over to W.W. White Road where Team Four is. Johnson, Murray, Dickson, and I will stay here and fingerprint, photo, and document the unknown. The rest of the guys are going to head back to the substation, Boss."

Dominguez smiled and nodded. "Good job, Nick."

Nick nodded, turned, and walked off.

Dominguez turned back to Travon and folded his arms. "So, what's your story?"

Travon shook his head. "Nothing."

"What are you? I don't see any tattoos, bullet scars, or any other kind of markings. Let me guess, you're Kirby posse."

"No."

"Lime Street?"

Again, Travon shook his head. "No."

"A BTP?"

Travon smiled smugly, and again shook. "No."

"Skyline?"

"Nope."

Dominguez unfolded his arms and frowned. "Well, you're too damned clean to be an RCG, a BSV, or a Bounty Hunter." He threw his hands up into the air. "Okay, I give up, which one are ya?"

"I ain't in no gang," Travon told him.

"Bullshit!" Dominguez bellowed. "C'mon, kid, don't play games with me. I've been doing this stuff since before you were born. I can smell a Blood!"

Travon shook his head. "I'm not!"

Dominguez exhaled forcibly. "Okay, look here, kid. For one, Lil Fade would have killed you if you were anything else. Two, there are a shit load of red bandannas in the car, along with a bunch of red baseball caps. So I suppose that none of that stuff is yours? You can't bullshit me, Blood, it only pisses me off. I've been doing this stuff for too long to fuck around with kids like you. Watch this, and learn."

He turned to Lil Fade. "Say, Lil Fade, what set you claim?"

"That's a dumb fuckin' question," Lil Fade told him. "My heart pumps Blood, fool!"

Dominguez turned back to Travon. "You see! He knows that he's a fucking low-life, gang-banging, cocksucker, and he ain't afraid to admit it. If you joined it, then claim it!"

Travon shook his head. "I ain't joined shit!"

Darius finally spoke up. "He hasn't been put on the hood."

Dominguez lifted his eyebrows in surprised. "How long you been out in the Heights?"

"For a while now," Travon acknowledged.

"Where are you from?" Dominguez queried.

"San Antonio."

"No, numb nuts, where did you live before you moved into the hood?"

Travon hesitated for several seconds before answering. "Wheatley Courts."

Dominguez turned to one of the deputies. "Look in the WCG files."

The deputy tapped away at his computer for several moments before finally peering up at his boss. "Negative, Boss."

"Try his full name, it's Travon Robinson!" Dominguez ordered.

The deputy tapped at his computer again. "Negative, Boss. I keep coming up with a Davon Robinson, WCG, deceased."

Dominguez quickly turned toward Darius. "Davon was your cousin, wasn't he?"

Darius nodded.

"You say that this here is your cousin, and he says that he is from the Wheatley Courts, so that means Davon was your brother," Dominguez said, pointing to Travon. "It ain't too hard to figure out, once you put all of the pieces into place. So, Too-Low was your brother, huh?"

Travon smiled and nodded. Dominguez *was* good.

"So, let me guess," Dominguez continued. "Too-Low gets smoked, so Elmira panics and sends you to live in the Heights with your aunt. And now you're hanging around with your low-life cousins and their homeboys in the Heights, wearing red and listening to that god-awful '*Piru Love*' shit!"

He turned to the other deputies. "Put him down as a Blood. No set yet, just place him into the general Blood category. He's probably active, but not dangerous yet, so make him an *A* for active. We'll give him a medium-to-high danger level, because he's hanging around with Darius and Lil Fade."

Dominguez exhaled forcibly. "You boys finish up here; I'm going over to the other stop, where Team Four is. From there, I'll head over to Team Three. I'll see you guys later. Good clean job you boys did."

"Thanks, Lieutenant," one of the deputies replied.

Dominguez waved the deputy off. "I'm still Sarge until Monday."

An officer whose name tag read Dickson, approached Travon with an armload of material. The deputy filled out a large index card with Travon's name, date of birth, nickname, mother's name, cousins' names, place of residence, aunt's name, social security number, and his suspected gang affiliation.

Then he took Travon's hand, pressed it into a large ink pad, and pressed the same hand onto a large, thick, manila card. The deputy repeated the process with Travon's other hand, and then once more, going finger by finger.

"Now, I just need for you to sign this form," Dickson told Travon, handing him a pen.

Travon scribbled his signature on the form, and then handed the pen back to the deputy. A second deputy approached, and snapped a couple of pictures of Travon. A third deputy took Travon's hand, turned his palms up, and waved a bar-type scanner over them.

"What's that for?" Travon inquired.

"It uses a laser to scan your fingerprints directly into our systems," the deputy explained.

"Okay, listen up," Dickson told them, clapping his hands loudly. "Since you have all been so cooperative, we are going to forget about the noise pollution ticket. You gentlemen have a nice day, and stay out of trouble."

"Y'all young brothers be careful," an officer named Johnson told them. "Cooney, Preto, Greyhound, and Kong are patrolling the area around the park for SAPD today. So you might not even want to head that way."

"Especially since y'all ain't got no money on y'all," another deputy added.

Dickson nudged McCray in his side. McCray and Johnson exchanged knowing glances and laughed.

"Y'all kids go home and stay out of trouble," Johnson said. "There are enough of us in trouble as it is."

The deputies turned and slowly made their way to their cars.

"They shouldn't even let guys like those have badges," McCray told Dickson.

"I know, I know." Dickson nodded. He opened his car door, and peered over the roof at his partner. "I'd really love to bust those crooked, prejudiced muthafuckers myself."

"Me too," McCray agreed.

Travon, Darius, Marcus, and Lil Fade climbed back into the Cadillac.

Marcus turned to Travon. "You might as well get down now, shit. Your ass is in the gang file as a Blood now."

Travon stared out the window, allowing Marcus's statement to go without comment.

"Where y'all want to go now?" Darius asked.

"To the park," Lil Fade told him. "Hell, fuck Preto and Cooney!"

Darius started the car, pulled back onto the road, and headed off in the direction of the park.

"And cut the fuckin' music up too, Blood," Lil Fade added. "I gotta get my G up."

CHAPTER THIRTEEN

Pletz Park

Cars were everywhere. Every gang in South Central Texas was represented in the park today. The gangs occupied their own individual sections, and each group stayed to itself, without any violence or hostility toward the other groups. As per agreement among the leaders of the individual gangs, the park was neutral ground.

Skimpily clad young ladies strolled about, making acquaintances, renewing old ones, and generally flirting with all they came into contact with. They brought a festive atmosphere to the park, and provided a much-needed calming effect. As long as there were girls to impress, the guys maintained their composure.

At any given moment, at least one hundred cars circled the park's perimeter, showcasing shiny new rims, hydraulic suspension systems, and booming stereo systems. Pletz Park was about showing out. The new hairstyles, bikini tops, booty shorts, fresh haircuts, and crisp, starched T-shirts were a testament to that. But mainly, it was about catching women.

"There go the homies over there," Lil Fade announced, pointing toward a significant gathering of red clothing on the other side of the park.

Darius wound his vehicle around the park, creeping, past some of their rivals on the way.

The ETGs were the first group that the boys passed. Lil Fade gave his enemies hateful glances, and made several Blood signs with his fingers.

The ETGs returned his looks and gestures with some of their own. Like the Bloods, the rival ETGs were out in numbers today.

Next up were the DOGs, a gang that was neither Bloods nor Crips, that was also out in significant numbers today as well. Their numbers mattered little to Lil Fade. He made a Blood sign with his fingers, and received a couple of *fuck you* middle fingers in return.

"Man, you making my shit hot!" Darius told him. "I just got the muthafucka, and you want somebody to put some bullet holes in it already."

Darius drove past the WCGs, which was the most numerous gang in the park today. There appeared to be a wall of burnt orange. Undeterred, Lil Fade leaned out of the window to taunt them as well. By habit, most of the WCGs ducked upon seeing him leaning out of the car window, until they realized that he was unarmed.

"What's up, Blood?" Lil Fade shouted. He made a Blood symbol with his fingers, and then formed the letters for BSV.

The WCGs returned his taunts by forming the symbols for their own gang. Lil Fade laughed, and continued to taunt the other smaller gangs, as they drove past.

When they finally arrived at their section of the park, Darius backed into a vacant parking space within walking distance of the main crowd. The Bloods were out in numbers today as well.

"That's my nigga!" Lil Fade shouted out of the car window. "That's my muthafuckin' nigga!" He threw open the door and bounded out of the car. He rushed to a heavily muscled individual standing amidst the crowd, and embraced him tightly.

Travon climbed out, and closed both his and Lil Fade's doors. He walked to where the majority of the crowd was assembled, and stood just on the fringes.

"My muthafuckin' nigga!" Lil Fade repeated. "What's up, Blood? When did you get out?"

The heavily muscled Blood shook his head. "Shit, about two days ago."

Lil Fade took a step back from his friend, and Travon maneuvered himself through the crowd in such a way as to be able to view this impromptu reunion. He could now read the letters over the pocket of the ex-felon's red T-shirt. The boy's name was Suga.

"What?" Lil Fade shouted. "Two days ago, and you ain't even called me? What's up with that shit, Blood?"

Suga shrugged his massive shoulders. "Shit, Blood, I just been doing the family thing. You know, banging the baby momma, kicking back with the T-Lady, all that good shit."

"I see you got your swoles on," Darius told Suga.

"Hell yeah, Blood." Suga crossed his equally massive arms. "That's all I was doing, lifting and jacking off. After awhile I even had to quit jacking off, just so I could get my yokes on."

Several of the boys in the crowd laughed.

Who was this Suga? Travon wondered. Who was this person that had made that lunatic Lil Fade, so happy?

Suga's tight red T-shirt showcased his bulging muscles and numerous tattoos. He had several gold teeth, and his hair was tied into two large Afro-puffs. He was half surrounded by fawning girls rubbing on his chest and arms.

"Hey, Suga, let me do your hair tonight?" one of the girls asked.

Suga smiled and nodded. "Yeah, but first I got to let Peaches do it, then I'll come by and let you do it."

Laughter shot through the crowd.

Lil Fade turned toward the girl and frowned. "Fuck, can't you see we talkin'? Move on, bitch!"

"Damn, Lil Fade, I didn't mean to step on your toes, girl," she shot back. "I'll get to it after you." She stormed away.

No one laughed out loud. No one dared to.

"Fuck you, you nappy-headed trick!" Lil Fade shouted.

Several of the girls in the crowd broke away and chased after their friend as she steamed off into the park.

"What's up, Tre?" someone called out.

Travon turned in the voice's direction and his cousins, Romeo and Capone.

"What's up, kinfolk?" Travon called out. He lifted his arms into the air.

"Just chilling." Romeo shrugged.

Loud music suddenly erupted from behind, interrupting everyone's conversation. It was the song "Mackin' to Slob Bitches." The Bloods quickly turned in the direction from which it was coming. Frowns and scowls shot across the faces of everyone present. It was a song that they hated with a passion.

Several Bloods reached for weapons hidden beneath their shirts, while others opened the trunks of their cars just slightly, making their large-caliber weapons more readily accessible. Many in the crowd maneuvered into better firing positions. Travon watched it all unfold in amusement, and then shifted his gaze toward the oncoming car that was playing the offensive song.

It was a Chevrolet Impala, with a gorgeous aquamarine candy paint job that had billions of blue glitter-like flakes sparkling throughout. Chrome one-hundred-spoke Dayton Wire Wheels, shiny chrome trim, and a cocaine-white convertible rag top completed the show car. The Bloods couldn't help but smile; the car was clean as Hell.

The Impala stopped just before the crowd of Bloods, and began to perform. Its hydraulic suspension system allowed the car to maneuver and dance in all kinds of ways. It bounced, hopped, rocked from side to side, and from front to rear, while its stereo system continued to boom loudly, drowning out many of the other cars' stereos in the park. Travon covered his mouth with his fist; the ETGs were flossing uncontrollably today.

Capone squinted at the vehicle as it started its approach again. "That's Pooh-Pooh, Nuke Dog, C.J., and Lacy in the '64."

"I think that's Big Mike, Shorty, C-Low, Deuce, and Mike-Mike in the first Caddy," Lil Fade added. "And Michael Vay, Lil Loc, B.K., Slim, and Shan in the other Caddy."

Travon was startled. He had been so busy paying attention to the first car that he had not noticed the other two. *Slipping again*, he thought. He had been caught off guard for the third time in just as many weeks. He would have to pay more attention. Suga, Lil Fade, Darius, Killa B, and

Capone maneuvered to the front of the crowd, and raised their hands into the air.

"What's up, Blood?" Lil Fade shouted.

Big Pimpin stepped behind Lil Fade and slid a pistol into the small of Lil Fade's back, tucking it in snugly into his waistband.

"Good looking, Blood," Lil Fade told him, without turning around or looking back.

The Crips in the first two vehicles rode by mad dogging the Bloods, who returned their stares with equally poisonous glares. Michael Vay's Cadillac stopped just in front of the crowd. It was a dark blue DeVille, with a white vinyl top. Gold and chrome Cadillac disc were shrouded in Vogue tires, and a massive gold CC grille sat prominently in the front of the car. The gold emblems throughout the car and the gold buttons on its vinyl roof complemented the gold on the grille and the rims.

"What's up, cuz?" asked Michael Vay, as he leaned out of the window. His bald head, gold teeth, and numerous pieces of gold jewelry gleamed brightly in the South Texas sun.

"Nigga, I'm your mother fucking kinfolk, not your mother fucking cuz," Suga replied, approaching the blue Cadillac.

Travon maneuvered past the others, so that he could gain a closer look. The Deville's passengers all had long curls in their hair, which had been sectioned off with blue rubber bands. Two wore Dallas Cowboys jerseys, while the others wore rich, royal-blue T-shirts. All of them had numerous gold teeth and wore a significant amount of gold jewelry.

The two rear passengers, both of whom were leaning toward their respective windows, had large AK-47 assault rifles sitting in their laps. The front passenger twisted and twirled and played with a sawed-off shotgun that he had sitting on the floorboards between his legs. They were armed to the teeth.

Travon examined Michael Vay and Suga closely. There existed no visible resemblance between the two. Suga was tall and muscular and tan, while Michael was husky, of medium height, and had very dark skin. Michael's nose was wide, and his eyes were huge, almost like a frog's; while Suga had a small nose, and eyes so narrow that they looked Asian.

Travon's thoughts turned toward himself and his cousins, and their strong family resemblance. All of them had their family's trademark slanted eyes, wide noses, and pale yellow skin. And their mothers could all pass for twins.

Suga began cursing out Michael Vay, and Travon thought it best that he step away from the vehicle. He sincerely hoped, for Suga's sake, that the two were in fact real cousins. It would be really unpleasant to get hit with a round from one of those AK-47's.

Suga finished his conversation with Michael Vay and backed away from the car laughing. Michael turned up the volume on his stereo, and slowly pulled away.

"That nigga is crazier than a muthafucker!" Suga told the rest of the group.

"What's he talking about?" Lil Fade asked.

"He wanna kick me down with some yea, but he wants me to go to the Terrace and pick it up," Suga explained.

"Fuck that nigga, I'll kick you down, Blood," Fro Dog told Suga. "It's all good in the hood, you know that."

"Shit, I got a lick for us too," Lil Fade announced.

Romeo nudged Travon. "Hey, let's go walk around the park and catch some hoes."

"Shit, what if them niggaz start tripping?" Travon asked. He shook his head. "I ain't down for no bullshit."

Marcus smiled, wrapped his arm around Travon, and led him off into the park. "C'mon, fool. Ain't nobody gonna trip in this park, unless they some damn fools. Everybody is strapped to the fullest." He waved his arm through the air. "Besides, with all of these park rangers around, you'd be crazier than a mutherfucka to shoot in this park anyway."

Travon, Marcus, and Romeo continued off into the park's interior, walking, talking, laughing, and having fun. Soon, they spotted a group of red bikini tops strolling just ahead of them.

"Say, there go Peaches and them," Romeo announced excitedly.

"Man, why do you want to fuck with them Bounty Hunter hoes?" Marcus asked. "Them bitches is scandalous and cross action. Plus, we can catch them hoes in the hood." He dismissed the girls with a wave. "Let's peep out something different."

"Fuck that, I been after Peaches for the longest," Romeo told them. "Come on, niggaz!" Romeo began to double-time it, in order to catch up with the girls.

"Say! Say!" he shouted, waving.

The girls turned to see who was calling them, and waited. Marcus, Travon, and Romeo caught up quickly, and together with the girls, continued their walk through the park.

Romeo placed his arm around Peaches and smiled. "What's up, girl?"

Peaches folded her arms. "Nothing."

One of the girls maneuvered herself in position next to Travon. "What's your name?" she asked, nudging Travon with her shoulder.

"Travon," he replied. "What's yours?"

"Pussy," she told him with a smile. "Actually, everyone calls me PussyKat, but you can just call me your Pussy."

Travon lowered his head and blushed. He thought of how wild these girls were, and how they were nothing like the girls in the Courts. A second girl wedged herself in between Travon and PussyKat.

"My name is Passion," she told Travon.

"Child, new meat, and these hoes go crazy," one of the girls said to another.

"Now, your name is Passion, yours is PussyKat, I know that's Precious, and that's Peaches, and I heard y'all call her Punkin," Travon said, pointing. "Do all of y'all's name begin with a P?"

"Yeah, my name is Poison, and this is Peanut, and that's Popcorn, and that's Paradise over there," Poison told him, pointing out the other girls.

Travon nodded and smiled at her. She was cute, and not as overt as the others. She was the one that he liked.

Poison was short and thick, although far from being fat. She wore her hair in two gigantic Afro-puffs, which accented her almond-shaped face and gorgeous hazel eyes. Today she wore a red overall short set, with a white T-shirt and some red Skechers clogs.

She caught Travon staring at her. "What?" she asked with a smile.

Travon shifted his gaze toward the ground and shook his head. "Naw, I was just trying to figure something out."

Poison nodded. "I'm both; Black and Hispanic. My dad is from Haiti, and my mom is from the Dominican Republic."

"Oh." Travon nodded and turned away. She was smart and pretty. Unless of course she was just used to everyone asking her that. He decided to ask her something else. "How old are you?"

"Old enough," she replied with a smile.

Travon shook his head. Things did not seem to be going right. He was coming weak, and he had *never* come that weak before. He had to think of something to say or do that would impress her.

Poison knew that Travon was crashing and burning. He didn't know what to say, which in her experience, was unusual for a Blood. He wasn't like the rest of them, she thought. He wasn't trying to be a ghetto superstar. She lifted his arm and placed it around her shoulder.

"Uh-uh, girl!" Passion told her with a frown. "Kilo is gonna kill you if he sees that boy's arm around you!"

"Girl, fuck him!" Poison frowned back. "I ain't got no time for no nigga who wanna trip all of the time."

"Oh, girl, there go Russell and them!" Peanut shouted in her shrill, high-pitched voice. "I gots to go and get my mack on!" She turned to Poison. "Girl, do my hair look all right?"

Poison frowned and recoiled. "Yeah, bitch, now go!" She turned Peanut in the direction of the boys, and shoved her forward.

Peanut rushed toward the group of boys sitting on top of a black Jeep Cherokee. "Hey, Russell!"

She was followed by PussyKat, Paradise, Popcorn, and Passion. Travon and the remainder of his group continued on their leisurely stroll through the park.

"So, why all of y'all's names start with a P?" Travon asked.

"It's a Piru thang," Poison answered.

"I thought that y'all was Bounty Hunters?"

Poison shook her head. "Naw, our men are all Bounty Hunters, but we are Piru."

"Blood Clot! A me means that literally!" a voice called out from behind them.

Travon froze. He recognized the voice. It was a voice that he hadn't heard in quite a while; a voice that he hadn't heard since middle school; a voice that he never wanted to hear again. It was the voice of trouble.

Slowly, Travon turned in the direction from which that voice had come. It was him.

"Me thinks dat was you, Tre," Re-Re told him with a smile. He brushed at some imaginary lint on his royal-blue T-shirt and black Dickies shorts. The five other boys standing just to the rear of him folded their arms and stared menacingly at Travon and his group. Blue bandannas hung low from their back pockets, almost touching their blue Chuck Taylor tennis shoes.

"Re-Re, I thought I smelled you," Travon told him.

Marcus, Romeo, and the girls let out a quick laugh. Re-Re and his companions did not. A couple of Re-Re's companions lifted their hands to their heads, and began twisting at their dookie curls. This allowed their shirts to rise up and display the weapons that they had tucked away. They were members of the notorious East Terrace Gangsters, sworn archenemies of the Blood Stone Villains.

"You always was de class clown, Tre," Re-Re told him. "Always makin' de people laugh. You was on top of de world, man, and now look at ya. Ya slobbin'!"

The ETGs laughed. Romeo took a step toward Re-Re, but all five of the ETGs quickly placed their hands beneath their shirts, halting him in his tracks. Romeo stepped back. He and Marcus were furious, not only because of Re-Re's derogatory remarks, but at their own stupidity. They had allowed themselves to get caught without their weapons.

"I never thought dat you'd turn into a fuckin' slob, mon. I thought you was better dan dat." Re-Re turned to his friends, who were standing just behind him laughing and enjoying the show. "Dis was me homeboy in elementary, and in middle school. Him was real cool with me back den, but now 'em slobbing."

Re-Re threw his head back in laughter. Then he stepped in closer, until he and Travon stood nose to nose. "Who's on top now, Tre?"

"You'll always be a fuckin' punk, Re-Re," Travon told him. "You'll always be just another goat-smelling son of a bitch."

"Wrong answer." Re-Re reached beneath his T-shirt and pulled out a black H&K pistol. He leaned forward and whispered into Travon's ear, "Who's on top now, Tre? East Terrace is on top. Can you say dat, Tre? Can you say East Terrace? C'mon, let me hear you say East Terrace is on top."

Travon stood his ground.

Re-Re slowly walked around Travon and his group until he came full circle and once again faced Travon.

"Let me hear you say East Terrace is on top," Re-Re told him. Again, he stepped closer to Travon, until they stood nose to nose. "Da only reason I don't smoke you right now is because Too-Low got a baby by me sister. If it wasn't for dat, you'd be a dead Slob right now."

He leaned back, folded his arms, and nodded in the direction of the park's exit. "Get de fuck outta me face."

Travon, Marcus, Romeo, Peaches, Precious, and Poison slowly filed past the group of ETGs. Travon turned and glanced back at Re-Re and his compatriots, who were still facing the other direction. He could read the words on the back of their royal-blue T-shirts: *E.T.G. Every Thang Goes.*

Travon shook his head and wiped away the tear that had formed in the corner of his eye. "Okay, every thang goes," he whispered, nodding. "From here on out, everything goes. I'm tired of this shit!" he shouted. "I'm tired of this fuckin' shit!"

The group's rapid steps quickly turned into an all-out sprint, as they raced through the park, back to where their friends were. Romeo was the first to speak.

"Say, Capone!" he called out to his brother. "Lil J, Nuke Dog, Lil Loc, Slim, BK, and some muthafucka named Re-Re just pulled straps on us!"

Suga pounded the air with his fist. "Fuck!"

Travon, breathing heavily, turned to Darius. "Gimme a muthafuckin' strap, Blood!"

Darius, Romeo, Marcus, and Capone turned and stared at Travon in shock. Travon turned away and silently wondered if that last word was an accident. The answer he came up with was no. It had not been an accident; he had used that word deliberately.

Someone from the crowd handed Travon an Intratech Tech Nine. Marcus reached into a nearby trunk and availed himself of a twelve-gauge shotgun, and then stuffed several loose shells into his pockets. Romeo was tossed a nine-millimeter Glock, and Lil Fade grabbed a Norinco SKS with a one-hundred-round drum clip. Once armed, the boys took off running through the park at full speed, searching for the ETGs.

Everybody saw them running through the park with all of their weaponry, and began to jump into their cars and flee. The assembly of Bloods had already done so, as they were fully aware of what was about to take place. A traffic jam quickly developed.

Once the boys were about forty yards from where the ETGs were parked, several of the female ETGs started screaming. The Bloods opened fire.

"Fuckin' crab-ass bitches!" Travon shouted. His thoughts were not only on Re-Re, but also on his brother. These were Too-Low's killers.

Sparks flew from the bullets ricocheting off of the ETGs' parked cars, and a loud, deep, rhythmic thump began to fill the air, as the 7.62 millimeter opened up.

Girls were screaming, people were running, and the ETGs were falling in droves. Suddenly, there was a small popping sound to the left of the boys. Lil Fade turned and spotted a park ranger firing at them. He quickly shifted his SKS toward the ranger, and a loud thud penetrated the air. The park ranger fell dead.

Lil Fade turned back to the assembly of blue cars, most of which were now trying to leave the park. There were several whose owners were dead, or wounded, or whose motors were too shot up to function. Most of the cars were riddled with bullets, and had numerous bodies littered around or hanging out of them. Smoke from the SKS filled the area.

A car horn sounded, and they turned to find Darius in his Cadillac waving at them. They ceased firing and ran for the Cadillac. Another popping sound began to emanate from the rear of them. Darius pointed behind the sprinting boys; another park ranger firing at them.

"I'm hit!" Romeo shouted.

Travon grabbed his cousin and helped him to the car. Lil Fade lifted his SKS and sent a deadly barrage toward the crouched park ranger. The ranger received Lil Fade's present, and died in the line of duty. Calmly, Lil Fade turned, walked to Darius' car, and climbed inside.

"Take me to my mother's house!" Romeo shouted. He yanked a red bandanna out of his back pocket and tied it around his bleeding arm.

"You need to go to the hospital!" Travon said nervously.

"No!" Romeo shook his head. "My mom's a nurse, have you forgot? She'll stop the bleeding, and then take me to a hospital in another county far away from here. Or, she'll sneak me into the hospital where she works and have one of her doctor friends take a look at me. If I just go to a hospital around here, they'll have to call the police because it's a gunshot wound. The police will know it's from the park shooting. Trust me; we've done this with Capone a few times."

Darius nodded, and made the turn onto the highway, where he headed for his Aunt Chicken's house.

Travon kicked the bottom of the front seat. "Fuck!" There seemed to be no escaping it.

CHAPTER FOURTEEN

"Shit, here comes a blue Caddy!" Darius shouted, as he peered into his rearview mirror.

Lil Fade turned and peered out of the back window. "It's Mike Vay and them!"

Darius mashed his foot on the gas pedal, trying to get his big Caddy up to speed. He had decorated his Cadillac with tons of accoutrements, but had done nothing to the car's motor. It was something that he now regretted.

Michael Vay's Cadillac had already been traveling at a high rate of speed, and so it continued to gain on Darius' car. Michael Vay *had* tinkered with his car's motor.

Travon grabbed the back of Darius' seat and pulled himself forward. "Shit, slow down, Darius!"

"Lil kinfolk, how old are you right now?" Darius asked.

"Sixteen, soon to be seventeen, if it makes any difference!" Travon told him.

"If you want to live to be seventeen, then let me drive and get us the fuck out of here!" Darius shouted.

Marcus peered out the back window and began squinting. "It's Mike Vay and Mike-Mike in the front seat."

"Fuck!" Romeo shouted.

"It looks like C-Low."

"Fuck! Fuck! Fuck!' Romeo shouted.

"And Pooh-Pooh in the backseat," Marcus finished.

"Shit! Shit! Shit!" Romeo shouted.

Darius turned toward his cousin. "Calm the fuck down!"

"Fuck!" Romeo shouted again.

Lil Fade smiled. "Don't worry, y'all got me."

Romeo turned to Lil Fade. "This ain't no time for no fuckin' jokes!"

Lil Fade turned toward Darius. "Put on some Ghetto Boys, so I can get my G up."

"It sure in the hell ain't no time to listen to no fuckin' music!" Marcus shouted. "You *are* fuckin' crazy!"

Lil Fade smiled serenely. He leaned forward, lifted some red bandannas from the floor, and began to pass them out.

"Surrender flags are supposed to be white, I don't think these will work," Romeo told him, clutching his wounded forearm.

Lil Fade tied a red bandanna around the lower half of his face, as Darius screeched onto an interchange at one hundred miles per hour. He leaned forward, pressed a button on the stereo system, turning it on. Scarface began to play, Lil Fade's favorite.

Lil Fade smiled broadly beneath his red bandanna, and lifted his SKS from the floorboards. "Did they take the interchange?"

Romeo, who had been crouched down in the backseat, lifted his head and peered out the window. "Yeah."

Lil Fade pulled back the bolt on his SKS and released it. The bolt slammed forward violently, chambering a round. "Then may God have mercy on their fuckin' souls!"

Lil Fade stood up in of Darius' sunroof and began firing. "Fuck you, Blood! Yeah, fuck you!"

Travon turned and stared at Marcus who was already staring at him. Marcus shrugged, and Travon shook his head. Both let out deep breaths as they tied their bandannas around the lower half of their faces. Resigned, they both leaned out of their respective windows and began firing.

The sound of gunfire filled the highway, and sparks danced off the front of Michael Vay's Cadillac. Soon, smoke began pouring from beneath the car, and the hood flew off and smashed into another vehicle. Lil Fade's bullets danced across the entire front half of the car, riddling it completely, but it continued to gain ground.

Out of the sunroof of the pursuing Cadillac popped Mike-Mike, while out of the rear passenger windows came Pooh-Pooh and C-Low. Pooh-Pooh was firing a fully automatic Cobray M-11, while C-Low was using a fully automatic AK-47 assault rifle.

More gunfire filled the air, and sparks flew off of the rear of Darius' Cadillac as the AK-47 and M-11 hit home.

"Shit! Shit! Shit! Fuck!" Romeo shouted, when he heard the thud of the bullets.

Mike-Mike was having trouble pulling his weapon through the sunroof. When he finally managed to get it through, the boys were able to see that it was a Fabrique Nacional FAL .308 assault rifle. Even with the wind whipping around the vehicles due to their high rates of speed, the noise from that gun was deafening. Chunks of Darius' car disintegrated as the .308 rounds found their target. Darius' car shuddered dramatically with the impact of each round.

"Fuck! Fuck! Fuck!" Romeo screamed. "Tell 'em we sorry! Tell'em we sorry!"

"I'm out!" Travon shouted. He pulled the magazine out of his weapon and examined it.

"Shit, join the club!" Marcus shouted. "I been out."

"Then get down!" Travon shouted.

"Shit, I been done did that!" Marcus replied.

Travon turned and spied Marcus and Romeo both crouched down near the floorboards.

"Hit the tires, Lil Fade!" Darius shouted. "Hit the got damned tires!"

"I been done did that!" Lil Fade shouted back.

"Fuck!" Romeo shouted. "You had to go to school with that fuckin' Jamaican! You couldn't have gone to school with Americans! No, Tre is special! I'll bet your ass wishes that you would have played hooky all those years like the rest of us!"

"Shut up!" Marcus shouted.

A loud, distinctive boom sounded; glass from the blown-out rear window fell on top of the boys.

"Oh, good, now I'm not only shot, but I'm cut too," Romeo told them. He turned toward Travon. "Thanks a lot, kinfolk."

"I'm out!" Lil Fade announced. He lowered himself back into the vehicle, turned toward Darius and shook his head.

A continuous group of extremely loud explosions shook the vehicle, as more .308 rounds found their way home. Sparks flew off of the back of Darius's Cadillac, and the trunk lid was completely blown off. It flew through the air and slammed into Michael Vay's windshield.

"That'll show 'em," a smiling Lil Fade announced.

Darius's car shuddered again, as more .308 rounds hit. This time, however, his car began to slow down.

"What the fuck's happening up there, D?" Travon shouted. "This ain't no time to stop and talk!"

"I don't know what the hell's going on, I got the gas pedal all the way down to the floor!" Darius shouted back.

He began weaving from side to side, in order to keep Michael Vay from pulling alongside of them. The driver's side window on Darius' Cadillac was shattered by bullets. Glass flew everywhere.

"Shit!" Darius cried out, as he and Lil Fade ducked for cover. When he sat up again, his front windshield was riddled with bullet holes, and Michael Vay was driving alongside of them grinning.

Pooh-Pooh sat on the windowsill of the blue Cadillac on the opposite side, aiming his weapon over the roof toward the occupants of Darius' backseat. C-Low hung out of the rear driver's side window, with his AK-47 also aimed at the occupants of the backseat. Mike-Mike was standing out of the sunroof, with his mini-cannon aimed directly at Lil Fade.

This was it, Darius told himself. He sat cringing, waiting for the rifle burst that would end his life. Lil Fade, on the other hand, turned toward Michael Vay, smiled, and lifted his middle finger. The smile on Michael Vay's face evaporated. He frowned, turned toward the gunmen inside of his vehicle, and began issuing instructions.

Suddenly gunfire erupted once again on the highway. Darius closed his eyes for a brief moment, anticipating the hot bullets. Mike-Mike reeled, dropped his FN FAL .308, and began reaching for his back. Pooh-Pooh fell back and then slid inside of the back window. Michael Vay and C-Low quickly shifted the gazes to the right. Fro-Dog's '64 Chevrolet Impala was on the scene, with Capone standing in the rear seat, firing two Glock model 23, forty-caliber handguns. Suga was sitting up high in the passenger seat, with a fully automatic Styer AUG assault rifle, and Red Rum was standing in the seat next to Capone, holding a Sig Sauer semiautomatic pistol in one hand, and flipping the ETGs off with the other. Red bandannas were tied around the lower half of their faces to conceal their identities. Suga opened up with his assault rifle.

Michael Vay took a hit in his right arm, and immediately lost control of his vehicle. The Cadillac slammed into a divider and quickly caught fire. Capone, Suga, and Red Rum continued to pour fire into the burning Cadillac until it was out of range. Fro-Dog turned toward Darius, honked his horn, and raised his fist into the air. The Impala took the next exit off of the highway.

"Fuck yeah, Blood!" Lil Fade shouted. "Fuck yeah! That's why I love your brother, Romeo! That's why I fuckin' love Capone!" Lil Fade leaned over the seat and kissed Romeo on the top of his head.

"Whooooeee!" Darius shouted. He pulled off of the highway two exits later, and headed for his aunt's house.

❖❖❖

The boys pulled up at Chicken's. Darius hopped out of his car and ran into the living room. "Aunt Chicken! Aunt Chicken!"

"What, boy?" Chicken walked out of the kitchen, wiping her hands on a dish rag.

"Romeo got hit in the arm!" Darius said excitedly. "He's all right though."

Romeo walked into the house, followed by Travon, Marcus, and Lil Fade. Chicken saw the blood on her son's arm and grabbed her chest.

"Oh my God!" Chicken exclaimed. She rushed to her son.

"I'm okay," Romeo told her. "Don't trip."

Darius lifted his aunt's keys from the coffee table and walked out to the garage. He lifted her old wooden garage door, and backed her car out into the street in front of her house. Then he climbed into his shot-up vehicle, pulled it into the garage and closed the garage door. When finished, he ventured out into the yard and examined the block, to make sure that no one had been watching. Once satisfied, he went back inside of the residence.

Chicken held the telephone between her chin and shoulder, speaking with one of her coworkers from the hospital as she examined her son's forearm.

"Yes, Martin, it's a clean wound. The bullet went straight through, no bone fractures or anything," she said into the receiver. "Tonight? Right now? Okay, Martin, and remember, this has to be kept hush-hush."

Chicken paused for several seconds, listening to her coworker. "I'll do it myself, and if you think it's bad, then I'll do the assist," she told him. "Okay, Martin, I'm on the way. And thanks again, you're a real sweetheart. 'Bye."

Chicken hung up. "Go and change shirts," she said angrily. "No, go and change all of your clothes! And when you come back downstairs, bring my black nurse's bag."

Romeo hesitated. "Are you sure that he ain't gonna call the cops?"

Chicken shook her head. "No, this is Dr. Larimey, the same one who treated your brother the last time. I'm going to sneak you through the delivery entrance, and then I'm going to do all of the work myself. He's just going to examine the wound and make sure that you don't need surgery, and that nothing is damaged."

Chicken pointed her finger into her son's face. "You're lucky I'm a nurse, or you'd be fucked! And you know what? I hope that it hurts like hell! That will teach you about going out and getting into all kinds of shit!"

Romeo headed up the stairs, and Chicken turned to Darius. "Go and call Vera, tell her that you're drunk, and that you and Marcus, and Tre will be staying over my house tonight."

A news brief broke into the regular show. An anchorman with a serious expression stared into the camera.

"One of the worst incidents of gang violence this city has ever seen occurred today on the Eastside. Two park rangers lost their lives in the line of duty, trying to stop two rival gangs in a shootout. It happened at County Park Number Six, also known as Pletz Park. We'll go live to Christine Parker who is at the scene right now. Christine."

The scene switched to a blonde white woman in a gray suit who was wearing too much makeup.

"That's right, David," the journalist led off. "Details are still sketchy right now, but this is what Channel Five has learned. Eyewitnesses say that the park was crowded earlier this afternoon, when shooting broke out between two rival gang factions. Seven people were killed, including the two park rangers, and thirteen wounded. Many of the wounded are in very serious condition right now, and the final death toll is expected to climb. Police say that they are coming up blank on suspects, because all of the potential eyewitnesses were trying to flee the carnage, so no one was able to get a good look at the assailants. That's all we have right now, I'll be at the scene for quite some time, so I'll keep you up-to-date on any new developments. Back to you, David."

"Thanks, Christine. Once again, gang violence erupts on the city's Eastside, that'll be our top story tonight on News Five at Ten. We'll keep you up-to-date, as more information becomes available." The anchorman turned to his right. "Dan."

The camera switched to another anchor, this one a white balding fifty-something male in a cheap gray suit with a red tie.

"In a related story. Police find a bullet-riddled, abandoned Cadillac on Interstate Thirty-five today. It was believed to have been involved in a high-speed, gangland shootout that occurred earlier. Police arrived to find a wrecked, burnt-out Cadillac, riddled with bullet holes. They cannot confirm who the occupants were, or whether this shooting was directly related to the shooting at County Park Number Six earlier."

Chicken lifted her remote and turned the television set off. She stared at Lil Fade, Travon, Marcus, and Darius in disappointment.

"Anyone want to explain this?" she asked.

"I got jumped, and they pulled guns on me," Travon told her.

Chicken nodded. "Okay, that explains one. What about the other seven dead and twelve wounded?"

"There were six of them," Travon said softly.

Romeo bounded down the stairs, and seated himself on the couch next to Travon.

"What about the seven dead and the other seven wounded?" she asked.

The boys remained silent. Chicken jabbed her finger at the television.

"Tonight, there are seven mothers crying, Tre!" she shouted. "Seven! Do you remember when it was your mother's night to cry?"

Travon, Romeo, Darius, and Marcus looked down. Lil Fade looked away.

"I'm an emergency room nurse," Chicken told them. "I see this shit every day! Every time a child comes in lying on a stretcher, I pray that it isn't one of you! I walk out and I see the family waiting and praying, and I know what the doctor is about to tell them. What do you say to a woman, a mother, who has just been told that her baby is never coming home! And worst of all! Worst of all! It's over a God damned color! Look at me!" Chicken screamed.

The boys quickly shifted their gazes toward her.

Chicken pointed her finger at them. "There are no medical or dental benefits in gang banging! There is no 401(k) plan, and you sure in the hell don't get paid for it! If you get wounded, you don't get a God damned disability check from your gang! So what the hell is it for? What's it all for? Why are you kids killing each other? Why?"

Chicken shook her head and walked out of her front door in tears. From the front yard, she called out to her son. "Romeo, get my nurse's bag, and my keys, and bring your ass on!"

CHAPTER FIFTEEN

Aunt Vera's House
The Next Day

"Yeah, Blood!" Suga shouted. "We served them hoes!"

"I gave Mike-Mike and Pooh-Pooh at least five shots apiece!" Capone bragged.

"But the news people said that the car was abandoned when the po-po's got there," Lil Fade told them.

Travon exited the house, and joined the others on the front porch.

"You think them niggaz made it?" Darius asked.

Lil Fade shook his head. "Shit, ain't no telling." He shifted his gaze to Capone. "Did y'all take all of the straps to Mr. C already?"

Capone nodded. "Yeah, we did that last night. He said that he was gonna re-thread the barrels for us, and put new barrels on the ones that he couldn't re-thread."

"Where y'all straps at?" Suga asked.

"We buried them hoes in a creek out in Lakeside," Darius answered. "We'll pick 'em up and take 'em to Mr. C next week. He should be through with the others by then."

"One Time says that they ain't got no witnesses," Lil Fade told the others. He threw his head back in laughter. "A park full of muthafuckas, and they ain't got no witnesses!"

"I watched the news this morning," Marcus commented. "The sheriff and the chief of police was on there begging for fuckin' witnesses. They was puttin' up reward money and damn near promising their firstborn child, if somebody would come forward."

"Man, if they offering rewards and shit, we'll beat that shit in court so easy, it won't even be fun," Capone said.

"Even if somebody did come forward, they wouldn't live to testify during trial anyway," Lil Fade announced.

"Man, this shit is getting boring," Capone told them. "We can do just about anything we want to!"

Capone and Lil Fade shared a laugh.

Marcus turned toward Travon. "You got down for yours yesterday, Blood! You was bustin' like a muthafucka!"

"Hell yeah, Blood, I had to go for mine!" Travon told them. "Everything goes, from now on." Travon turned and stared down the street. He had used that word again.

Suga grabbed Travon, wrapping his massive right arm around his head. "Shit, lil homie put in work yesterday. He got his cherry popped!"

The boys broke into laughter. Suga released Travon, leaned back, and stared at him for several moments.

"Your name ain't Tre no more, you're too dangerous to be called Tre," Suga told him. "From now on, your name is T-Dog. You gonna be my little trigga nigga from here on out."

"Don't worry, I'm a bring it out of him," Lil Fade said. "He got more of it inside of him, just waiting to get out. So I'm a bring it out of him." Lil Fade stared at Travon with his cold, penetrating blue eyes. Travon turned away.

"You getting down for the hood no, Tre?" Capone asked.

"Yeah, I keep hearing you say Blood this, or Blood that," Darius added.

"Shit, you done put in work as a Blood, and your new hood is a Blood hood," Marcus told him. "You're on the gang file as a Blood, and all of your cousins are Bloods. You might as well, kinfolk. It's all good in the hood."

"We all get down for each other, and protect each other," Darius added.

Lil Fade stood. "Don't convince nobody to be down with my hood! Either his muthafuckin' ass is, or he ain't! We don't need no half-ass dedicated muthafuckas running around the hood. You either love your homies and your hood, or you don't. I was a Blood the day I came outta my momma's pussy. Nobody made me one, or talked me into a muthafuckin' thing! Blood is in the heart, and BSV is in the soul. It's for life! It's BSV until the day I muthafuckin' die!" He approached Travon, and stood just before him. "I killed for you."

"And I for you," Travon replied.

"Then let it be done." Lil Fade waved his hand through the air in a grand sweeping gesture, motioning toward the yard.

Travon nodded and rose. He walked down the porch steps and into the yard.

"Let the lil homies do it!" Lil Bling shouted.

Lil Fade, Robert Jr., Cibon, and Antwon walked down the porch steps and into the grass, where Travon waited. Robert Jr. swung first, but missed. Travon had been anticipating it.

Cibon and Antwon, who were twins, both took swings at Travon. Their punches were immediately followed by one from Lil Fade. Travon was ready, but could not possibly dodge all three fists. Lil Fade's and Antwon's connected.

"What up, Blood?" Lil Fade shouted.

Travon absorbed the blows and then charged at Lil Fade. Before he was able to reach him, though, he was punished by a barrage of fists from all three boys. Hit from all directions, he stumbled back and began to swing wildly.

Robert Jr. landed a left hook on Travon's right cheek, while Antwon managed to land a right jab on Travon's left eye. Travon's wild swing struck Lil Fade on his nose.

"Fuck!" Lil Fade shouted. He stopped and clutched his nose.

"C'mon, Blood!" Voices shouted from the crowd. "Get 'im!"

Cibon was able to get in close and give Travon a strong right to his stomach. That, along with a kick from Antwon, caused Travon to stumble back.

"Don't fall, Blood!" Lil Bling shouted.

"C'mon, Lil Fade, get 'im!" Suga shouted.

Lil Fade entered into the fray again. Travon threw a right punch and missed. Punches from all directions began to land all over Travon's upper body. Several fists struck Travon's face in rapid succession. He stumbled and fell.

"BSV for life!" several of the boys shouted, as they descended upon him.

The boys punished Travon with kicks and blows for several minutes, before Darius and Capone declared the initiation over. Lil Fade continued to kick.

"That's enough!" Darius shouted.

"That's enough!" Capone repeated more forcefully.

The boys backed away from Travon, who was lying on the ground curled into a ball. Marcus was the first one to reach him. He helped his cousin up.

"You BSV now, baby!" Marcus said excitedly.

"Yeah, boy!" Cibon shouted. "You a villain now!"

Lil Fade approached Travon and hugged him. "Welcome to the family, Blood."

A car pulled into the driveway, and Travon quickly dusted himself off. It was one of his aunt's cars, and five of the seven sisters were inside.

Regina was mother to Cibon, Antwon, Robert Jr., Niesha, and RaLisa. Vera was mother to Darius, Marcus, LaTonya, and JoBeth. Chicken was mother to Capone, Romeo, Erica, and Jeanette. Elmira was Travon's mother, while Clarissa was the mother of Red, Omar, Spliff, Maurice, and Caesar. Two of the sisters were not present. Irma Lee, who was Winky, Boss, Lil Daddy, J-Bird, and Carlwell's mother, and Martha Ray, who was Frank, Buddy, Urisa, Candy, and Lashonda's mother. Regina exited the car first.

"Oh, girl," Regina exclaimed. "You got all of these hoodlums in the front of your house!"

"Hell, two of them hoodlums is yours!" Chicken told her.

"I'd rather have them right here safe, and know where they are, than to have them out there in them streets getting into all kinds of shit," Vera added.

The women were greeted by several indistinguishable "hello Mrs. Robinsons," "hi Aunties," and "hi Mommas" as they filed past the boys and into the house.

Regina shook her head. "Oh, girl. I couldn't have this shit at my house."

Clarissa shook her head in agreement. "Me neither."

"That's because you got enough bad-ass kids of your own living there," Chicken told them. "And besides, this ain't your house, so shush up. You two always did think that you was better than everybody else."

The last of the sisters filed past into the house, and the door was closed.

"Damn, all y'all's moms look alike," Lil Bling said. "That shit is weird, like they was cloned or something."

Several of the boys broke into laughter.

"Say, let's smash to the spot," Lil Fade told them.

"C'mon." Suga nodded.

Everyone except Travon, Marcus, and Darius filed out into the street, and climbed into various vehicles. Robert Jr. turned back toward his cousins.

"Y'all coming to the spot?" he asked.

"Yeah, we'll be there later, kinfolk," Marcus told him.

"All right then, I'll holler at y'all later." Robert lifted his fist into the air, then climbed into Lil Bling's car.

After all of the cars had pulled away, Marcus said to Travon, "So, how do you feel?"

Travon lifted his head. "About what?"

"About getting down?"

Travon turned away and began to examine his surroundings. The street was quiet and peaceful, the sky was clear, and the evening was warm with a cool, gentle, moderating breeze flowing through the air. The stars were starting to appear, and the retreating sun was meandering across the sky, painting it different shades of red, yellow, orange, and purple. It was a beautiful South Texas evening.

Travon turned back to Marcus and started to speak, but was interrupted by the sound of his mother and aunts enjoying themselves inside. It was the sound of family. It was also the first time that he had heard his mother laugh that much since the death of his brother. His mother was happy, and so he was happy.

"I feel like I'm home," Travon told them. "I feel like I'm finally home."

Marcus slapped Travon across his back. "All right, Blood!"

Marcus, Darius, and Travon shared a smile, and then an embrace.

CHAPTER SIXTEEN

T hat night, Travon, Darius, and Marcus did not go to the part of the neighborhood where all of the other boys were hanging out. Instead, they went to their own private spot that Darius had found for them. It was the middle of the month, so business was average.

"What was that one?" Darius asked.

The car Travon serviced drove away, and he walked back into the yard.

"That was a fifty," Travon told Darius, counting his money. "But on the real, the cuts is dead tonight."

The house that they were using to sell their wares belonged to a heavily addicted drug abuser who allowed the boys the use of his property in exchange for a small amount of drugs for his personal use. On average, Darius gave the dude about a hundred dollars' worth of crack cocaine every week.

"Shit, ain't nothing poppin' tonight," Marcus told them. He seated himself on the front porch of the crackhouse.

Soon, another car drove up, an old Ford Thunderbird, with three of its four hubcaps missing. A skinny, dusty white man with torn jeans and a filthy aqua T-shirt climbed out. He walked up to Travon and smiled, releasing a torrent of bad breath, and revealing a mouth with three missing teeth.

"Got a twenty?" the man asked.

"Yeah." Travon nodded. He walked to a small bush near the house and bent down to get his stash.

"Who's in the car with you?" Marcus asked. He walked to the car and peered inside.

A smiling dirty white woman waved at him. She, too, was missing several teeth.

"It's my wife," the man told them. He smiled nervously at the woman.

Marcus turned toward Travon and nodded. "It's cool."

Travon pulled a small white piece of cocaine base from his tiny plastic sack and handed it to the man.

The man examined the small piece of crack, and nervously rolled it around in the palm of his hand. "It's too small; can you add another piece?"

"Hell no!" Travon shouted. "Now where's my fuckin' money?"

The man nodded toward the car. "My wife's got it. Hold on."

The man walked to the car, with Travon following closely behind. Once the man was close enough to his vehicle, he leapt through the passenger side window.

"Go! Go! Go!" he shouted to the woman.

Travon and Marcus grabbed the man's legs and began to pull. The woman drove off just as Darius reached inside of the car and opened the passenger side door. The man was pulled away from the moving vehicle, and hit the ground hard. Like a pack of wolves, Darius, Travon, and Marcus surrounded the man and began to kick him brutally.

"Muthafuckin' geeker!" Travon shouted.

"Yeah!" Darius added while delivering a blow. "I bet you won't try to beat no one else!"

"Yeah, fuckin'g stupid-ass geeker!" Marcus yelled.

The man's wife stopped the car down the street and began honking the horn. Travon, Marcus, and Darius continued to kick brutally, until too many lights from the surrounding houses began to come on. Doors began to open, blinds began to crack, and the once dark and peaceful street began to come alive.

"Let's go!" Darius shouted. "Fuck this trick!"

The boys took off running into the backyard of the crackhouse and hopped the fence into an adjacent alley. They continued to scale fences and cut through trails, until they reached the main hangout spot. Out of breath, they emerged from the shadows between two houses.

"Man, y'all better cut that shit out!" Lil Fade shouted. "Y'all asses almost got mowed down by this muthafuckin' chopper!" He showed them the AK-47 assault rifle cradled in his arms.

"All of that running out from in between the houses almost got y'all killed, Blood!" Lil Bling shouted.

Travon, Marcus, and Darius slowly walked to where the rest of the boys were standing around and hanging out.

"What's poppin'?" Darius asked.

Lil Fade shook his head. "Shit, nothing. Everybody done boned the fuck out, that's what's happening."

"Where y'all coming from?" Capone asked.

"Shit, we was on our way here, and we had to stop and whip this geeker," Darius lied. He wanted to keep his other drug spot a secret.

"Oh, yeah?" Lil Fade asked. "Damn, I missed all the fun."

A car pulled up in front of them and the passenger flashed a cigarette lighter twice.

"Shit, I'm out," Capone announced, extending his arms out to his sides.

Lil Fade shook his head. "I ain't got nothing."

Marcus turned to Travon. "Go on and get it."

Travon strolled up to the driver's side and examined its occupants. There were two young, attractive women inside. They both smiled at Travon.

"Hey, baby, what's up?" the driver asked, fondling Travon's zipper.

"You wanna do something?" the passenger asked.

"Fuck!" Travon smacked his lips, and walked back into the yard where the others were standing.

"What's up?" Capone asked.

Travon smacked his lips once again. "They ain't got no money; they wanna get busy and shit."

Capone peered over Travon's shoulder, examining the occupants of the vehicle. He liked what he saw and turned back toward Travon. "Say, lil kinfolk, let me get a piece from you and I'll pay you back tomorrow."

Travon shook his head and pulled out his small plastic sack, which was filled with pieces of crack cocaine. He unwrapped the sack, and handed Capone a twenty-dollar piece. Lil Fade hurried over.

"Break it in half and give me a piece," Lil Fade told Capone.

Using his fingernail, Capone snapped the twenty-dollar piece of crack cocaine in two, and handed Lil Fade one of the pieces. Together, they approached the car.

"Yeah, boy!" Lil Fade said excitedly. "I'ma get my duck sick tonight!"

"So, what y'all wanna do?" one of the ladies asked.

Lil Fade held up his palm. "Hold on, bitch!"

Capone, who had walked to the passenger side window, quickly examined the ladies, and then headed over to the driver's side. "I wanna get my jimmy waxed."

"Me too," Lil Fade told the passenger.

"You got a dime?" the passenger asked.

"Yeah, just come on!" Lil Fade told her.

"Hold on!" she begged. "Let me hit it first."

Lil Fade shook his head. "Nope, first I handle my business, then you can handle yours." Lil Fade grabbed her arm, pulled her out of the car, and then led her around to the side of the house.

"Get in the backseat, and take your mutherfuckin' pants off," Capone told the driver.

"You got a twenty?" she asked.

"Bitch, please!" Capone told her. "You better be happy with this dime I'm a give you."

The driver climbed into the backseat, and removed her blue jeans.

"Ho, open your muthafuckin' legs!" Capone told her, as he climbed on top of her.

A second car pulled up, and the man inside held up two fingers, then cupped his hands into a circle. He mouthed the words *two* and *zero*.

Travon nodded and pulled out a twenty-dollar piece of crack from his little plastic sack, and then handed it to the driver. The driver handed Travon a twenty and then pulled away.

"Let's go to the weed house, and the bootleg," Lil Bling suggested.

Marcus, Darius, and Lil Bling rose, walked to the Chevrolet Impala, and climbed inside. Marcus turned back toward Travon, who was standing in the yard.

"You coming?" he asked.

Travon shook his head. "Naw, y'all go ahead, I'm a stay down."

"All right, BSV out then, Blood!" Marcus told him with a smile.

Lil Bling flipped a toggle switch on his dashboard, activating the hydraulic suspension system on his car. The car bounced up, lifting itself off the ground. After a few seconds, the booming stereo system came alive, and Lil Bling pulled away.

Another car pulled up to the house where Travon was standing. This one was a late-model Nissan Maxima with chrome rims, tinted windows, and a ground effects kit. It looked more like a dealer's car than a drug. The window slid down.

"You got a two-oh," the passenger asked.

Travon removed a twenty-dollar piece of rock cocaine from his small plastic sack and walked to the passenger's side. Both driver and passenger were wearing military uniforms. Remembering what Darius had told him about military customers, Travon added a few pieces of loose chips from the bottom of his sack, to make it appear as though they were getting a lot more. He handed the merchandise over to the passenger.

"Look at this!" the passenger said excitedly. He held out his hand so that the driver could see the amount that he had been given. "I told you that this was the spot!"

The driver looked up at Travon. "What will you do for a C-note?"

Travon pulled out six pieces of rock cocaine and added several loose pieces from the bottom of his sack.

"Bet!" the driver said happily. He handed Travon a one-hundred-dollar bill and Travon handed over the crack. "What's your name?"

"Rico," Travon told them.

"All right, homeboy, the next time we come through, we are gonna ask for you," the driver told him.

Travon nodded and returned to the empty porch. Soon, the car pulled away, leaving him alone with his thoughts.

Travon sat quietly, thinking about his life, and the direction it had taken. Too-Low had been dead for less than a year, and in that short period of time, he had gone from being one of the favorites in the Courts to being its sworn enemy. In that short time period, he had gone from not knowing anything about drugs to sitting on a porch in one of the city's hottest dope spots. In that short amount of time, he had gone from being an unaffiliated innocent to being a member of one of the state's most notorious and violent gangs.

This time last year, he would have been sneaking out of the house to meet Frog, Justin, and Re-Re in the park. Now, with the exception of Frog, the others wanted him dead. He never saw it coming, and he didn't really understand how it happened. Everything was moving at warp speed, and it was so hard to get a grip on things, to gain his bearings. He felt like a bullet. Traveling fast, not knowing where he was going, when he was going to stop, how he was going to stop, and worst of all, not being in control of his own fate. His life was spiraling out of control, faster and faster with each revolution. He would be dead within a year, he told himself. Dead within a year.

"Why you do it in my mouth?" the young lady from the passenger seat asked.

"Shut up, trick!" Lil Fade told her, as they emerged from the shadows. "Just swallow and be happy."

Travon peered in the direction from which they came. Lil Fade was zipping his pants; the girl was spitting. She huffed, and stormed back to the car, where Capone was climbing out and pulling up his pants. Capone tossed the young lady in the backseat her payment, and then returned to the porch where Travon and Lil Fade were now sitting.

"Y'all tricks hurry up and get the fuck outta here!" Lil Fade shouted.

The young lady in the backseat emerged from the vehicle, and put her pants back on in the middle of the street. Then she climbed in the driver's seat, and turned to the passenger, who was already inside.

"Bitch!" the driver shouted. "I knew you would start smoking without me, give me some of that!"

They sat for a few moments and quickly ingested some of the payment for their services, before finally driving away.

Lil Fade opened the front door, grabbed a radio, along with his AK-47 and an extra thirty-round magazine. He turned on the radio, rose, and then walked to some nearby bushes and stashed the AK-47. When finished, he returned to the porch, where they all sat quietly listening to the radio and bobbing their heads. Soon, they heard the distant rumbling of some deep bass notes.

Lil Fade rose, walked over to where the AK-47 was hidden, and waited patiently as the bass notes grew louder. Soon, Lil Bling's car turned the corner, and Lil Fade rejoined Capone and Travon on the porch.

Lil Bling's car pulled up in front of the house and slowly lowered itself to the ground when he hit the switch for it to pancake. Laughing loudly, the boys climbed out of the burgundy lowrider, and strolled up to the porch carrying bags of beer, liquor, and marijuana.

"What the fuck took y'all so long?" Travon asked.

"We ran into some hoochies at the store," Marcus told them. "Plus, Lil Bling had to call his baby's momma back at the pay phone. She kept blowing his shit up."

Lil Bling set a bag of beer, chips, and other items down on the porch, and then headed back toward his car. "I'll holler at y'all later."

"Where the fuck is he going?" Travon asked.

"Shit, he's probably going to go and whip that tripping bitch of his," Lil Fade answered.

Capone peered up from the bag in which he was rummaging. "Say, fool! Don't go and catch no ho-bashing case!"

Darius shook his head. "Man, I couldn't have no broad like that!"

Marcus reached into his pocket and pulled out a large plastic bag filled with marijuana. Some of it had already been rolled into joints. "I rolled some up already, but I ain't about to roll no more," he told them, holding the bag in the air. "That shit got my fingers cramping."

Lil Fade snatched the bag away from Marcus. "Shit, nigga, give it here. You ain't said nothing, I'll roll the rest." He turned to Capone. "Puffing is an art form. You have to be able to roll the shit just right, plus you have to be able to puff all night."

The boys laughed at Lil Fade's rhyme.

Capone turned to Marcus. "You can't roll no weed anyway, youngster. You be rolling baby joints. Yo shit so tight, a nigga can't even get a decent pull off a one."

Marcus pulled out a Swisher Sweet cigar that had been emptied and stuffed with marijuana. "That's cool, y'all keep on cutting, while I sit here puffin'. And since y'all wanna talk about the way I roll, y'all gets none of this here."

"Naw, dog, you know I'm just fuckin'g with you," Capone told him.

Marcus pulled out five more Swisher Sweet cigars, and tossed them to Lil Fade, who immediately began removing the tobacco from them.

"I got more 'gars if you need 'em," Darius told him.

Lil Fade nodded. "Bet."

Capone popped the top on a bottle of gin, took a drink, and then passed it around. Darius turned up the volume on the radio, and the boys commenced to getting drunk and high.

❖❖❖

Later that night, Travon was helped inside the house, where he was laid on a couch. He quickly fell asleep again. This time, he dreamt of his brother.

"Don't ever join a gang, Tre."

"I do this shit, so you don't have to!"

"I better not ever hear about you joining a gang, or selling any kind a dope, do you hear me?"

"Tre Tre Tre"

Travon tossed and turned in his sleep. He dreamt of the gunshots that he'd heard the night of his brother's murder. He dreamt of the shootout in the Courts between himself and the others. He dreamt of the shootout in the park. He dreamt of the shootout on the highway and of the words that his aunt spoke to him afterward. His dreams, and his sleep, came to an abrupt end when a thunderous roar ripped through the house, as the front door was busted open.

"Everybody get down on the floor now!" Now! Now! Now!" the first officer through the door shouted. "This is a search warrant! Search warrant! Police Department! Everybody on the floor now!"

Travon's heart began to beat a million miles per hour. His first thought was that it was actually a jack move by some rival gang. Those thoughts were quickly erased when he spied two officers wearing black jumpsuits, ski masks, gloves, boots, helmets, and utility vests entering into the room. They were also wearing bright yellow jackets with "police" printed across the front of them, and they carried large black bulletproof shields in their left arms. One of the officers was pointing a Glock semiautomatic pistol at him, from behind his shield.

"Get down on the ground now!" the officer shouted through his black ski mask. "This is a narcotics search warrant! Keep your hands where I can see them!"

Travon quickly felt himself being searched; his arms were pulled back and his wrists were cuffed.

"Get up!" one of the masked officers told him.

Another clasped Travon by his forearm, and pulled him up from off the floor.

"Yeah, we got you muthafuckers now!" shouted the officer who was holding Travon's arm.

Travon was led into the kitchen; Marcus, Darius, Capone, and Lil Fade were already seated around the breakfast table with their hands cuffed behind their backs. He stared at Darius, who smiled at him. Travon shook his head in disbelief, and then peered down at the floor.

"Sit down over here," one of the masked officers told Travon, pointing toward an empty chair.

As Travon was seated, the old man to whom the house belonged was led in. All of the chairs around the small breakfast table were occupied, so a chair was brought from the living room for the old man to sit in.

"We're clear," one of the officers announced. "This is everybody."

One of the masked officers walked to the front door, and waved his hand signaling that everything was clear. All of the officers with the exception of two holstered their weapons. The officers leaned their massive ballistic shields against the dirty off-white refrigerator, just as an old fat white man in a beige Guayabera shirt hobbled into the kitchen. The old man held a long, official-looking piece of paper.

"Canine unit is five minutes out, sir," one of the officers reported.

The old man nodded, and the officer turned sharply on his heels and departed. The old man shifted his gaze toward the boys.

"Listen up!" he barked. "I'm Sumner Bowlman, and this here's a narcotics search warrant. It was signed last night by municipal court Judge Homer Falls. You can make it easy on us and tell us where the dope is, or we can tear the place apart. But before you say anything, I'm a gonna read you your rights. You got the right to remain silent, because anything you say can and will be used against ya in a court a law. You all have the right to an attorney, an' if'n you can't afford an attorney, they have to give you one. Do you fellers understand these here rights as I have read them to ya?"

The boys stared at one another; all remained silent.

"Good," Bowlman said. "Now down to business. Where's the fuckin' dope at?"

The boys remained silent. Bowlman turned to the owner of the house.

"Waters, do you know where these boys keep their dope at?" Bowlman asked, in his heavy, good-old-boy accent.

Waters shook his head.

Bowlman squinted and shrugged. "Okay, if that's the way you want it. I guess we'll be here all day then." Bowlman turned to the unit of masked officers. "Okay, boys, tear the place up."

"All right!" one of the officers exclaimed.

Another officer brought a chair from the living room, and sat it down just behind Bowlman. The commander seated himself in it, and began to rock back and forth and stare at the boys.

The noise from the officers' overly enthusiastic search soon became deafening. They broke, smashed, tore, ripped, slashed, cut, and destroyed everything in sight. It was what the Waffen SS once termed "Youthful Exuberance." They merrily destroyed the entire house.

After a while, Travon began to wonder about the small pieces of rock cocaine that he'd had in his pockets when he fell asleep. The police had searched him thoroughly, and yet they had found nothing.

Waters, Travon thought. The old man must have peeled him while he was sleeping. He could almost kiss the old fool.

Lil Fade did not have anything, Darius had sold out before they left their other spot, and so had Marcus. Travon now knew that he was clean, so he was able to sit back and relax a little bit. He found that he was even able to smile now.

"Bingo!" one of the officers strutted triumphantly into the room. He held the AK-47 up in the air, displaying it to his boss. "Look at what we have here."

Bowlman grunted approvingly. "Now we're talking fed time. And since you boys wouldn't cooperate, as soon as I get back to my office, I'm calling the U.S. Attorney. I'm going to ask him to pick up the case and prosecute your little asses to the fullest."

"What?" Waters shouted. "I can't even have a gun in my own house, to protect myself?"

Travon smiled at Waters. He felt as though he were falling in love with the old man.

"I went to Vietnam and fought for my country," Waters continued. "I got a Silver Star, a Bronze Star, and two Purple Hearts, and you mean to tell me that I can't have a gun in my home! Is that what you're telling me?"

Travon promised himself that he would give Waters an entire quarter-ounce of crack, so that the old man could smoke until his heart was content.

"I'm not saying that, Mr. Waters," Bowlman told him. "But I do seriously doubt that this here gun is yours."

"What? Are you calling me a liar?" Waters asked. "Who's your boss? Who's in charge of this breaking into my home?"

"I'm in charge of this task force," Bowlman told him.

Waters shook his head. "No, I want *your* boss. I'm gonna sue your ass for everything you've got!"

"Mr. Waters, if we find anything in this house, I'm taking you to jail," Bowlman told him. "And then I'm going to try my damnedest to seize this house from you."

"When you don't find anything, all of the shit you are letting your boys break, you will pay for, and then some," Waters countered.

The only time that Travon had any dealings with old man Waters was when he was already doped up. Waters' current actions compelled Travon to think about the old man's life. He wondered what had happened to him to drive him into so deep of an addiction. Who was the man before he became a crack addict? Where was his family? Did he have any children, and if so, where were they? He would never allow something like this to become of his mother, Travon told himself. How could people slip so far, and how could their families allow them to?

Travon thought about all of the people that he had met since beginning his new occupation. Who were they, and what had happened to them? How could it have happened to so many? What would their lives have been like, if they weren't strung out? How would their lives be, if it weren't for drugs, or drug dealers for that matter? How would their lives be, if it weren't for him?

❖❖❖

Two hours later, an officer entered the room. He stared at Bowlman and shook his head. "Nothing, boss."

Waters smiled, and Bowlman tightened his lip. He rose from his chair rapidly.

"Send me a bill, Waters! But you'd better hurry, because I'll be back!" Sumner knocked over the chair in which he had been seated as he stormed out of the room. "Take those grinning little bastards to juvenile!"

The confused officer stared at his boss. "What charges?"

"Curfew violation, firearms charges, hell, I don't know!" Bowlman shouted. "Be creative!"

The officer turned back toward the boys. "Okay, you three juveniles, let's go."

Travon, Marcus, and Lil Fade were led outside and placed into a large, black van. On the way to the juvenile detention center, Travon peered out of the dark tinted window. It was still morning outside. Marcus hit Travon's leg with his knee, in order to get his attention. Travon turned and stared at his cousin.

"Don't worry, kinfolk," Marcus told him. "We'll be out by lunchtime."

CHAPTER SEVENTEEN

"Travon Robinson!" shouted the slightly overweight guard.

"What?"

"You're going before the judge," the guard told him. "C'mon!"

Travon rose from his bed. He was wearing a bright orange jumpsuit with *BCJDC* stenciled on the back in big, bold, black letters. It stood for Bexar County Juvenile Detention Center. Travon carefully walked to where the guard was standing and waiting. It was imperative that he step with caution, or risk a terrible fall. The orange sandals he wore were made two sizes too small by his thick gray institutional socks.

The guard took Travon by his arm and escorted him to the elevator, where a second guard was waiting. The elevator arrived and the doors opened to reveal a smiling Marcus, along with his stern-looking escort. Forbidden to talk to each other, Travon and Marcus were content to simply exchange comforting smiles during their elevator ride down to the courtroom floor.

The cousins were led out of the elevator and through a hall filled with social workers in cheap suits. They passed a holding cell, with four other juveniles inside, and walked straight to a desk with another overweight guard seated behind it.

"These are the two late ones that Judge O'Connor wanted to see," Marcus' escort told the guard.

The desk guard nodded. "Okay, and when they are done, take 'em to the visitation area. They both have parental visits."

Marcus' escort nodded. "Okay."

The desk guard punched a button and a loud buzzer sounded; the thick metal door to the right slid open. The boys and their escorts walked through the steel door and a large white metal detector that was positioned just on the other side of it. They turned right and walked down another corridor and through a set of massive wooden double doors.

Their mothers were seated in the center of the courtroom, and waved to them as they entered. Vera pointed her finger at Travon, and mouthed *"You're gonna get it."* Travon joined a balding gentleman in a cheap gray suit who was seated at a scarred wooden table.

"Hi, I'm Anthony Conway Jr., your attorney. I've been looking over your case file since it was given to me five minutes ago. You have been charged with possession of a dangerous weapon, lying to a Texas peace officer, curfew violation, membership in a dangerous criminal organization, and obstructing justice. I've talked to the prosecutor, and he wants to send you to boot camp for six months, or TYC for a year, and then place you on a monitor until you turn eighteen. I recommend that you take the boot camp, because I think that it's a pretty good deal. He said that if we take it right away, he'll drop everything but the obstructing of justice."

The lawyer reached into his briefcase and pulled out some papers and a pen. "Just sign these and we're done."

Travon turned and peered over at Marcus, who was arguing with his attorney. He turned back toward his attorney. "I ain't pleading guilty to shit. I ain't did shit, and they ain't caught me with shit."

The lawyer tapped the papers he held. "But it says here that they found a Norinco AK-47 in your house!"

Travon shook his head. "Bullshit! It wasn't my house; it was the old man's house, and the old man's gun."

Conway stared at Travon, tilted his head to the side and sighed. "Do you have any money? It says here that you live on the Eastside."

Travon frowned. "Hell yeah, I got money. I got enough to hire a real lawyer, and get rid of your sorry ass!"

Stunned, Conway leaned back in his chair. "You have enough money to hire a lawyer?"

Travon nodded. "Yeah."

"Can you bring me two Gs to my office before the week is up?" Conway asked.

"Can you get me and my cousin outta this bullshit?" Travon demanded instead.

"Maybe." Conway smiled.

Travon leaned forward. "I'll tell you what. Get us the fuck outta here, and I'll have your two Gs waiting for you tomorrow morning when you get to the office."

Conway returned Travon's smile. "Keep this between us. I'm not really supposed to be taking money from you. So just drop it off, and we'll consider it a gift."

Travon nodded. Conway went to the prosecutor's table and sat down next to the state's attorney. He opened his briefcase, pulled out Travon's file, and began to flip through it while talking to the prosecutor. Both men looked up as the defense attorney pointed toward Travon, and returned their focus to the file.

Conway continued to flip through the folder and point things out. He and the state's attorney shared a few laughs during the process, as well as a few pats on the back. Another prosecutor and defense attorney stood before the judge, and Travon focused his attention on them.

What a mean bitch, was Travon's first impression, as he listened to the judge berate both men. Conway rejoined Travon, followed by Marcus and his attorney.

"Mike has dismissed the charges against both of the boys, on the grounds of insufficient evidence," Conway told Marcus' attorney. "C'mon, I'll buy you a beer."

Marcus' attorney grabbed his hand. "No, let me buy you a beer. I couldn't have gone before the judge with that kid; she'd have torn our asses off."

Conway turned toward Travon and Marcus. "You boys are free. I just have to take care of some paperwork, and then your mothers can sign you out. Stay out of trouble."

The attorney extended his hand toward Marcus, who shook it firmly. He did the same to Travon, and then leaned forward and whispered into Travon's ear. "My office, tomorrow morning, two grand, and not a penny less."

Travon nodded.

"Good luck, son!" Conway told him, as he turned and walked away. Midway he turned back. "I'll tell your mothers the good news."

Later That Day
Aunt Vera's House-Denver Heights

"Shit, I was scared," Marcus said.

"You wasn't alone." Travon nodded. "Po-po everywhere, all jacked up, wearing ski masks and destroying everything in sight. Hell, I was scared as a muthafucka."

"Boy, they got hot when they didn't find nothing," Darius said. "I thought that they was gonna plant something. That task force is known for that shit."

Darius turned toward Travon. "That reminds me; I been meaning to ask you, what happened to you yeayo?"

"I think the old man peeled me," Travon told him. "But trust me, I ain't mad at him."

Darius shook his head. "Man, I just knew we were gone."

"Shit, I wanted to kiss Waters when they didn't find nothing," Travon told them. "Hell, they didn't find no crack pipes or nothing!"

"That's because old man Waters in a primo man," Darius explained. "He won't touch a pipe, but his ass will get geeked as hell on them moes."

"How much money did you lose?" Marcus asked.

Travon shook his head. "Nothin' but a couple a hundred. I gotta holler at that lawyer tomorrow though. He want me to take him two grand. Shit, I gotta get me some wheels. I don't wanna bum a ride or catch the bus. I'm a have to rent me a geeker car tomorrow or tonight if I can find one."

Darius shook his finger at Travon. "Boy, you playin' with fire, fuckin' with some dope tonight."

"Yeah, you can't get lucky two days in a row," Marcus added.

Travon shook his head. "Shit, I need a car though."

"I know where a clean-ass six-four is," Darius told him.

"Naw, fuck that," Marcus said. "Everybody is pushin' fours. I know where a clean-ass Olds Regency is. Stay away from them hot-ass fours and battle-lacs."

A small white Subaru pulled up. Darius reached for his Ruger P-89 nine-millimeter handgun, until he recognized the car. It was Lil Fade's sister's car.

The Subaru stopped in front of Aunt Vera's house, and out leapt a smiling Lil Fade, pulling up his sagging pants.

"What's up, Bloods?" Lil Fade shouted, extending his arms into the air. His smile was wider than the Grand Canyon.

"What up, B?" Darius replied, extending his right arm into the air, and using his fingers to form the letter *B*.

"What happened?" Marcus asked.

"Shit, they dropped the charges, but I had to stay until my sister could come and get me," Lil Fade explained.

His sister rolled her eyes at Darius, and pulled away. Darius turned to Lil Fade and smiled.

"She wouldn't even wave at me," Darius told him.

"She'll get over it, I know she still cuts for you," Lil Fade told him. "So, what are y'all getting in to?"

Darius shook his head. "Nothin.' Tre was talking about getting a ride."

"Oh, Blood!" Lil Fade shouted. "Did you tell him about that black six-four over there by Jolly Time?"

"Yeah," Marcus answered. "But we need a ride over there."

"Hell, we just rode past Cactus Street, and Big Pimpin is home," Lil Fade told them.

"Shit, let's go!" Darius said.

The boys set off for Big Pimpin's house.

"Shit!" Marcus shouted. "I forgot my strap!"

Darius stared at him. "You know we are goin' over there by Jolly Time, and you forgot your shit?" He shook his head. "Tre, Lil Fade, are y'all strapped?"

"Yeah." Travon nodded.

"Hell, yeah!" Lil Fade answered.

The boys continued toward Big Pimpin's house. A beige Ford Escort drove past them and slowed down. A hand came out of the window, held up two fingers, and then formed an *O*. Lil Fade waved his arms in the air, and then turned to Travon.

"You got some yea?" he asked.

Travon nodded. "Yeah, but it's at the crib."

"Fuck Big Pimpin, here's our ride right here," Lil Fade told them.

The Ford Escort backed up, and the passenger nodded. "What's up?"

Travon walked to the driver's window. "Shoot me to the crib, and I'll hook you up if you let me rent your car for two hours."

The passenger stared longingly at the driver.

"How much?" the driver asked.

"A fat forty," Travon told him.

The driver nodded. "All right, but only for two hours. I gotta get back home."

Travon hopped on the hood of the Escort. "Take me two blocks that way, and then make the block until I meet you back at the corner."

The Escort turned around, and took Travon in the direction in which he had pointed. Once at the corner, Travon leapt from the hood and ran to his Aunt V's house.

Travon bounded up the stairs and into his room, where he lifted his mattress. Beneath the top mattress were several thousand-dollar bundles of money. Travon grabbed four wads.

Travon headed back down the stairs, out of the front door, and into the backyard, where he approached Tank, Darius's pit bull. Travon lifted Tank's dog bowl and dug up his sack of drugs. He removed a hundred-dollar bag of crack, then reburied the sack and replaced the dog bowl. Confident that no one had witnessed his actions, Travon bolted from the backyard and raced down the street, where he met up with his ride.

"You got it?" the driver asked.

Travon handed the driver two rocks from his sack, and the driver quickly climbed out of the vehicle.

"We'll be at Dave's Barbecue joint, right around the corner," the driver told him. "Just bring the car there when you're through." The driver and passenger turned and headed down the street.

Travon climbed into the car, and then backed up to where Darius, Marcus, and Lil Fade were sitting patiently on a curb waiting for him. Then they headed off toward Jolly Time, a small gambling shack in the heart of the city's Eastside.

"Shit, Tre, I still think that you should peep out that nine-eight first," Marcus told him.

"Naw, man, get you a four," Lil Fade countered. "Paint that ho lime green and dip it, like the one in Cube's video."

"Naw, hook it up like the one in that Black Superman video," Darius suggested.

"Man, get that nine-eight, and paint it black cherry," Marcus told him. "Throw you a white vinyl on it, and buy you some gold and chrome disc and vogues, a white interior, some sounds, and you got you some shit."

"Turn left here." Lil Fade pointed.

"Shit, Tre, you gonna be seventeen soon," Darius said. "Do you want us to throw you a party? You know we can have it at Big Pimpin's house."

Travon shrugged. "Shit, I don't care. You know that it don't make me none."

"Turn right at the next street and slow down," Lil Fade told him.

The boys began looking from driveway to driveway, trying to spot the car. About halfway down the street, Lil Fade found it.

"There!" Lil Fade said excitedly. "Right there, at the purple and white house."

"Pull right up here in front of the house," Darius told Travon. "I'ma go up to the door with you."

Travon parked the Escort, and he and Darius climbed out of the car and ventured up the sidewalk toward the front door. Darius knocked, while Lil Fade and Marcus watched anxiously from the car.

Darius banged on the door a little harder, and then turned toward Travon. "Someone has to be home; there's a brand-new Cadillac in the driveway."

He knocked again.

"I'm coming," a high-pitched female voice declared from the other side of the door. "Who is it?"

"It's Dwayne," Darius told her.

The door slowly crept open, and an elderly woman in a housecoat and slippers stood before them. She looked to be in her eighties.

"Yes?" she asked, shifting her questioning eyes between Travon and Darius.

"Ma'am, we're sorry to bother you, but we just wanted to know if your car was for sale. The sixty-four Chevy Impala? We are willing to pay you good cash money for it."

Travon smiled at his cousin. *Go ahead, spend all of my money for me,* he thought.

"Well, boys, everyone has been asking me if they could buy it, but I'm afraid the car isn't for sale," she told them with a smile. "It belonged to my late husband. He loved to work on that car, so I'm gonna keep it for a little while longer."

Darius smiled back and nodded. "Okay, ma'am. Sorry to have disturbed you."

"Thank you, ma'am," Travon added. He and Darius turned, and returned down the path to the rented Escort. They climbed inside, and closed their doors.

"What she say?" Marcus asked.

"She said that she wanted to keep it," Darius explained. "She said that it belonged to her husband who died."

"Keep it!" Lil Fade exploded. "How long can she keep it? The old bitch is gonna croak any minute now! Fuck that shit, Blood! This is BSV. That old bitch is gonna come off the car, or I'm gonna smoke her ass!"

Lil Fade quickly climbed out of the car. "I put that on the set!" he told the others.

Travon panicked. "Naw, man! It's cool! I didn't want it anyway!"

"Yeah, we can go get that nine-eight up there on New Braunsfels Street," Marcus added. "It's cleaner anyway."

"C'mon, get back in the car, Blood," Darius told Lil Fade. "Let's bail."

Lil Fade waved them off. "Naw, fuck that shit! I put it on my set."

He stormed up the path toward the front door. Travon reached for his weapon.

"No!" Travon shouted. He pulled out his handgun, and tried to exit the vehicle. Darius and Marcus grabbed him.

"No!" Travon shouted. "You can't let him do it! Stop him! Stop him!" He struggled violently to break free.

"Tre!" Marcus shouted.

"Travon," Darius said to him through clenched teeth, "you are going to kill me. This gun is going to go off by accident, and you are going to kill me."

Travon continued to struggle and try to break free from their grasp, but removed his finger from the trigger of his weapon. Darius and Marcus were finally able to pull the gun away from him. Marcus leaned over the seat and spoke directly into Travon's ear.

"Tre! If you get out of this car, he will kill you. Do you hear me, Tre? He will kill you! Let it ride, Tre. Let it ride."

Through tear-filled eyes Travon watched the events on the porch unfold. Lil Fade and the old woman stood talking.

"Please, God, no! No!" Travon begged. "Don't let it happen, don't let it happen!"

He watched as Lil Fade reached for his weapon, and the old lady slammed the door. He watched as Lil Fade pumped twelve shots through the front door.

"No! No!" Travon shouted. Tears flowed from his eyes, saliva from his mouth, and mucus from his nose. "Noooo! Noooo!"

Suddenly, Travon lurched, and Marcus and Darius quickly released him. He opened the car door and vomited.

"What's wrong with him?" Lil Fade asked, as he climbed inside the vehicle.

"Nothin'," Marcus told him. "Probably just some bad juvenile food."

"Well, let's go!" Lil Fade told them.

Marcus climbed out of the backseat, and slid behind the wheel of the vehicle, scooting Travon over. Darius climbed into the back, and Marcus pulled away.

The old woman's name was Mrs. Jackson. She was eighty-nine years old; however, due to multiple gunshot wounds to her back, she would not live to be ninety.

CHAPTER EIGHTEEN

"Drop me off at the hood store," Travon told them. He was leaning against the passenger-side window, staring out of it lethargically.

"Okay," Marcus said, acknowledging Travon's request. They were the first words that had been spoken since they'd left the old woman's house more than eight minutes ago. They were now motoring through the Denver Heights.

Marcus pulled into the parking lot of Mrs. Chang's, and Travon slowly opened his door and staggered out. He feebly headed for the entrance.

Marcus climbed out of the car and peered at Travon over the roof. "Do you want us to wait for you?"

Travon shook his head, and Marcus climbed back inside of the car and pulled away. Travon turned, and staggered into the store.

"What's up, Tre?" Mr. Chang asked.

Travon shook his head. "Nothin', Mr. C."

Mr. Chang squinted his eyes and examined Travon carefully. "Are you all right? You don't look so good."

"I'm okay," Travon replied. "I just need a beer."

He walked to the beer freezer, threw open the door, and grabbed a Crazy Horse. He unscrewed the top, and immediately began to guzzle it down.

"How's Vera?" Mr. Chang asked, as Travon returned to the counter with his half-drunk beer. "Haven't seen her in here in a while."

"She's okay," Travon replied.

"You usually talk my ear off, Tre," Mr. Chang told him. "Are you sure you're all right?"

Travon bit down upon his bottom lip and stared off into space. "I'll be okay again, eventually."

Mr. Chang placed his hands flat on the counter top and leaned forward. "Tre, look at me."

Travon lifted his head and stared Mr. Chang in the eyes. Mr. Chang could tell that he had been crying. He could also see deeper.

"You're one of them now," Mr. Chang said softly. "I can see it in your eyes."

"What?" Travon asked, turning away. "You can see what, Mr. C? What are you talking about?"

"You're one of them," Mr. Chang repeated, pointing out to the streets. "You've done too much; you've seen too much; you've *been through* too much."

He shook his finger at Travon. "I remember when you first came to this neighborhood. You were different. You were innocent. Always asking questions, helping out around the store, so full of energy. Now, you look tired, worn. You look like the kids I served with in Vietnam. Just like a lot of the other kids that come through here."

Leaning forward he whispered, "Too much war, Tre. Don't let it drag you in, don't let it engulf you, don't let it destroy you. It will eat you alive, trust me, I've seen it."

Mr. Chang waved toward the front door, motioning toward the neighborhood. "You don't have to become a part of this 'jungle,' as they call it. Don't become a predator. Don't become a monster."

Travon stared at Mr. Chang coldly. "And the guns you sell us? What are they for?"

Chang looked down at the counter, and a deep sadness spread across his face. After several moments, he lifted his head and returned his gaze to Travon.

"Not one time has my store been robbed, and I have been here twenty years. My wife has not been assaulted, or murdered, and she works here alone, sometimes at night." He pointed toward the ground. "We live in this neighborhood. We could have moved away to the Northside, but why? We are welcomed, loved, and protected here. Not once has my home been shot up or burglarized."

Mr. Chang paused for a moment, and then held up his index finger.

"Then, there is my son, Johnny. He loved this neighborhood, and he loved your buddies. I know that you've heard them talk about my son."

Mr. Chang pointed toward the ground. "He grew up here. He was a BSV, just like you. My son gave his *life* in this war!" he shouted. "He died with a red rag tied around his head. He died right at the bus stop at the corner of Pine and Dakota Street. All of the boys were so nice to my wife and I after the funeral. When they were children, these same boys played in my front yard, spent the night in my home, ate at my dinner table, and accepted my Asian son as one of their brothers."

Mr. Chang's voice turned cold. "I will give them whatever they need to protect themselves, so that their families will not have to go through what my family did. That is why I do what I do."

Travon took a step forward. "And the families of the people they use them against?"

"I don't know them, I know you," Mr. Chang told him coldly. He sighed. "Take my advice, Tre. Protect yourself, get a job, move out of the hood, raise a family, and grow old. Live your life and grow old."

Chang removed his glasses and sat them down on top of the counter. "Son, I survived my Vietnam." He poked Travon in the chest with his index finger. "Now you have to survive yours."

Travon lowered his gaze to the floor, as he allowed what he had just been told to sink in. After a moment, he lifted his head again and smiled.

"Thanks, Mr. C."

"For what?"

"For keeping it real," Travon told him. He put two dollars on the counter, turned, and walked out of the store.

❖❖❖

Travon began to think about his life, about what he had just been told. He thought long and hard about what Mr. Chang said about him not having to become a monster. There were other ways out of the hood. He knew what his first step would have to be. He would have to physically extricate himself from Darius, Marcus, Romeo, Capone, and especially Lil

Fade. He needed to get back in school, but first of all, he needed a plan. Something he could follow, something he could use as a guide. The steps wouldn't have to be major; they could be baby steps at first. Anything would be progress.

"Hey, boy, ain't you about three payments late?" a voice called from the side.

Travon looked up. Cooney and Preto were driving along the side of him.

"Help your black ass out of trouble, and look how you repay us! By not paying us!" Cooney told him. "What kind of nigger shit is that?"

"Boy, stop walking when we're talking to you!" Preto shouted.

Travon stopped, and the patrol car stopped beside him. Cars had to swerve around the patrol car, because it had stopped in the middle of the street.

"Look, nigga boy, did you think we were fuckin' with you?" Cooney asked. "We'll string your fuckin' ass up on the tallest Texas oak we can find, and not give a shit if it's in the middle of downtown."

The thought of his brother having to deal with these two angered Travon. He could picture them calling his brother some of the names that they had called him. His thoughts shifted to the old lady who died that day, her only sin being that she loved her husband and wanted to keep a memento of him. His thoughts shifted to the little girl, whose only sin was that she wanted to go to the park and swing that day. He thought of his mother, who had to bury her son, because of bullshit like this. He thought of his brush with death and the painful beating that he took at the hands of Tech Nine, Quentin, and Lil Texas. He thought of the car chase, the park shootout, the hospital stay, the trip to juvenile, and decided that he had had enough. He turned toward the patrol car.

"Martin Cooney, eighteen twenty-one Artesia Way, Sky Harbor subdivision," he said.

Cooney and Preto exchanged glances.

"Yeah, I found your address in my brother's wallet," Travon continued. "I also have all of the straps you sold him, along with Preto's fingerprints on the Beretta from the day that little girl got shot in the Courts. That, along with the videotapes I stole from Mrs. Chang's store of y'all shaking her down, should get you twenty to thirty in a Federal prison. A few statements from the other neighborhood businesses you two honkies have been shaking down will just seal the case up airtight."

Travon stepped closer to the patrol car. "They will just love your fat, pale white ass in U.S.P. Atlanta, Cooney. The brothers will be fighting over you for the first two weeks after you get there. I imagine some big strong Georgia buck will wind up becoming you husband though. And I guarantee, all of that nigga shit you been talking? Well, it'll just ooze right out of ya after the first couple of times that he runs up in ya."

Cooney and Preto were stunned into silence.

"The deal's been changed," Travon told them. "The new contract is this. You leave me the fuck alone, and I'll leave you the fuck alone. If anything happens to me, even accidentally, I have already set it up so that one of my relatives will send my little information package to the newspaper."

"Bullshit!" Preto spat.

Travon shrugged. "You may get a lot of time, you may get a little, you may even get none at all. But your careers as bloodsucking pigs will be over. And your legal bills, well, they'll be so fuckin' outrageous that you'll spend the rest of your miserable lives trying to pay them off."

He jabbed his finger at them. "Don't fuck with me, you white sacks of shit!" Turning, he briskly walked away.

After a few moments, Cooney and Preto pulled alongside him again.

"Nigga boy, you have just declared a war you cannot win," Cooney told him. "If I catch you at night with your shirt on, I will swear that I saw you reaching for something, and I am going to blow your black face off!"

The officers accelerated past Travon, turned onto a main thoroughfare and sped off. Travon threw his arms into the air and smiled. He felt good. His thoughts immediately shifted to his next battle, the battle that mattered the most. It was the battle to get away from his cousins, the battle for his future; it was the battle for his life.

Aunt Vera's House

Travon walked into the yard.

"What's up, T?" Romeo greeted him. "Where have you been?"

"Just walking and thinking," Travon replied.

Marcus opened the screen door and stepped outside. Travon stared at him in silence.

"Tre, he would have killed you," Romeo told him. "Don't cross him, that muthafucka is crazy. Marcus told me what happened, they did the right thing."

"If he's so crazy, then why do we still fuck with him?" Travon asked. "He's our age, and everybody is scared of his white ass! Fuck him!"

Romeo extended his hands in a calming motion. "Tre, calm down. He's crazy, but he *is* the homie, and he *is* BSV."

Travon jabbed his finger in the air. "Fuck that albino muthafucka!"

"Tre, calm down," Romeo told him.

Travon pointed accusingly toward Romeo. "You're just taking up for him because he's Capone's best fuckin' friend! Your brother is a lunatic just like him!"

Romeo's face turned to stone. "And what was Too-Low?" he asked calmly. "Anything Capone does, or has already done, can never, and will never, be able to match the blood on Too-Low's hands."

Travon stepped forward, leaning into Romeo's face. "That son of a bitch killed an old lady, Romeo! In cold fuckin' blood! She wasn't banging, he just got pissed. No, change that. He wasn't even pissed, he just killed her!"

Romeo, still offended by Travon's attack on his brother, pointed toward the Wheatley Courts. "And Too-Low is better than Lil Fade because the people he killed were young? Is that what you're trying to say, Tre? Killin' those five guys in the country execution-style was okay? They were on their knees, with their hands tied behind their backs! And Too-Low, your fuckin' sainted brother, put a bullet in the back of their heads, one by one. Two of them were brothers. One brother had to watch the other die!"

Travon's mouth fell open, but he could not speak. He wanted to call Romeo a liar, but deep down inside, he was not sure if he could.

"And what about the motel jackin'?" Romeo continued. "Another execution-style killing. And the two girls found dead in their car in the Courts? What about the two bodies found in the dumpster in the Courts?"

"That's enough, Romeo!" Marcus shouted.

Travon wanted to run away. He wanted to run away from this foul truth, from this exposure, but he could not. The truth had to be known, and it held him in its vise-like clutches, refusing to let him go. His legs felt as if they were two-hundred-year-old tree stumps rooted deeply into the ground. They could not move even if he wanted them to.

"What about the bodies behind the middle school?" Romeo continued. "The security guard at Windsor Apartments? The two Crips from Austin? The..."

"That's enough!" Marcus repeated, but Romeo ignored him.

"What about the time Too-Low got into it with Mike-Mike, and Mike-Mike ran back to California, so Too-Low kicked in the door to Mike-Mike's baby momma's apartment and killed her. *In front of their kid, while she was pregnant with the other!* The amount of bodies Too-Low left behind for his master Dejuan and their beloved Wheatley Courts runs past the one fifty mark. Too-Low left bodies in California, Virginia, Louisiana, Oklahoma, Arkansas, Missouri, Georgia, Florida, Carolina, Tennessee, and Texas. There are scars from your brother's trips all over Texas. Dallas, Houston, Waco, Midland, Lubbock, Austin, Fort Worth, and of course, good ole San Antone. Dozens of people in dozens of towns all across Texas will always have something to remember Too-Low by!"

Romeo jabbed his finger at Travon's face. "Don't you ever again put your fuckin' lips together and call *my* brother a murderer!"

He turned and stormed into the house, leaving a shocked Travon to digest what he had just been told. Travon turned to Marcus, searching for answers. Marcus just walked away.

The fact that Marcus could not face him told him enough. He too walked into the house. He ran up the stairs and into his bedroom, where he closed the door.

Travon seated himself on the edge of his bed, and then opened his night-stand drawer. He removed his massive Desert Eagle fifty magnum hand-gun, placed the weapon to his temple, and slowly squeezed the trigger. *Click.*

Travon squeezed the trigger once again, and again nothing happened. Angrily, he threw the weapon against his bedroom wall, and then buried his face into his pillow, where he cried himself to sleep.

CHAPTER NINETEEN

The Next Day
Aunt Vera's House

"C'mon, Tre," Marcus shouted through the bedroom door. "We gonna go up to Caesar's on New Braunsfels and peep out that nine-eight."

"Come in," Travon told him.

Marcus opened the door and stood just inside of the doorway. Travon was sitting on his bed. He still wore the previous day's clothing.

"Shit, we ain't got no wheels," Travon told him. "How are we gonna get there?"

"Robert Jr. got his car," Marcus told him. "Him, Ace, and Frog are downstairs right now."

Travon bolted from his bed. "Frog! What the fuck?" He quickly gathered his tennis shoes from the floor. "All right, here I come!"

Marcus smiled, and closed the door behind him. Travon retrieved his handgun from off of the floor. He was glad that Marcus had not noticed it, because he would have hated the questions that would have followed. He had no answers for them. Besides, yesterday was a day that he desperately wanted to forget.

Travon took several extra clips from his nightstand drawer, and stuffed them in his pockets. Then he reached beneath his mattress and grabbed four of the thousand dollar wads that he kept hidden there. He placed the money rolls into his already bulging pockets and then bounded down the stairs and out of the door.

"What's up, Jr.?" Travon greeted his cousin. "What's up, Ace?"

Robert Jr. turned to see who had spoken to him. "What's up, kinfolk?" he asked, after seeing that it was Travon.

Ace nodded. "What's up, Tre?" He greeted his friend with a broad smile.

"Shit, nothing," Travon replied. "Where's Frog?"

"He's in the car," Robert Jr. told him.

Marcus bounded out of the front door. "Y'all ready to bail?"

Robert Jr. nodded. "Yeah, let's go."

The boys walked down the front porch steps to Robert Jr.'s small gray Hyundai and climbed inside. Travon slid into the backseat.

"What's up, my nigga?" Travon shouted to Frog, who was seated in the front passenger seat, fiddling with the radio.

"Shit, nothing, Blood!" Frog replied, turning and raising up in his seat.

Travon leaned forward and the two boys embraced.

"What have you been up to?" Travon asked.

Frog shrugged his thin, knobby shoulders. "Shit, nothing but chilling. Trying to get my shit straight."

Robert Jr. started his car, and the boys headed for Caesar's auto lot.

"Man, I ain't seen you since you left the Courts and went to Cali," Travon told Frog. "Man, how was it?"

Frog shook his head and smiled. "Shit, same as here. I liked it. Fine-ass bitches, and hardheaded-ass niggaz killing each other. You know how it is, the world is a ghetto, baby! Ain't nothing changing but the location and the name."

Travon nodded. "I hear you, fool. Trust me, I hear you." He turned and peered out of the window. "So, how long have you been back?"

"For about a month now," Frog told him. "I got me a little shorty now. He and his momma came back with me."

Travon sat up in his seat. "Bullshit! You ain't got no muthafuckin' kid, nigga!" He slapped Frog across his shoulder. "I doubt if yo ugly ass even got some pussy yet!"

The boys laughed.

"Yeah, man, I seen his little shorty." Ace nodded. "He looks just like this nigga."

Travon shook his head. "Damn, that's fucked up. Why you do that kid like that?"

"Nigga, fuck you!" Frog told Travon. "I'ma handsome muthafucka!"

The boys laughed and talked until finally; they arrived at the car lot. It was a small mom-and-pop car lot, consisting of a trailer, the surrounding parking lot, and about ten to fifteen cars ranging in ages from three to more than ten years old.

"I see that muthafucka now!" Marcus told them, pointing out the Oldsmobile.

"Damn!" Travon said excitedly. "That muthafucka *is* clean!"

"Hell yeah," Robert Jr. added.

The boys climbed out of the Hyundai and walked to where the Oldsmobile was parked. They surrounded the car and examined the body for any dints or dings.

"He only wants two grand for it?" Ace asked, peering at the sticker. "Shit, Tre, that's a win."

"Man, it is on hit," Frog added.

The door to the trailer swung open and a short chubby gentleman with an oily S-Curl strutted out. He was forty-something, with graying strands of hair interspersed within the black. He flashed a quick grin at his potential customers, displaying a rather shiny gold tooth sitting prominently in the front of his mouth.

"You like that one, huh?" Caesar asked.

"I'll give you fifteen hundred dollars for it, right now," Travon told him.

The salesman shook his head, declining Travon's offer. "I can't go no lower than two thousand for it. The A/C blows cold, has power everything, and it even has a power sunroof."

Travon nodded. "All right then, I'll give you eighteen hundred for it."

The salesman folded his arms, lifted his hand to his chin, and thought about the offer for several moments. "I think I can swing eighteen hundred. But you have to pay for the title change and get it done yourself."

Travon shrugged. "Cool."

"What's your name, son?" the salesman asked.

"Tre."

Caesar nodded toward the trailer. "C'mon inside and we'll do some paperwork. Do you wanna take her out for a spin first?"

"No," Travon shook his head. "My kinfolk says that it's all right."

"Do you wanna start her up and hear how she sounds?" Caesar asked. "That motor is so quiet, you'll forget that the car is running."

Again, Travon shook his head. "Naw, it's cool."

Caesar led Travon into the trailer, leaving the others to look around and examine the other vehicles on the lot. Caesar seated himself behind his cheap faux-wood desk, while Travon took the metal folding chair opposite him.

"You look kind of young. Whose name are you gonna put this car in?"

"My aunt's," Travon told him. He pulled out his money, counted out eighteen hundred dollars, and handed it to Caesar.

"Okay." Caesar stood. "That's about all the paperwork we really need to take care of." He pulled a pair of keys off of a key holder that was mounted on the trailer wall, and tossed them to Travon. "I want you to take this title and the bill of sale that I'm going to give you, and go down to the title office. There, pay the tax on your vehicle, and the fee, and then you're straight. But you'll need to take your aunt down there with you; don't forget that."

Travon nodded and rose. "All right, cool. Hey, I appreciate your help. I'll holler at you another time."

"Thank you," Caesar told him. "It's good doing business with you. If you have any other partners looking for some wheels, shoot 'em my way."

"I'll do that," Travon told him, exiting the office.

"Hey, you forgot your bill of sale!" Caesar told him.

Travon turned and hurried back to the trailer door, where Caesar handed him the sales slip.

"You'll need to take that with you, don't forget," Caesar told him.

"Alright," Travon replied. He turned, and hurried over to his newly purchased vehicle, beaming with the pride of a new father. "I'm going to put some humps in it right now!"

"Aw shit!" Frog shouted. "Don't do it like that, Tre! Look at my homie Tre balling!"

"I'ma roll with you," Marcus declared.

"Me too," Frog told him.

"Say Jr., when you hear me coming through the hood pounding, just pull your shit over and cut the stereo off," Travon told his cousin with a gigantic smile.

Robert Jr. smiled back, and then shot Travon the finger.

The boys piled into their vehicles, and Travon headed for the stereo shop, just off of Interstate 35. Robert Jr. followed just behind. The boys were caught by a traffic light at the intersection of New Braunsfels and Houston Street. On one corner of this busy thoroughfare sat a liquor store, on another sat a pawn shop. An H.E.B. grocery store occupied one of the corners, while a Jack in the Box fast-food restaurant sat on the other.

"Tre! Tre!" Marcus tapped frantically at his cousin's shoulder.

Travon peered over his shoulder at Marcus. "What's up?"

Marcus pointed. "Look who just got out of the car at Jack in the Box!"

Travon turned toward the hamburger joint. It was Re-Re, with a female companion.

Travon rolled down his window and waved his hand frenetically, in order to get Robert Jr.'s attention. Robert lifted his hand into the air asking his cousin what he wanted. Travon activated his right turn signal, turned, and then made a quick left up into the parking lot of the restaurant. Robert Jr. followed.

The boys parked, climbed out of their vehicles, and met in the parking lot.

"That's the muthafucka from Pletz Park," Travon explained. "He's one of the ones that pulled straps on us and made us catch out."

"If it wasn't for him, Romeo wouldn't have gotten shot, because we wouldn't have had to wreck shit," Marcus added.

"What do y'all want to do, kill that nigga in broad daylight?" Robert Jr. asked.

"We can make it look like a robbery," Ace suggested.

Travon shook his hands like an umpire calling an out. "Naw, we still one up on them niggaz. I just want to make him bow down and catch out, like he did us."

Robert Jr. knew that they were about to play a dangerous game. He lived by the maxim, *"You don't pull out a gun, unless you're going to use it."* He was the most experienced of the boys present, and he far outranked them. But still, he acquiesced.

"Okay." Robert shrugged.

"Let's mob," Marcus said, leading them inside.

Re-Re and his girl were just sitting down with their food, when Travon and the boys approached. Travon took the seat next to the girl, while Marcus seated himself next to Re-Re. Robert Jr. seated himself at the table directly across from them, Ace found a seat next to Travon, and Frog occupied a booth just behind Re-Re. They had him surrounded.

"What's up, Re-Re?" Travon asked. He placed his arm around the shoulder of Re-Re's female companion. "Hey, baby, what's up? What's your name?"

"Nikki," she replied bashfully.

Re-Re had been stunned into silence. His eyes bulged from their sockets and his mouth hung open. Fear prevented him from speaking.

"Close your mouth," Frog told him. He too was a former classmate of Re-Re. "You're attracting flies."

"What's in the bag, Re-Re?" Marcus asked. He lifted the sack from the table and began rummaging through it. "Ooooh, fries! I love Jack in the Crack's fries!" Marcus began to eat the French fries one by one.

"Don't be rude, Marcus," Travon told him. "Give the lady her food."

"What's yours?" Marcus asked her.

"The chicken sandwich and some fries," Nikki answered. She lifted her drink from the table and sipped from it.

Marcus rumbled through the bag and found her food.

"This one must be yours, Re-Re," Travon said, reaching for the remaining cup on the table. He lifted the cup and swirled the contents around. "Mmmm, milkshake. I'll tell you what. If it's strawberry, I'll let you eat your food before I kill you. But if it's chocolate, we'll eat your food before we kill you."

Marcus leaned over and spoke directly into Re-Re's ear. "Either way, you're gonna die, ass wipe." He handed Nikki her food.

Travon lifted a straw from the table and removed the paper wrapping from around it. He inserted the straw into the cup.

"I hope that it's chocolate, Re-Re, because I am kinda hungry." Travon lifted the cup to his lips and sipped. "Bingo! It's chocolate!"

Marcus took Re-Re's hamburger, tore it in two, and handed Travon half. They immediately began to wolf the burger down.

Robert Jr. rose, walked to where Re-Re was seated and began searching him. Re-Re had no weapons on him, so Robert Jr. reseated himself. Travon and Marcus devoured the burger and then Travon leaned to his side and kissed Nikki on her cheek. He turned and faced Re-Re.

"Who's on top now, muthafucka?" Travon asked. He pulled from his waistband the massive fifty magnum Desert Eagle he carried, and placed the weapon on the table just in front of him.

Robert Jr. pulled out his Taurus nine-millimeter and held it in his hand, just in case Re-Re managed to grab hold of Travon's weapon.

"Can you say BSV is on top?" Travon asked Re-Re. "Come on; let me hear you say BSV."

Marcus, who was seated next to Re-Re, nudged him in his side. Re-Re jumped and passed gas loudly.

"You can say it, Re-Re," Marcus said. "C'mon, let's hear it. BSV is on top."

"Say BSV is on top, Blood," Travon repeated.

Marcus pointed to Travon's weapon. "Can you imagine the size of the hole from that thing?"

Re-Re cut his eyes toward the gun, and then shifted his gaze back to Travon.

Travon leaned forward. "I'll tell you what. If you can say BSV is on top, we might let you make it."

Re-Re, who like most Crips was scared to death of Robert Jr., shifted his gaze to the floor and relented. "You on top. You got me, it's BSV."

"That's good," Travon told him. "That's real good to hear you say that. Now, can you say East Terrace ain't shit, Blood?"

Re-Re looked at Nikki, and then back at Travon. "You know me can't say dat, Tre."

"So, you do have some nuts somewhere," Marcus told him.

"I guess I'll let you make it," Travon told him. "You gave us a pass, so now I'm a give you one. But no more passes, Re-Re. If I see you again, it's on!"

"Don't get caught slippin' again, Blood," Marcus told him. "And to make sure that the message sinks in, break yourself!"

Re-Re removed his jewelry and emptied his pockets onto the table. Marcus raked the jewelry and money off of the table and put it inside of his pockets.

"Say, baby, you want something else to eat?" Travon asked Nikki.

"No," she replied shyly.

Travon stood and placed his gun in his waistband. He turned to leave.

"Tre, you slippin'!" Robert Jr. told him. He turned toward Marcus. "Y'all supposed to be teaching him what's up."

Marcus was puzzled. "What are you talking about?"

Robert Jr. turned back to Travon. "Rule number one, never trust a crab bitch!" Robert Jr. rose, and walked to where Nikki was seated. "You's a cute bitch, but you're still a crab bitch. Give me the muthafuckin' purse, ho!"

Nikki lifted her purse into the air and Robert snatched it. He seated himself and began to ramble through the purse. Inside, he found a Lorcin .380 semiautomatic pistol. Robert Jr. stared at Travon, and then at Marcus.

"The reason why this nigga ain't packin' is because his bitch is." Robert Jr. held the pistol in the air, allowing it to dangle loosely between his thumb and forefinger. With his other hand, he tossed Nikki her imitation Dooney & Bourke purse and turned to Travon. "Shake the ho down."

Travon pat searched Nikki. "She's clean."

"This could have been one of us, as soon as we turned our backs to leave," Robert Jr. told them.

"It would have been for all y'all slobs!" Nikki shouted.

Robert Jr. punched Nikki in her jaw, sending her crashing back onto the table. Re-Re stood, but Travon, Marcus, Frog, and Ace all drew their weapons. Re-Re plopped back down into the booth.

"Let's go," Robert told them.

The boys concealed their weapons, turned, and walked out of the restaurant.

"Say, Tre," Robert Jr. called out to him, as they were climbing into their respective vehicles. "I'll see y'all back in The Jungle in a little while."

Travon rolled down his car window and closed his door. "All right, kinfolk. We'll get with you later."

The boys pulled out of the restaurant parking lot, and Travon headed for Custom Sounds.

"Man, did you see that dude's face when we sat down?" Marcus asked.

Travon laughed. "Yeah, I thought he was gonna shit himself."

"He almost did when I nudged him!" Marcus laughed.

The rest of the boys joined in the laughter, as they continued toward their destination.

CHAPTER TWENTY

The Stereo Shop
Two Hours Later

Bass notes resonated loudly throughout the area.

"Is that my shit?" Travon asked.

A short young white guy peered out of the shop's large glass window. "Yeah, I think that's yours." He turned back to Travon. "The Oldsmobile, right?"

"Yeah," Travon answered proudly.

"Boy, Tre, your shit is hittin'!" Frog told him.

"I think your shit might be louder than Fro-Dog's," Marcus added.

Travon beamed proudly. A slim Asian installer with a white T-shirt, a pair of blue jean shorts, and a white baseball cap turned backward walked in. He pointed at Travon.

"We are just about finished with your alarm system," he informed Travon. "The stereo system is done."

Travon walked out to his car, where he marveled at the loud, crisp sounds emanating from the speakers. Another young Asian technician was lying on the floorboards, working on something beneath the dashboard. A tall, slim white technician was working beneath the hood. Travon could tell that it had to do with the alarm's siren, because of the intermittent chirps that pierced the air. He walked to the rear of the car, where he peered into the trunk and watched the subwoofers work.

Inside the trunk sat four fifteen-inch subwoofers, mounted in what the technicians called an isobaric configuration. In this configuration the subwoofers were mounted facing one another, and one of the speakers within each pair had their polarities reversed, so that they could help one another push and pull. The effects were tremendous.

In addition to the subwoofers, the trunk also played host to four amplifiers, on very large electronic crossover, and a twenty-disc CD changer. Travon marveled at the seemingly built-in installation, shook his head, and then ventured back into the waiting area.

"Here's your receipt, Mr. Robinson," the clerk said, handing Travon a yellow slip.

Outside, the alarm system blared loudly as the technicians put the final touches on it. Inside, the boys fiddled with the stereo systems on display until they were finally told that the car was ready.

Travon was the first one out of the store. He strutted to his car with all the pride of a victorious fighting cock and climbed inside.

"Say, I know y'all hungry," Travon told Marcus and Frog. "So we gonna go and get something to eat, my treat."

"Shit, yeah!" Marcus replied.

Frog nodded. "Cool."

"We'll go to Bob's barbecue," Travon told them. He started his car and pulled into traffic.

"Oh, hell yeah!" Marcus told him. "Bob's is on!"

Travon cranked up the volume on his new stereo system, and the noise became deafening. The boys sank down into their seats, and began bobbing their heads and throwing up gang signs to the music.

Travon exited the highway, turned down W.W. White Road, and headed for Rigsby Road, home to South Texas's most famous barbecue eatery.

"Combo plate, here I come!" Marcus announced, rubbing his stomach.

His fuel light blinked on. "Damn!" Travon exclaimed.

He had gone straight from the car lot to the stereo shop, and had yet to visit a filling station. The needle on his gas gauge was now pleading for him to do so. He maneuvered into a One Stop filling station and convenience store, and pulled up next to a gas pump. He peered into the backseat at Marcus.

"Say, kinfolk, you pump and I'll go pay," Travon told him. "Do you want something outta here?"

Marcus shook his head. "Naw, I'm cool. Besides, I'm a try to break your ass when we get to Bob's." Marcus laughed, climbed out and headed to the gas pump.

"Stop it on fifteen dollars," Travon told him, as he and Frog headed for the store.

"Damn, T," Frog said, as they walked into the store. "Your shit be hittin'. Man, my ears are still ringing."

"I'ma try to enter into that bass contest that the radio station be having on Fridays and Saturdays," Travon told him. He headed to the beer freezer, pulled three bottle of Bull from it, and then returned to the counter where he handed the clerk a twenty-dollar bill. "Put fifteen in the tank."

"He stopped the pump at fifteen twenty-seven," she told him with a flirtatious smile.

Travon nodded. "Okay, that's cool."

The clerk rang up the total and handed Travon his change.

"Thank you," he told her with a smile.

"Thank you," she told him seductively. "And thank you for shopping at One Stop."

Travon stepped to the side and waited, as the clerk rang up Frog's merchandise, and returned to him his change. Together, he and Frog walked out of the store.

A dark blue Honda Accord pulled up just as the boys were exiting. As Travon walked past the car, he glanced inside. The occupants looked familiar.

Travon's memory served him poorly for several moments, and then it struck him. He picked up his pace toward his own vehicle. He could hear the doors to the Accord slamming.

"It *is* him!" a voice called out. "That's the little nigga from the park!"

Travon dropped his bag of beer, pulled out his Desert Eagle pistol, and spun. Frog did the same. Marcus had pulled his weapon as soon as he saw the boys exit the blue Honda. Gunfire erupted.

Travon and Frog fired in the direction of the Accord as they raced back to Travon's car. Marcus used the car as a shield and took his time. His aim was deadly.

"Aaaargh, I hit!" one of the boys from the Accord cried out.

Marcus aimed again.

"Aaaargh! Fuck, cuz, I'm shot!" another boy screamed. "It burns! It burns!"

Travon and Frog leapt over the trunk of the nine-eight and hunkered down. Travon immediately reloaded his weapon, by slipping in another clip. Screams echoed from the other side of the nine-eight, as Marcus continued to fire with deadly accuracy. Soon, the sound of screeching tires filled the air, and Marcus stopped firing.

"Fuck, Blood!" Travon rose. "I hope they didn't hit my shit!"

"Say, Frog, they gone," Marcus said. "You can stand up now."

Frog shook his head. "I can't, Blood. I'm hit."

Travon smiled. "Bullshit!"

Marcus walked to where Frog was crouched down and helped him stand. Frog's once pristine white T-shirt, turned crimson red.

"Fuck!" Travon screamed. "Aw, fuck!"

Frog fell back into Marcus's arms. His pink lips were now pale blue.

"Go on, Blood," Frog told them. He grabbed Travon's hand. "I'm not gonna make this one."

Travon's mouth fell open and he shook his head.

Frog let out a half-smile. "Leave now," he told them. "The po-po is coming."

Frog tried to smile again, but this time a cough interrupted him. Blood shot from his mouth and nose onto Travon. Marcus stepped back and gently lowered Frog to the ground. Travon dropped to his knees and lifted Frog's head into his lap.

"Naw, Blood, fuck this shit!" Travon shouted. "Fuck this shit!"

Blood poured out onto the concrete and soaked Travon's pants.

"You gonna make it, just breathe," Travon said nervously. "Breathe!"

Marcus heard the sirens in the distance, and gently tugged at Travon's shirt. Travon yanked away and began crying heavily.

"Stay awake!" he told Frog, shaking his head slightly. "C'mon, Frog, fight!"

The store clerk ran outside. "I saw what happened," she told Marcus. "Those boys started shooting at you first."

Marcus pointed at Frog. "Stay with him!" he told the clerk. He pulled at Travon's shirt again. "C'mon, Tre, we gotta go! You hear those sirens? Let's go!"

Travon gently lowered Frog to the ground and rose. He held out his arms and examined himself, only to find that he was covered from head to toe in his friend's blood. He turned to the store clerk. "Lady, don't leave his head like that. Get his head outta the dirt, please."

Marcus grabbed Travon and shoved him into the car. He turned back toward the clerk. "Tell the police what you saw. Forget about our car, our names, our descriptions, and our license plates. But tell them that Frog was innocent. Thanks, lady."

Marcus quickly climbed inside of the car, cranked the motor, and raced away.

The boys drove through the Skyline residential area instead of taking the main street. Marcus knew that the police would be crawling all over the place.

"Fuck! Fuck! Fuck!" Travon screamed. He began kicking and banging on the dashboard of his car.

"He'll make it, Tre," Marcus told him.

Travon continued bawling.

Marcus glanced over at his cousin. "Let's just get back to the hood, posse up, and go and serve them muthafuckas."

The boys headed back to the Heights as fast as the streets could take them. The trip home was a silent one.

❖❖❖

Before Marcus could bring the car to a complete stop, Travon leapt out of the vehicle and ran upstairs to his room, stripping his clothes off along the way. Marcus parked and ran into the house after him.

"Tre! Tre!" Marcus followed him. "Say something! Speak to me!"

Travon ignored his cousin's pleas and continued to strip. When he finished, he bolted into the bathroom. Marcus listened as the shower went active, and then turned and shouted down the hall.

"Darius! Darius!"

"What's up?" Darius shouted back from his room down the hall.

"Come here real quick," Marcus said nervously. "Let me holler at ya!"

"Where you at?"

"I'm in T's room."

Seconds later, Darius appeared at Travon's door. "What's up?"

He followed Marcus's eyes down to the floor, where he spied the pile of bloody clothing.

"Fuck!" Darius said. He stepped into the room and quickly closed the door behind him. "What in the hell happened?"

"We stopped at the gas station to get gas," Marcus explained. "Me, Tre, and Frog."

"What happened to Ace and Robert Jr.?"

Marcus shook his head. "They weren't with us. Tre bought this nine-eight and we split up. Anyway, we stopped at One Stop on W.W. White to get some gas." Marcus began pacing. "Tre and Frog went in, while I pumped. We was getting ready to leave when Mike Vay drove up in a little blue car."

Marcus stopped pacing, stared at Darius, and shook his head. "Them fools just started busting at us."

Darius tilted his head to one side. "Where did Tre get hit?"

"He didn't get hit, Frog did." He swallowed hard. "I don't think he made it."

Darius shook his head. "Fuck! Where's Frog now?"

"We had to leave him, because the po-po was coming."

Darius leaned forward. "Y'all left him?"

"We left him with the lady at the store," Marcus explained. "The ambulance and police was coming. We had to! We had to get the fuck outta there! The ambulance was almost there, plus he was hit bad."

Marcus twirled his index finger toward his body. "I think he was bleedin' on the inside, 'cause blood didn't come out 'til he stood up."

Darius pounded the air with his fist. "Shit! Are you sure it was Mike Vay?"

Marcus nodded rapidly. "Yeah! I think I shot BK, Pooh-Pooh, and Lacy. I'm not sure, but I think I hit one of them fools in the head, and the other two in the chest." Marcus pounded his fist into the air. "Fuck, D! They just came outta nowhere." He held up his hand. It was trembling.

"It's okay." Darius extended his hand in a calming motion. "It's okay, just sit down and take it easy." He turned and walked to the bathroom door. "Tre, are you all right?"

No answer.

"Tre?" he called out again.

Silence still.

Darius opened the bathroom door, and was hit with a tremendous wave of steam. He fought through it, walked to the shower, and pulled back the curtain. Travon was scrubbing himself with a steel wool pad, in steaming hot water.

"Got to get the blood off," Travon mumbled. "Got to get the blood off."

Darius cut the cold water on and turned the hot water down. He removed the steel wool pad from Travon's hand, causing Travon to acknowledge him.

"Got to get the blood off," Travon repeated. "Got to get the blood off!"

"Tre! It's all off!" Darius told him. "Tre, it's all off!"

Darius tossed the steel pad to the floor and grabbed Travon by his arms. He shook him. "Tre! Tre! It's over. It's over! All of the blood is off!"

Travon shook his head. "No, no. I'm still sticky. It, it's sticky." Travon broke down into tears. "It's sticky. The blood is so sticky."

He raised his hands and stared at them. "They killed Frog. They killed him, Darius. They killed my friend!"

Tears streamed from Travon's eyes, mixing with the water from the shower. Darius grabbed his cousin and hugged him.

In the bathroom, in the shower, soaking wet they stood, and together, mourned the loss of their friend.

CHAPTER TWENTY-ONE

Next Day
Frog's Mother's House

Travon parked along the curb across the street. There were several cars parked in the driveway of Frog's mother's house, and many more parked in front of the residence. Travon climbed out of his car, crossed the street, and walked up the long pathway leading to the front door. He carried with him a large shopping bag and some flowers.

Yvette, Frog's oldest sister, answered the front door. Today she wore a white T-shirt, a pair of blue jeans, some pink house shoes, and a scarf tied around her normally well groomed hair. Makeup was completely absent today, and her usually sparkling emerald green eyes were bloodshot and tired.

"Hey, Tre," she greeted him softly. "C'mon in."

Travon stepped into the living room and was greeted by several of Frog's relatives. Sheila, Frog's other sister, rose from the couch, rushed into Travon's arms, and burst into tears.

"Oh, Tre!" Sheila cried out through her heavy weeping. "They killed my brother!"

Travon wrapped his arms around Sheila and tears fell from his eyes. "I'm sorry, Sheila," he whispered. "I'm sorry."

An aunt rose from the couch, grabbed Sheila, and began to comfort her.

"Momma's in the kitchen, Tre," Yvette told him. "She'll be glad to see you."

Travon nodded and walked through a set of double doors into the kitchen.

Mrs. Davis was seated at the breakfast table alone. Travon could tell that she had not slept. She looked up at him and smiled.

Travon lifted his hand and wiped the tears from his face. Mrs. Davis quickly rose from her seat and embraced him.

"C'mon, baby, it's all right," she told him. "It's all right. Freddy is with God now, baby. He's run his race. He's okay now, baby. Trust me; he's in a much better place. Now come on over here and sit down."

Travon broke down and began crying again. "They killed him, Mrs. D," he said through his heavy weeping. "They killed him."

"I know, baby. I know." Mrs. Davis clasped his hand. "Come on over here and sit down by me."

They walked to the small Formica breakfast table. Travon took the seat across from hers, and lowered his face into the palms of his hands.

"Tre, I know you were there," she said softly, as she reached forward and patted his hands. "I know that you and Freddy were together when he got shot. The police say it was a big shootout. Two of the boys y'all were shooting at died. Another is at the hospital in critical condition. Listen to me, Tre. They know that Freddy wasn't by himself."

Travon lifted his head and stared at her. His eyes were now bloodshot.

"They don't know who was with him, but they found shell casings from three different guns by where Freddy was lying," Mrs. Davis continued. "My point is this, Travon. I helped raise you. You and Freddy were like two peas in a pod, when y'all were growing up. Me, Elmira, and Vera all grew up together, and went to all the same schools when we were younger. You are like my child, Tre."

Mrs. Davis leaned forward and cleared her throat. "My Freddy is dead. He ain't never coming back. Two other mothers are crying right now, because they child ain't never coming back. I ran into them at the hospital last night. Even after I was told that my baby was dead, I stayed there with them. We held hands together, and we all prayed together. Tre, it's over."

She shook her head and stared Travon in the eyes. "Our babies are never comin' home. Now don't you go out there and get yourself hurt or killed, or hurt somebody else, all in the name of my son. If you want to do anything for Freddy, Tre, you finish school for him."

Mrs. Davis softly jabbed her finger in Travon's direction. "You go to college for him, and you help take care of his son, and you make sure that he goes to college. That's what you can do for Freddy."

Yvette strolled into the room. "Momma, do you want some more coffee?"

Mrs. Davis shook her head. "Naw, child. I'm caffeined out. Tell Tamara to bring Lil Freddy here."

"All right." Yvette nodded and left the room.

Mrs. Davis turned back to Travon. "I've shed my tears, Travon. Last night, I shed enough tears for all the rest of the mothers in this city. I've paid their bill for them. So now, they shouldn't have to cry. I don't want them to cry." She lifted her thin, worn, wrinkled hand to her face and began to cry. "Nobody! Nobody should have to bury their child!"

Travon rose.

"I have to bury my child," she whispered softly through her sobbing.

Travon wrapped his arms around her. "I'm sorry, Mrs. D."

Mrs. Davis shook her head. "No, I'm the one who's sorry." She quickly wiped away her tears. "I shouldn't be acting like this around you kids."

"It's okay, Mrs. D," Travon told her. "It's okay."

Tamara walked into the room holding Little Freddy. Her hair was twisted into long, thin micro braids and tied up in a French roll. Three of the braids hung loosely in the front, with gold balls attached to their tips. Like the others, Tamara was wearing blue jeans, a T-shirt, and some house shoes.

Little Freddy wore tiny blue jean overalls over a white T-shirt with tiny blue and red teddy bears sewn into it. On his feet he wore tiny Michael Jordan tennis shoes, while a red pacifier hung loosely out of his mouth. Travon lifted him from his mother's arm and held him tightly.

"He looks just like his dad," Travon declared with a smile.

Mrs. Davis and Tamara smiled.

"Mrs. D, I brought something for you to have, but instead, I'm going to give it to the baby," Travon told her.

Mrs. Davis leaned back. "Oh?"

Travon handed the baby back to Tamara and grabbed the flowers that he had brought with him. "These are for you," he told Mrs. Davis, handing her the bouquet.

She smiled. "Thank you, baby. I'll have Yvette put them in some water for me."

Travon reached into his bag, pulled out two sympathy cards and handed them to Mrs. Davis.

"Thank you, baby," Mrs. Davis told him. "Here, give me some suga."

Travon leaned forward and kissed her on her cheek. He then reached inside of his bag again, and this time produced an old, worn football.

"Remember when you took me, Too-Low, and Freddy to the mall that time, and Freddy cried the whole time about this football? He cried until you turned around and went back to the store and bought it for him. Well, I won it six months later while we was shootin' marbles. It's the football we was always playin' with in the Courts, even up 'til last year. I kept it all this time. It has everybody's signature on it, even my brother's. It was Freddy's football, and now it's Lil Freddy's."

Travon sat the ball on a chair. Mrs. Davis rose and embraced Travon tightly. She began crying again.

Tamara covered the lower half of her face; tears streamed from her eyes as well. Travon and Mrs. Davis stood hugging and crying for several moments, until finally, Mrs. Davis released him and began wiping away her tears. She seated herself again, and pointed toward the ceiling.

"Travon, you go upstairs and look in Freddy's room, and see what you want out of there. Anything you want, you keep." Mrs. Davis waved her hand from side to side. "Don't tell me, just take it. As a matter of fact, I want you to search his room real good for me, and take everything out that you think I shouldn't find. I'm afraid to go in there and look around. When I clean his room, I'll need you and the rest of the boys to come over and help me."

"You don't want to keep none of his stuff for memories?" Travon asked.

"I remember my baby," Mrs. Davis told him. She touched her hand against her heart. "I'll always remember my baby. Plus, I'm bringing my son home. We are going to set up a shelf in the family room for his urn. It's going to have his pictures all around it, and pictures of his friends. I'm gonna have it so that all of you boys can come over on his birthday, and holidays, and be able to pay your respects."

Travon's eyes were wide with shock. "You're gonna cremate Frog?"

Mrs. Davis nodded solemnly. "Yeah. The family talked about it, and we all decided this morning that it would be best."

Travon smacked his lips and turned away. "Aw, man. Why you gonna do that?"

"Well, for one thing, it's a lot cheaper," Mrs. Davis explained. "We'll be able to give him a nicer funeral this way. We won't have to pay for a burial plot, or any of that kind of stuff. Tre, I didn't have any insurance on Freddy. I'm already having a hard time as it is, and now I have to pay for a funeral?"

She began sobbing again. "Plus, I just want my baby home with me. He was always running the streets and living here and there, and so now, I just want him home."

Travon clasped her hand. "It's okay, Mrs. D. We are gonna help you with everything. We are all gonna put in and help you."

Mrs. Davis tilted her head to the side and nodded. "Thank you, baby," she told him, gently patting his hand. "Thank you."

Travon stood. "Well, I'm gonna go and holler at everybody and start getting everything together. So, when is the funeral?"

"Three days from now," she told him. "The wake is the day after tomorrow."

Travon leaned forward and kissed Mrs. Davis on her cheek. "I'll be by tomorrow." He turned to leave, and she grabbed his hand.

"Travon, remember what I said," Mrs. Davis said softly. She shifted her gaze toward the baby. "That's what you can do for Freddy. Nothing stupid. Don't ruin my son's memory by trying to get revenge in his name."

"Yes, ma'am," Travon replied. He slowly walked out of the kitchen and into the living room.

"Have something to eat, baby," an aunt told him, pointing to a table filled with food.

Travon lifted his hand and shook his head. "No thank you, ma'am. I'm not hungry right now."

She nodded. "Okay, baby. You be careful, and tell Elmira that I said to call me."

Travon nodded. "Yes, ma'am." He turned to leave, but heard his name being called. It was Sheila.

"Tre." She clasped his arm, interlacing it with her own. "I'll walk you to your car."

Sheila wore a large T-shirt, some blue jeans, and a pair of slippers. Her hair was braided into a scrunch, with large gold butterfly clips pinned in a row down the front. Even though she had been through hell over the last twenty-four hours, she was still extremely attractive. She and Travon headed out of the front door and down the pathway toward his vehicle.

"Tre, I know my mother is talking all of this peace shit, but I want you, and Darius, and Robert Jr., and Lil Fade to kill the rest of them mutha-fuckers. Tell Darius that if he ever loved me that I said he would do this for me."

Sheila halted and faced Travon. "You know what happened between me and Darius? Tre, we were both young and scared. I know that I shouldn't have gotten an abortion, but I didn't know what else to do. Tell him that I still love him, and that I know he still loves me. Tell him to please just accept my calls."

Travon lifted his hand. "I don't want nothing to do with you and Darius's problems."

"I know, I'm sorry." She shifted her gaze toward the concrete pathway. "Just tell him that I said to do this for me. I need for y'all to get the niggaz who killed my baby brother." Tears began to fall.

"We gonna handle our business," Travon told her.

"Good!" Sheila leaned forward and hugged him. Travon held her tightly, comforting her. After a few moments, Sheila pulled away from him, and then pulled from beneath her T-shirt a submachine gun.

"I want you to use this," she said excitedly. "It belonged to my brother. He loaded it at my apartment the day before he died. When the police check the fingerprints on the bullets, they will be Frog's. It will be like my brother killed them niggaz from the grave."

Travon nodded, and carefully removed the weapon from her hands.

"Sheila, promise me something," Travon said softly. "If I do this for you, will you do something for me?"

Sheila nodded.

"I want you to go inside and get some sleep," Travon told her. "After this is all over with, I want you to go and talk to somebody. I want you to let somebody help you deal with all of this. Those are my conditions, and I want you to swear to me that you'll do it."

Sheila shifted her gaze to the ground and nodded. "I will."

Travon leaned forward, kissed her on her cheek, and turned and headed for his vehicle.

CHAPTER TWENTY-TWO

Later that Night
Denver Heights' New Dope Spot

"This is for my nigga Frog," Lil Bling announced. He took his forty-ounce bottle of Bull and poured some beer out onto the curb.

"Yeah, this is for my homie," Suga said as he followed suit, pouring some of his beer onto the street.

"This is for all of the homies who ain't here," Capone added, as he and all of the others present joined in the ghetto ritual of offering libations to their lost comrades.

Ace kicked a rock, sending it scampering across the street. "Fuck! I can't believe he's gone! Me, him, and Robert Jr. was just kicking it the other day."

"I'ma get my nigga's name tattooed on my back, along with the names of the other dead homies," announced Tate, a slim, freckle-faced Blood from the Rigsby. "I'ma put it inside of a scroll, like it's some kind of ancient list. I'm a hook it up clean."

"Say, I went by his T-lady's house and she says the funeral is in three days," said Charlie, a tall, slim Bounty Hunter Blood from the Westside. "We need to go to the mall and get some T-shirts made for the funeral."

"Say, y'all, I called Sheila today, and she says that the family is hurtin' for cash to bury the homie," Darius announced. "We need to dig deep, plus whatever cash we make tonight, we need to just put it in the pot."

"Nigga, you didn't know?" Suga asked rhetorically. "That's automatic. That's why we all out here."

Darius turned to Marcus. "You and Tre been collecting; how much y'all got?"

"We got three Gs so far," Marcus answered. "Tre put in five hundred, Missy and the ladies at her beauty shop all put in five hundred, Mrs. Chang gave us a thousand, plus other people been throwing money our way."

"Oh yeah, Bull, Lil Bling, and Big Pimpin brought me fifteen hundred today," Travon told them. "So really, it's a little over forty-five hundred, because I also got a couple of loose twenties from other people."

"Y'all know they planning to cremate the homeboy?" Red asked.

"Bullshit!" Lil Fade exclaimed. "Man, fuck that shit! Them niggaz is gonna pay for this shit!"

"Why they tripping like that?" Lil Bling asked.

"Mrs. D says that she just wants her son home," Travon answered.

"Man, that's fucked up!" Charlie said.

"We gonna serve them hoes good tonight!" Lil Fade declared.

"Maybe we should wait until after the funeral," Travon suggested. "Mrs. D say that she don't want that shit. She don't want no revenge on the part of her son. We need to respect her wishes, and then serve them niggaz after the funeral."

The group shifted their gazes toward Travon, and silence fell over the entire assembly. Lil Fade was the first to speak.

"What, nigga?" he shouted. "Are you afraid or something?"

Although Travon was afraid of Lil Fade, at that moment he felt more angry than afraid.

"Nigga, fuck you!" Travon shouted. "Frog was my muthafuckin' partner! Me, him, and Marcus went out like soldiers! We popped three of them muthafuckas. I ain't afraid of nothing, or *nobody!*"

A frown shot across Lil Fade's face. He started to reach for his weapon, but instead glanced to his right. Robert Jr. was staring directly at him. Lil Fade quickly weighed the odds. It would be Suga, Charlie, and himself against Robert Jr., Capone, Travon and Darius. He decided to let Travon's remarks slide.

"We gonna serve them hoes *tonight*, with or without you," declared Killa

B, another Bounty Hunter Blood from the city's Westside. Killa B wore his hair in an enormous afro, and sported a muscle shirt that showcased his dozen or so tattoos, as well as his numerous scars from various bullet wounds. He had almost as many teardrops tattooed down his back as Lil Fade.

"Big Pimpin, Quick, and Fro-Dog are getting the straps ready right now," Lil Bling told them.

"As a matter of fact, they should already be here to pick us up," Killa B told them. "What time is it?"

"Nine thirty," Tate answered.

"We gonna hit them niggaz at ten, when the po-po's changing shifts," Charlie announced. "Then we gonna bail to the club where the rest of the homies are, and just blend in like we been there. We gonna have to change clothes in the parking lot."

"Marcus, what kinda cars did y'all lil niggaz steal for us to use?" Red asked.

"Don't worry, we got some clean-ass shit." Marcus smiled. "I stole a Maxima for me, Capone, and D to ride in."

Travon examined the crowd of boys and finally realized that he was the only one not wearing all black. Darius noticed the look on his cousin's face, leaned over, and whispered in his ear.

"You was over Frog's house when we got all of this shit together. Here." Darius handed Travon a black T-shirt and a black bandanna. "I brought you some shit to wear after the hit too. It's in the back of Fro-Dog's car."

Four cars turned the corner trailing one another.

"There them niggaz go right there," Lil Bling announced.

Marcus squinted and examined the approaching cars. "We ain't steal none a them cars," he told the others.

The cars quickly sped up and extinguished their headlights.

"Get down!" Marcus shouted. "Drive-by!"

Gunfire erupted, and the sound of automatic weapons quickly filled the air.

"This is for Pooh-Pooh and Lacy, muthafuckas!" voices shouted through the sound of the gunfire.

The Bloods were armed, but pistols against fully automatic AK-47s and SKSs were futile. The boys remained under cover.

Bullets peppered the car Travon was hiding behind. The assault rifles that were being fired turned the house in the background into something resembling Swiss cheese. A fragment from the concrete leapt up and stung Travon on his forehead. For a brief moment the blood pouring down his face led him to believe that he had been hit. He lifted his hand to his forehead, and felt the cut from the chunk of cement. He thanked God that it hadn't been a bullet.

After the shooting continued for more than a minute without any signs of letting up, some of the Bloods began to fire back. Travon removed Frog's Uzi from his waistband, lifted the weapon over the hood of the car that he was hiding behind and began firing. The gun burped rapidly, and to his surprise, he realized that the weapon was fully automatic. He had to insert another magazine.

The sound of handguns and other small-caliber weapons returning fire, started to fill the air. It was then Travon felt his pants leg jerk, and felt a sudden burning sensation in his left leg. He stopped firing and quickly examined his leg. There was a small black hole inside of his pants, but there were no visible traces of blood. Still, he hunkered down behind the car, and this time, he stayed down.

The sound of automatic-weapon fire lasted for more than three solid minutes. Now, for the first time in his life, Travon wished that the police would come. Unfortunately, he knew that they would wait until the shooting stopped, and then come in and pick up the bodies. He didn't want to become another statistic, he turned to prayer.

Soon the sound of automatic weapons ceased, and several of the boys stood, while others continued firing their weapons down the street at the fleeing vehicles. Travon stood, pulled up his pants leg, and examined his wound. The fabric pulled away from his bloody, mangled flesh, causing him to wince.

There was a deep gash on his leg where the bullet had burrowed through his flesh. The wound burned immensely; it felt as though someone were raking a fiery hot coal back and forth over his leg. But the important thing, he told himself, was that he was alive. He turned and spied his cousin Capone lying balled up in the middle of the yard.

"Capone! Capone!" Travon cried out. With great pain and effort he hobbled over to where his cousin lay motionless.

Travon dropped to his knees and began to shake his cousin. Not again,
he told himself. Oh please, God, not again. "Capone! Capone!"

"What?" Capone shouted. He leapt to his feet and dusted himself off.
"Gotcha!"

The others laughed uproariously. Travon frowned and lowered his head.

"Capone! Capone! Oh, I love you kinfolk, don't die!" Capone teased.

Travon rolled his eyes at his cousin for several moments, before a smile
slowly crept across his face. He imagined how dramatic he must have looked.

"Anybody hit?" Lil Bling asked.

"Yeah, me."

The boys turned. Red was standing in the middle of the yard holding
his arm.

"Shit, me too," Charlie declared.

"Where?" Darius asked, thinking it might be another practical joke.

"Here." Charlie grabbed the hem of his shirt and lifted it. There was a
large bloody hole in the center of his stomach.

"Fuck!" Darius leapt back.

"Sit down, Blood!" Lil Bling told Charlie. He, Marcus, and Capone
rushed to where Charlie was standing, grabbed him, and gently lowered
him into the grass.

"Naw, y'all bring him over here," Tate told them. "I'll watch him."

"What's wrong with you, Blood?" Lil Fade asked Tate.

"Shit, they wounded me in my pride," Tate told him.

Lil Fade peered down and examined himself. There was a grass stain
on his shirt from where he'd slid down into the yard. "Fuck, we really
gonna kill them muthafuckas now, this is my best black T-shirt!"

"Shit, they grazed my leg," Travon announced.

Darius walked to where Travon was standing, dropped down to his knees,
and examined Travon's wound.

"Yeah, you need to go." Darius told Travon. "C'mon, I'll take you home."

"Naw, leave him here with me, I'll watch him," Tate told him. "Y'all
niggaz go on."

"You ain't coming with us?" Killa B asked.

"Naw, nigga!" Tate shouted. "They shot me in the ass!"

Laughter broke out amongst the boys. Travon turned and stared at Tate, who was lying in the grass on his side. Lil Fade, who stood just behind Tate, peered down and examined his friend's derriere.

"Yep, they got this nigga right in his left butt cheek," he declared.

Again, the boys laughed.

"Y'all hear them sirens?" Tate asked. "Them hoes'll be here any minute now. Y'all take our straps and we'll say that they was shootin'; at us. We'll keep the po-po here as long as we can."

"What if them crabs come back?" Marcus asked.

"It's cool," Travon told him. "Just hurry up and blaze, them sirens is getting louder."

"We probably won't even be able to find them niggaz," Lil Bling said. "They riding around here somewhere."

"Fuck it!" Lil Fade told them. "We'll hit they hood and do a mutha-fuckin' walk-through. Any crab we see, we kill!"

The boys filtered into the streets and piled inside of various vehicles and drove away. Travon limped to where Tate, Charlie, and Red were lying. He sat down in the grass next to the others, and waited for the arrival of the police and the paramedics.

"Think we going to jail tonight?" Travon asked.

"For what?" Tate asked. "We was just minding our own business, when all hell broke loose."

"Besides," Charlie added. "What are they going to charge us with, bleed-in' to death?" Charlie began to laugh, but quickly stopped because of the pain.

Tate noticed the pained expression on his friend's face, and leaned over and placed his hand on Charlie's chest. "Be cool, Blood. Just lay back and chill."

Travon turned away from them and glanced toward the street. "Oh my God."

There were thousands of shell casings lying around.

"They must have had at least twelve to sixteen AKs with hundred-round drum clips in them, to do that," Red told them.

"Just what we was gonna use on them tonight," Tate said, shaking his head. "They just beat us to the punch."

"We forgot that two of their homies got killed too," Travon told them. "We should have known that they was gonna come for revenge."

Tate shifted his gaze toward the corner, where the flashing red lights and bright spotlights of the police cars could now be seen. "Here they come."

A patrol car turned the corner, followed by another, and then a third. Soon, there was a line of patrol cars approaching from every direction. The police cars stopped just short of where the boys were lying, and shined their spotlights on them. The whole area was bathed in bright light, as the police officers exited their vehicles with their weapons drawn.

"Put your hands up and lie down on your stomachs!" one of the patrolmen shouted, using his patrol car's public address system.

The boys lifted their hands high into the air and watched as the shadows from beyond the spotlights approached.

"We can't lie down on our stomachs," Tate shouted. "I'm shot in the ass, one of us is shot in the stomach, one of us is shot in the leg, and as you can see, my buddy here is shot in the arm!"

"Very well, officers will approach you from the rear and side," the officer replied. "If any of you move your hands, you will be shot!"

"Is anyone inside the residence?" another voice asked over a loudspeaker.

Tate shook his head. "No!"

"You with the arm wound. Keep your hands above your head and walk toward my voice," the first officer ordered.

Red stood. He walked into the bright lights and disappeared from the view of the others. Suddenly, Travon felt one of his wrists being cuffed. It was quickly pulled down behind his back, where it was cuffed to his other wrist. He turned and stared at Charlie and Tate, whose hands were cuffed to the front. An officer kneeled next to Charlie and examined his wound. After checking the wound for several moments, the officer turned to the others and shook his head. Travon felt himself being pat searched.

"Where did you get hit at?" the officer asked.

"In the leg," Travon told him.

"Just hang loose," the officer told him. "Are the cuffs okay?"

Travon nodded. "Yeah."

Paramedics began to approach in numbers. Two hustled over to Tate, while four of them began working on Charlie. A seventh paramedic began to treat Red; another approached Travon.

"Say, boss, can we remove these cuffs?" the paramedic asked.

The officer nodded. "Yeah, we can do that." He removed Travon's handcuffs. Other officers began removing handcuffs from the rest of the boys.

A small crowd of neighbors began to gather, and several of the officers began to herd them back.

"Look at this shit!" one of the officers declared. "There's gotta be a thousand fuckin' rounds here!"

"Just like fuckin' Beirut," another one of the officers declared, shaking his head.

The officers marveled at the number of spent shell casings.

"Who else was with you guys?" an officer asked.

"Nobody," Travon answered. "It was just us."

"So, you four were shooting from here, there, over there, behind the house, on the other side of the house, and from behind these two cars as well, huh?"

Tate shook his head. "Naw, they was shootin' at us from all those places."

"Who were *they*?" the officer asked, pulling out his notepad.

"I don't know, I was too busy running for my life to ask for ID," Tate told him.

A sergeant who was standing nearby monitoring the conversation stepped forward. "Okay, smart-ass. We just want to know who shot you. If you wanna tell us, fine. If not, then I really don't give a shit. As far as I'm concerned, they can come back and finish the job. I got paperwork to fill out, that's why I'm asking."

"*Shots fired!*" the radio blared. "*Shots fired in the East Terrace. Reports of fully automatic weapons, with possible gang members involved. Suspects are armed and extremely dangerous. All units in the area are to respond.*"

The officers exchanged glances, and several shook their heads.

"It's gonna be a long night," one of the officers declared.

"I told Ginger that I would be home by ten-thirty," said another.

"You can forget that," one of the sergeants told him.

"At least we get overtime," another officer replied.

"Well, kid," the first sergeant told Tate. "At least we know who shot ya. And now I know where all of your buddies are at."

Tate shook his head. "Maybe the same guys who shot us is shootin' at them? Have you been through the Wheatley Courts tonight?"

"Several fatalities in the East Terrace, all units roll." The radio crackled again. *"Possible uniform down. Repeat, possible uniform down. All cars roll."*

All of the police officers with the exception of four who stayed with the paramedics, raced to their patrol cars and screeched off into the night with their emergency lights blazing and their sirens wailing.

Tate turned toward Travon and they shared a knowing smile. Frog had just been avenged.

CHAPTER TWENTY-THREE

Next Day
Aunt Vera's House

Travon woke late. He had spent all of the previous night at the hospital and all of the morning being questioned by the police. The death toll at the East Terrace last night had been horrendous.

Travon lifted the envelope filled with the donations for Frog's funeral and placed it on top of his bed. Along with the forty-five-hundred-plus they had already collected, he added the total that the boys had earned prior to the shooting. It came out to more than six thousand dollars.

Slowly, Travon rose from his bed and hobbled into the bathroom to brush his teeth and wash his face. When finished, he grabbed his crutch, limped down the stairs, and hobbled out of the front door to his car. The trip to the Davis' home was a quick one.

❖❖❖

Travon pulled up to the house, parked, and hobbled to the front door. Yvette answered the doorbell.

"Why, Tre?" she nearly shouted. "Why did y'all have to do it?"

Travon recoiled. He hadn't been prepared for such questions, nor for such hostility. It took him a few seconds to collect himself.

"I was at the hospital last night and the police station all morning," he told her. "I didn't do anything. Those dudes from the Terrace shot me last night, while I was chilling in the Heights."

Travon reached into his pocket and pulled out his wallet. He removed his discharge papers and handed them to her.

Yvette snatched the papers and quickly read through them. A smile slowly stretched across her face the more she read. She returned her gaze toward Travon, and he lifted his hand, displaying the hospital band still wrapped around his wrist. Yvette became ecstatic.

"Oh thank you, Tre!" She hugged him, bouncing up and down slightly. "Thank you! Momma will feel so much better to know that you wasn't involved. C'mon in!"

Yvette stepped to the side and allowed Travon to enter. He followed her into the kitchen where Mrs. Davis was seated at the table, drinking a cup of steaming hot coffee.

"You just couldn't do like I asked you to!" Mrs. Davis shouted, once she looked up and saw Travon standing before her. "You couldn't leave well enough alone!"

"Mrs. D," Travon began. "I didn't do noth..."

She flew from her seat and slapped him. "You God damned killer! You get the hell outta my house!"

"Momma, he didn't do nothing!" Yvette screamed. "He was at the hospital!"

Travon turned and stormed out of the kitchen.

"Why, Tre?" Mrs. Davis shouted. "Why?"

Travon barreled through the living room and out of the front door. Yvette chased him down.

"Tre! Tre! Tre, wait!"

Travon stopped and turned to face her.

"Tre, I'll let her know what's up," Yvette told him. "I'll let her know that you didn't have anything to do with this." She held up the front page of the local newspaper. Travon snatched it from her hands.

"Six dead, nine wounded in gangland shootout," he mumbled. Travon lowered his head and handed the paper back to her.

"Tre, this is why she's upset," Yvette said softly. "Don't stop coming around and being a part of this family. She needs you. You and Freddy were so close."

Travon pulled the envelope containing the donations from his pocket and handed it to her. "Here, give her this. Not right now. Wait until after she calms down, and when you have explained to her that we weren't involved, then you give it to her. It's over six thousand dollars in there for Frog's funeral."

Yvette's eyes widened. "Tre, it's not going to cost that much!"

"Whatever's left, tell your mom it's hers, and ask her to buy a few things for the baby from all of us. I'll do whatever I can as far as diapers, milk, and clothes go. You got my Aunt V's number. Whenever the baby needs something, let me, Darius, or Marcus know. And give the number to Tamara too."

Tears fell from Yvette's eyes, and she leaned forward and kissed Travon on his cheek. "Tre, you are a real friend to my brother. Thank you."

Yvette turned and walked back into the house. Travon limped to his car, climbed inside, and pulled away.

❖❖❖

He pulled up to his Aunt Vera's house, parked, and hobbled to the porch. Marcus, Darius, Romeo, Capone, and Lil Fade were all gathered there.

"C'mon, T, we all gonna smash to the mall and buy some T-shirts," Marcus told him. "We gonna have Frog's picture put on the front of them, with *Gone But Not Forgotten* airbrushed around it."

"On the back of the shirt we are gonna have BSV in black, old English letters," Romeo continued. "We are gonna wear those red T-shirts over some black Dickie suits. That shit is gonna look sweet."

"A lot of the homies already went and got they shit done," Darius added. "We just need to get ours."

Travon nodded. "All right. I guess y'all want me to drive?"

"Yeah, fool," Capone told him. "What do you think we're sittin' here conversing with yo ass for?"

The boys laughed.

Travon shook his head and hobbled back to his car. He knew that he should be trying to pull away from them. He knew that he shouldn't be going anyplace with them anymore. He would just take them to the mall, he told himself. A quick trip to the mall, and then he would slowly try to pull away from them. He would get a job and he would stay at work all of the time, and that way it wouldn't be so obvious that he was trying to get away from them. He would simply just be too busy. That's what he would do. He would stay at work, eat at work, and damn near sleep at work, if that's what it took.

Travon, Romeo, and Darius climbed into the front seats, while Lil Fade, Marcus, and Capone climbed into the back. Travon cranked the ignition, and the boys headed off to Windsor Park Mall.

Lil Fade tapped Travon's shoulder. "Say, Blood, kick the system."

Travon leaned forward and turned up the volume on his stereo system. He hoped that the music would keep his occupants content. He did not feel like holding a conversation with them today.

Frog's death had taken a lot out of him. The pain medication for his leg wound had him doped up, and the trip to Mrs. Davis's house had broken his spirits. The quieter this trip was the better for him.

"Say, what's up with the concert?" Lil Fade asked. "Y'all smashin'? Tickets go on sale next week."

"Who's all coming?" Romeo asked.

Travon shrugged. So much for silence.

"Nine Ball and NJG, MC Seven, AMW, Mayhem and Tragedy, and the RCC plus Cube. It's gonna be the shit!" Marcus told him.

"Boy, stop lying!" Darius said.

"All them Crabs ain't gonna come down here with that bullshit," Capone added. "It's muthafuckin' DJ Slick who's coming."

"Aw yeah, then we can kick it at the concert and hit they muthafuckin' ass up!" Romeo said, making a Blood sign.

"Say, D?" Travon called out. "What happened last night?"

Darius contorted his lips and gave Travon a strange look. "I'll tell you about it later."

"You know, I been thinking," Travon started.

"What I tell you about that?" Romeo asked.

"About what?" Travon asked.

"About thinking!" Romeo said loudly. "You know you not properly equipped to do that!"

The boys laughed.

Travon, realizing that his conversation could be heard by the passengers in the backseat, leaned forward and increased the volume on his stereo. He did not want Lil Fade to hear the coming conversation.

"J-Bird and Lil Daddy are going back to Houston in about two months," Travon told Darius. "You think that Aunt Irma Lee will let me go and stay with them?"

Darius nodded. "I don't see why not. Lil Daddy and them is always comin' up here to stay with somebody. Why you wanna leave the Heights? What's up, lil kinfolk, talk to me."

"It's cool in the Heights, but I just need a change," Travon answered. "I need to get away for a while, get my shit together. I need to get my head together, you know?"

"I hear you, lil kinfolk," Darius told him. "Do the right things, get your life together, and see if you can talk Marcus into going with you and get his shit together too."

Travon focused on his driving, thinking about his life for the rest of the trip to the mall. He knew that he had to get away from them. He could feel it.

Windsor Park Mall
The T-shirt Shop

"Yeah, Blood, that shit is on!" Capone said, while holding his T-shirt in the air and examining it. "That shit came out good."

"Mine's came out good too!" Lil Fade announced.

Darius leaned against the counter and smiled. "So, when can I call you?" he asked the girl working behind the counter.

She returned his smile. "Tonight. I'll be home by ten."

Darius held up the paper she had given him with her number on it. "So, how do you pronounce this again?"

"Chrishanda," she told him. "If you forget, just ask for Chris."

Darius nodded. "All right. And thank you again for doing such a good job on our shirts."

"You're welcome," she replied. "And I'm really sorry about your friend."

Chrishanda was kind of cute, Travon thought. The fake ponytail, green contacts, and press-on nails did a lot to help her, but she still would have been okay without those things. Fuck it, he thought, she had given the number to Darius anyway.

The boys collected their shopping bags, and headed out into the mall. Windsor Mall was a fairly large and modern shopping center, located on the city's Northeast side. It catered to a primarily urban clientele, and over time had found itself becoming the primary weekend hangout spot for the city's youth. It was for this reason that the mall was particularly crowded today. But not so crowded that individuals could not be picked out of a crowd.

"Oh look!" Lil Fade said. "It's Dejuan!"

"That fool is slippin'!" Capone announced. "He's all by himself. Oh, we gotta get him, Blood!"

"And he has on a whole lot of that expensive jewelry that he likes to floss," Lil Fade added. "I agree with you, Blood, we gotta get him."

"If somebody tosses a peach in your lap, it'd be rude not to take it," Capone declared.

Travon shook his head and shifted his gaze to the floor. Darius noticed Travon's expression.

"Say, Tre," Darius said. "You, Marcus, and Romeo go and start the car. If we get chased, y'all blast at whoever's chasing us. Y'all still get y'all cut."

"Man, Dejuan don't go nowhere by himself," Travon warned. "Him, Tech Nine, and Quentin is cool again. I'll bet you a gang of other WCGs is in this muthafucka."

"Fuck Tech Nine!" Lil Fade shouted. "It's about time me, him, and Quentin bumped heads anyway. SaTown ain't big enough for all of us."

"I'ma help get that fool," Romeo told them. "I ain't waitin' in no muthafuckin' car."

The boys continued to follow Dejuan from a safe distance. After several minutes of trailing and observation, Travon's apprehensions were validated.

"Yep, I told you," Travon said. "There goes Lil Anthony, Pay Day, Dupriest, and Stephon. I told y'all them niggaz travel deep."

"Fuck them niggaz!" Lil Fade nearly shouted. "That's just more jewels for us."

Travon turned to Darius. "Say, D. I know Quentin, Tech Nine, and Short Texas is around here somewhere. We don't need to get caught slippin', and we don't need a war with the Courts. We already fightin' with East Terrace."

"Speaking of which, they just walked in," Romeo announced.

Lil Fade turned and began searching. "Where? Which ones?"

"Ahhh, it looks like, all of them," Romeo said, pointing in their direction.

Travon turned. "Shit!"

There was a massive ocean of royal blue floating toward them.

"Okay, we got WCG in front and East Terrace behind us," Darius told them. "I think that we need to detour sideways at either the next left or right, whichever comes first."

Lil Fade pointed. "Ooooh, look! Dejuan is going into the restroom. I know they love their mighty king, but they ain't gonna go in and hold his dick for him."

Capone nodded in agreement. "Let's get him."

"Fuck!" Travon exclaimed. He knew that he could not run with his leg in the condition that it was in. Even more important, Dejuan had saved his life, and now he had failed in his effort to return that favor. He did not want Lil Fade to kill Dejuan, but how could he stop it? How? Think, Tre, he told himself. He had to think.

Darius tapped Travon on his shoulder. "Bring the car around to the food court exit. When we leave the building, we are gonna run to the right, toward the expressway. Make sure that you are coming from that direction." Then he turned toward his brother. "Marcus, you and Romeo wait around the corner, and bust at whoever's following us. We are gonna run past y'all and take cover, then we'll cover y'all while y'all run to the car. Once y'all get to the car, then y'all cover us. Remember how Leo showed us when he came from the Army?"

Marcus nodded. "Yeah, he called it the shoot and scoot, or tactical withdrawal, or some bullshit like that."

Darius said, "Well, that's what we're gonna do. We're outnumbered, so we are gonna have to try some crazy shit."

Travon, Romeo, and Marcus broke away from the rest of the group, and quickly made their way outside.

"I got another idea, since we are so outnumbered," Marcus told Travon and Romeo. He gathered them close, placed his arms around their shoulders, and began to explain.

❖❖❖

Darius stood just inside of the restroom door, while Lil Fade and Capone rushed into the main restroom area with their weapons drawn.

"Don't be stupid, Dejuan!" Capone said, with his weapon aimed at Dejuan's head.

"Naw, be stupid, Dejuan," Lil Fade told him. "Please be stupid and give me a reason."

"You never needed a reason before," Dejuan told him.

Lil Fade frowned. "Whatever! Just break yourself, Blood!"

Capone peered beneath the doors of all of the stalls. They were empty. He walked to where Dejuan was standing and pat searched him. He found a Smith & Wesson nine-millimeter semiautomatic handgun tucked into Dejuan's waistband. Capone carefully removed the weapon and then slowly stepped away from him.

A thirty-something white male wearing glasses, strolled into the restroom. Darius quickly grabbed him and shoved him against the wall. The man began to panic.

Darius placed his fingers over his lips. "Shhhhh." He searched the newcomer and found nothing. "I'm sending one in to you!" he shouted. He turned the man around, and stared him in the eyes. "You go in there, and you do exactly what they say, do you hear me?"

The man nodded.

"They will kill you," Darius continued. "Do you understand me? They will kill you. Don't make any foolish moves, don't say anything stupid, just shut the fuck up and do exactly what they say."

The man understood. He slowly walked into the main restroom area. Capone and Lil Fade now had red bandannas tied around the lower half of their faces.

"You let me see your faces," Dejuan told them, as he continued to remove his jewelry.

Lil Fade smiled. "We kill you, the police won't give a shit. But if we kill Bob here, then they'll be all over us."

"I won't tell," the newcomer told them. He removed his glasses. "And I'm blind as a bat too."

"Dejuan, just hurry the fuck up so we can be on our way," Capone said.

"You want my money?" the white guy asked.

"Naw, just shut the fuck up, peckerwood!" Lil Fade shouted.

"Yes sir!"

Dejuan tossed Lil Fade two extremely large wads of money, along with his bulging wallet. Thinking that they had been following him the entire time that he had been inside of the mall, he gave up money that he did not have to.

"The rest of the money is in the shopping bag," he told Lil Fade.

Capone and Lil Fade exchanged glances, and then Capone snatched the shopping bags that were resting near Dejuan's feet. He quickly began rummaging through them.

The first bag contained two tennis shoe boxes from Foot Locker; to his surprise, they were both filled with thick wads of money. Capone closed the boxes, and placed them back into the bag. He then concentrated on the second bag. It, along with the remaining bags, was filled with merchandise. He tossed the bags of merchandise at Dejuan.

"Don't nobody want that Texas shit!" Capone shouted. "Burnt orange is a fuckin' sissy color!"

Dejuan stared at both of them and frowned. "You know what this means, don't you?"

"Yeah, it means that you're mad at us now," Lil Fade answered. "Who gives a fuck, you know the routine. Lay your greasy, curl-wearin' ass on the floor and count to fifty." He turned to the white guy. "You too, Opie!"

"And another thing, stay your muthafuckin' ass away from my kinfolk!" Capone added. "He don't need your damn help!"

"Is that what this is all about?" Dejuan asked. "Tell Tre that he can keep those five ounces, I don't need 'em. I drop more dope than that just walkin' to the shitter."

"If I could take your bitch ass outta this mall, by the time I got through jacking you, you would need 'em," Lil Fade replied.

"We out!" Capone shouted.

"Remember, count to fifty!" Lil Fade shouted, heading out of the door.

The boys tucked away their weapons, as they hurried through the food court toward the exit. Behind them, they heard a loud commotion. Capone turned to see what it was. Dejuan was out of the restroom pointing toward them. Travon had been right: Quentin, Tech Nine, Dupriest, Alonzo, Stephon, Short Texas, Lil Texas, Lil Anthony, DT, Boss, Lil Burst, Money, and quite a few other WCGs began to pull out their weapons.

"Run!" Capone shouted.

They hit the exit doors and ran to the right, with the WCGs in pursuit. Just as the boys were about to turn the corner, the WCGs opened fire.

Bullets whizzed past the boys, ricocheting off of the corner of the building. They turned the second corner, only to find that Romeo and Marcus were not there.

"Fuck!" Darius shouted, breathing heavily. "They should have been here."

The boys continued their all-out sprint toward the garage. Soon, they were able to see the front of Travon's car sticking out of the garage. Gunfire erupted again as the WCGs turned the second corner.

"Oh shit!" Darius shouted. "They going to eat us up when we get to the car!"

Suddenly, two AK-47s opened up from the parking lot, and four of their pursuers fell. The remainder of the WCGs scrambled back around the corner of the building to safety.

Marcus and Romeo, hiding behind cars in the parking lot, effectively laid down suppressive fire in a moving ambush and took the fight out of the WCGs. They moved covertly from vehicle to vehicle, firing their weapons, and brought gang warfare into an entirely new era.

Travon pulled out of the parking garage, and Darius, Capone, and Lil Fade leapt inside. Travon then raced into the parking lot and picked up Marcus and Romeo at the prearranged rendezvous point.

"Fuck yeah, Blood!" a jubilant Lil Fade shouted. "We got that muthafucka!"

"Whoooooeeeee!" Capone shouted. "We pulled that shit off!" He emptied the shoe boxes into his lap and began counting money.

Darius turned to Marcus. "What happed to the shoot and scoot?"

"Marcus came up with another plan," Romeo explained. "We did something else Leo taught us. And we used three-round bursts and everything, just like he said to. That shit worked beautifully!"

"I decided it would be better if we set they ass up like this instead," Marcus added. "That way they would be too shook up to follow us. I wasn't down for no more car chases, so we came to the car with Tre and got two of the AKs out of the trunk."

"They are gonna come after our asses like crazy," Romeo told them.

"How many?" Darius asked.

"Four the first round, and three the second," Romeo answered.

"Well, don't worry about it," Lil Fade told them. "They just lost seven homies; they won't be in a hurry to lose any more."

"They was all still moving," Marcus told them. "All of our shots hit kinda low."

Marcus and Romeo exchanged knowing glances. Neither wanted to reveal that Travon would only let them get the AKs out of the trunk, if they promised to aim for the legs.

"Damn, Marcus," Lil Fade exclaimed. "I know you can shoot better than that."

Romeo changed the subject. "So, how much did we win for, Blood?"

A wide grin crept across Capone's face. "That muthafucka had four Gs in his wallet, and six in his pockets. He musta just one a deal because he had *sixty* muthafuckin' Gs in the shoe boxes!"

"Whooooeeee!" Lil Fade shouted. "Fuck yeah, Blood! I knew we shoulda got that nigga! Somethin' inside a my head said, 'Fade, get that mutha-fucka'!'"

Darius smiled and shook his head. "Seventy muthafuckin' Gs for ten minutes' worth of work! I love this shit!"

Travon nodded. "No wonder all of them muthafuckas was there. I knew they traveled deep, but not *that* deep! That dude was either about to meet his connection and score, or he did some business with some niggaz he didn't trust."

"I'll bet you he was gonna make a shitload of money from whatever he was doing, and wasn't gonna pay them niggaz shit for watching his back," Darius told them. "That's one stingy-ass muthafucka!"

"Yeah, but I'll bet you one thing," Travon told them. "I'll bet you that he splurges on guns and ammunition to come after our asses."

Capone finished examining Dejuan's jewelry and sat it inside of one of the shoe boxes. "This is about fifty thousand dollars' worth of jewelry right here. We won big-time, Blood."

Travon nodded in agreement, then said, "Yeah, but for how long?"

CHAPTER TWENTY-FOUR

The Funeral

Travon and his mother squeezed into a pew in the rear of the chapel. Although large, the chapel was already filled to capacity, and mourners were beginning to stand along the sides of the room.

Frog was dressed in a black suit and white shirt, with a crimson red tie. A large, freshly clipped red rose was pinned to his lapel. It matched the rest of the bouquets inside the chapel today.

"The funeral home did a good job on him," Elmira whispered in her son's ear.

Frog's casket was surrounded by thousands of red roses, and appeared as though it were floating on a bed of flowers. The exterior of the casket was a deep sparkling red, with glistening chrome fixtures throughout. The interior was lined with a light rose-colored satin. It was not unlike the material that one would find on the beds inside of an expensive hotel. Yvette approached.

"Auntie Mira," she whispered to Elmira. "We want you and Tre to come and sit with the family. My mother has saved y'all some space up front."

Travon and Elmira followed Yvette. When they arrived at the section reserved for the family, Elmira leaned forward and hugged Mrs. Davis.

"Patricia, girl, how are you doing?" Elmira asked, as they embraced.

Patricia Davis shook her head. "I don't know. Elmira, I don't know how you did it, girl." She pointed toward the casket. "I'm trying to be strong, but that's my baby over there!" She broke down and began crying again.

Elmira sat next to her friend, placed her arm around her shoulder, and began to comfort her. Soon, the reverend approached the podium and began his sermon.

"Can we say, amen?" the reverend asked.

"Amen," the crowd responded.

"We are here to say farewell to a young man whom God called home early," the reverend told them. He continued by telling the gathering what a wonderful person Frog was, and recollecting childhood stories about Frog. Once the reverend was finished, and group of young men walked to the front of the church and harmonized Boyz II Men's "It's So Hard To Say Goodbye."

The young men were followed by the choir from Frog's mother's church, which rose and sang "Soon We'll be Done," and "Jesus Is Calling." Tamara, the mother of Frog's child, journeyed to the podium and spoke of the love she had for Frog, and the love that he had for her and their son. She was followed by Yvette, who spoke beautifully of her brother, and consoled the mourners with several selections of poetry.

The minister returned to the podium and spoke, and was once again followed by the choir. Finally, Vera rose and walked to the podium and spoke, and then conducted the ceremony for the viewing of the body. She asked that everyone remain seated, so that the family might view the body first and then leave.

After the family had made its mournful sojourn past the body, Vera called the rest of the congregation up, row by row, and allowed them to pay their last respects as well.

When Big Pimpin arrived at the casket, he placed a red-and-black BSV T-shirt inside. Lil Fade stuck some blunts in Frog's jacket pocket, while Lil Bling placed fifty dollars inside. Capone leaned over and put a small pint of gin in the casket, while Charlie placed a fifty pack of cocaine base inside Frog's jacket pocket.

"Get your hustle on, Blood," Charlie told him. He made a Blood sign, and filed out through the side door with the rest of the congregation.

Suga leaned over the coffin and placed a twenty-two-caliber semiautomatic inside. "Just in case there are some Crabs in Heaven, which I seriously doubt," he told Frog. He made a Blood sign and filed out with the others.

When the last of the BSV had gone, Frog had amassed a total of three hundred dollars, a quarter of an ounce of crack cocaine, two handguns, an all-black Dickie suit, six red bandannas, four red T-shirts, two red baseball caps, and twelve photographs of him with various women.

The pallbearers carried the casket outside, where it was set upon another stand, which was also surrounded by numerous roses. Dozens of bandannas that had been sewn together were draped over the casket as if they were a national flag.

The casket was oriented toward the street. As cars began to drive down past, they performed their best maneuvers with their hydraulic suspension systems. The cars were all juiced up today, polished to an unbelievable level of finish. Sparkling and looking their best, they gave Frog his last car show.

The cars continued to perform as they trailed the hearse to the cemetery, where Frog's remains would be cremated. At the cemetery, a brief service was held and then the crowd dispersed, the majority heading back to Frog's mother's house to eat.

Patricia Davis' House

While everyone was busy talking, eating, and reminiscing about Frog, Mrs. Davis summoned Travon.

"Tre, come with me and let's talk for a minute," she told him.

Travon rose from the couch and followed her out of the living room, through the kitchen, and into the back yard. She seated herself on some old white wrought-iron lawn furniture, and Travon took the seat just across from her.

"I'm so sorry that I behaved like that toward you the other day," she said softly.

"It's okay." Travon nodded. "You had every right to be angry. Plus, I know you were upset about Frog and everything."

"Well, actually, I was really upset about the shooting in the East Terrace," she told him. "I meant what I said about that, I just should not have taken it out on you."

Mrs. Davis leaned back in her seat and exhaled forcibly. "Yvette told me that you weren't involved and she gave me the money that you raised for Freddy's funeral. It was such a beautiful service, and it was all because of you. Thank you, Tre."

"You're welcome, Mrs. D," Travon replied. "You know I would do anything for Frog."

Mrs. Davis nodded her head. "I know that, baby, but Freddy's gone now." She patted Travon's hand. "So, what I want to talk to you about is doing something for Tre."

Patricia Davis leaned back in her chair, squinted her tired, wrinkled eyes, and peered off into space. "I need for you to make it, Tre. Frog is gone. Davon is gone. You are all Elmira has left, and all I have left, as far as a son goes. Somebody has to make it, Tre. I need for you to live and be successful. I need to know that Freddy could have done that. I know it's an unfair burden to put on you, but, Tre, you're it now. Baby, you're the last of a dying breed. You're a young African American male who is not dead or in prison."

She jabbed her finger at Travon. "You have to carry the torch. I have to know and Elmira has to know, that there is nothing wrong with us. That we are not failures. Our babies are killing each other, Tre. You're dying in the streets like...like animals. We need to know it it's us that's lost our way, or whether it's society."

Solemnly, Mrs. Davis lifted her arm and pointed out toward the streets. "Something out there is eating up our children, some unseen monster. But you," she said, shaking her wrinkled finger at him. "You, he will not get. I have a brother who is a professor at Grambling, and I also have a sister who is an admissions counselor at Prairie View. I can get you into either one, but first I need for you to get your GED or high school diploma. Once you do that, I'll make some phone calls and you're in."

She leaned forward and clasped Travon's hand. "Don't worry about tuition or anything; I have a few churches lined up for that. You just do your part and go to school and study. I don't know if Freddy told you, but he was going to go back to school. He wanted to be able to get a good job and take care of Tamara and the baby."

Travon shifted his gaze toward the lawn. "I been thinking about finishing up school in Houston with my Aunt Irma Lee, or up in Dallas with my Aunt Martha Ray."

Mrs. Davis enthusiastically slapped Travon across the top of his hand. "That's good! What does Elmira say?"

"I ain't told her yet. She's kinda hard to talk to, and she's busy with school and work." Travon shifted his gaze toward her. "I'm trying to work things out for myself."

"Oh, bullshit! You can't tell me that Elmira is too hard to talk to, and don't give me any of that macho crap either. Everybody needs somebody, Tre. You're seventeen years old, baby. You don't have all of the answers, although you may think that you do. Every once in a while we all need help to sort through our problems. I needed help, and you helped me. Besides, if you really feel like Elmira is hard to talk to, you've got me, Vera, Regina, and Chicken."

"You forgot Clarissa," Travon told her.

Patricia Davis shook her head. "No I didn't. Clarissa's got her ass on her shoulders. She's been like that since we was little girls. Hell, I can't even talk to Clarissa, so I know you can't!"

Together they shared a long laugh.

"Baby, finish school, get your GED, and if you need anything, come and talk to me. I'm here for you, Tre."

Travon stood and embraced Mrs. Davis tightly.

"Now, let's go inside and eat!" she told him. Together they walked to the door. "Your Aunt Clarissa brought over one of her red devil cakes, and a cold oven cake. She might be a Miss Goody Two-shoes, but she sure in the hell can bake!"

They shared another laugh, and they ventured into the crowded house.

Later That Evening
Aunt Vera's House

The entire family was gathered at Vera's house, including Martha Ray and Irma Lee and their children, who'd come for the funeral. Travon, Marcus, Winky, Lil Daddy, Frank, Robert Jr., Cibon, Omar, Caesar, and Buddy were all seated around the front porch. The conversation was about girls.

It was another beautiful South Texas evening. The sun's golden rays were retreating slowly to the West, and the sound of nature's orchestra permeated the temperate evening air. For the first time in a long time, Travon was truly happy. He was surrounded by family.

Chicken stood in the front yard surrounded by several of his female cousins, while Martha Ray, the oldest of the sisters, was venturing back inside of the house. Martha Ray was forty-two, but acted as if she were sixty-two, and so the fun had taken a brief hiatus during her presence. The rest of the cousins and aunts were scattered throughout the house, and if it had not been for the funeral, Travon would have counted this day amongst the most perfect days of his life.

Tonight he was going to ask Martha Ray if he could go back to Dallas with her. The hints he had thrown to her earlier had been received positively. She had thrown out to him how much room she had and how nice the schools were in her area. She had also mentioned how many nice young ladies lived in her neighborhood. Tonight, it would be all systems go, he was certain of it.

"Say, let's go to the backyard and blow some of this Bubonic," Antwon told the others.

His twin, Cibon, turned to him. "How much do we have left?"

"Shit, enough to roll ten fat blunts and a couple a joints," Antwon answered. "Let's bail then," Omar said, as he rose and headed off to the backyard. He was followed by Caesar, Cibon, Antwon, Marcus, J-Bird, Frank, Robert Jr., Buddy, and Winky. Travon, Lil Daddy, and Romeo stayed.

The stereo inside the house came alive, and Denise LaSalle's *Down Home Blues* CD blared from the speakers.

"They are getting drunk tonight," Lil Daddy said.

"Getting?" Romeo asked. "Hell, they already *are* drunk."

Urisa, Jamitra, Niesha, RaLisa, LaTonya, Tracey, and Jeanette left the front yard and headed up the street. Chicken walked to the porch where the boys were seated.

"Where they going?" Travon asked her.

Chicken turned and watched the girls walk up the street. "They going to the store." She cringed and turned toward the boys. "Ooooh, listen to the old fogey music they listening to. Tre, go get your radio, we gonna get our party on out here. I like listening to Ice Water."

"Chicken, that's Ice Cube," Lil Daddy told her.

"Momma, you know his name!" Romeo told her.

"I know, boy, I'm just teasing," she said, slapping Romeo across his arm. "Where are your CDs at?"

"I left them at home," Romeo told her.

A white diamond late-model Cadillac pulled up in front of the house. Travon, Lil Daddy, and Romeo rested their hands on their hidden weapons without Chicken noticing. She was too busy watching the car.

The passenger door flew open, and Tamika leapt and raced to the porch.

"Tre, I got something I need to tell you," she said, grabbing his hand and leading him down the porch steps away from the others.

"What's up, Tamika?" he asked, placing his arms around her waist and pulling her close. He leaned forward and kissed her.

A large, well-dressed African American woman climbed out of the driver's seat. She appeared to be in her forties.

"That's why you in the trouble you in now!" she shouted as she headed toward Tamika and Travon.

"Tre, I'm pregnant, don't be mad!" Tamika blurted out. "Pretend like you been knowin'. Please."

Travon was stunned into silence. The woman approached.

"Excuse me, young man, but I presume that you are the one responsible for my daughter's condition?" she asked.

Travon nodded. "Yes, ma'am."

"Well, what do you suppose we do about it? My daughter is trying to get into Spelman, but now she is six months' pregnant. It's too late to terminate the pregnancy, so I would like to know what your plan is."

Travon remained silent.

"That's what I thought," the woman told him, nodding her head. "Are your parents home, and may I speak with them?"

Chicken walked down the porch steps and approached the woman. "Hello, I am Cynthia Robinson, and you are?" She extended her hand toward the woman. Her hand was ignored.

"Mrs. Johnson," Tamika's mother replied. "Are you this young man's mother?"

Chicken pulled her hand back, dropping it to her side. "No, but I am his aunt and legal guardian."

"Well, your nephew has ruined my daughter's life. He has gotten her pregnant and I want to know what we are going to do about it." Mrs. Johnson pointed at Travon. "Did you ever think to teach him about safe sex?"

Chicken reeled.

"Excuse me, ma'am, but what I teach him is none of your business. I am well aware that Tamika is pregnant," Chicken lied. "Now since there is nothing that we can do to change that, I suggest we move on."

Mrs. Johnson placed her hand on her hip. "Well, that's easy for you to say, your daughter isn't the one who's pregnant by some hoodlum!" She pointed toward herself. "I'm the one that's going to be stuck raising that child, not you! So all of that 'move on' shit ain't gonna cut it. I want answers!"

Chicken placed one hand on her hip and lifted her other hand, sticking her finger into Mrs. Johnson's face. "Look, bitch! My nephew ain't no God damned hoodlum. If you want to see a hoodlum, you just keep talking crazy to me. Now, you want to talk about values, and how I raise Tre, and what I teach him? Well, in case you didn't know, it takes two to tango. It looks to me like you ain't been doing too good of a job at teaching yourself. Especially since you the one standing up here whining about your daughter being pregnant."

Chicken pointed toward Tamika. "Now what you need to do is stop telling this child that her life is ruined, because it's not. She can still go to college and be whatever the hell it is that she wants to be. As far as taking care of the baby, you don't have to worry about that. I'll be glad to take the child off of your hands and give it all of the love and affection it needs."

Chicken stuck her finger in Mrs. Johnson's face again. "Now, since you want answers, let me give you one last piece of advice. If I were you, I'd get my fat ass back in that Caddy and drive off, before I got whipped."

Chicken turned toward Tamika and placed her hands on her shoulders. "Anything you need; money, diapers, milk, a ride, a place to stay, anything, you just call me. You go to college, you study hard, and you make something of yourself, you hear me? It's not the end of your life, it's the beginning. You are just starting the most wonderful part of your life off early. But don't let anyone tell you that your life is ruined. I was sixteen when I had my first child. I was able to enjoy my children, grow with them, and be real close to them. I went back and finished high school, and then I went to college. I got my degree in nursing, I own my own home, and my life is far from being over."

Chicken pulled Tamika close and embraced her tightly. "Congratulations and good luck, baby."

Mrs. Johnson grabbed Tamika's arm, pulled her away from Chicken, and stormed off to her car. Tamika turned and smiled at Travon.

"Call me!" she shouted.

Travon nodded.

Tamika and her mother climbed into the car, and pulled away. Chicken turned, walked up the porch steps and stopped just at the front door.

"Tre, honey," Chicken called back to him.

"Huh?"

"Come inside with me so I can kick your ass."

"Huh?"

CHAPTER TWENTY-FIVE

Aunt Vera's House
Weeks Later

"We smashing deep, Blood," Winky exclaimed.

"Hell muthafuckin' yeah!" Omar agreed.

"Did anybody pick up the Ks from Fro-Dog?" Caesar asked.

Lil Daddy nodded. "Tre did that last night."

"What we smashin' in?" Omar inquired.

"Let's smash in our black Dickie suits with the red BSV T-shirts over them," Lil Daddy suggested. "The shirts with Blood Stone Villans on the back in big, black, old English letters."

"What are them Crabs wearin?" Winky asked. "We gots to look cleaner than them muthafuckas."

"They probably gonna wear some black Dickies with them royal-blue T-shirts that gots *Every Thang Goes* on the back of 'em," Caesar answered.

"Then let's smash in those brand-new burgundy Dickie suits we bought the other day," Winky suggested.

"Hell yeah!" Omar agreed. "That shit a look sweet. We just gotta tell the homies where to go buy them."

"Anyway, back to them Crabs, did anybody hear what's up for tonight?" Caesar asked.

Lil Daddy nodded. "Yeah, Darius said that Big Mike called Big Pimpin and they agreed on a truce for the concert, the afterparty, and everything else, all the way up until twelve o'clock tomorrow afternoon."

"Dejuan called Missy at her beauty shop and told her to tell Big Pimpin and Lil Bling that they want to call off the pistol play for tonight too," Omar added.

Winky peered around the yard. "Where'd Tre disappear to?"

❖❖❖

"Yeah, baby, it's cool," Travon said into the receiver. "Yeah, two more months until Lil Tre is born."

"What did your aunt say about us staying with her?" Tamika asked. "Have you even talked to her about it?"

"Yeah, I talked to my auntie; she said of course we can come and stay with her," Travon replied. "Well, me and the baby can go and stay with her, and you can stay with us during your summer breaks and during the holidays and stuff."

"Boy, you don't know how to take care of a baby," Tamika told him. "I'll bet you can't even change a diaper."

"I do know how to take care of a baby," Travon told her. "And yes I do know how to change a diaper."

"And when he cries at night?" Tamika asked. "Who's going to get up with him?"

"I'll get up with him," Travon told her. "Tamika, quit tripping. You're worrying too much. Look, I'm a come by and holler at you later, okay?"

"Okay." Tamika exhaled. "I'll see you later. Love you."

"Yeah," Travon replied. "I love you too."

Travon placed the telephone back into its cradle, rose from the couch, and walked out onto the porch. "Where's Marcus?"

"Him and Romeo went with Robert Jr. to take Darius to pick up his new ride," Lil Daddy told him.

"Damn. Well, y'all wanna ride with me?" Travon asked. "I got to go to the Courts and get something."

Caesar stood. "What the fuck are you going to the Courts for? Nigga, is you crazy?"

Travon shook his head. "Naw, we sneaking in the back way. I'm a run in and pass y'all something through the window of my momma's house. If she ain't there, then I'm a run in and run right back out."

"What are you going to get?" Winky asked.

Travon turned and peered off into the distance. "I'ma get my Street Sweeper."

That Night
The Concert

"Damn, everybody is here," Marcus exclaimed.

"I feel naked without my strap," Darius told them.

Travon walked in behind them. "Yep, they searching us, but they ain't searching the broads. I sent Romeo back to tell the girls. They gonna bring in all of the straps. Poison brought her big Dooney bag. She gonna try to get my Sweeper in."

Travon shook his head and laughed. "That girl is crazy."

"Trust me, we are gonna need all of the firepower that we can get in here if something jumps off," Darius told them. "You know that this is Tweetie's club, so all of them WCG's is strapped. He probably brought they shit in for them this afternoon when he opened the club up."

The music inside was almost deafening. Though the club was rated to hold sixteen hundred people, it was clearly over its capacity by at least half that much. People were everywhere.

The majority of the club's patrons were wearing some sort of clothing indicative of their gang affiliation, but a few had dared to dress up for the occasion. There were people dancing, carrying drinks and mingling, while many others were seated around one of the massive bars. Many were seated at tables that were spread throughout the establishment.

"There go the homies over there," Darius announced, pointing at a massive sea of red across the room. He and the rest of his entourage made their way across the crowded room.

"What's up, Blood?" Lil Fade shouted, as he and Capone embraced.

"What's up, Darius?" Suga nodded.

Darius returned Suga's acknowledgment and the two pretended to be friendly.

"What that Blood Stone Villain be like?" a familiar voice shouted from behind.

The boys turned. It was Fro-Dog, Big Pimpin, Bull, Lil Bling, and an entourage of about fifty plus. As the night progressed their numbers continued to grow, as did everyone else's. Soon, a drink arrived at the table. The girl delivering the drink caught everyone's eye. She wore a formfitting bodysuit beneath a pair of high-cut Daisy Duke shorts, and her hair was styled in a short pixie cut. Her curvaceous figure made all the boys go silent. She pointed.

"It's from that boy over there," she told them. "He says that it's for Big Pimpin."

The Bloods turned and stared. There was a massive crowd of ETGs across the room. Seated at the center table amongst them, were Big Mike, Michael Vay, Lil BK, Half Dead, C-Low, and Mike-Mike. Big Mike lifted his glass in a toast toward Big Pimpin, and then sipped from it. Big Pimpin raised his glass and did the same.

"What the fuck's that supposed to mean?" asked Suga.

Big Pimpin turned to Charlie. "Say, Charlie, go to the bar and send Big Mike a drink. Tell the waitress to tell him that it's from me. Since he sent me a Blue Hawaiian, send his ass a Blood Mary."

Soon, the concert began. The lesser groups performed first, and did quite well. The entire crowd was pumped up, on its feet, waiting raucously for the main artist to perform. Finally, DJ Slick made his appearance.

The rapper taunted the crowd, and performed his act flawlessly. The entire crowd was whipped into a festive frenzy. The rapper's entourage soon got into the act, and began to throw gang signs into the air with their fingers. They repeatedly formed the symbols for Treetop Piru and a few other Blood gangs as well. The atmosphere inside the club quickly reached a crescendo. And then the alcohol took over.

"Fuck Crabs! Fuck Crabs! Fuck Crabs! Fuck Crabs!" Alonzo, Baby T, Stephon, Dupriest, and a few other WCGs began chanting along with the music.

"What did you say?" Half-Dead asked Alonzo.

"Nigga, I said fuck Crabs!" Alonzo answered with an intoxicated slur. "Now what's up? It's Wheatley Courts on mines!"

"Nigga, fuck Wheatley Courts!" Dupriest shouted.

A shoving match ensued, quickly elevating itself into a full-blown fist fight. Travon grabbed Poison and immediately headed for the exit. Romeo, Marcus, Winky, and Precious followed.

Chairs began flying through the air. DJ Slick was struck in the head and members of his entourage were quickly pulled off of the stage and beaten. People began fleeing, and panic engulfed the entire club.

Travon made it out of the door and led Poison around the side of the building. They stood just around the corner and watched for their friends and relatives. He removed her large bag from off of her shoulder, placed it on the ground, and quickly removed his Street Sweeper from it.

People were storming out of the club; many were trampled. Then gunfire erupted inside.

Darius, Capone, and Charlie ran out together, holding their weapons in the air. They quickly scrambled into the parking lot and melted into the darkness. More gunfire erupted inside, and people began screaming.

"Fuck!" Travon shouted. "Where are they?" He was desperate to find Omar, Caesar, Antwon, and Cibon. Soon, he spied C-Low, Slow Poke, and RJ running from the parking lot, back toward the club. The gunfire inside of the club was almost continuous now.

Several people ran out of the club, including DJ Slick. The rapper happened to be running out of the club amidst a group of burnt-orange T-shirts, and as a result was next to Baby T when C-Low lifted his shotgun and blew Baby T's face off. The rapper's face and clothing were covered with blood and brain tissue. He ran past Travon screaming.

Travon turned to Poison. "Wasn't he just rapping all of that gangsta shit?"

Together they laughed.

Slow Poke lifted his shotgun and began firing into the fleeing crowd. A red shirt fell and Travon's heart skipped a beat. Robert Jr. walked calmly out of the club and up to RJ, and put a bullet in RJ's face at point-blank range. Cibon, Antwon, Caesar, and Omar ran out of the club together, firing their weapons. Red shirts, blue shirts, orange shirts, and black shirts were all falling.

"Over here, Blood!" Travon shouted. "BSVs!"

The cousins made an all-out sprint toward Travon.

C-Low, now finished reloading his shotgun, lifted it and took aim at Omar. Travon, unable to fire at C-Low because his cousins were in the way, shouted and waved his arms.

"Look out!" Travon shouted. "Behind you!"

Lil Daddy ran out of the club firing rapidly. He held a weapon in each hand, and fired both with an adroitness that was almost uncanny. C-Low shifted his weapon toward Lil Daddy, but a massive crowd rushed by and subsequently bore the brunt of C-Low's shotgun blast. C-Low quickly pumped his gauge again, but Lil Daddy was lost in the crowd. Furious, C-Low backed away and descended into the shadows of the parking lot.

"C'mon, Blood, let's go!" Robert Jr. shouted as he, Cibon, Antwon, Caesar, and Omar ran past Travon.

Darius drove up with Marcus, Lil Daddy, Romeo, and Precious inside of his car. "Don't go to the Heights, go to Chicken's," he told Travon. "The po-po will be all over the Eastside tonight."

Travon shoved Poison toward the car. "Go with them!"

Poison shook her head.

Travon opened Darius' car door and forced her inside. "It's too dangerous for you to run through the parking lot. Go with them!"

"Be careful, kinfolk!" Darius shouted. He revved his motor and raced off into the night.

Travon bent down, lifted Poison's bag, and ran off into the parking lot toward his car. He spied Robert Jr.'s car pulling away, and sighed with relief. They had all made it.

Travon turned back and examined the club. No one was running out anymore, but there were several people lying on the ground in front of the club, many more lying throughout the nearly empty parking lot. Some were dead, some were dying, and many were severely wounded. Some were Blood, some were Crips, some were WCGs, and some were DOGs, and some were members of other gangs. Gunfire was still erupting sporadically throughout the parking lot and from the nearby highway and surrounding streets. Gun battles were raging all over the area tonight, as people bumped into each other while trying to flee the carnage and get back to their respective neighborhoods.

Travon turned toward his car and spied a burnt-orange shirt standing near it. Another burnt-orange shirt was running toward the first. Travon ducked behind a nearby vehicle, lifted his Street Sweeper and let it roar.

One of the burnt-orange shirts cried out, and the second one grabbed him. They both ducked, and retreated like jackals into the night. They had wisely chosen to not engage the Street Sweeper.

Travon rose and ran to his vehicle. Lying on the ground next to his car where the burnt-orange jackals were gathering, was Slow Poke, a notorious ETG. He was breathing laboriously, bleeding profusely, and holding his stomach. Travon lifted his Street Sweeper and pointed it at the wounded boy.

"Quentin and Tech Nine was about to finish me off. I guess you wanted the pleasure instead, huh?" Slow Poke asked. "Well, go on and handle yo muthafuckin' business! I'm ready to die for the Terrace, nigga!"

"Where's your strap at?" Travon asked.

Slow Poke broke out into laughter. "If I had a strap, do you think Quentin and Tech Nine would have been standing over me? If you're jackin' for straps, then you're shit outta luck, cuz."

Gunfire erupted nearby and Travon jumped. He turned back toward Slow Poke. "C'mon!"

Travon leaned over and helped Slow Poke to his feet with one hand, while holding his Street Sweeper in his other hand.

"Ooow!" Slow Poke cried out in pain. "Shit! That hurts!"

Travon walked Slow Poke to the other side of his car, opened the door and helped him in. He then turned and walked to the driver's side and climbed inside.

"You know, if I had a strap, I would have killed you when you opened that door to get in," Slow Poke told him. "I just wanted you to know that."

Travon started his car and pulled away. They could see flames from automatic weapons here and there, as they exited the club's parking lot. Inside of the parking lot, there were several cars riddled with bullet holes, and a few wrapped around a light posts.

"So, where are you taking me?" Slow Poke asked him. "To the country to kill me, or to the Heights so you and your Slob-ass homeboys can torture me first?"

"I'm taking your Crab ass to the hospital," Travon told him.

"What?" Slow Poke shouted. "Awww, ain't this some sweet white-ass movie shit! I just smoked two of your homeboys tonight! If I live to see you on the streets again, I'm a smoke your Slob ass too!"

Travon smacked his lips. "Shut the fuck up!"

"A fuckin' Slob, taking me to the hospital! I don't believe this shit! What the fuck have you been smoking, cuz?"

Travon shook his head and maintained his silence.

"You know what?" Slow Poke told him. "That's why East Terrace is on top, 'cuz y'all Slobs is weak!"

Travon kept silent.

"If you was a real soldier, you'd a let Quentin and Tech Nine smoke me, and then you would have smoked them," Slow Poke told him. "That's what I would have done."

Travon still did not respond.

Slow Poke became angry. "What movie have you been watchin'?"

Travon turned toward him. "I'm not doing this for your Crab ass, I'm doing this for my homeboy's T-lady."

"What homeboy?" Slow Poke asked.

"My nigga who got killed."

Slow Poke turned and stared out of the window. "Hmmm, a Slob that got smoked?" He turned toward Travon. "The one we killed in the Rigsby last week?"

"No."

"That nigga we killed at First Stop last month?"

Travon nodded. "Aw hell, I smoked that bitch myself!" Slow Poke told him.

Travon's grip on his Street Sweeper tightened. He was beyond angry now. "No you didn't. One of your Crab-ass homeboys got off a lucky shot."

"Okay, but I wish I would've been the one to smoke your homeboy!"

Travon's anger had built to the point where he could do one of two things. He could either pull the trigger, or laugh. He laughed.

"You're trying hard, ain't you?" Travon asked.

"Man, what is this cornball cracker shit?" Slow Poke shouted. "Let me the fuck out!"

Travon leaned forward and placed his Blood and Crip *Bangin On Wax* CD inside of his CD player. He selected the "Piru Love" track and turned up the volume.

Slow Poke turned toward Travon and frowned. "Fuck that bullshit, cuz. I'm a smoke your ass good for disrespecting me by playing that ho shit."

"Not if I smoke you first," Travon told him. He turned to Slow Poke. "Let's get something straight. I don't know you and I don't know you. I don't like you and I really don't give a fuck about you. If I see you in the streets, I'm a smoke your bitch ass. I'm giving you a pass. A one-time-only pass. This is just for my homie's T-lady."

"Your homeboy must'a not been much of a soldier if this is for him," Slow Poke told him. "You supposed to smoke my ass for your homeboy."

"Just shut the fuck up, we're almost there!" Travon shouted. "And be the fuck still! You're leaking that Crab juice all over my seats, Blood!"

Slow Poke turned and stared out of the window, and smiled. "What's your name, cuz?"

"Why?" Travon replied. "And, nigga, I don't answer to that muthafuckin' 'cuz' shit either."

The boys sat quietly for the remainder of the trip. Soon, Travon pulled up to the emergency room entrance. He turned toward Slow Poke.

"Get the fuck outta my shit," Travon told him.

Slow Poke smiled, displaying all twelve of his gold teeth. He might actually live through this, he told himself. He knew a bad wound when he saw one. And *he* had a bad wound. He opened the passenger side door and climbed out of the vehicle, and then quickly turned back toward Travon, pointing a nine-millimeter Sig Sauer handgun at his face. Travon was petrified.

"I didn't smoke Tech Nine and Quentin because I couldn't reach it. It was in the small of my back. I don't know why I didn't smoke you. You get a pass, a one-time pass. If I see you again on the street, it's on. No passes, we're even. I'm going to kill you, and I'm going to enjoy doing it."

Slow Poke uncocked the pistol's hammer and then released the clip, which slid out of the weapon and onto the passenger's seat. He laid the weapon down on the seat next to the clip. Travon's eyes were bulging out of their sockets.

"One last thing," Slow Poke told him. "Get out of the game; you don't belong in it."

Slow Poke closed Travon's car door, and slowly staggered into the hospital holding his stomach. Travon laid his Street Sweeper down and lifted Slow Poke's weapon. There was a round inside of the chamber.

Travon carefully moved the slide forward again and tossed the weapon back onto the seat. He shook his head. He couldn't save the old lady, he told himself. He couldn't save the little girl in the park. But at least there would be one less funeral. That one was for you, Mrs. D. Now, he thought, he would do something for himself. He was going to take Tamika and their child, and he was going to get the hell away from this place.

Travon shifted his car into gear and drove off into the night.

"I *am* going to get the hell away from this place," he whispered.

CHAPTER TWENTY-SIX

Aunt Vera's House
Days Later

"Shit, one time is still sweating us," Darius said. "They have been running up on us every fuckin' night since the concert."

"Say, Tre, I thought you was gonna break camp on us and head to Big D?" Marcus asked.

Travon nodded. "I was, but Tamika is trippin'. She don't wanna go now. She wants to wait until she has the baby, and then leave."

"Man, everybody done got ghost and bailed outta town," Lil Fade said.

Suga nodded in agreement. "Ain't too many of us around. I'm a catch out myself, and head back to Florida for a minute."

Darius turned to Suga. "Where Big Pimpin take off to?"

"Shit, him, Fro-Dog, Red Rum, and Bull went back to Cali," Suga told him. "Charlie Brown bailed to Atlanta, Kilo went to Mississippi, and Goldie went back to Memphis. Shit, I heard that some of the homies bailed to Kansas City, Tulsa, and Little Rock."

Darius shook his head. "Damn, we probably won't hook back up for at least a couple of months."

"We got to get the fuck outta town, D," Marcus told him. "Man, I ain't down for taking the blame for what went down at the concert. A muthafucka get electrocuted a thousand times for all that shit."

"We gonna need some snaps to get gone," Darius told him. "I spent my ends on getting another ride."

"Say, Blood," Lil Fade said enthusiastically. "I know a real quick lick we can hit, and get away cleaner than a muthafucka."

Darius turned and stared at Lil Fade like he was crazy. "One time is already hot, we can't make no money because they keep running up on the cuts, the straps is getting low, and you wanna pull off another lick?"

"We got paid hittin' Dejuan's ass," Lil Fade told him. "We got over ten grand a piece for five minutes' worth of work. Think about how many nights we'd have to spend on the cuts to get that. You get another ride and hook it up, just like that. It's a win. We can hit, divvy up the snaps, and be in the wind before anybody knows anything."

Travon did the numbers inside of his head. He had ten grand from the lick on Dejuan, plus the money that he got from Too-Low, plus the yea that he had already sold. He had forty thousand dollars cash, and about eight thousand dollars' worth of jewelry. Still, it wasn't enough to quit forever. He wanted to quit and walk away for good. He turned to Lil Fade.

"How much we talking?" Travon asked.

"Eighty grand in cash, plus jewelry, plus straps!" Lil Fade replied.

"Bullshit!" Darius told him.

"I'm not bullshitting," Lil Fade told them. "I don't fuck around when it comes to money."

"Who is it?" Marcus asked.

Lil Fade shook his head. "What is it, would be a better question. It's the Easy Pawn on Austin Highway. It's a pawn shop, a jewelry store, a gun shop, and a check cashing place all rolled into one."

Travon began adding again. The pawn shop job would net him another sixteen thousand, and that would put him over the top. With that kind of money, he was sure that he could convince Tamika to leave with him. She could go to school in Dallas, and he could go back to school, obtain his diploma and work. He turned to Lil Fade.

"When?" Travon asked him.

Lil Fade shrugged. "Shit, this Friday is payday. They will have stacked up on money to cash all of them damn checks."

Travon nodded. "I'm down."

"I'm with it," Suga told him.

Darius folded his arms. "Let's hear it."

"We need some sacks, some towels, gloves, masks, hammers, and some flu wear," Lil Fade explained. "We get a couple a cars, and some of our silenced straps. Tre and Marcus will steal a car from the mall, and we'll follow them to another mall, where we'll park D's car. We'll park some fresh plates from a car at that mall, and bail to the pawn shop. We gonna do it early, while everybody is still at work. That way we get more money because they ain't started cashing checks yet. We'll mob in the store dressed like Crabs. Marcus, you'll stay in the car and pop anybody that tries to roll in or run out of the store. Tre, you will hold the door open, just in case it has an automatic lock on it, plus you'll watch our backs from the door. Suga will mob straight to the back room and keep everybody there under wraps. You'll also have one of them crack the safe for you. Just in case you have to drop somebody, you'll use the H&K-MP5 with the silencer built into it. I'll use one, and Tre will use the other."

Lil Fade began pacing. "Marcus, you'll use the Smith and Wesson nine-millimeter with the silencer on it. Me and D will mob through the store with some hammers, break the display cases, and bag the jewelry and straps. D will get the jewelry and I'll get the guns. Then we'll get the registers, while Tre times the whole thing. We want to walk in, get the shit, and walk out. We don't want to be in the store no more than two minutes," Lil Fade told them.

"Then we'd better bring Capone," Marcus told him. "He'll clean out the registers, while you and D hit the display cases, and Suga takes care of the safe in the back."

Lil Fade nodded. "Good idea. I'd like to have Capone in on something like this anyway."

"I'll call and hip him to the game," Darius told them. "So who's gonna use the other pistol with the silencer?"

"We ain't gonna take it," Lil Fade answered. "We just gonna use the three silenced HKs, and the one silenced pistol."

"So what am I gonna use, my finger?" Darius asked.

"Naw, you're gonna use the FAMAS, and Capone will carry the AKM," Lil Fade explained. "We are gonna need some fully automatic shit in there, just in case things don't go right. The nine-millimeter HKs just won't do the trick when in comes to slicing through walls and intimidating people."

"Why do I gotta use that French piece of shit?" Darius protested.

Lil Fade shrugged. "Then use one of the L-8s."

Darius laughed. "Now you're really trying to kill me."

"Then use one of the Styer AUGs," Lil Fade told him. "I just need for you to carry something small, but with enough firepower to help regulate shit. Remember, it has to be small so you can sling it over your shoulder and move around when it comes time to use the hammers. You know we don't have a lot of shit left. Mr. C is changing barrels on almost everything we got. That's one of the reasons why we gotta hit this lick!"

Darius shook his head and smiled. "I'm down, but if you wanna get rid of me, then shoot me. Don't have me go in there with some French piece of shit that's gonna break down after two shots."

The boys laughed.

"All right, Friday we are doing this," Lil Fade told them. "And then we are all gonna get the fuck outta town, right?"

"Right," Marcus agreed.

"Yeah." Darius nodded.

"Cool," Suga agreed.

Later That Evening

"Yeah, but what about your aunt in Colorado?" Travon asked. He shifted the telephone away from his now tired right ear to his left one. "What did she say?"

"She said that she would love for us both to come and stay with her," Tamika told him. "But my mom doesn't want me to leave until after I have the baby and finish high school."

"You're gonna finish school, you're just gonna do it in Colorado," Travon told her.

"I don't understand what the big deal is about leaving, Tre. Why can't we wait? You know that it's always been my dream to go to Spelman. I want to join a sorority like the one my cousin is in. You said that you'd watch the baby for me while I was in school, and that I could come and live with you and the baby in Dallas. Those were our plans, and I don't see why you are trying to change them."

"Tamika, I got to get away from here," Travon pleaded. "I got to get outta this place. You don't understand, it feels like I'm running out of time. It feels like the walls are closing in on me or something. I have to get away, I'm running out of air."

"Boy, what's wrong with you? What are you talking about? Why are you tripping? I want to go to college. I want to go to step shows, and foot-ball games, and pep rallies. Why are you trying to ruin things for me, Tre?" Tamika said.

"I'm not," Travon replied. "I thought that you wanted to be with me, that's all. I want to take care of you and I want to take care of my baby. I thought that you wanted to be together forever and have a family with me."

"I do, but there are other things I wanted to do with my life too. Things that I wanted to do before we even started going together."

"Okay, Tamika, we'll do it your way. You're right, you're always right. I've just been looking at it wrong. I have to go, I'll call you later."

"Tre, don't be mad at me. I don't want you to hang up mad."

"I'm not mad, I'll talk to you later."

"Okay, I love you."

"Yeah, same here. 'Bye."

"'Bye."

Travon turned and slammed the phone down onto its base. "Stupid, spoiled bitch!" He fell back into a nearby recliner and rubbed his tired eyes. Soon, he drifted off into a much-needed sleep.

CHAPTER TWENTY-SEVEN

Friday
Easy Pawn

The door flew open and the four males entered quickly. All wore blue ski masks, blue flannel shirts, black gloves, black Dickie pants, and blue Converse All Stars. They were carrying a variety of weapons.

"Get down!" Number One shouted. "Get down on the floor now!"

Paralyzed by fear, a lady stood in the middle of the aisle screaming. Number One grabbed her and threw her to the floor.

"Bitch! Get yo ass on the floor now, and shut the fuck up!" he told her.

Suga ran to the rear area, while Travon stood just inside of the entrance holding the door slightly open. To his horror, Suga's HKMP-5 released an almost continuous flash of blue and orange in several directions. It was capital murder now.

A knot formed in Travon's stomach as he glanced at his watch.

Darius began smashing the glass counters on the right side of the store, while Lil Fade smashed those on the left. There were four hostages lying on the floor in the middle of the shop. Capone gathered the others from behind the counters, and made them join the four already on the floor. It was Travon's job to annihilate them if they moved. He prayed that they acted like statues.

Capone returned to the area behind the counters, where he began opening the cash registers and emptying them. Darius and Lil Fade continued to smash counters with their hammers, and bag the numerous guns and pieces of jewelry.

"Thirty seconds!" Travon shouted.

Ten seconds later, Lil Fade and Darius completed their part of the job.

"Number One, done!" Lil Fade shouted.

"Number Two, done!" Darius shouted.

"Bitch, keep your head down!" Travon shouted to one of the hostages.

A silenced burst was heard in the rear of the store. No one inside the store, except for the boys, knew what it meant.

Suga had just executed the last of the hostages in the rear, after they had opened the safe. Fifteen seconds later, he burst from the rear.

"Safe is secured!" Suga shouted.

"One minute!" Travon shouted, his voice cracking.

"Number Three done!" Capone shouted.

Travon threw open the door, and Suga, Darius, and Capone raced out of the pawn shop. Travon nodded at Lil Fade, and motioned toward the door. It was time to go.

Lil Fade walked down the line of hostages and fired two shots into the back of each of their heads. Travon closed his eyes and his legs began to give. That hadn't been a part of the plan. No bodies. Lil Fade had promised them that there would be no bodies.

"Five, let's go!" Lil Fade shouted into Travon's ear.

Travon snapped to, and ran for the car. Lil Fade removed a hand grenade from his pants pocket, pulled the pin, and tossed it inside of the store. He turned and ran like hell.

On the way to the car Travon raced past a young white couple lying dead in the parking lot. They had chosen the wrong day to go to the store and shop for an engagement ring. Marcus had shot each one of them in the head twice.

Travon climbed into the car, followed shortly thereafter by Lil Fade. A deafening explosion filled the air as they pulled off, and the car was peppered with glass fragments from the pawn shop's windows.

"We did it, Blood!" Lil Fade shouted. "We did it!"

"Whooooeeee!" Capone shouted. "Fuck yeah!"

The boys celebrated as they drove to the mall to change clothes and cars. After being on the highway for several minutes, Lil Fade tapped Marcus on his shoulder.

"Pull over here," Lil Fade told him. "Exit right here!"

Marcus exited the highway.

"We ain't got time for this shit!" Darius told Lil Fade.

"Yeah, in case you've forgotten, this car is stolen," Marcus added.

"We gonna put the clothes in the Dumpster behind the movie theater," Lil Fade explained.

Suga turned to Lil Fade. "I thought we was gonna burn them?"

"Just chill," Lil Fade replied.

Marcus drove behind the movie theater. It was completely deserted. A high wooden fence shielded the area further.

"Pull in that space right there." Lil Fade pointed. "Pull all the way up in between those two buildings, up near the Dumpster."

Marcus navigated the car in between the two small air conditioning buildings, so that they could be totally shielded from view.

"We'll change right here and put the clothes in the Dumpster," Lil Fade told them. "When y'all change clothes, don't forget to put on the surgical gloves too. Don't touch shit in the car without gloves."

The boys climbed out of the car and began to strip their clothing off. While they were occupied with removing their clothing, Lil Fade eased back to the car, and removed a silenced pistol from his bag.

No one paid Lil Fade any attention. He slowly crept up behind Suga, lifted the silenced pistol, and fired twice.

Travon felt Suga's blood and brain fragments fly onto his face, neck, shoulder, and chest. He looked to his left, where Lil Fade was standing over Suga, holding the silenced pistol. Travon shifted his gaze to the ground, where he witnessed Suga's last spastic movements. Blood poured from Suga's head. Slowly, Travon peered down at his arm, and saw the thick crimson liquid oozing down it. He lifted his right hand and wiped his face. His hand was covered with blood and soft, pink brain tissue. His stomach heaved and he fell to his knees and began to vomit.

Lil Fade gathered Suga's belongings and passed Suga's clothing to the rest of the boys. "Wipe the blood off with this. And don't worry, we gonna burn it all anyway."

The boys took the clothing and wiped the blood off of their bodies. They then dressed in all black, bagged up the blue clothing, and placed it inside of the car.

Marcus walked to where Travon was kneeling and wiped him off. He lifted Travon up off of the ground and helped him get dressed. Darius grabbed some of the clothing that they were going to burn and wiped Travon's vomit off of the ground. He then kicked dirt over the remainder of the vomit and finally poured oil over it from a bottle that they had found in the trunk.

Together he and Marcus placed all of the clothing that they were going to burn back inside of the bags, and then helped Travon climb into the vehicle. Once all of the boys were inside, Marcus pulled away, leaving behind the naked, bloody corpse of their former comrade.

"Can I ask why?" Travon asked weakly.

Darius shrugged, indicating that he did not know anything. Travon shifted his gaze toward Marcus, who shook his head.

"I talked to the homie Edmond yesterday," Lil Fade explained. "He called me from the pen. Him and Suga was on Bido One together. Suga was not only a snitch, but a transformer. He got up there and was hanging with some Crabs and claiming Disciples. That snitching and transforming shit pisses me the fuck off. Nobody disses the BSV, and nobody leaves. It's BSV until the day you die. Blood in, Blood out."

"He, he was your friend," Travon told him.

"Fuck that nigga!" Capone shouted. "It's all about BSV. A'int nobody greater than the set. Besides, if he snitched once, the muthafucka will snitch again."

Lil Fade smiled. He stared at Travon with his cold, penetrating blue eyes.

"Remember that," he told Travon. "Blood in, Blood out."

CHAPTER TWENTY-EIGHT

Aunt Vera's House
Days Later

"Police, FBI, sheriffs, and ATF have been raiding the East Terrace every night since the robbery," Darius told them. "The news say that they have executed sixty-eight search warrants and will possibly be executing another one hundred and thirty before it's all over with. They are taking all of them Crabs' guns and dope. They have even laid off everybody else and forgot about that concert shit."

"While we won for almost a hundred straps, a hundred grand, and who knows how much jewelry!" Marcus laughed.

Travon bolted from the house, headed for his car.

"Where you going, T?" Marcus asked.

"I gotta run to Tamika's house real quick, I'll be back," Travon answered. He carried his backpack with him, which he removed from his shoulder and placed in the front seat. He quickly climbed into the driver's seat, cranked up the volume on his stereo system, and pulled away.

Tamika's House

"Tre, I don't understand all of this," Tamika told him. "Where did you get all of this money?" She tossed a thick wad of rubber-band-wrapped twenty-dollar bills back onto a pile of similarly wrapped wads.

"Don't be stupid, girl, you know how I got this," Travon replied.

"But this is sixty-five thousand dollars! You made all of this from selling drugs?"

Travon leaned forward and kissed her on her cheek. "What? Are you wearing a wire or something?" He lifted his hands to her chest and began pat searching her. "You trying to give me a case, girl?"

Tamika pushed his hands away. "Stop, Tre, don't get on my stomach." She turned back toward the money. "That's a lot of money, Tre. What do you want me to do with it?"

"Put it away, hide it," Travon told her. "It's for us and the baby. I was gonna buy my mom a house and get her out of the Courts, but she'll be finished with school in a few months. She'll be making some decent money, and she'll be able to move out of the Courts after a couple of paychecks. Especially since she's by herself now."

"Tre, are you sure?" Tamika asked, caressing the side of his face.

"She's gonna be okay." Travon nodded. "So now the money is for us and the baby. Besides, she wouldn't take any of it anyway, unless I could explain to her exactly where I got it from. Anyway, now that we're having a baby we'll need it, so everything works out for the best."

Tamika sat up in bed. "Tre, that's kinda what I wanted to talk to you about. I went to the doctor and I finally let him show me the sonogram. I know that I said that I didn't want to know what I was going to have, but I just couldn't help it."

Travon sat up. "Is everything okay with the baby?" he asked nervously.

Tamika laughed. "Yes, boy. Relax."

Travon reclined back onto the bed, interlaced his fingers, and rested his head on his palms.

"Well, it's not just *a* baby," Tamika told him. "It's *two* babies. That's why my stomach is so big."

Travon's eyes widened and a smile slowly crept across his face. "We're having twins?"

Tamika smiled and nodded.

Travon sat up and wrapped his arms around Tamika. "That's good, baby! Expensive, but good!"

"The doctor asked me if twins ran in my family, and I told him no. Do twins run in your family?"

"Hell yeah!" Travon exclaimed. "I got three sets of twins in my family right now. I got two sets of cousins who are twins, and my mom is a twin. What did your mom say?"

"She's happy. As a matter of fact, she's really beginning to get on my nerves with all of the attention. She's already dropping hints that she wants to keep the babies while I'm in school. She's been talking about all of the fun she's going to have with the babies and she's been calling everybody and telling them that I'm having twins. She called Varika in Hawaii, and my other sister in Virginia, and all of my aunts."

"That's good. I could kind of tell that she was coming around." Travon smiled. "She even pretends like she actually likes me now."

Tamika waved her hand through the air, dismissing Travon. "Boy, she does like you. If she didn't like you, she wouldn't even let you inside the house, let alone spend the night."

"So what are we gonna do about leaving, Tamika?" Travon asked. "I gotta get outta here. At least for a little while. The longer I stay, the more shit I get into. If I stay with another aunt, I'm still in the same boat. I need to get away. I have to get away. *We* have to get away."

Tamika exhaled forcibly. "I know, baby, I know." She lifted her hand and caressed his cheek. "I don't want you to get into trouble. I don't know what I would do if something happened to you." She kissed Travon upon his cheek.

Travon smiled at her. "Now you sound like my Tamika."

"I'm sorry, I've just been moody lately," she said softly. "I've been thinking about me, me, me, and not about us. If I have to leave and put school on hold, I will. Or, I'll go to school wherever we move to."

Tamika smiled, and Travon replied with one of his own.

"I fell in love with a gangsta, so I'll just have to go on the run with you, and lead the life of a gangsta bitch."

Together they laughed. Travon tugged on the sleeve of her shirt.

"Where did you get this outfit?" he asked. "It looks real nice on you."

Tamika ran her hand across her white maternity shirt and traced her finger over several of the blue teddy bears, yellow ducks, and red sailboats that were embroidered into the fabric. "You gave me the money to get some maternity clothes, and this is one of the outfits that I bought with it."

Travon leaned forward and gave her a peck on the cheek. "You look beautiful to me."

Tamika peered down at her belly and pouted. "I look fat."

"You look pregnant and beautiful," Travon told her, as he kissed her belly through the shirt.

"Stop that!" Tamika told him. She reached for the lamp on her nightstand and extinguished the light. The room became pitch-black.

"Hey!" Travon shouted. "Watch your hands!"

"When you get pregnant, you get real horny," Tamika explained. "I'm having twins, so I'm twice as horny."

Hours Later

Travon spied a convenience store on his way home from Tamika's, and pulled into the parking lot to top off his gas tank. It was past one a.m.

Tired, Travon climbed out of his vehicle and walked inside the store, where he received a friendly nod from the night clerk. He nodded back and continued on to the soda freezer. A patrol car pulled up outside.

The officers exited their patrol car and began to examine Travon's vehicle. The custom paint, large chrome rims, tinted windows, and numerous chrome trim pieces drew their attention. It was obviously a car that did not belong in this area.

Travon grabbed a Big Red soda from the freezer and then walked to the chip stand and he grabbed a bag of Cheetos from the rack. He then headed over to the candy aisles, where he grabbed a bag of M&Ms with peanuts. Now finished with his shopping, he headed up to the checkout counter. The officers watched as he pulled a small wad of bills from his pocket and handed the clerk a twenty.

"Put the change on gas," Travon instructed the clerk. He turned and peered out toward the gas pumps. "I'ma pull up to pump number five."

One of the officers approached. "That's an awful lot of money to be carrying all rolled up like that."

The clerk rang up Travon's merchandise and handed him a receipt.

"Is that your car outside?" the officer asked.

Travon nodded. "Yeah."

"Has some pretty expensive-looking rims on it," the officer commented. "Where do you work?"

"Who said anything about working?" Travon asked.

"Are you saying that you don't work?" the officer asked.

"No." Travon shook his head. "I work at the convenience store in my neighborhood."

The second officer approached. He handed the first one a cup of coffee.

"What neighborhood is that?" the first officer asked.

"The Heights," Travon told them.

"That's kinda far from here," the officer told him. "What are you doing way out here at one o'clock in the morning?"

"You got any identification on you?" the second officer asked.

Travon pulled out his wallet, and handed the second officer his ID.

"You got a driver's license?" the officer asked.

"No," Travon told him.

"What are you doing driving?" the second officer asked.

"I'm not," Travon told him.

"I thought that you said that was your car out there?" the first officer asked.

"It is," Travon confirmed.

"You just told me that you weren't driving!" the second officer told him.

"I'm not," Travon replied calmly.

"All right, smart-ass, turn around!" the second officer ordered.

Travon turned and placed his hands on top of the counter. The officers pat searched him, and found a pager, wallet, set of keys, and a total of two hundred dollars. They handcuffed him, led him outside, and placed him in the back of their patrol car.

Officer number two took Travon's keys, walked to his car, and began searching the vehicle. The officer found Travon's Glock model twenty-three, forty-caliber semiautomatic pistol beneath the driver's seat. He tossed the weapon on top of the passenger seat, and continued his search. Nothing else was found.

The officers took Travon to the county magistrate's office, where they charged him with driving without a license, driving without insurance, and unlawful carrying. A hold was placed on him, and he subsequently denied bond in order to investigate a warrant on him from the district attorney's office. It was a warrant for murder.

CHAPTER TWENTY-NINE

Next Day
Bexar County Courthouse

Travon was taken before a county judge for arraignment. The court clerk called his name.

"Robinson, Travon!" the clerk bellowed.

A sheriff's deputy walked to where Travon was seated in the jury box, uncuffed him from the twelve other prisoners that he was shackled to, and escorted him to the center of the courtroom.

"You are aware of your rights?" the judge asked.

Travon nodded. "Yes, sir."

"You are charged with unlawful carrying, a Class A misdemeanor punishable by up to twelve months' incarceration. Mr. Robinson, to this charge, how do you plead?"

"Not guilty."

"You are charged with murder in the first degree, a Class A felony punishable by life imprisonment or lethal injection. Mr. Robinson, to this charge, how do you plead?"

Travon was stunned into silence. The first thing that came to his mind was the pawn shop.

"Not guilty, Your Honor," Travon stammered.

"Mr. Robinson, do you have an attorney?" the judge asked.

"Uh, no, sir. Your Honor, what's this about a murder charge?" Travon asked.

The judge lifted his finger. "Just one moment," he told Travon. He turned to a group of attorneys standing in the corner to his left. "Which one of you is the least busy?"

None of the attorneys spoke.

"Mr. Kaufman, can you take this case?" the judge asked.

A tanned, trim lawyer with graying sideburns stepped forward. "Ah, yes, Your Honor. I can take it."

The judge nodded, handed the lawyer the case file, and then squinted. "Here, get with Mr. Robinson and go over things with him. Do it right now, while we're all in the courtroom."

The lawyer frowned as he stared at the judge and accepted the case file. "Yes, sir."

The judge turned to Travon. "Mr. Kaufman will go over things with you, young man. I'm sure he'll be able to answer all of your questions. This trial is set to begin thirty days from now." The judge banged his gavel and turned to the clerk. "Call up the next defendant."

The deputy escorted Travon back to where the rest of the orange jumpsuit-clad defendants were, and reshackled him to the group. He then moved on to unshackle the next prisoner that had to go before the judge. The attorney walked to where Travon was seated and extended his hand.

"Hi, I'm Gary Kaufman and I'll be representing you for this case."

Travon extended his hand and gripped the lawyer's firmly. Kaufman handed Travon a business card. It was thick, tan, and custom-made with raised gold letters. It read: The Law Firm of Schuster, Goldberg, Kaufman, Jacobs, Steinberg, and Spiel. Another lawyer approached.

"Congratulations, Gary," he told Travon's attorney. "I hope that you're appointed."

Three more attorneys approached.

"Stop kissing butt, Greg," one of them teased. "He isn't on the bench yet."

"Can we still call you Gary, or do we have to call you O Great One?" another asked.

"Will we have to bow when we approach from now on?" asked the third.

"O Great One will do, and yes, a slight genuflection would be appropriate," Kaufman told them.

All four attorneys laughed and bowed.

"Congratulations, Gary, you deserve it," the first attorney told him.

Another winked his eye at Travon. "The judge must like you."

The attorneys departed, and Travon turned toward Kaufman.

"What was all of that about?" he asked.

"Oh nothing." Kaufman shrugged. "I'm on a very short list for a federal judicial appointment. I'm not even a prosecutor; I just got a call from the White House's lead counsel, telling me that I'm the leading candidate out of the remaining three."

"Shit, that's cool. So, what is all of this murder stuff about?"

Kaufman seated himself in the empty chair next to Travon and began rifling through the case file. After a couple of minutes of silent reading, he turned to Travon.

"Okay, the unlawful carrying is bad," Kaufman told him. "The DA's office should have rejected that case outright. It's a bad search. You weren't in the vehicle, it was parked, and you were buying a soda. There was no probable cause, no nothing. They're just trying to stack shit on you, that's probably what pissed the judge off and made him give me the case. He doesn't like it when one side doesn't play fair. They're going to come to us and say that they'll drop the unlawful carrying and drop the first-degree murder to a manslaughter, if we plead guilty right away and save them a whole lot of trial preparation. You know how the game is played."

Kaufman shifted in his seat and cleared his throat. "Well, I can tell you this, they'll be wasting their time. For one, the judge is gonna throw this unlawful carrying so far out of his courtroom, they'll have to send their secretaries into the parking lot to look for the case file. As for this murder charge, well, they are accusing you of shooting a Tyrone 'Baby T' Warfield in the face with a shotgun at some nightclub. No murder weapon, no nothing. Just a single eyewitness who saw you firing a shotgun the night of the shooting. It's weak, but you have a gang jacket and since this guy was in a rival gang, they are betting that a jury will buy it; which they will."

Kaufman patted Travon's knee. "So, we're not gonna let this get to court, are we? The case is weak because she saw you firing a shotgun, but not who you were firing at. In other words, she didn't actually see you shoot the guy. As your attorney I need to know, did you shoot the guy?"

"Hell no!" Travon said. "I was there and I was blastin', but not at him. I was tryin' to get my cousins out of there and save my own ass. But dude got blasted by somebody else."

"And you wouldn't be willing to tell the State who, because then you'd be a snitch, right?"

Travon nodded. "Right."

"If it comes down to your ass or his, we are going to give them his," Kaufman told him. "I don't like losing. In fact, I never have. You're being railroaded so the judge wants me to make sure it's fair."

"Yeah, me against the State of Texas." Travon snorted. "How is that fair?"

Kaufman shook his head rapidly. "No, no, no, my dear boy." He laughed. "You don't understand. We're your attorneys now. The law firm of Schuster, Goldberg, Kaufman, Jacobs, Steinberg, and Spiel. All one thousand two hundred and seventy-three of us. Plus our secretaries, paralegals, researchers, investigators, writers, and money. The State of Texas doesn't stand a chance."

Kaufman laughed again. "Now, what I need from you is a list of witnesses and a few other things. I'll set up a motion to suppress hearing for two weeks from now, and see if we can squash this thing before it gets in front of a jury. Juries don't like guns and gangs. I'll get back to you in a few days; right now I'm going to go and talk with the judge and get rid of this unlawful carrying. I'm also going to get us a discovery hearing."

Kaufman rose. "Have my list ready when I come and see you in a couple of days. And see if you can dig up some dirt on Tyrone Warfield. I'll get my investigators to start doing the same. We gotta make this guy out to be a real scumbag. I'll see you later, Mr. Robinson. If you need anything, you have my card. Try not to get into any trouble in the meantime."

Bexar County Jail
"Travon Robinson!" the guard shouted.

Travon climbed out of his bunk and hurried over to the officer's desk. "What?"

The guard smiled at him cynically. "Pack your shit, you moving to the sixth floor!"

"Fuck!" Travon exclaimed. "Why are they moving me again?"

"You're moving to the gang floor," the guard said with a smile.

Travon walked back to his bunk, pulled off his sheets, and folded them along with his other meager jailhouse possessions into his blanket. He then folded his blanket into a ball, tossed it over his shoulder, and returned to the officer's desk.

"I'm ready," he told the smiling guard.

"Walk to the elevator and wait," the guard told him as he reached beneath his desk and pressed a large red button.

The massive steel door that controlled entry into the jail pod slowly slid open. Travon walked out of the unit and down the hall to the elevator, where he stood and waited for its arrival. Soon, the elevator's doors slid open, and Travon boarded the empty lift.

There were no numbers to press, he noticed upon climbing on board. Only a single, steel-covered speaker mounted into the wall and a large camera encased in steel occupied the elevator with him.

"What floor?" a gruff male voice with a deep Southern drawl asked over the crackling speaker.

"Sixth," Travon answered.

The doors slid closed and soon the car began to move. When the doors opened once again, Travon was greeted by an overweight Hispanic guard.

"Robinson?" he asked, while checking the name on his clipboard.

"Yeah." Travon nodded.

"Six D." The guard pointed. "Go down that hall, right up to the door at the end of it, and ring the buzzer."

Travon followed the directions given, and waited patiently as the massive steel doors next to the buzzer slid open. They were slower than the doors on the floor from which he had just come, and seemed infinitely more ominous. Hesitantly, he entered the pod, approached the officer's desk, and presented himself.

"Robinson?" the guard asked, without looking up from his crossword puzzle.

"Yeah."

"Take twenty-eight," the guard told him. "It's upstairs and it's empty."

Travon turned and walked past the telephones, where all of the guys were either yelling and cursing, or talking baby talk. He strolled past the card tables where there were a variety of games being played, with guys doing even more yelling and cursing. He went up the stairs with his over-sized bundle of bedding, and surveyed the numbers painted on the steel door of each room, until finally he arrived at number twenty-eight.

Inside were two empty bunks made of steel, bolted to a steel wall. There was a sink and a toilet built together out of a single piece of steel, bolted to the corner wall just to the right of the door. A steel desk and a built-in stool occupied the left side of the room, where it was also bolted to the steel wall.

Travon threw his linen on the top bunk, and proceeded to make up the bottom one. When this was done, he ventured out of his room, and down the stairs to examine his new surroundings.

At the card tables inside the day area, the prisoners were playing dominoes, tonk, spades, blackjack, and gin. Other prisoners were standing around talking, some were reading books. Travon spied the book cart to his right, and it was there where he headed.

Most of the books on the cart were old, which mattered little because he had done little reading in the last year or so. This would be the perfect time to catch up. He lifted *The Color Purple* and *Whore Son* from the book cart, and turned to go back to his room to begin his reading, but was surprised by two familiar faces that had been standing just behind him. Alonzo and Lil Texas.

"What's up, Tre?" Lil Texas greeted him with a smile. "I knew that we would run into each other again. That was some fucked-up shit you pulled in the Courts that time."

"Whatever," Travon told them. He brushed past them and walked back up the stairs to his room, where he fell onto his bed and opened the first book. A shadow danced across the page of the book, causing him to leap up. Lil Texas was standing in his doorway.

"When you least expect it, expect it," Lil Texas told him, and then turned and walked away.

Travon took the small bag of personal hygiene items that he had been issued and poured them out onto his bed. He took the shaving razor and bit the plastic until he could remove the blade from the plastic handle. Then he used the razor to carve the end of his toothbrush into a sharp point. Travon took the sharpened toothbrush and began scraping it against the concrete floor of his cell.

After an hour of scraping, Travon took his newly created weapon, placed it beneath his pillow, and returned to his novel. If they tried anything, he would be ready for them, he told himself. If they tried anything, he was going to kill Lil Texas.

CHAPTER THIRTY

Bexar County Courthouse
Two Weeks Later

"Your Honor, our suppression issue is intertwined with our discovery motion," Kaufman told the judge. "Unless we have full disclosure, how can we prepare? The whole case revolves around this witness they say exist. We need to be able to investigate this witness in order to examine her credibility. We don't know if she wears glasses, and if she does, how old the prescription is? We don't know whether she's on some type of medication, and if that could have impaired her vision on the night in question. Was she drinking, and if so, how much? What was her exact location at the scene, and how does that affect her perception of what really happened? Is she in a rival gang, and does she have some type of grudge against my client? There are many things we have to know, and the State has provided us with absolutely nothing."

The State's Attorney rose. "All of that can be obtained under direct examination, Your Honor. The State has to protect the witness. Mr. Robinson is a member of the notorious BSV gang. Her safety is our primary concern."

"She is going to testify for the State, Your Honor, so she will have to come forward eventually," Kaufman told the judge. "If she is in fact in such grave danger, then why have her testify at all? My client is incarcerated, he can do no harm. He has never professed to being a member of any gang, nor does he have a history of violence. In fact, he has never been convicted of anything!"

Kaufman pushed his glasses up on his nose. "Your Honor, we don't want to know what she's going to say, we only want to know about her judgment on that night. There was a lot of panicking going on all around her. People were trampled, there was shooting going on all around; was she panicking? Was she running around? Your Honor, it is imperative that we be able to depose this witness. If she proves to be not credible, then her testimony should not be allowed, and furthermore, the statement she gave to the police should be suppressed."

"Your Honor, her credibility is for a jury to decide," the State's Attorney said. "It's obvious that Mr. Kaufman does not want our witness to get in front of the jury to tell her story. He wants to depose her, so he can tear her down and destroy her credibility. He's reaching, Your Honor. He's trying all of his fancy lawyer tricks so that his client can go free and kill again."

Kaufman bolted from his seat. "I object to that last remark, Your Honor! In fact, I object to Mr. Coonts' last statement!"

The judge waved his hand in a settling motion. "What are you objecting for?" He waved his hand around his nearly empty courtroom. "There is no one here. The Motion to Suppress is fair game, counselor, you know that. You can say what you want, just like the State can say whatever it wants. But I warn both of you, in my courtroom, when that jury is seated in that little box over there, you'd both better watch what you say!"

"Your Honor, the State wants to put their witness up on the stand and let her cry her heart out to the jury," Kaufman argued. "We won't be able to question her about gang affiliation, because then they will be able to bring that gang stuff into play. They are going to say, 'Well, since you brought it up,' and they are going to use that to prejudice the jury against my client. They say that I'm the one using fancy lawyer tricks? My client won't stand a chance in hell then. Gang affiliation is another crime in and of itself and it has no reason being brought into this trial."

The prosecutor leapt to his feet. "Wait a minute, you want to question the witness about her gang affiliation and now you say that it has no reason to be brought up? Which is it, counselor? We plan to bring forth witnesses to testify to that fact that Mr. Robinson is a gang member, and that this was a gang-motivated shooting! Bexar County Sheriff's Department records indicate that Mr. Robinson and Mr. Warfield were both gang members. *Rival* gang members."

The prosecutor seated himself with a smile on his face that would make the Grand Canyon seem like a crack in the pavement of a quiet residential street.

Kaufman rose. He harbored a rather large smile of his own.

"Mr. Coonts, I'm glad that you agree with me," Gary Kaufman told the State. "This was a gangland murder, and all of the participants are possibly gang members. It is imperative that we be able to question your witness as to her knowledge, motive, and gang affiliation. That's what this entire trial is basically going to boil down to, isn't it? That's what you're basing your entire case on; using gang affiliation as the motive. So what gang is your witness affiliated with, and what is her motive?"

Kaufman turned and winked at Travon. "These are the things we would like to find out, Your Honor. And to play this out in front of a jury would only confuse matters. This issue is a loose cannon, and it really needs to be resolved beforehand."

The prosecutor turned beet red. "Your Honor, our position is simple. The defendant and his fellow gang members are a threat to society, and to our witness in particular. We feel that her life would be in danger if we bring her forward."

The judge cleared his throat and leaned forward. "There are many confusing issues in the trial, and one thing in particular is most bothersome and confusing to me," he told them in his high-pitched, nasal tone. He turned toward the prosecutor. "So, let me see if I understand this correctly. The State is saying that the witness is in danger if she testifies at this hearing, but that she is not in danger if she testifies at the trial? She will be okay after the trial? These gang members are dangerous now, but they will not be dangerous during or after the trial? Or, is the State saying that after she testifies, it no longer cares if she is in danger?"

The judge frowned, Kaufman smiled, and the two DAs turned even redder.

"That's not what we're saying, Your Honor," the prosecutor said, as he rose from his seat. "The State is concerned about the safety of all its citizens. That is why we are here today, trying to get Mr. Robinson off the streets."

The second DA rose. "Your Honor, we do feel that her life is in greater danger now, if she comes here and testifies. Studies have shown that the danger subsides substantially after the person has been convicted."

"There are remedies, Your Honor," Kaufman told the judge. "We can close the courtroom while she testifies, for one."

The judge turned to the DA. "How do you feel about that? I think that it is logical, if you are worried about her safety. And we won't use her real name. The defense gets to depose the witness, we protect her identity, and everything is fine."

A clerk approached the judge and whispered into his ear. The judge nodded and leaned forward again.

"Gentlemen, another matter has come up, that demands my attention. We'll have to reschedule this hearing, how does Monday look? No, make that Wednesday of next week. If your calendar is full for that date, call my office and let the clerk know. I want this out of the way on Wednesday though, so you'd better be ready. Keep in mind that this is a murder trial, and because it is, I'll be granting wide latitude to both sides, to let each of you prove your cases."

The judge eyed the attorneys sternly. "But before anything is said out of line in front of the jury, I want you to think carefully. I want to see every piece of evidence and know every witness' testimony, beforehand. No wild and loose stunts from either of you."

The judge cleared his throat. "Now back to the issue at hand. Both sides have your witnesses here and ready to take the stand on Wednesday. If you have to cut holes in a paper bag and place it over your witness' heads, then I suggest you do so. But be ready on Wednesday! This goes for both sides. This hearing is adjourned!" The judge banged his gavel, rose, and exited the room through a door to the rear of his courtroom.

Kaufman, standing in the center of the courtroom in his three-thousand-dollar Brioni suit, wheeled and walked to where Travon was seated. "We got this in the bag. We'll tear her apart and discredit her when she gets on the stand. We'll either get it suppressed, or have the State so scared to put her on the stand that they'll dismiss it."

"The judge seemed like he was on our side," Travon told him.

"Well, he doesn't like the shit they're trying to pull. They really don't have a case, plus, he doesn't like the DA who's trying the case. Coonts is a pompous ass."

Kaufman gathered his materials. "Last but not least, the judge and I went to law school together, we worked in the same law firm together, we play golf together, and we live two blocks away from each other. Besides that, once I get on the bench, I'll overturn every God damned case he sends to me." Kaufman threw his head back in laughter.

"If I was paying you, how much would it cost me?" Travon asked.

Kaufman squinted. "This is such an easy case...probably about three hundred grand."

"Shit!" Travon exclaimed. "What in the hell were you doing here that day? I mean, what made you take this case?"

"I was here visiting Judge Weitzer," Kaufman told him. "I'm not even on the list to do pro bono work. So, when the judge asked me to take it, I knew that there was probably something fishy about this case. Judge Weitzer doesn't like it when somebody is getting run over. And he doesn't like prosecutors who try to convict everybody, whether they are guilty or not. A lot of these DAs are just racking up convictions so that when they run for office, they can say how tough they were on crime. The judge doesn't like that."

Kaufman patted Travon on his back. "You're very lucky, because he's a good judge and a fair man. So, now that I have answered your question, why don't you answer mine? You seem like a smart kid; why are you out there getting into trouble? I'm going to get you outta this one, but the next time you might not be so lucky. Next time, you could end up with one of these hanging judges, and some court-appointed lawyer who doesn't give a shit. Make sure that there isn't a next time, kid. Anyway, I'll see you on

Wednesday. Stay outta trouble." Kaufman rose, slapped Travon across his back, and left.

The Weekend

A heavyset Hispanic guard hung up the telephone and shouted: "Robinson, visitation!"

Travon was already dressed and groomed. Tamika told him that she would be coming today, so he had risen early to prepare. He walked to the massive metal door as it slid open, and strolled down the hall to the elevator. When finally it arrived, he climbed on board. There were three others already inside.

"Visitation?" asked a gruff voice over the loudspeaker.

Travon nodded. "Yeah."

The elevator was already moving.

"That's where we're going," one of the other men told him.

The elevator came to a stop and the door opened. A guard was standing at the elevator door with a clipboard in his hand.

"Robinson, number five; Johnson, number eight; Washington, number fifteen; Garcia, number three," the guard barked, reading from the clipboard.

The prisoners walked to a room with numerous glass booths inside. On the other side sat identical booths for each of the visitors. The thick, industrial-strength glass, had thick strands of steel wire running through it. Inside each booth sat a telephone handset for communication with the visitor. Travon lifted his handset and waited.

Tamika strolled into the visiting room, examining each booth as she passed it. Finally, she arrived at Travon's booth. She lifted her telephone handset, wiped it off on her blouse, and placed it to her ear. She could see Travon's lips moving, but could not hear him. She lifted her hand and told him to wait.

Tamika left her booth and walked into an adjacent stall, where she un-plugged the telephone and carried it back with her. She plugged it into the wall and smiled as it came alive.

"What's up, baby?" Travon asked.

"Nothing. How are you?"

"I'm okay," Travon replied. "Why do you sound so sad?"

"I don't know." Tamika shrugged. "I guess I just miss you."

"I miss you too, baby."

"What is the lawyer saying about you coming home?" Tamika asked. "What was all of that stuff about in court yesterday?"

"My lawyer wants the witness to testify at the suppression hearing, but the prosecutor doesn't want her to. The judge says that he wants her to testify, so we gotta go back this Wednesday. I can't wait to see who this bitch is."

"What did I tell you about calling women bitches all of the time?" Tamika admonished him. "You picked up that habit hanging around with those boys over there in the Denver Heights."

"But, baby, this time I'm right. She is a bitch. A nosy, lying one at that. I didn't shoot that dude!"

Tamika nodded. "I know. But you know what? I told you not to go. I had a feeling that it wasn't going to be nothing but trouble. Especially when they said that it was going to be at a nightclub."

"I know, I should have listened to you," Travon told her. "But I will next time. My lawyer says that we are gonna beat this case."

"Tre, they always say that. What am I going to do with two babies and a man in prison for life?"

"You got the money, use it to go to school. Buy the kids some birthday and Christmas presents from me. Bring them to see me every once in a while, and send pictures of them at least twice a year. Things will be all right."

Tamika frowned. "That's not funny."

"I didn't say that it was funny."

She pointed her petite, well-manicured finger at him. "You sound like you're giving up. Don't you give up on me. I thought you just said your lawyer could beat it?"

"I thought you just said that they always say that?"

They shared a laugh.

Tamika gently banged upon the glass with her tiny fist. "Travon, don't tease me. You better hurry up and get outta here. I don't wanna raise two babies alone."

"I'll be out. And after I get out, we are gonna go straight to the court-house and get married."

"I don't wanna hear any jailhouse promises."

"If I get out, I'm going to marry you. But if I get a lot of time, I love you enough to let you go on with your life and find someone else."

Tamika began to sob. "Tre, I'll always be here for you, no matter what. You know I'll marry you."

"I love you, Mika." Travon lifted his hand and touched the glass. Tamika lifted her hand and touched the glass in the same spot.

"I love you too," she said softly.

They lowered their telephones to the counter, turned, and walked out of their respective booths. He turned and watched as she headed for the door. At the door she stopped, turned, and waved sadly. Travon lifted his hand and waved back. He tried to smile, but only sadness spread across his face. Tamika turned and walked away.

"Are you Robinson?" a guard holding a large clipboard asked.

Travon nodded. "Yeah."

"You got another visit," the officer told him. "Use the same booth. You got twenty minutes."

Travon turned and walked back into his designated booth. He was puzzled, because he knew that his mom had to work today, and he could think of no one else who would come to see him. Vera, he thought. It was probably his Aunt Vera. He hoped that she wouldn't become all mushy and begin crying. After his visit with Tamika, more crying was something that he could not take.

Red shirts entered the visitation room, and slowly made their way to his booth: Lil Fade, Capone, and Robert Jr. To his surprise, his cousins did not pick up the telephone, Lil Fade did.

"What's up, Blood?" Lil Fade greeted him cheerily.

Travon shook his head. "Ain't nothing."

"I would send you some snaps, but ain't no need," Lil Fade told him.

"I got some good news for you, Blood. After your court hearing was over, I overheard the prosecutor talking to this bitch inside of this little side office, telling her that she might have to testify on Wednesday. I figured that this was the witness bitch, so me, Capone, and Robert Jr. followed the bitch home. We saw where she lived, and we paid her a little visit. You don't have to worry about no witness anymore, Blood."

Travon turned pale. His stomach became nauseated and he lowered his head.

"Don't be so sad, you'll be outta here next week," Lil Fade told him. "No murder weapon, no witnesses, no motive, no nothing. Don't thank me, though. It's all part of that homie love that I have for you."

Travon lifted his head and his eyes met Lil Fade's. "My lawyer said that we had it beat. You didn't have to kill her."

"Now we know you got it beat for sure," Lil Fade told him. "Besides, it was my pleasure."

Travon shifted his gaze toward his cousins. He searched their eyes for a reason, and pleaded with his own for help. Robert Jr. and Capone both turned and walked away.

"Now listen to me, Travon. This is the second time I've killed for you," Lil Fade told him. "Now I really don't mind, because I enjoy it. It's easy. It makes me feel good. When I have a gun in my hand, I decide who lives and dies. I am one of the gods. Robert Jr., Capone, C-Low, Slow Poke, Quentin, Tech Nine, Lil Anthony, Charlie, Winky, Lil Daddy, Frank, Omar, and Caesar are all gods. It's part of the game. We kill, and we do it often and without remorse. It's inside of you to do these things also."

Lil Fade shook his head, looked down, and smiled. "I love your family. You have so many killas in your family that I wish I was a part of it. And the greatest killa of them all, was your brother Two Low."

Lil Fade lifted a clenched fist and pounded the air. "I know it's inside of you too, I just have to bring it out. Too-Low was so perfect at it. He'd kill just to try out a new gun. It was his high."

Lil Fade pointed toward Travon. "You have the same blood inside of you; you're going to be my Too-Low. If your brother had been a Blood, we would have been unstoppable together. We would have crushed all other sets. But, he was a WCG, and now he's dead. That leaves us with you."

Lil Fade shook his head and leaned in closer. "Don't fight it any longer, just flow with it. The more you fight it, the more people I will have to kill in front of you. Just think of it like this: You will kill to save lives."

He threw his head back and let out a demented laugh. "I'm going to make you immune to feelings. I'm going to make you indifferent to killing. Indifferent to caring about life and death. If I do it, I'll kill mercilessly. But if you do it, then at least you will have a say in who lives and who dies. I love BSV, and I'm going to do whatever it takes to put it on top. I need for you to be my Too-Low, I'm going to make you into my Too-Low. When these people release you, I will be waiting for you in the parking lot. We are gonna take a little ride, and I'll show you how easy it is to control life. We'll decide who lives and who dies on our way home. I'm going to turn you into one of the gods."

Lil Fade slammed the receiver down onto the counter, stared at Travon for several seconds, and then turned and walked away. Travon stood inside the booth with the telephone still to his ear. His entire body was shaking.

CHAPTER THIRTY-ONE

Tuesday

A young African-American guard hung up the telephone. "Robinson! Pack your shit, you're outta here!"

Travon rose from his bed and began to gather his belongings.

"No the hell you ain't!" a familiar voice shouted from behind.

Travon fell forward when the unexpected blow struck him on the back of his head. He cried out, rolled over, and immediately began swinging. Fists struck him all over his body. One landed on his lip and split it on the inside.

"Muthafucka!" Travon shouted. He began kicking desperately. His kicks were landing solidly and his attackers paused.

Suddenly, one of the attackers leapt over his thrusting legs and landed on top of him, neutralizing his only effective defense. He remembered that he had another one.

Travon thrust his hand beneath his pillow and felt around until he found his sharpened toothbrush. One of the attackers struck him in his face again, and instinctively, Travon thrust with his toothbrush, striking flesh. He tried to pull his toothbrush free, but it was lodged deep. The room instantly became silent, the only noise a clogged, choking, gurgling sound. He pulled harder, and finally the toothbrush was freed.

Travon was finally able to shove off the boy on top of him. The second boy saw the blood spewing from his friend's neck and quickly fled. Breathing heavily, Travon stood and turned toward the remaining boy, now spread out across his bed writhing in pain. It was his childhood friend, Justin Robles, also known as Lil Texas, who lay upon his bed dying. Tears fell from Travon's eyes.

"Robinson! I told you to pack your shit! You don't got time to visit with."

Travon turned and faced the six-foot-six, two-hundred-and-sixty-pound, bald-headed guard standing in his doorway. The guard looked at Travon, shifted his gaze toward Lil Texas, and finally, to the bloody shank resting in Travon's trembling hand. Slowly, Travon closed his eyes and tilted his head back. His thoughts shifted to the children he would never be able to teach how to ride a bicycle. The children he would see take their first steps through a thick prison glass window. The children he would never walk in a park with, fly a kite with, or play football with. Tamika would marry someone else, his children would grow up without him, and he would spend the rest of his days trying to survive on some gladiator farm.

The guard stepped inside the cell and extended his hand. Travon handed him the sharpened toothbrush. The guard peered into Travon's eyes and shook his head.

"I said pack your shit," the guard told him. "Go to the elevator and tell the muthafucka to take you to the basement so you can process out."

Travon glanced over his shoulder toward Lil Texas, who had stopped gurgling, and then turned back toward the guard.

"I grew up in the Lincoln Courts as an LCG Blood," the guard said softly. "I know what's up. I saw them when they ran in here, and I saw Alonzo when he took off outta here. I can pretty much figure out what happened." He pulled a handkerchief from his back pocket and tossed it to Travon. "Wipe the blood off of your lip and throw the handkerchief in the trash can on the way out. When you get downstairs, keep sucking on your lip so that no one sees the bleeding."

Travon nodded and pressed the kerchief against his lip.

"These white folks got enough of us in prison already," the guard continued. "I'll take care of this shit, you just get the fuck outta here and stay outta trouble. Get past that gang banging shit real quick too, because all you stupid muthafuckas is doing out there is killing each other. Go on."

Travon quickly gathered his belongings and bolted for the elevator.

❖❖❖

Travon was in the last processing cell when he heard the alarm go off. Officers dressed in all black paramilitary gear ran out of the processing area to assist the officer in trouble. He had no doubt in his mind that the officer on the sixth floor had just been attacked by an inmate with a shank. The guard, while fighting for his life, accidentally stabbed the inmate with the shank. The remaining guards continued to process inmates in or out of the facility.

Once finally processed out, Travon walked to the rear of the processing area, where another guard let him out into the lobby area of the first floor. Travon walked straight to a pay phone where he called Tamika collect.

"Hello?"

"Tamika?"

"Yeah, Tre?"

"Yeah, baby, it's me. Listen, I need for you to come and pick me up. Use my car and bring all the money with you. We gotta leave and disappear for a few days. We'll go to Houston and I'll buy another car there, then we'll sneak back into town in a couple of days and stay with your mom while we look for an apartment. I don't want anyone to know where we live, or what kind of car we drive. We'll sell the old car when we get to Houston, but the main thing is, we gotta leave right now!"

"Tre, you didn't escape, did you?"

"No, girl! I'm calling from the jail's lobby area. Just hurry up and don't let nobody see you, or know where you're going."

"What about my mom?"

"We'll call her from Houston; I'll explain things to her then."

"What about your Aunt Vera?" Tamika asked. "Do you want me to go by and get some clothes for you to wear?"

"No!" Travon shouted into the receiver. "That's the last place I want you to go! Tamika, I need to disappear. I don't want Marcus, Darius, or nobody else to know."

"Tre, why? I don't understand what the rush is. What's with all of this sneaking around?"

"Tamika, I'm leaving them," Travon told her. "I'm leaving the Heights. If they find out, they'll kill me!"

"What? Who? Tre, they're your cousins."

"Not them, Lil Fade. Just hurry up!"

"Okay, baby, okay. Just calm down, I'm on my way."

Travon slammed the telephone down into its cradle and walked to the front of the lobby, where he peered out of the massive glass windows. Soon, a black coroner's van pulled up.

"Shit." He had forgotten about the body upstairs.

Travon began to pace back and forth. He sat for a short period of time, and then rose and resumed his pacing. She seemed to be taking forever.

Finally, a horn blew. It was a familiar horn, from a familiar car, with a familiar face seated behind the steering wheel. It was Tamika.

Travon raced down the steps of the Bexar County jail to his car, where he flung open the passenger side door and leapt inside. He and Tamika embraced.

"Tre, what happened?" she asked. Her tears began flowing.

"I have to get away from Lil Fade. He's crazy. He killed her, he killed the witness."

Tamika gasped and covered her mouth with both of her hands. "Oh my God, Tre! Are you sure?"

Travon nodded. "Yeah, he told me in the visitation room, right after you left."

"I saw Robert and Capone in the lobby when I was leaving that day, but I didn't see him."

"He was there, trust me. He was there." Travon turned and stared out of the window. "C'mon, baby, let's go. Let's get out of here."

"We need gas, Tre."

Travon laughed. "That's right. I was about to get some gas when I got arrested. My luck with gas stations hasn't been too good."

Tamika joined in the laughter. "We can make it to Stop N Go on I Thirty-Five. That way, we can get on the highway, and stay on the highway."

"We're not going to Dallas, baby," Travon explained. "We're going to

Houston. We got to take Interstate Ten to Houston, so go through down-town and we'll stop and get gas at that Diamond Shamrock across from the Alamo dome."

"Okay, and then you get behind the wheel," Tamika told him.

❖❖❖

They drove through downtown, where traffic was light for a Tuesday afternoon. The ride to the filling station took only ten minutes. Tamika pulled up next to the pump, and turned off the car. Travon opened his door and climbed out.

"I'll be right back," he told her.

"Wait, I'm coming in."

"Girl, just tell me what you want and I'll get it. It takes ten minutes just for you to get out of the car."

"We're hungry, and we haven't eaten lunch yet," Tamika protested. "Besides, I don't even know what I want yet."

"We'll stop for something to eat once we get out of the city."

Tamika waddled past him. "C'mon, boy."

They entered the store and Travon walked to the soda cooler, where he got a Big Red soda. He then walked to the stand where the chips were, and grabbed himself a bag of Munchies. He peered over the aisle at Tamika, who was still trying to decide what type of candy she wanted.

"Get me a pack of M&M's with peanuts," Travon told her. "I'ma go and start pumping the gas. I'm gonna pay the man for the stuff, so don't forget to get my change."

Travon walked to the register, where he handed the clerk thirty dollars. He turned and pointed toward Tamika. "Give her my change. It's just this, whatever she wants, and twenty in the tank. I think it's pump number four."

The clerk nodded, sat the money to the side, and Travon turned and walked out of the store. He pulled open his bag of potato chips, wanting to eat a few before he started pumping the smelly gas.

"Well, well, well, look what we have here," a familiar voice called out.

Travon peered up from his bag of chips to find Dejuan standing outside of his big white Mercedes, which was parked on the other side of the gas pump from his car. Quentin was seated in the backseat, while Tech Nine was standing outside with the passenger side door open. Dupriest was nestled in the backseat on the passenger side.

Travon's first instinct was to run back inside the store, but then he remembered that Tamika was there, along with his unborn children. Besides, running inside would be pointless, as Quentin and Tech Nine would simply get out of the car, walk inside of the store, and blow his brains out in front of everyone.

Quentin lifted an M-16 A2 Shorty assault rifle and pointed it at him. Dejuan walked around to the driver's side of his car, where he climbed inside.

"You jacked me for five ounces, your punk-ass homeboys got me for eighty grand and all my jewelry, plus your little ass is a turncoat!" Dejuan told him.

Tech Nine climbed into the big Benz and closed his door, just as Dejuan cranked the engine. Travon's heart slowed down to a semi-normal pace when he realized that they were about to leave, and that there existed a marginal chance that they would not kill him.

Dejuan peered over his shoulder toward Quentin. "Do that muthafucka!"

Quentin smiled and took aim, just as Tamika exited the store. He peered up from his rifle and stared at her for several seconds, before a sadistic smile slid across his face.

Travon watched in horror as Quentin's rifle slowly slid to the left, moving away from him to Tamika and the twins.

"Noooo!" Travon screamed. He raced toward Tamika, desperately trying to be in the path of the gun. The bullet was faster.

Quentin's assault rifle released its energy, and instantly, Tamika fell. Slowly, Dejuan's S600 Mercedes pulled away, with laughter pouring from the backseat.

Travon dropped to his knees and lifted Tamika's head into his lap. He began to move her hair out of her face.

"Tamika, talk to me!" he shouted.

Tamika smiled, and Travon began crying uncontrollably. He pressed his face against hers. Slowly, Tamika's angelic smile drifted from her face, and she closed her eyes.

CHAPTER THIRTY-TWO

Downtown Baptist Hospital

Travon paced nervously around the hospital waiting room, waiting for Tamika to come out of surgery. A doctor wearing green surgical garb walked in and approached the waiting room desk. The nurse behind the desk pointed at Travon and the doctor turned and approached him.

"Hi, I'm Dr. Markowitz. Are you the young man who rode inside of the ambulance with Ms. Johnson?"

Travon nodded nervously. "Yeah, Doc, how's she doing?"

The doctor frowned. "Are you her brother?"

"No." Travon shook his head frantically. "No, I'm her fiancé."

Travon's age gave the doctor pause. "Well, sir. Your name is?"

"Tre. Travon Robinson. How is she?"

"Well, Mr. Robinson, by the grace of Almighty God, we were able to save the babies. Luckily, she was close to downtown and the paramedics were able to revive her long enough. The boys will be fine. They will have to stay here for observation for a while, but they are going to make it."

"Wait a minute, what do you mean, long enough? What's wrong with Tamika? Please tell me she's okay, Doc."

The doctor looked down and shook his head. "I'm sorry, son. We did everything we possibly could."

"But they said she would be okay! They revived her, Doc, I saw them!

They revived her! God damn it, that's not fair!" Travon fell to his knees and began crying heavily. "It's not fair!"

He leaned forward, until his head rested against the cold, white, sterile tile floor. "Oh, God, nooooo! Take me instead!" Travon pounded the floor with his fist. "Take meeee!"

Tamika's mother and two of her aunts ran into the waiting room. They spied Travon on the ground crying hysterically, and Tamika's mother fell into the arms of her sister.

"My baby!" she screamed. "My baby!"

❖❖❖

Travon remained at the hospital through the night and well into the morning. He stayed long after Tamika's mother had identified the body and left. He stayed long after the detectives had questioned him and left. He stayed long after the shifts had changed and the tears had dried. He sat alone in the corner of the waiting room, staring at a blank wall. In his mind, the doctor continuously walked into the room and told him that Tamika was okay and that he could go in and see her. Over and over again the scene was replayed inside of his mind, as he wished for the alternative, as he wished for what was not to be.

Darius strolled into the waiting room, spied his cousin seated in the corner, and approached him. "It's time to go. C'mon."

Travon continued to stare at the wall.

Darius leaned forward, grabbed Travon's arm, and gently pulled him up. Travon turned, and stared into Darius' eyes.

"Why, Darius, why? Why not me?"

Darius shook his head. "I don't know why, T. I don't know."

Travon's tears returned, and he and Darius embraced. They stood in the hospital lobby and held each other for a long time.

"C'mon," Darius told him, nodding toward the exit.

The boys walked out of the hospital, climbed into Darius' car and slowly pulled away.

"People are saying it was Dejuan," Darius told him.

"It was," Travon confirmed. His voice cracked. "He gave the order, and Quentin pulled the trigger. He told Quentin to kill me for the five ounces and the mall jacking. Quentin aimed at me, and then Mika walked out, and he killed her."

Travon's tears came again. "He killed her."

"We'll take care of it, don't worry about shit. We'll get them niggaz." Darius turned on his stereo, but kept the volume low.

Travon leaned against the passenger side window, and cried the rest of the way home.

Darius pulled up to the house. There were people everywhere. Robinson's cousins had been arriving since the previous evening, bringing with them a sizable arsenal and many friends. Aunt Vera, JoBeth, and LaTonya had abandoned the house, and went to stay at Chicken's house, in order to make room for all of their out-of-town relatives and guests.

Travon climbed out of the car, walked into the house and up the stairs to his bedroom. It had been turned into a war room. Robert Jr., Frank, Caesar, Winky, Lil Daddy, Capone, Omar, Marcus, and Romeo were all there.

"What's up, kinfolk?" several of the boys asked.

"Hey, what's up?" Travon asked, acknowledging them back. He walked to his bed, which he climbed into and covered up.

"I'm telling you, the way to get this muthafucka is through his wallet!" Robert Jr. told the assembled boys. "All of them muthafuckas revolve around money. It's their whole life, it's they whole world, and that's how we get them. All of this shoot-'em-up, bang-bang shit y'all are talking ain't gonna cut it."

"Man, we can find out where this dude stays, kick in the door, kill his ass, and it *will* be final!" Winky declared.

Darius and Lil Fade walked into the room.

"We gotta get all of them at once," Darius told them. "Just getting Dejuan won't do. Quentin pulled the trigger."

"The only time they are all together is if they are smashin' somewhere like the mall, or to a concert or something," Marcus added. "And then they'll be too deep."

"I want this shit over with in one swoop," Robert Jr. told them.

"We all know that these dudes think money, so all we need to do is set a money trap," Frank suggested. "Bring them fools to us."

Lil Fade snapped his fingers. "I got an idea. They don't know Frank or his homeboys, so we use them to set these niggaz up. We put out the word that they are some outta-town ballers and that they are trying to move some weight. Remember, Dejuan is eighty grand short, and Dupriest, Quentin, and Tech Nine can't resist a jack."

"How can we guarantee they'll bite?" Frank asked. "How do we make sure they'll get the word; and even if they do get it, how do we know when they'll try something?"

"If we put the word out through Missy at her beauty shop, then it will definitely get out," Lil Fade told them. "Just tell her fat ass not to tell anybody, and she is guaranteed to tell everybody. Secondly, we put a time limit on how long y'all will be in town. Let's say, three days. Then we just sit and wait for the rats to come to the cheese."

"Where do we plant this cheese?" Omar asked.

"That's easy, the Sky Ridge Motel," Marcus answered. "It's near the highway, not too cheap and sleazy, not expensive, and it's privately owned. It's also quiet and isolated. Just the kind of place out-of-town ballers would stay in, if they were carrying weight. It's perfect."

Robert Jr. turned to Romeo. "Get in touch with the girls, we'll need them for this. They'll have to go to Missy's with the guys, get their hair done, and run their mouths."

Romeo nodded. "Something they'll be good at."

"We'll need a mini van for this one, and some fake driver's licenses to rent the room," Darius told them.

"I'll take care of that," Lil Fade said.

"I want in."

Everyone in the room turned toward the bed.

"I wanna kill the bastards who killed Mika," Travon told them. "I wanna kill Quentin. I wanna do it myself."

"Are you sure you're up to this?" Marcus asked. "We can handle it, dog."

"It might be better if you just rested up and let us handle this, Tre,"

Darius told him. "You're angry now, and anger brings carelessness. I don't need any fuck-ups on this."

"Darius, you know I have to go," Travon told him. "You know I gotta do this."

Darius shifted his gaze to the floor and nodded. "Okay."

CHAPTER THIRTY-THREE

Sky Ridge Motel
Night Two

Robert Jr., Lil Fade, Capone, Romeo, and Travon were inside a stolen, burgundy Toyota Previa minivan. It was their night to watch the motel room.

"They gotta hit tonight," Lil Fade told them. "If I was gonna jack in this situation, I would do it as soon as possible. The quicker you hit, the less dope they will have sold, and the better chance of you hitting them first."

Romeo checked his watch. "One time is about to change shifts, so they gotta hit soon. If they're smart, that is."

"If they don't hit tonight, then Darius, Marcus, Winky, Tre, and Omar will just have to come back tomorrow night," Robert told them.

"Do you think they got the word?" Travon asked.

"Hell yeah!" Lil Fade answered. "That bitch Missy can't hold water."

Romeo, who was seated behind the steering wheel, began tapping on the dashboard excitedly. "Uh-oh, peep this, peep this!"

A white Cadillac had pulled into the parking lot and was creeping along slowly. The boys watched with a fierce intensity through the van's tinted windows as the Cadillac parked and its occupants climbed out.

"Bingo!" Romeo announced.

Hatred swelled inside of Travon as he watched Quentin creep in between the cars parked in the motel's parking lot, and make his way up to the motel room. Travon grabbed his .308 Galil assault rifle and tried to exit the van. Capone grabbed him.

"Tre! Tre! You are gonna fuck things up! Wait!" Capone told him. "We'll get them all, just like we planned. Just be patient."

Lil Fade turned toward Travon. "Don't fuck things up, Blood."

For a brief moment, Travon debated whether he should kill Lil Fade, and just try to catch Quentin another time. In the end, he decided that killing Quentin was more important. He relaxed.

"Dejuan ain't with them," Romeo announced.

"We know that," Lil Fade told him. "We got another plan for Dejuan; this is for his boys."

"Dejuan ain't gonna get his hands dirty; he's a pussy," Robert Jr. declared. "He just gives the orders, and his brainless followers carry them out."

Travon shifted uncomfortably in his seat. Robert Jr. had apparently forgotten that Too-Low had been one of Dejuan's most devoted followers and trusted friends.

"Well, it looks like he sent Tech Nine, Quentin, Dupriest, Pop, and his brother Shawny to take care of this one," Romeo announced.

Capone sat up and watched the boys maneuver the last remaining yards to the motel room. "It's almost show time. They're getting ready to kick in the door."

"There they go!" Romeo shouted.

"Go! Go! Go!" Capone shouted, hitting Romeo's shoulder.

Romeo started the van and raced through the parking lot, bringing the van to a screeching halt just in front of the motel room door. Lil Fade slid open the van's huge rear sliding door, and he, Travon, Capone, and Robert Jr. commenced firing.

The fire from the automatic weapons turned night into day again, and quickly decimated the motel room. Bullets from the boys' high-powered rifles penetrated the thin motel walls striking wood, drywall, tile, and flesh. Some continued through the first set of walls and penetrated others' walls, where they struck down unintended victims. When finally the boys had expended all of the rounds from their magazines, they loaded new ones. All with the exception of Lil Fade, who leapt from the van and lobbed a hand grenade into the motel room. As the grenade flew inside, Quentin and Tech Nine flew out. Lil Fade quickly drew his handgun from his waistband and fired four shots into Tech Nine's back. Tech Nine fell to the ground instantly.

Lil Fade placed his handgun back in his waistband and leapt back into the van. Romeo hit the gas and pulled away from the motel room, just as the grenade exploded. The section of the building where the explosion detonated was transformed into a gigantic blue-and-orange inferno. The explosion shattered many of the windows of the nearby buildings and cars.

"Pull around!" Travon shouted.

Romeo peered over his shoulder. "What?"

"Pull around!" Travon shouted again.

"Tre, we gotta go!" Romeo told him.

Travon lifted Lil Fade's shirt and snatched the pistol from his waistband. He pointed the weapon at Romeo. "I said, pull around."

Out of the corner of his eye, Travon spied Capone moving. Using his free hand, he reached over the seat, grabbed Romeo's pistol from his lap, and then pointed it at Capone.

"Don't fuck with me, Capone!"

Reluctantly, Romeo turned the van around and headed back into the parking lot of the demolished motel.

"Step on it!" Travon told him.

Romeo accelerated. They could now see Quentin running through a neighboring field. Travon removed the pistol from Romeo's head and pointed it toward a sprinting Quentin.

"Catch him!" Travon ordered.

"What?" Romeo shouted.

"Drive through the fuckin' field, Romeo!" Travon told him.

The van jumped the curb and raced into the field. They rapidly closed the distance between themselves and Quentin, who was now merely twenty yards away. Quentin came to a large wooden fence that separated the field from a neighboring residential area and rapidly scaled it. Romeo drove up to the fence and stopped.

Travon threw open the sliding rear door of the van and leapt out. Romeo,

Capone, Lil Fade, and Robert Jr. watched in amazement as Travon scaled the fence in pursuit of Quentin.

"Fuck it, he'll be all right," Robert Jr. told them. He tapped Romeo's shoulder. "Let's go."

Romeo turned the van around and headed out of the field toward a strip filled with fast-food restaurants. From there, they entered onto a main strip, and then the highway heading home.

❖❖❖

Travon ran through the dark alley between the large wooden fence and the chain-link fences that marked the boundaries of the nearby houses. Quentin, unaware he was still being pursued, slowed considerably. Travon continued his pursuit at full stride until he came within ten yards of his prey. He didn't want to fire his weapon just yet, because it would only bring the police. He did not want the police anywhere close tonight, as he was determined to finish Quentin off.

Quentin hopped a chain-link fence and entered into a nearby backyard. Travon hopped the same fence. Hearing the rattle, Quentin turned and spied Travon in pursuit. He quickly picked up speed and hopped a gate leading into the front yard, where he pulled his weapon from his waistband. Quentin headed for the safety of a parked car and ducked behind the front fender.

When Travon emerged from the shadows of the side of the house, he received a welcome present from Quentin. Bullets struck the corner of the house near Travon's head, causing splinters to fly into the side of his face. Travon immediately dropped down and returned fire. His bullets sprinkled the front of the car from which Quentin had fired. Quentin himself was no longer there, as he had fled after he fired. The hunt was no longer a quiet one.

Hearing the rattle of a chain-link fence, Travon rose and ran into the backyard of the house directly across the street. He arrived in time to see Quentin hopping another fence. Travon fired, missed, and continued his pursuit.

Quentin jumped another gate and ran across the front lawn of this home. Travon followed. They ran across the street and entered into another backyard, but this time, it was not empty. A large Rottweiler attacked Quentin, and he quickly silenced the dog by putting a bullet through its head. Travon fired again, and this time, Quentin was struck. He cried out but continued to run.

Quentin scaled another fence, ran into the front yard, and again waited just around the corner. Travon hopped the gate leading to the front yard, and Quentin stepped from around the corner and fired. Travon fell. He could feel a burning sensation in his side where Quentin's bullet had grazed him deeply, but he was alive.

Travon rose from the dirt, cursed, and continued forward. Quentin was crossing the street just as he was charging through the front yard. Upon seeing Travon, Quentin cursed, stopped, turned and fired again. Bullets peppered the house just inches away from Travon's head. Quentin turned, ran up to the front door of the nearby house, blew the lock off, and ran inside. Travon ran up to the home and entered. Upon noticing that the back door was open, he continued through the residence, and ran into the backyard. Quentin's gamble had failed; Travon had not paused as he had hoped he would.

Two houses down, Travon heard another growl, and then a gunshot, followed by a loud yelp as a dog cried out in pain. He ran toward the gunshot and hopped two fences without even touching them. He happened upon the wounded dog, and spied Quentin running through a nearby alley. Without pause, Travon leapt the fence and headed into the alley.

Bitten, shot, and exhausted, Quentin had slowed considerably. Travon quickly gained ground on him. Hearing a splash from a puddle of water, Quentin turned and spied Travon behind him. He quickly lifted his weapon and fired, but after only three shots his weapon clicked. He cursed and through it down in the mud.

Now defenseless, wounded, and even more desperate, Quentin emerged from the alley and ran to a nearby house, where he began to pound upon the door. Travon emerged from the alley and fired twice. After the second shot, his weapon clicked, so he discarded it and pulled out Romeo's gun.

Travon fired again, and bullets struck the door just inches away from Quentin's left arm. Frightened, Quentin took off running again, but this time only as far as two doors down, where he dove through a large, living room window. Travon, like a wild animal who had tasted blood, dove through the window right behind his prey.

"Please." Quentin lifted his hands into the air and pleaded for mercy. He lay on the living room floor between the coffee table and the couch. "I'm sorry. I'll pay you! Don't kill me, please!"

Travon rose from the floor, walked to where Quentin was lying, and pointed his weapon at him. "Lil Fade says that you're one of the gods, so resurrect yourself, muthafucka!"

Travon emptied Romeo's sixteen remaining shots into Quentin's face, and then turned and walked calmly out of the house, by way of the window from which he had entered.

After struggling with himself for so long, Travon the human had lost. He had now become a full-blooded monster.

CHAPTER THIRTY-FOUR

Next Day
Aunt Vera's House

It was two o'clock in the afternoon. Lil Fade, Marcus, Romeo, Cibon, and Antwon were all seated around Aunt Vera's porch. Romeo stopped in mid-sentence, although his mouth remained open. The others quickly turned and stared in the direction in which he was staring.

Travon was walking down the middle of the street clutching his side. He walked with a pronounced limp, and the elastic waistband of his normally white boxers was a deep, crimson red. Lil Fade smiled.

The news had given a fairly decent account of the incident, except they, like the detectives, were at a complete loss as to who had chased down the victim and why. Travon walked into the yard.

"What's up, Blood?" Marcus greeted him. "The news say that you pumped seventeen shots into that sucker."

Travon walked his gaze across the assembled group of boys. He did not return Marcus's smile. "Where's everyone else at?"

"Out looking for you," Antwon told him. "We was all worried when you didn't make it back last night."

"I told y'all he would be all right!" Lil Fade told them. "Tre is a mutha-fuckin' killa."

"You should have seen him in action last night," Romeo said. "Tre took off after that fool like a madman. You really wasn't gonna smoke me last night, was ya, kinfolk?"

Travon shifted his gaze to the street, allowing Romeo's question to hang in the thick humidity. Lil Fade broke the tension.

"I knew you had it in ya, it just needed to be brought out. It was inevitable. From now on, we gonna call you Baby-Low."

A sarcastic smile spread across Romeo's face. "Yeah, just like Too-Low."

"Dejuan called Darius today, he says that he wants to call it quits between us and them," Marcus told Travon. "He says that he didn't tell Quentin to kill Tamika and that he thought that it was fucked up that he did. He lost his brother and a couple of his homeboys last night, and now he just wants to bury his brother and homies in peace; and then he's leaving town."

"In peace? Doesn't he mean, in pieces!" Lil Fade let out a demonic laugh.

"He offered two keys to call it quit so he can leave," Marcus continued. "He says that he just wants us to respect his brother's funeral, and leave his other two brothers alone after he leaves."

"What did Darius say?" Travon asked.

"He said of course, leave the two birds with Missy," Marcus told him. "And then he hung up the phone and we started thinking about how we could kill this dude before he left town."

Travon laughed and shook his head. Deep down, he knew that Darius wouldn't sell him out.

"I got an idea," Marcus told them. "Remember what Lil Fade said at the mall that time we jacked Dejuan?"

Travon shrugged. He didn't know which thing in particular Marcus was referring to.

"Yeah, well, they ain't gonna hold his dick for him when he fucks either," Marcus told them.

"What do you mean?" Travon folded his arms and shifted his weight to one side.

"His bitch!" Marcus told them.

Travon shook his head. "Nobody, and I mean nobody, knows where Dejuan lives."

"Not that bitch, I'm talking about his piece of candy on the side," Marcus explained. "Sympathy pussy is the best pussy, and Dejuan's been trying to push up on Tangela's fine ass lately. I'll bet you anything he's gonna run up over there for a little TLC in the next couple of days. All we gotta do is catch his ass over there, and pop him."

"Why come nobody ever did this before?" Travon asked.

"Because we never had any reason to just outright kill them niggaz," Marcus told him. "We just used to serve them niggaz to get the message across to not fuck with us. Sometimes we would ride by and pop one of their homeboys whenever they popped one of ours. There's a difference between banging and murder, Tre. Some of us just don't know the difference."

Lil Fade smiled at Marcus's little dig at him.

"Whatever, just let me know what's up," Travon told him. "I gotta go and take a shower and get some rest. Mika's wake is tonight, and the funeral is tomorrow."

Travon turned and went inside.

Next Day

Travon, Marcus, and Darius rode home together from Tamika's funeral. Her family had totally shunned Travon during the services, and did not allow him to sit with the family. They blamed him for Tamika's death, which disturbed him deeply.

Travon reached into the front seat and tapped Darius upon his shoulder. "Drop me off at Poison's apartment."

Darius shook his head. "I don't understand you, Tre. Your ass is in love with Poison, but you was acting like you really cutted for Tamika. What's up with that?"

"I did cut for Mika. Me and her was having kids together. She was my heart, but Poison is my heart also."

"I think both of them is cool, but I just don't understand how you can cut for both of them," Darius told him. "They are like night and day. One is ghetto and one was Gucci."

"Shit, you know how it is. Sometimes I need to kick it real, and sometimes I needed to kick it different. Mika was from a whole different world. She turned me on to a whole lot of different things. For me, she kinda represented want I wanted to be and what I wanted to have. Poison reminds me of who I am, and where I come from. She keeps it real."

Darius nodded. "Yeah, if it's one thing Poison does, it's keep it real." He pulled into the parking lot of Saddle Ridge Apartments, and Travon climbed out of the car.

"All right, I'll holler at y'all later," Travon told them. He closed the car door, turned, and ran up the stairs to Poison's apartment, where he pounded on the door.

"Hey, baby," Poison greeted him when she opened the door. "Come on in."

Travon bounded into the apartment, kissed Poison on her cheek, and then seated himself on the couch. She sat next to him and began to caress his arm.

"I wish that I could have gone with you and comforted you," she told him.

Travon shifted his gaze to the carpet. "That wouldn't have been right, you know that."

"Yeah." Poison nodded. "So how are the babies doing?"

"Better. The doctor says that it's a miracle that they both survived."

"Have you given them names yet?"

"Yeah, I named them Travon and Davon, after me and my brother."

"Oh, baby, that's so nice!" Poison exclaimed. She wrapped her arms around him. "I can't wait to see them, and hold them, and play with them."

"Huh?"

"I said that I can't wait to play with them. I really want to help you with them."

"You're moving a little fast, ain't you?"

"What? Wait a minute," she told him. "I didn't say that I wanted to be their mother, or take their mother's place, or anything like that. I'm not trying to be all up under you either, I just wanted to help you. If you don't want my help, then cool."

Poison shrugged, rose from the couch, and walked into the kitchen.

Travon rose and followed her. "There you go; tripping."

"I'm not tripping." Poison pulled a large steel pot down from her cabinet and slammed it onto the stove. "I'm just thinking what a fool I am."

Travon extended his arms into the air. "What's that supposed to mean?"

Poison waved her hand dismissing him. "Nothing."

"Naw, don't nothing me. Last time you nothin'ed me, we argued for two days."

"I know that you are going through a lot today, so let's just drop it."

"Man, what's with this attitude all of a sudden?"

Poison pointed her finger at his face. "I'm just thinking how funny it is that I'm good enough to fuck, but I'm not good enough to touch your kids."

"I didn't say that."

"You didn't have to say it, I know what you meant." Poison turned away and walked to the refrigerator.

Travon stepped into her small kitchen area. "Don't put words in my mouth."

Poison closed the refrigerator and turned to face him again, holding two steaks. "I'm not putting words in your mouth."

She walked to the sink and sat the steaks down in the basin. Then she faced him again. "You know what, things have changed between us, Tre. It's not your fault, it's mines. When I met you, I was talking to Kilo, and you was already talking to Tamika. I fell in love with you, and I had already quit talking to Kilo."

She extended her finger into his face again. "But you kept on messing with me and Tamika at the same time. I should have stopped it then, but I didn't. I liked being with you, the few moments that we did spend together, so I kept on. I accepted Tamika, because she was there first, and I knew about her. But now she's gone, and I still feel like I'm second. That shit I will not stand for!"

"I love you too!"

Poison waved him off. "Bullshit!"

"I do," Travon whispered. "I love you."

"How the fuck can you love two people?"

"Tamika gave me something that you couldn't. You gave me something that Tamika couldn't. I loved both of you for who you are."

Poison waved her hand through the air again. "That shit sounds like a bunch of bullshit! An excuse. And a weak-ass one at that!"

Travon turned away. "I knew that I shouldn't have come over here today! I don't have to take this bullshit!"

Poison jabbed her finger toward the door. "Then get the fuck out! There's the door, nigga!"

Travon stormed past her. "Crazy bitch!"

"Bitch? Bitch?" Poison opened one of her kitchen drawers and pulled out a large revolver. She pointed it at his face. "Bitch? Nigga, don't you *ever* disrespect me like that again. I don't know who in the fuck you think you are talking to, but I'm not one of your little hood rat tramps. If you ever, ever call me a bitch again, I'll blow your muthafuckin' face off. Do you understand me?"

Travon nodded solemnly.

"Good. I'm from the muthafuckin' streets too, don't ever forget that." Poison lowered the revolver and un-cocked the hammer.

Travon walked to where she was standing, and once they stood nose to nose, began to kiss her passionately. With the gun still in her hand, she wrapped her arms around him and squeezed him tightly. He wrapped his arms around her waist and lifted her into the air. Kissing and breathing heavily, Travon carried her off into the bedroom.

CHAPTER THIRTY-FIVE

Later That Evening

Someone knocked on the bedroom door, rousing them.

"What?" Poison asked.

"Girl, y'all come on out here and eat this shit before it gets cold," Peaches shouted through the bedroom door.

"All right." Poison nudged Travon in his side.

"All right, I'm up," he told her.

Together they climbed out of bed, got semi-dressed, and walked into the living room. Lil Fade was seated on the black leather sectional, eating a hamburger. Peaches was on the floor across from him, removing food from the McDonald's bags and placing it on the coffee table.

"What's up, girl?" Poison asked.

"Here." Peaches handed her some bags. "Y'all need to quit making all that noise when y'all fuckin'."

"Girl, just put a pillow over your head, I gots to make noise when I'm getting my groove on," Poison told her, as she rummaged through the bags. She pulled out a burger and handed it to Travon. "Where's the sodas and fries?"

Poison pulled out an order of fries and handed them to Travon, who was already devouring his burger. Satisfied, Poison unwrapped her burger and bit down into it. She chewed for a few moments, and then turned to Peaches.

"Girl, this got tomatoes in it?" Poison asked.

"I ordered yours with no tomatoes," replied Peaches, shaking her head. "You must've given Tre the wrong one."

Poison spat the moist glob of chewed food into her hand, jumped up, and ran to the bathroom. Travon sat his food down on the coffee table, and walked after her. He arrived at the bathroom door just as she was flushing the toilet.

"What's wrong?" he asked.

"Nothing." She shook her head. "Tomatoes just upset my stomach." Poison turned on the faucet and proceeded to rinse her mouth out in the sink.

"Since where?" Travon asked. "We done ate a million burgers together and they never bothered you before."

"I just realized something; you're a very nosey fellow." Poison removed her toothbrush from its holder, rinsed it off, and then applied a generous amount of toothpaste.

Travon stood in silence and stared at her. His staring made her uncomfortable.

"What do you want me to say?" she asked. "They bother me now, okay?" She lifted the toothbrush to her mouth and began brushing.

Travon extended his hands into the air. "What's with the attitude? I thought I worked all of that out of you earlier." He laughed.

Poison stopped brushing and frowned at him.

"Damn, your mood swings are worse than Mika's, and she was...pregnant." Travon's gaze turned into a glare, and he frowned and shook his head.

Poison stopped brushing, glanced at him, and upon noticing his expression, resumed her brushing at a much more frantic pace.

"Uh-un, this is bullshit," Travon told her. "I recognize the symptoms. How long? And don't bullshit me either!"

Poison ignored him and continued her frantic brushing. He grabbed her arm, stopping her in mid stroke. She pulled the toothbrush from her mouth.

"Okay, I'm pregnant!" she shouted, spitting toothpaste everywhere. "Is that what you want to hear? I'm pregnant!"

Travon stepped back. "Is it mines?"

Poison rinsed the toothpaste from her mouth. When finished, she stood erect and stared at him. "I'll bet you didn't ask Tamika that. Thanks a lot, Travon."

Poison brushed past him and stormed from the bathroom.

Travon followed. "I mean, it could be Kilo's, right?"

Poison halted. "No it couldn't. I had just started talking to Kilo a month before I started talking to you. I never did nothing with him, because I didn't trust him. Before you, I hadn't had sex for damn near ten months. Regardless of what you and your little friends like to say about us, we ain't hoes." Poison turned and continued walking.

Travon followed. "I'm sorry, I didn't know. Why didn't you tell me before?"

"Tell you what? That I'm not a ho, or that I'm pregnant?"

"You know what I'm talking about!" Travon shouted.

"Because I didn't want nothing from you, Tre!" Poison snapped. She pointed her finger in his face. "Do you hear me? I don't want shit from you! Besides, you and *Mika* already had y'all the perfect little family."

"That's bullshit!" Travon shouted, flailing his arms through the air. "That shit is fucked up and you know it! I have a right to know, that's my kid too!"

"Oh, so now you're sure it's yours?" She placed her hand on her hip. "A minute ago you weren't. You went from '*is it mines*,' to '*I have a right to know*.' Nigga, you crazy."

Poison turned and stormed off into her bedroom. Travon followed close behind.

"What are you gonna do? I mean, are you gonna keep it?"

"Of course I am! Why in the hell would I kill my baby?" Poison pointed to her bed. "I laid down and made it. I love my baby. I'll kill you before I kill her."

"Her? You already know what it's gonna be? How many months are you?"

"Don't worry about it. When she gets here, if you want to, you can see her."

Travon threw his arms up into the air. "What are you tripping for? I wanna help you."

"I wanted to help you with yours earlier, and you acted as if I said something wrong. Now you wanna help me with mine?" Poison waved him off. "No thank you, we'll be fine."

"How? What the hell are you gonna do?"

"Well, if you came by in the daytime, instead of just at night when you wanna get your rocks off, you would know all of these things," Poison told him. "For one, I'm in school. I have only two years to go, and then I'll have my degree."

"What? Bullshit! How old are you?"

"Now you ask? You should have been trying to ask that kinda shit months ago. Anyway, I'm nineteen, if it makes any difference."

"What are you doing hanging out in the Heights and banging?" Travon asked incredulously.

"I'm real about mines!" Poison replied. "I know who I am, where I come from, and where I'm going. I'm trying to get my life together, but that don't mean I'm a cut my home girls loose. We sisters. We been through the same shit y'all been through, and got the same bonds y'all got. I may not be some preppy little cheerleader, but I can still have a future. Why don't you wake up before it's too late."

"You didn't have to go there with that cheerleader comment," Travon said softly. "You know you was wrong for going there."

Travon turned and walked out of the room. Poison rushed up behind him and wrapped her arms around him.

"Tre, I'm sorry," she said softly. "Wait, baby. I shouldn't have went there, I'm sorry."

They continued into the living room, where Lil Fade and Peaches were kissing. Upon seeing them enter, Lil Fade turned toward Travon.

"C'mon, homie," Lil Fade said. "Let's drink to the kids, all of them. May they grow up happy and healthy."

Lil Fade handed Travon a glass full of gin. Travon accepted it, and gulped it down like soda. Lil Fade poured him another, and lifted a second glass that had been resting on the coffee table.

"To the kids!" Lil Fade raised his glass and Travon returned the gesture.

Lil Fade poured drink after drink, with Travon tossing them down one after another. They drank until after nightfall. They drank until long after Poison had gone to her room and fallen asleep. They drank until Travon began to stagger and slur his words.

"Say, Peaches," Lil Fade called to her. "Where are them straps I gave you to hold for me?"

"They're in the closet. Look in that big box at the top. Them masks and gloves, along with the rest of your illegal shit, is in there too."

"Good." Lil Fade smiled. "I'ma need you to take me and Tre somewhere and drop us off. We got some business to handle."

"Boy, he's drunk!" Peaches protested, pointing at Travon. "He can't handle no business."

"Yes he can. This is when he's at his best, watch." Lil Fade turned to Travon. "We gonna get Dejuan tonight, ain't that right?"

"That muthafucka," Travon slurred. He began crying. "Tamika, he killed Tamika."

"That's right, and Lil Fade is gonna help you get him. Who always kills for Tre?"

"Fade…"

"Good, good." Lil Fade nodded. He turned to Peaches. "Help me take him in the room and get him dressed."

"Boy, what if Poison wakes up tonight?" Peaches asked, pointing at the bedroom door. "What am I gonna tell her?"

"She won't, and if she does, just tell her that you took us home."

They helped Travon into Peaches' bedroom, where they dressed him in some dark clothing, a mask, and some gloves. Travon was inebriated, but still able to walk and stand.

"Let's go, Tre," Lil Fade told him.

"Let's get him," Travon slurred.

CHAPTER THIRTY-SIX

Dejuan pulled into the driveway, exited his big white Mercedes, and walked to the front door. He and his friends had been up all night drinking, trying to ease the pain of losing their family and friends. He rang the doorbell.

The front door swung open quickly, to reveal Lil Fade holding a massive handgun, which he had pointed at Dejuan's face.

Lil Fade smiled satanically, and placed his finger over his pale lips.

"Shhhh," Lil Fade told him. He lifted his hand and waved for Dejuan to enter the dark house.

Dejuan stepped inside. "Where's Tangela?"

"Bitch, shut up!" Lil Fade told him. He waved his handgun to a spot across the room. "Go sit your ass on the couch."

Dejuan slowly walked to the living room couch and sat. Travon, who had been seated in a chair across the room, rose slowly.

"Muthafucka!" he shouted, slurring his words.

Lil Fade lifted his hand. "Hold on, T."

Dejuan shook his head. "Lil Fade, I know it's you already, so you can take off the fuckin' mask! Where's Tangela? If this is another one of your jacks, then get it over with and don't involve these people!"

"Nigga, this ain't no jack, it's a muthafuckin' multiple homicide!"

Dejuan shook his head slowly. "You better not have."

Lil Fade stormed over to the couch where Dejuan was seated. "How in the fuck you gonna tell me what I better not do? Blood, I think you forgot who's holding the pistol." Lil Fade struck Dejuan across the face with his gun.

"Fuck!" Dejuan cried out, grabbing his jaw.

"Get up!" Lil Fade shouted. "We taking you out to the country, so we can blow your ass away."

Holding his jaw, Dejuan rolled his eyes at Lil Fade. "If you gonna do it, then do it here. I'm not going nowhere with you."

"I figured you would say that. That's why Darius and Capone took that bitch Tangela out there. When we get you out there, they'll let her go." Lil Fade nodded toward the door. "C'mon."

"Fuck that bitch!" Dejuan shouted. "Kill her ass, for all I care."

"I knew you was a sorry-ass ho!" Lil Fade struck him with the pistol again.

Dejuan screamed in pain, grabbed his face, and buried his head in the couch cushion.

"Get your bitch ass on the floor!" Lil Fade commanded. "Now!"

"Yeah!" Travon added. He staggered to where Dejuan was kneeling and punched him in the face. "You killed Mika!"

Dejuan looked up in surprise. "Is that what this is all about? I didn't kill her, and I didn't tell Quentin to kill her either. I swear." He shifted his gaze from Lil Fade to Travon. "Tre, you heard me, I told him to smoke you, but that's because y'all jacked me."

Dejuan extended his hands into the air with his palms facing Travon. "Tre, I swear, you gotta believe me."

"Shut your whining ass up," Lil Fade told him. "At least die with some nuts."

Lil Fade pulled a second handgun from his waistband, which he handed to Travon. "Do this fool."

"Do this fool!" Travon repeated. He began crying again. "That's what you said, you said, 'Do this muthafucka.' And he killed Mika, he killed my Mika!" Tears streamed down his face.

"That's right!" Dejuan said excitedly, "I didn't tell Quentin to kill that girl! He did that on his own." He pointed out of the window. "Quentin killed her, not me. And Quentin is already dead!"

"Kill him, Tre," Lil Fade said softly. "Lil Fade gave him to you, now kill him."

"No, Tre!" Dejuan's hands flew into the air. "I saved you! I took you to the hospital, and I stopped Quentin from killing you!"

The frown slowly drifted from Travon's face, and the gun he held to Dejuan's head slowly fell back down to his side.

"Yeah, Tre, I took you to the hospital, and I even tried to look out for you when you got out," Dejuan told him. "You was my little homie."

Lil Fade smiled. He was enjoying himself immensely. He walked up behind Travon and whispered softly into his ear, "He wanted to use you. He wanted to use you, like he used Too-Low."

The frown returned, shooting across Travon's face like a bolt of lightning. "Too-Low," Travon muttered. His tears came again.

"That's right, Too-Low!" Dejuan jabbed a finger toward Travon. "Too-Low was my homeboy. He was like a brother to me. I looked out for Too-Low."

Dejuan crossed his index and middle fingers and held up his hand. "Me and him was always together, remember that? I used to always go over to your house with Too-Low."

Lil Fade frowned. He leaned forward and whispered into Travon's ear again. "He's not Too-Low's friend. He tried to kill Too-Low's little brother. He tried to kill you, Tre. He made you leave the Courts. You can't even go back over there to see your mother. They didn't help pay for Too-Low's funeral. They just used Too-Low to kill. Dejuan made Too-Low kill." Lil Fade smiled. "He hurt Too-Low."

Anger spread across Travon's face, and once again, the gun rose to Dejuan's head.

"No!" Dejuan exclaimed. "Don't listen to him, Tre. Whatever he tells you, don't listen!" Dejuan jabbed his thumb toward himself. "Too-Low was my friend. We served the East Terrace after they killed Too-Low."

Being heavily inebriated, Travon blurted out the first name that came to him upon hearing East Terrace. "Re-Re," he said, slurring.

Dejuan did not know who Re-Re was, so he provided another name. The correct name. "Slow Poke did it. It was C-Low, Jermaine, Turtle, and Slow Poke. Slow Poke is the one who pulled the trigger."

Although intoxicated, it was a name Travon easily recognized. It was the name of the boy whose life he saved after the concert. It was too much for him. Travon broke down into tears, and the gun fell back down to his side.

Lil Fade shook his head and frowned. He placed his left arm over Travon's left shoulder, resting his hand upon Travon's chest and making a Blood sign. His right hand glided down Travon's right arm until it came to rest upon Travon's right hand. Lil Fade slowly lifted the gun back up until it was once again pointed at Dejuan's face. He slid his finger into the trigger guard with Travon's, and then slowly squeezed until the pressure built, and the gun popped, releasing its energy.

Together, they repeated the process over and over again. Squeeze and release. Squeeze and release. It was sensual, sexual, powerful, and rhythmic. Together they squeezed and released, consummating their relationship with Dejuan's blood. When finally they tired, Lil Fade walked to Dejuan's body, and took his money, jewelry, and car keys.

Lil Fade and Travon exited the house and walked to the big, beautiful Mercedes; they climbed inside and drove away. Inside of the home, they left Dejuan, Mrs. Collins, and her two daughters. Their only sin being that one of them had been a mistress to Dejuan.

Inside the car, Lil Fade turned to Travon.

"Tre, who kills for you?" he asked softly.

"You do," Travon slurred.

CHAPTER THIRTY-SEVEN

Next Day
Aunt Vera's House

"Tre," Aunt Vera called out to him. "Tre, get up!"

"Huh?" Travon rolled over, opened his eyes, and tried to focus.

"Get your ass up and clean off this porch!" she commanded.

Slowly, Travon sat up. His Aunt Vera stood over him, glowering at him.

Vera pointed at the floorboards of the front porch. "I want this mess cleaned up by the time I get back! No, change that. I want it cleaned up now!" She stepped around Travon and stormed off to her car.

Travon quickly deduced that he was on his aunt's front porch, but how he came to be there, he could not recall. In fact, he could recall little from the previous night. Slowly, he braced himself and stood.

Both the front of his shirt and the white, wooden floorboards of the porch were covered with vomit, and he felt as if he were toting a thousand-pound anvil on top of his head. He staggered out into the front yard, where the sun's fresh beams slapped him across his face. The brightness caused him to reel, lift his arm and cover his face. Clumsily, he made his way over to the garden hose.

Travon turned on the water, then leaned forward and twisted the nozzle on the hose, which sent water gushing out from the end of it. He inhaled deeply, and then lowered his head into the stream of water, rejoicing in its cleansing effects. He quickly removed his shirt, doused it with water, and then proceeded to the front porch, where he cleaned off the result of the previous night's excesses. When this was done, he returned the hose to its holder, turned off the faucet, and headed inside. With his head still pounding, he ascended the creaking stairs to the bathroom. He brushed his teeth, rejuvenated himself with a quick shower and some fresh clothing, and then headed to his bed for some much-needed sleep.

Later That Day

Travon woke, stretched, and glanced at the clock. Two o'clock. He slowly climbed from his bed, where he ventured into the bathroom and freshened himself. He was still tired, and still aching, but more than anything he was hungry. He left his room, struggled down the stairs, and headed for the kitchen. While passing through the living room, he heard voices coming from the front porch. Curiosity defeated hunger, and Travon turned to see who had gathered this early in the day. It was Marcus, Darius, Romeo, Capone, Lil Fade, and a stranger. Darius interrupted the stranger and introduced him.

"Say, Taariq, this is my cousin Tre," Darius said, waving toward a disheveled Travon. "Tre, this is my homie Taariq. Me and Taariq used to be untouchable back in the day. We used to get into all kinds of shit."

"Yeah, Spook was downer than a muthafucka," Lil Fade added.

Travon nodded at Taariq. "What's up, Blood?"

"What's up, my brother?" Taariq greeted.

"So, that's yo hustle now?" Lil Fade asked Taariq.

Taariq shook his head in disappointment and stared at Lil Fade. "If you wanna call it that. In fact, it's the greatest hustle of all, young blood. It's the hustle that saved my life. It's the *only* hustle that can save us all."

"Can it save me?" Lil Fade asked cynically.

"He can save anybody, you just have to believe," Taariq told him.

"Man, after all the shit we been through, it's a trip to hear you talking like this," Darius told Taariq. "You was the shit. It was me and you, baby!"

"I'm still the same, but different," Taariq told them. "It's hard to explain.

I've been through the belly of the beast, and I saw what it likes to eat. It likes to eat us, Darius. It likes to eat young brothers like ourselves. I fell with the attitude, *I'm gonna do my bid, get out, and then get my hustle on.* But as time passed by, I got to thinking. If it's one thing prison does, it gives a person time to think. My eyes opened, D, and I saw us. I saw what was happening to us. Bloods, Crips, and everybody else. We all die alike. We all human, and we all in this together."

Taariq waved his hand through the air in a grand sweeping gesture, pointing out the neighborhood around them. "Our women are being strung out on crack and made to sell their bodies in the streets for it. While we, all of the young brothers, are killing each other. We sell that poison to our people, and then wonder why our mothers and sisters are on it. *We* doing it to them! Sure, them folks is bringing it over here by the shipload, but that don't mean we got to fuck with it. They bring that shit, and guns, and weed, and a whole lot of other shit that's bad for us, over here by the shipload. They also bring oil, cars, and consumer electronics over here by the shipload, but do you think they are letting us get as much of that shit as we want?"

Lil Fade shook his head. "Man, what in the fuck is you talkin' 'bout?"

"It's a conspiracy, and it's controlled from the highest levels!" Taariq told them. "Give them dope, string out the women, and lock up the men. They give us astronomical release dates, and then take our women. They put food on the table by given our women food stamps. They put a roof over their head, by giving them housing. And then they pay all of their bills by giving them welfare. They are trying to take the place of the black man."

Taariq leaned forward and tapped Darius on his knee. "Peep it, they strung out our pops in the seventies, and made sure that we grew up without dads. Now they locking us up in the nineties, and making sure our kids grow up without dads! They are afraid! If our kids grow up right, with moms and pops in the house, they'll become lawyers, doctors, and scientists. They'll take jobs away from they kids. More importantly, our kids will look around and realize that they can be doctors, lawyers, and scientists too. The stereotypes and claims of mental inferiority will be shattered. The playing fields will be level, and they know they can't play on the same field with us."

Taariq lifted his hand and gave Darius a high-five. "Every time we concentrate on something, and are determined to excel at something, we dominate. They let us on the baseball field, and there goes Jackie Robinson. They let us on the basketball courts, and there goes Kareem and Mike. The list goes on and on. Now imagine, if instead of our kids wanting to be the next Mike, they all wanted to be the next Charles Drew, or Benjamin Banneker. We'd blow up, baby! But you know what, that'll never happen, because we killin' each other. How many future leaders have we shot dead in the streets over a color? We need to stop. The same guns they are puttin' in our community and the same kids they are turning into battle-hardened soldiers, need to stop killin' each other and start using those guns to protect our women. Let our mothers and sisters and grandmothers feel safe enough to walk down the streets at night again. They need to become soldiers in the right war, and fight the right fight."

Taariq began tapping at his fingers, as he ticked off the things that he felt needed to be done. "The fight to save our people from welfare, food stamps, drugs, poverty, and illiteracy. Being shot at by bullets ain't nothing compared to being bombarded by that shit. An old man told me in prison that the hand that rocks the cradle rules the world. That's why crack cocaine has nearly destroyed us. It puts our women in the streets, it takes them away from their jobs as mothers, and makes them turn out crack babies. We men can't do a damn thing about it, because we are either dead or in prison. You know who it's going to take to stop this shit?" Taariq asked.

"Us," he answered himself. "Darius, you said it yourself, it's me and you, baby. It's up to us to stop this, it's up to us to put down the guns and the crack. It's gonna take some generals like us to stop this war. If not, then who? Nobody else cares, and you know why? Because dead men and convicted felons can't vote. So we gotta grab our little knuckleheads and stop them. You know the saying: 'Each one, teach one.'"

Taariq lifted his arm and stared at the watch on his wrist. "Dang, I'm late. I didn't mean to preach to you brothers, but I ain't told y'all nothing wrong.

There's something else I want y'all brothers to think about too. There is something that falls in between Michael Jordan and being the neighborhood drug dealer. There is honor in being a plumber, a carpenter, an electrician, stuff like that. Ain't nothing wrong with getting a trade and working with your hands to take care of your family. Pick up them shorties with your big, dirty, rough hands and teach them how to be a man. Y'all come on down to the mosque and hear the imam speak. A Salaam a laikum."

Taariq waved to them as he left the porch and headed for his vehicle. Just as he reached his car, Poison and Peaches pulled up. Poison rolled down her window.

"Hey, Spook!" she shouted.

Taariq stopped and smiled.

Peaches parked, and Poison leapt out of the vehicle, ran to where Taariq was standing, and jumped into his arms.

"When did you get out?" she asked.

"A couple a days ago," he told her. "What have you been doing with yourself?"

"Going to school," she told him. "Have you talked to Preference yet?"

Taariq shook his head. "Naw, she didn't ride with me the whole bid. The truth be told, she only rode with me a year before she broke bad." Taariq glanced at his watch again. "Say, I'm a give you my number so you can call me tonight and we can finish talking."

"Okay." Poison stood and waited, while Taariq opened his car door, climbed inside, and scribbled down his telephone number.

Travon, who had overheard the conversation, was fuming with jealousy. He rose from the porch, walked to where Poison was standing, and wrapped his arm around her.

Poison accepted Taariq's number, and then turned toward Travon. "What's up, baby?" She kissed him on his cheek. "Why didn't you tell me you was gonna leave last night?"

"I really didn't know myself at the time, it just kinda came up."

Taariq honked his horn and pulled away.

"So what's up?" Travon asked Poison. "What brought y'all out here?"

Poison wrapped her arms around Travon and pulled him close. "We gonna go and wash this girl's car."

"Who, you?" Travon shook his head. "Uh-uh, you're pregnant. Hell, let Lil Fade do it, that's her man."

Poison smacked her lips and frowned. "You know Lil Fade ain't gonna do nothing for her but jump up and down on top of her and eat up her food."

Travon lifted his arms into the air. "Then what the hell is she fuckin' with him for?"

Poison folded her arms and shifted her weight to one side.

After a few moments of silence, Travon exhaled and relented. "I'll go with y'all and wash it for you."

Poison smiled and hugged him. Together, they walked over to the small red Geo Metro and climbed inside.

Lil Fade, who was talking to Peaches, opened the opposite rear door and joined Travon in the back. Peaches closed the door and pulled away.

"They sure are getting mighty close lately," observed Marcus from his seat on the front porch.

"I know," Darius agreed. "I wonder what that's about."

"Better him than me," Romeo added.

CHAPTER THIRTY-EIGHT

Car Wash
East Houston Street

"I'ma go get some quarters from inside the store," Peaches told them.

"Hold on, girl, I'm a go with you," Poison said. She turned to Travon. "Baby, you want something outta here?"

Travon shook his head. "Naw, I'm cool."

The girls turned and walked into the store, which was adjoined to the self-serve car wash. It was a large car wash, with ten carports. Travon and Lil Fade stood outside of the small car, neither one speaking to the other.

Travon dug inside his pocket, pulled out some change, and inserted two quarters; instantly, the high pressure hose came alive. He turned the knob that controlled the hose's functions, to the setting marked soap. He lifted the hose from its rack, and began spraying the car. After several moments of awkward silence, he turned to Lil Fade.

"Lil Fade, what happened last night?" Travon asked.

"You know what happened last night, Blood," Lil Fade answered. "We handled our muthafuckin' business."

"What happened to Tangela?"

A sinister grin spread across Lil Fade's face. "It's a bloody story; you might get queasy and throw up if I tell you."

Travon's nostrils flared. "Don't fuck with me, I'm not in the mood for any of your bullshit-ass psychopathic games! Just tell me what the fuck happened!" Travon stopped spraying the car and stared at him.

Lil Fade pressed his hand against his chest. "My psychopathic games?" He shook his finger at Travon. "You're the one who killed those people, one by one."

Travon shook his head in disbelief and turned his attention back to the car, where he started spraying again. "Bullshit! I was too drunk, I couldn't have."

"You did. You was so determined to get Dejuan, you took out anybody who got in you way." Lil Fade began following Travon around the small red car. "You're a pure killa now, Baby-Low."

Travon shook his head. "I knew I wouldn't be able to get a straight answer from you. You're all caught up in your twisted little games."

Lil Fade placed his hand upon his chest again. "I'm twisted? You killed them, not me."

Travon stopped and stared at him coldly. "And Dejuan, who killed him?"

"We did, together." Lil Fade's smile returned. "For the first time last night, we acted like true homies. Afterward, we celebrated by going on a little joyride. We took our little trip. The one I promised you when you were in jail. We rode by people in the streets last night, and each time we were about to pass one up, you decided whether or not they should live or die." Lil Fade's smile widened. "You killed mercilessly."

"Bullshit!" Travon walked away. "I'm through talking to you."

Lil Fade quickened his own pace, remaining just behind Travon. "I'm not bullshittin'; we took a hell of a ride last night."

A red Mustang GT convertible passed by the car wash, and Lil Fade hurried out of the stall so that he could be seen.

"What's up, Blood?" He waved his hands through the air, beckoning for the vehicle to return.

The Mustang's brake lights flashed, and the car quickly turned down a nearby street.

"Who was that?" Travon asked.

"Just the homies from the Rigsby," Lil Fade answered.

Travon shook his head. "Damn, what's taking them so long?"

"Shit, they probably in there shopping, you know them," Lil Fade answered.

The red Mustang pulled into the parking lot.

"Aw shit, there go the homies right there," Lil Fade told Travon.

Monsta was first out of the Mustang, followed by Tate. When Travon saw Tate, he began walking toward him. Peaches and Poison exited the store.

The Mustang was parked between the girls and the wash stalls where Travon and Lil Fade were standing, and as a result, the girls were able to see what Tate was hiding. Peaches' eyes flew wide.

"Lil Fade, look out!"

"Yeah, niggaz, what's up?" Monsta shouted, as he pulled a nine-millimeter handgun from his waist and began firing.

Lil Fade grabbed Travon, slung him back, and bore the brunt of Monsta's flurry of bullets. Travon fell and quickly began to crawl away.

"This is for Suga!" Tate shouted. He lifted a small sawed-off, double-barreled shotgun and fired.

The blast swept Lil Fade off of his feet. Travon, who had crawled out of the wash stall, now stood up to run. Monsta fired at him, but missed. Chips from the concrete wall struck Travon in his face, as the bullets from the nine-millimeter ricocheted off of it.

Tate ran up to a badly wounded Lil Fade, who was lying next to the Metro. He stood over him, and gave Lil Fade the second barrel of the shotgun from point-blank range. When Tate turned to run back to the Mustang, Poison was standing there. She fired once, and his blood and brain fragments sprayed the wet concrete walls of the wash stall. Peaches stood next to the Mustang, where inside Leonard Wright lay dead against the rear panel. Monsta fled on foot.

Poison began scanning the area. "Tre. Where's Tre?"

Peaches ran to where Lil Fade was lying in the stall. "I don't know, girl. I don't know." She dropped her weapon and knelt down beside her man.

"Tre! Tre!" Poison screamed. She quickly began moving from wash stall to wash stall, searching each one. She walked to the last stall and peered inside, where she found Travon seated on the ground, rocking back and forth nervously. His hands were cupped over his face, and his entire body was shaking.

Poison knelt and wrapped her arms around him. "It's okay, baby," she whispered softly. "It's all right."

"I got caught slipping," Travon told her. His voice broke with each of his words. "I didn't bring my strap, and I got caught slippin'."

Travon stood, walked to the far wall, and began kicking it. "God damn it! I know better than that!"

Poison rose. "Tre, it's okay." She walked to where he was standing.

Travon turned and stared at her coldly. "Is it? Listen."

They stood in silence, and both could hear Peaches crying loudly.

"Oooooh, girl, I'm coming!" Poison ran out of the stall with Travon and into the one where her friend was crying. When she arrived, Peaches was seated in a pool of blood with Lil Fade's head in her lap. Her pants and shirt, as well as her hands and face, were covered with blood.

Travon walked to the stall where the girls were kneeling and trying to care for Lil Fade. He watched for a moment, and then placed his arm against the wet concrete wall, where he leaned his head against it. "He pulled me out of the way," he told them softly. "It should have been me."

Travon shook his head. "Again, it should have been me." Tears began to flow, and his body began to shake violently. "Why? Why do I keep getting chances?"

He turned, slowly walked out of the stall, and peered up at the beautiful clear blue South Texas sky.

"What is it that You want from me?" Travon shouted. "What is it that You want me to do? I'll kill! I'll kill! I'll do whatever You want! Just stop killing everybody around me!"

Slowly he fell to his knees, and laid his head down upon the concrete. Tears poured from his shaking body. "Please! Please."

CHAPTER THIRTY-NINE

Aunt Vera's House
Days Later

Travon pulled up to the house, climbed out of his vehicle, and walked inside. The house seemed empty. No one was sitting on the porch, no one was watching television inside of the living room, and there was a general absence of noise.

Travon climbed the stairs to his room, where he pulled some clothing from his closet and tossed it onto his bed. He then walked to his dresser, removed some underclothes, which he placed on top of the others. He folded his clothing into a large bundle, struggled back down the stairs, and headed out the front door. This time, Darius was seated on the porch.

"You still hiding?" Darius asked him.

"I didn't come for any shit, I just came to get some clothes," Travon replied.

"So I guess that means yes."

Travon halted. "I don't need the lecture, and no, I'm not hiding. I'm taking it to them niggaz, and if you would come down off of the fence, we could get this shit over with. It looks to me like you're the one hiding."

"I've heard about some of your little escapades," Darius sneered. "You're out there shooting at everybody and building quite a little name for yourself. You shootin' at C-Low, Slow Poke, and Jermaine in the East Terrace. You're shooting at Snuff Dog, Lil Bullet, Lil Anthony, and Short Texas in the Courts. You're even into killing Bloods now, huh? I heard you shot up Pork Chop, Monsta, Daryl, and Filou yesterday. You're a real bad-ass now. I guess Too-Low would be real proud of you. Everybody is running from, or trying to kill Baby-Low. Congratulations."

"Jealous?" Travon asked.

"Jealous?" Darius rose from the porch banister. He pounded the air with his fist and his voice trembled with fury as he spoke. "Hell no, and fuck you! I don't want it, Tre, I never did. And the little shit I did do, I can't even do that anymore. I can't do it anymore, I can't."

"So you let Taariq talk you into that Muslim shit, huh?"

"It's not shit, and yeah, I've been going by the mosque to hear the imam speak. You should come with me one day."

"Thanks, but no thanks." Travon began to walk away.

"Lil Fade is awake now," Darius told him.

Travon stopped, paused for several seconds, and then turned back toward his cousin. "What do you want me to do about it?"

"You could go see him," Darius told him.

"What for?"

"Well, for stepping in front of that pistol for one," Darius told him sarcastically.

Travon shook his head. "I didn't ask him to. I didn't ask for any of this shit!"

Darius jabbed his finger at him. "But you got it, so now deal with it!"

Travon sat his bundle of clothing down on the porch, and then lifted his arms high into the air. "What do you want from me, Darius? What?"

"I want you to come back across the line. We do what we have to do, to protect each other and survive. We don't go out and just blow people away! We never did that!"

Darius jabbed his finger through the air toward his cousin. "You crossed the line, Tre. Just like Too-Low crossed the line, and Lil Fade crossed the line, and a whole lot of other muthafuckas just like y'all, crossed the line!"

Travon jabbed his finger back at his cousin. "You never said shit to Lil Fade about it! So why are you giving me a bunch of shit?"

"Because you're my cousin and I love you," Darius told him through clenched teeth. "There's a difference between how I feel about you and how I feel about Lil Fade!"

Travon sat down on the porch steps. He lowered his head into the palms of his hands. "I don't know how to come back, Darius. I'm afraid." He lifted his head and peered over his shoulder at his cousin. "How do I come back?" he asked softly.

Darius took a step toward his cousin and opened his hand. "Come with me tonight, Blood. But first, go and see Lil Fade."

Travon frowned. "Why?"

"Because, regardless of what he's done, he's still the homie. Besides, you owe him at least that."

Travon swallowed hard. "Have y'all already been up there yet?"

Darius shook his head. "No, I just found out a little while ago. His sister called; she was trying to get in touch with Capone."

Travon lowered his head and stared at the ground. "I can't face him," he whispered.

"I don't see why not," Darius told him. "You've become just like him." With that last biting remark, he went inside, leaving Travon sitting on the steps.

Brooke Army Medical Center
Fort Sam Houston Army Post

Travon paused at the door. "I've got to face him. I've got to face him," he whispered.

He pushed open the door to the room and stepped inside. Lil Fade was lying in a hospital bed, surrounded by a forest of electronic monitors and intravenous drip machines. There were tubes and electronic patches all over his heavily illustrated, pale body.

Lil Fade writhed in pain.

Travon walked to the bed. "Lil Fade," he called to him in a low, soft tone.

Lil Fade opened his eyes. They were bloodshot. He turned his head toward Travon and smiled.

"What's up, Blood?" he said, greeting him, in a hoarse, low tone. "I knew you would come."

"How did you figure I would come?" Travon asked.

"Because you let me get into your head, you let me get into your soul."

"Tell me why I shouldn't kill you?" Travon asked. "Because of you, Tamika's dead. I tried to run from you, and Dejuan killed her."

"Blood in, Blood out," Lil Fade told him. "I never said whose blood it would take for you to get out."

Travon stepped forward. "You made me kill those people. Because of you, a lot of people are dead who shouldn't be."

Lil Fade swallowed hard, and shifted his gaze toward the white ceiling. "Tre, if you killed me, I would consider you to be an angel of mercy. I would also die happy, knowing that BSV has you know, Baby-Low."

Travon shook his head and began to pace near Lil Fade's hospital bed. "I'm not no fuckin' Baby-Low. I don't want this shit. Mika's dead, Too-Low's dead, and the people who killed them are dead. I'm through."

Lil Fade smiled. "I see you've gotten good at killing. Aaargh." He writhed in pain. His hand grabbed a small rectangle-shaped box lying next to him. He pressed a little white button in the middle of the box, and this button sent a signal to the computer controlling one of his IVs, telling it to release more morphine. After a moment, he was able to speak again. He opened his eyes, and turned his attention to Travon.

"Baby-Low, you killed those people, no one made you. And you felt satisfied when you did it. You are who you want to be."

Travon took another step toward the bed. "You stepped in front of the gun for me. Why?"

"BSV for life," Lil Fade said softly.

Travon shook his head in disgust. "What happened to you?" he said through clenched teeth. "Why are you like this? What made you become like this?"

"Like what?" Lil Fade asked.

"A monster! A cold-hearted fuckin' monster!"

Lil Fade laughed, and pain shot through his body. His breathing became labored. "Look at me!" he commanded. His voice was raspy, clogged, muddled. "I'm an albino. I was born a monster. I'm a nigga with blue eyes and white skin. Do you know the hell I went through growing up? You'd be surprised at the names kids can come up with. I've been hating for a long time, Tre. I've been immune to feelings for a long time."

Travon frowned and tilted his head to the side. "You confuse the hell outta me. You're smart, but sometimes you talk like you're not. You use your intelligence to fuck with other people's heads. Since you like that shit so much, why don't you go back to school and become a shrink?"

Lil Fade smiled. He waved his hand at the blankets that covered his body. "Pull the covers down," he told Travon. "Pull this sheet all the way off of me."

Travon stepped forward and pulled the covers down. There was a large pink spot on the bandages covering Lil Fade's stomach, where the shotgun blast hit. Travon's gaze walked down Lil Fade's body, and saw that his right leg was missing below the knee. Travon's eyes flew wide and he jumped back. Once he became conscious of his actions, he stepped forward again.

"It's okay." Lil Fade nodded and turned away from Travon. "I feel like running away too. It's over for me, I'm finished." Tears streamed down his face.

Travon closed his eyes for a few moments, searching for the right words. There were none. He waved his hand over Lil Fade's body. "It's not over. All this means is that you have to slow down."

"And live like some fuckin' cripple?" Lil Fade shouted. He pounded the covers with his fist. "This ain't the way it's supposed to happen. I'm supposed to die in the streets like a soldier!"

Travon shook his head. "You mean like a fool!"

Lil Fade shook his head and pounded the covers again. "No, like a soldier! Believing in something. Believing in the hood, in the homies, in you! I'm not supposed to live to be some crippled old man; I'm not supposed to live past eighteen!"

Travon shook his head and turned away. "You're crazy."

Lil Fade shook his head. "No, I'm finished. It's all on you now, it's all on you." He lifted his bandaged hand and pointed at Travon. "You're Baby-Low, and no one will let you forget it. From now on, everybody will be gunning for Baby-Low. Everyone will want the honor of being able to say that they killed Baby-Low. You will go on killing, BSV will keep on growing, and the set will live forever, and so I'll live forever."

Travon shook his head and his eyes widened. "No."

"Yes." Lil Fade bit down upon his lip. "I was it, and I passed it on to you. You will die, and someone else will have it."

"Fuck you, and your psycho killa bullshit."

Lil Fade rapidly shifted his gaze toward Travon. "Is it? Think about it. When someone thinks of Wheatley Courts, they think Dejuan and Too-Low. East Terrace, they think Slow Poke and C-Low. BSV, they think Capone and Lil Fade. Now they think Capone and Baby-Low."

Travon extended his arms toward the ceiling. "Is that what this is all about? Nobody will fear you, because you have only one leg?"

Lil Fade turned away from Travon and again stared at the ceiling. "I didn't ask you to come here!"

"I know. I had to come."

"I know, because I saved you. Because you had to come and decide on the spot whether or not to kill me." Lil Fade stared into Travon's eyes, with his own tear-filled ones. "Please..."

Travon turned away from him. "What the hell are you talking about?" he asked nervously.

Lil Fade pounded the metal bed railing. "I can't bail outta the car any longer, I can't go anywhere or do anything anymore! My life is over. Everything I know how to do is over! Tre, I can feel again. I'm not a monsta."

Lil Fade began crying heavily. Tears streamed down Travon's face as he leaned over and embraced the one person in life who had touched upon his every emotion. The person who he feared the most, the person who had killed for him, the person who made him take lives, and the person who gave him life.

After all of the blood and all the killing, Lil Fade was human again. For several moments the two boys embraced, as Lil Fade let out years of pain. Tears flowed continuously from his bandaged body and broken soul. When finally they no longer embraced, Travon stared into Lil Fade's eyes. They were no longer the cold, lifeless, penetrating eyes that brought fear to many. Now they were the tired eyes of a scared boy.

"Tre, you can make it," Lil Fade whispered.

Travon recoiled. "What?"

"Everything I told you was wrong, and everything Taariq said was right. Go to him."

Travon frowned. "What?"

"Go to him," Lil Fade repeated. "Don't try to fight it by yourself, it's addictive. Once you've started, you can't stop. It'll always be your first resort, and your defense mechanism. You'll always use it to fall back on."

Travon lifted his shoulders and shook his head. "What are you talking about?"

"Violence, murder. You've tasted blood, you've tasted power. It consumes you." Lil Fade turned and stared into Travon's eyes. "Tre, you have to kill Baby-Low."

"Is that the medicine talking, or you?"

Lil Fade lifted his finger. "One last death. You have to kill Baby-Low, in order to save Travon."

Travon nodded and looked down. He understood.

"Tre, I need you to do me a favor. Capone is coming up here, and I don't want him to see me like this."

Travon turned, grabbed Lil Fade's bed sheets, and spread them back over his body.

Lil Fade shook his head. "That's not what I meant."

Travon stared into Lil Fade's eyes, and upon realizing what he meant, shook his head and stepped back. "No."

Lil Fade nodded. "Yes. You said it yourself, I'm a monster. And monsters need to be put to sleep."

Travon's eyes flew wide and he shook his head again. "No."

Lil Fade closed his eyes and nodded slowly. "Yes. If you ever thought you owed me anything, for the park, for the witness, for the motel, or for the car wash, then you'll help me. Please..." Tears streamed down Lil Fade's cheeks again.

"This is the easy way out," Travon told him. He shifted his eyes toward the floor.

Lil Fade lifted his hand and pointed out of the hospital window. "If I go back out there, they'll shoot me dead anyway. Let me spare myself the humiliation!"

Travon lifted his head and stared into Lil Fade's eyes. "You weren't merciful to none of those people, and now you want mercy? You even dragged me down into your twisted little world and made me kill!"

"You didn't kill those people, I did! I did! And now it's eating me up inside." Lil Fade began crying heavily again.

Travon shook his head, and his own tears cascaded down. "Even on your way out, you leave scars."

Travon reached beneath his shirt and pulled out his brother's nine-millimeter Beretta. He pulled back the slide and chambered a round, knowing that Lil Fade would be too weak to do so. He laid the gun in the bed next to Lil Fade's hand, and took the sheets and rubbed them over the gun, removing his fingerprints. It would be the last time that this gun would kill.

"Thank you," Lil Fade told him through tear-filled eyes. He lifted his hand, and Travon clasped it. Lil Fade shook his head. "I can't live like this. I don't wanna live like this. A one-legged albino?"

Travon laughed, and Lil Fade smiled.

"I'm scared, Tre. Can you believe that, I'm scared?"

Travon looked down. "I'm scared too," he told him softly.

"Of what?" Lil Fade asked with a frown.

"Of tomorrow. Of the next day, and the day after. I'm scared of the rest of my life."

Lil Fade closed his eyes and nodded. "I know. I'm more scared of living than I am of dying. I kinda feel sorry for you guys. At least for me it's over." Lil Fade shook his head and smiled. "No more killing, no more banging, no more drive-bys, no more funerals, no more cases, no more courts, lawyers, jails. No more pain, or worries, or trouble. It's all over."

Travon leaned forward and whispered into Lil Fade's ear, "BSV for life."

Lil Fade shook his head and broke down into tears. "Don't say that. Don't say that." He released Travon's hand. "Go now, just go."

Travon patted Lil Fade's shoulder, turned, and headed for the door.

"Take care of Capone for me," Lil Fade told him. "And I'll tell Too-Low…that you're gonna be all right."

Travon paused and closed his eyes, biting down on his bottom lip in an effort to hold back his tears. He walked out of the room, gently closing the door behind himself.

Travon walked rapidly to the elevator, rode it down to the first floor, and strode out into the parking lot. About halfway to his car, he heard the faint sound of a gunshot. He arched his back and stared into the sky. He was released. Blood in, Blood out. Lil Fade had fulfilled the grim prophecy with his own blood.

Travon closed his eyes and bit down upon his lip again, but this time it did not work. The tears came. They streamed down his face, as he climbed into his car and drove away. Inside of his car he began to think hard about his life, about tomorrow, and about his future. He thought about his children, and his family. He thought about Justin, and Frog, and of how they used to play marbles and toy soldiers together while growing up in the Courts.

Travon thought of the football games, the playground, and the basketball court. He thought of his brother, and his death, and the first beating that he'd received at the hands of Quentin and Tech Nine. His mind jumped to his arrival in the Heights, and all of the people he had met, the things he had learned, and the things he had done. He thought of the little girl swinging in the park, just like he used to do when he was her age. He thought about Tamika, the twins, and her death. He thought of Poison, and the baby that they were going to have. He recalled all of the things that Mr. and Mrs. Chang had told him. He thought of the old lady, the crooked lawyer, the crooked police officers, the drug raids, and the juvenile.

Travon thought of Mrs. Davis, and the mothers of the other boys who died that day. He thought about the park shooting, the concert, and all of the deaths before, after, and in between. Lil Fade was right, there had to be one last death. Mr. Chang was right, there was another way. Taariq was right; they were just young brothers killing one another over nothing.

Soon, Travon arrived at his destination. He stepped out of his car, closed the door, and peered up toward the sky. Those beautiful South Texas evenings were gone. Now, there was nothing but darkness and rain. The heavens opened, lightning illuminated the sky, and the loud awakening clap of thunder roared across the city. The thunder was deafening. It shook his soul and vibrated the very essence of his being. The lightning flashed again, and it illuminated all. It brought light to all of the dark hiding places within. It illuminated his mind, it illuminated his soul. And finally, finally the rains came.

The torrential waters flowed down upon him heavily, as he stood in the parking lot and extended his arms toward the heavens. He closed his hands, clenching them tightly. It was as though he were shaking the hands of God and forming a new covenant. The rains, they were purifying, drenching, and thoroughly cleansing. They washed away the blood upon his hands; they washed away the blood upon his soul. They mixed with the tears streaming down his face, washing them away as well.

Standing in the center of the parking lot, Travon shivered, as the tears and cool rains came falling down. Finally, he turned and slowly walked inside the mosque where Baby-Low would slowly die, and in his place would be born Shaheed. A man, a father, a SURVIVOR...

EPILOGUE

Travon Robinson Travon went back to school and received his high school diploma from Competency Based High School. With Poison's help, he was able to enroll in a local college, graduate, and go on to law school. He and Poison are now married, and live together with their three children on the city's North side.

Poison Whose real name is Camilla Jones, finished her last two years of college and went straight into her graduate studies. She recently graduated with a doctorate in computer science, and now works as a computer engineer at a local research center. Camilla adopted Travon's two sons and is now raising them as her own. She also volunteers religiously at the Eastside YWCA and is a Big Sister to several inner-city youths.

Darius He went back to school, and then on to college. He is now a schoolteacher in the poor San Antonio Independent School District. He married Sheila, Frog's sister, and they now have two beautiful children.

Marcus After Marcus rose to become head of the Blood Stone Villains, he then walked away from it all. He joined the Navy, served on an aircraft carrier during Operation Desert Storm, Kosovo, and Operation Enduring Freedom off the coast of Pakistan. He is now a Navy recruiter in Philadelphia.

Capone Alexander aka Capone was serving a sixty-year state prison term, for killing a Blood in the Rigsby in retaliation for Lil Fade's shooting. His case was recently reaffirmed on appeal; however, it has recently been dropped to a twenty-year non-aggravated sentence.

Romeo Jerome aka Romeo went on to college, but later dropped out. He is now married, and works for the city of San Francisco.

Chicken She is now in her third year of residency at University Hospital. She was recently married to a doctor at the hospital where she previously worked.

Elmira Travon's mother went on to finish school and become a registered nurse. She moved out of the Wheatley Courts and into a nice apartment complex on the city's Northeast side of town. She subsequently enrolled in a second work-study program, where she became a nurse anesthetist. She now drives a Lexus GS 450.

Vera Still a registered nurse at the same hospital, Vera lives in the same two-story Victorian-style home in the Denver Heights.

LaTonya Married a lieutenant who was stationed at Fort Sam Houston. She graduated from Incarnate Word College with a degree in biology. Today she and her husband live in Georgia where he is stationed. They have been blessed with a son.

Robert Jr. A major drug dealer, Robert Jr. is still dealing drugs and using violence to expand his narcotics empire. His ruthlessness and entrepreneurial spirit have made him a millionaire several times over. He uses Bloods from the city to move his product, and has bodyguards for protection.

Charlie Brown Was killed in a Los Angeles gang shootout shortly after Lil Fade's suicide. He was twenty-one.

Lil Bling His real name is Roderick, and he is now serving a fifteen-year stretch in a federal penitentiary in Atlanta for conspiracy to distribute nine ounces of crack cocaine.

Big Pimpin Melvin aka Big Pimpin is serving time in a federal penitentiary in Colorado. He received a twenty-year sentence for conspiracy to deliver eighteen ounces of crack cocaine.

Fro-Dog His real name is Christopher, and he's serving time at a federal penitentiary in Illinois. He was sentenced to twenty years for possession of crack cocaine. After the landmark *Brady* case, he was able to give back five years for the gun.

Big Mike He was killed in the East Terrace by C-Low, who jacked him for all of his money and then shot him.

C-Low His real name is Charles. He became a jacker and bank robber. Though no longer active these days, he still resides at the top of the federal authorities' most wanted lists.

Re-Re Reginald aka Re-Re married Nikki and moved to Houston. Today they have two children, and Re-Re is the owner of a Jamaican restaurant and club.

Gary Kaufmann Was passed over for his federal judgeship, but is now a United States Senator.

Judge Weitzer Became a federal judge. He is constantly at odds with the federal legislature because of his judicial activism. He is a very vocal opponent of federal minimum mandatory sentences, and the sentencing disparity between crack and powder cocaine.

Lil Anthony Now a major drug dealer, he took over the Courts and much of the Eastside's drug trade after Dejuan's death. He is currently engaged in a fierce turf battle for control of the project's lucrative drug trade.

Cooney He is now serving a life sentence in federal prison.

Preto He is now serving a twenty-year sentence in federal prison. He testified against Cooney and several other officers in exchange for a lesser sentence.

Mr. and Mrs. Chang They still run the store in the Denver Heights, although they now own several others across the city as well.

The East Terrace It was finally closed down and demolished. The area has been turned into a low-income, mixed-housing neighborhood, with the former tenants getting first choice to move back in. Gang members are slowly filtering back in.

The Wheatley Courts The Courts still stand, although a fence has been added. Another generation is slowly taking the reins.

The Denver Heights Another generation of Bloods is slowly taking over, as the younger kids join. Older people are dying, and their homes are being sold to younger couples with children.

The saga of the EASTSIDE will continue...

AFTERWORD

Eastside was the first book I ever wrote. I wrote the book, tucked it away, and then went on to write *Two Thin Dimes*, and another novel, which eventually became an *Essence* bestseller. I sold a couple of novels to a famous author/publisher, and then wrote a couple of television pilots, several screenplays, five more novels, and even parts two and three to the bestseller. In the back of my head over all of those years, however, was my first novel, my first love, *Eastside*.

I dusted *Eastside* off, read it again, and consulted with several people whose opinions I trusted. It had been years since I wrote the novel, and I struggled with the question of its relevance. Was *Eastside* still relevant? I found myself questioning the book's relevance, because like so many others, over the years I had allowed myself to become so focused on the packaging, that I forgot what really mattered, which was the gem inside.

On the exterior, *Eastside* appears to be a coming-of-age story, amidst the gang violence of the inner city; on a deeper level, *Eastside* is so much more. *Eastside* is about the gang violence that has plagued our community; it is about the hopelessness, the poverty, the desolation, and the destruction that has beset our society. *Eastside* is my scream.

I used my ability to compose words to point an accusatory finger at all of those who comfortably lie under a veil of security, a comfortable blanket of feigned ignorance at the events and activities that take place in our inner-city communities. *Eastside* is my yell at those who sit idly by, unquestionably devoted to maintaining the shackles and limitations imposed children are dying in the streets. I shout at those who have not lifted their voices and screamed to the top of their lungs, and called attention to the destruction taking place within our communities.

When I originally wrote *Eastside*, it was my intention to take the readers on an exploratory journey into the socio-economic conditions that incubate and produce Lil Fades, Dejuans, Too-Lows, and Travons. It was my intention to illuminate the wanton violence, the homicides, the illicit drug trade, the debilitating poverty, and in general, the miasmic conditions that result in an infestation of gangs, and gang affiliation, which are often multi-generational afflictions in many urban communities. *Eastside* is an alarming beacon to us all.

There exists a perpetual pendulum of violence that swings from one generation to the next, and for the sake of our survival, we must discover why. Why do our children kill and destroy? What is it within their world that makes them capable of committing such atrocities? Why can one grandmother sit on her porch and safely watch the sun set, whilst another must live in fear behind a barricade of chains, locks, bolts, bars, and weapons? How can there exist two different worlds within one city, or even within a few minutes' driving distance from one another? Why is it that in this day and age, an African American grandmother feels lucky if she has only one grandchild in prison? What have we as a people descended to?

I believe the true tragedy of *Eastside*, is that it is a mirror image of many areas within urban America. *Eastside* is not a special set of circumstances, nor is it particular to a certain geographical area. The saga of *Eastside* is being played out all across America, in all of its epic violence, and destructive tragedy. Our children are being forced to survive in concrete jungles, where they are rapidly devolving into one of two things. They are becoming either predator or prey.

There are no easy answers, nor easy solutions for the conditions described within this novel. Midnight basketball games, gun buyback programs, three strikes laws, and federal minimum mandatory sentences will not solve our problems. Those are someone else's solutions to *our* problems, and it is our political marginalization that forces us to accept those impositions. Dead men and convicted felons do not count; dead men and convicted felons cannot vote.

For the majority of our youth, those that survive to experience the ripe old age of eighteen, an even more precarious monster is awaiting them, a prison industrial complex, that is truly a multi-headed hydra of despair. This hydra has evolved into a jobs program for rural communities hit hard by BRAC, the Base Realignment and Closure Committee. It is a multi-billion-dollar boon for an already wealthy corporate America; it is a population control monster that removes the men from our communities when they are at their most productive ages; it is a political control mechanism, as convicted felons no longer have the right to vote; and it is a socioeconomic control mechanism, as most employers will not hire convicted felons, thus limiting upward mobility, and ensuring the prison industrial complex of a plentiful supply of inner-city youths from the next generation. This prison industrial complex is a living organism, because the more it eats, the more it grows. The more young African Americans it ingest, the more prisons that it will need to build, and thus, it grows. Again, the answers will not come easy.

In bringing this novel to the forefront, I also encountered a contingent of people who questioned why I would want to publish something so negative and damaging to the global perception of African Americans. Why not use my talents to write something more positive, I was asked. It is to this contingent that I quote James Baldwin.

"The responsibility of a writer is to excavate the experience of the people who produced him."

We, as a people, hail from a multitude of socioeconomic, educational, cultural, and geographical backgrounds. Our experiences are as numerous and varied as there are grains of sand in the Sahara. I chose to tell a story that would hopefully bring light to the debilitating conditions of one segment of my people. We do not all live in Prince George's County, or Montgomery County, Maryland; or in Stone Mountain, or Alpharetta,

Georgia; just as we do not all live in the Fifth Ward, Marci, Pink House, The Magnolia, or Watts. I chose to tell a story so that we could hopefully examine ourselves, our conditions, and if not find solutions, then at least begin to ask the questions that would eventually lead to the solutions. Again, I wrote this novel to scream.

I also decided to publish this novel for one other reason: Those of us who survived have an obligation to tell the stories of those who did not. We have an obligation to shout, to bring attention to their lives, to bring some kind of meaning to their lives, and to try to reach out to future generations on their behalf. We have an obligation to their families to not forget. The living owe it to the dead to never forget.

Across this nation, tens of thousands of young African American men donned red bandannas and blue ones, and went to war with one another over absolutely nothing. We actually fought a civil war with one another, over nothing. There was something inside of me that refused to allow those deaths to go unnoticed, unspoken of, to be meaningless. If this book changes one child, just one, then it has done its job.

I close by pointing something out to you. I intentionally left out any African American fathers in this book. It was done to highlight their absence in our communities. If I were to have included one father, just one good and decent African American male in this novel, I would have had to cut down the violence in the book, by at least fifty percent. That's how much of a difference just one good Black man being a role model within his community can make. Just one could change the lives of numerous children. Black men, grab our sons and our daughters. The task is daunting, but not insurmountable. Their greatest heroes are not the ones they see carrying a ball on television, it's that one who walks through the door in the evening, with his hands dirty from doing a hard day's work.

Our children are dying. They are dying young, and they are dying in droves. Each year, the shooters and the victims are getting younger and younger. Our babies are being born, and sacrificed to the inner city. They are, in essence, being born to die. This is the true tragedy of *Eastside*. Let us commit ourselves to working hard and rebuilding our communities, so that we can end this tragedy within our generation. Ten years from now, let there exist no reason for another novel like *Eastside*. Let this subject matter become an alien concept to our posterity.

Thank you for listening, and may God bless you and keep you.

Sincerely,

Caleb Alexander

ABOUT THE AUTHOR

Caleb Alexander resides in San Antonio, Texas with his family. He is an *Essence* No. 1 bestselling author and has written *Two Thin Dimes* (to be released in 2008), *When Lions Dance, One Size Fits All, Big Black Boots* and *Next Time I Fall*. The author has also written several television dramas, and the hilarious and touching screenplay, *Finding Gabriel*. He has also penned the action/adventure screenplay *The Team*, a political thriller titled *UNICOR* and several articles for various magazines. The author can be reached via email at Caleb@calebalexanderonline.com. For more information you can visit the author's website at www.calebalexanderonline.com

SNEAK PREVIEW! EXCERPT FROM

Two Thin Dimes

BY CALEB ALEXANDER

COMING FROM STREBOR BOOKS JANUARY 2008

CHAPTER ONE

Jamaica had always been blessed. Physically, emotionally, spiritually, financially, and mentally. From her beautiful, silky, copper skin, to her captivating emerald-colored eyes. She was blessed with smooth almond-colored hair, which flowed readily down her miraculously well-proportioned, sultry, sinewy figure. But most of all, she was blessed with a voice.

It was a voice that could deliver notes so high, that the bats which inhabited the cool dark Gotham night, danced and rejoiced at each melodious rendition. It was a voice that could resound so low, that walls shook, and a cannon's deep thunderous boom, would fall silent in envy. It was a harmonious voice, a melodious voice, a multi-platinum, over one hundred and fifty-million albums sold worldwide voice. It was the voice of Jamaica Tiera Rochelle, who to her tens of millions of fans worldwide, was simply known as Tiera.

"Cut! That's a wrap!" bellowed Tony Battles, the hottest young director in the entire music video industry.

Tony was young, black, gifted, and arrogant. His short-cut, wavy hair, and hip, urban fashions, which hung from his thin frame with just the right amount of cool bagginess, along with his quick devilish smile, made him feel that he was God's gift to women. ALL WOMEN.

Tony rose carefully from his director's chair, which had been custom made so that the word "*DIRECTOR*" loomed large on its front and back, and sauntered confidently across the set, stepping over cables and wires, dodging video cameras and lighting equipment, as well as personnel.

The video shoot had been a night one, outdoors. The weather was quite mild for New York this time of the year, and everyone was taking advantage of it. Dancers, lighting equipment, cameras, spectators, fill-ins, gophers, makeup artists, pyrotechnic experts, models, choreographers, animal trainers and animals, along with the usual assortment of bystanders and hangers-on filled the area.

Jamaica, tired and perspiring from the previous dance routine, as well as the intense heat of the lighting and the thick layers of commercial makeup, strode across the set to speak with her friend, publicist, and personal assistant, LaChina Anderson.

"Good job, Jai." LaChina clapped. She pulled several pieces of tissue from her pocket and handed them to her friend.

"Thanks," Jamaica told her. She took the tissue and wiped away her beads of perspiration. Along with them came thick globs of television makeup.

Jamaica exhaled a cool sigh of relief. "Ooooh, girl, I'm glad that's finally over." She smiled wearily at her friend. "No more videos?"

LaChina returned Jamaica's smile and nodded reassuringly. "No more videos...for now."

"I need a vacation," Jamaica told her. She rubbed her hand across her stomach, now realizing how little she was actually wearing, and how much she was actually exposing. Her black knit tights were almost see-through, while her white cotton half-shirt exposed her sexy, tight mid-section. Her well-proportioned figure was the product of natural endowment, as well as a dedicated and expensive personal trainer.

LaChina, on the other hand, was exquisitely dressed as usual. Chanel frames rested comfortably midway down her nose. They stylishly matched her DKNY pantsuit and Ferragamo shoes. And of course in her hand rested her ever-present, leather-covered, gold-embroidered Mont Blanc clipboard.

LaChina had been Jamaica's best friend since as far back as either could remember. They had grown up together in several of the wealthiest communities in New York state. Each of their futures had been decided by their mothers prior to their births.

Jamaica's mother had designed a future for her daughter that included singing, acting, dancing, modeling, and a life of sheer glamour. Hundreds of talent shows, music lessons, voice coaches, personal trainers, and performance academies later, here she stood.

LaChina's university professor mother had stressed education over all else, despite her daughter's natural beauty. Growing up, LaChina often tied and sometimes even defeated Jamaica in beauty contests. Her flawless skin, pearlescent smile, and long silky hair often caused men to stop and stare in the streets. Nevertheless, many honor rolls, academic awards, certificates, scholarships, and class presidencies later, here she stood.

LaChina had graduated magna cum laude from Spelman College in Atlanta, and returned home to New York with a degree in management, where she began working for her best friend.

"Jai, girl, Bev and I were just talking about how tired you've been looking," LaChina told her. "I think a vacation would be a pretty good idea."

LaChina lifted her index finger to her face and tapped lightly at the bottom of her chin. "How about a working vacation?" she asked Jamaica. "We want to shoot the next video in a sunny location, so…while we lounge around like tourists, we put on hats and sunglasses, and scout locations."

Jamaica clasped her friend's arms and shouted excitedly. "Yes! Yes! You know how I love the Caribbean; when do we leave?"

"Actually, we have to do the Sea World promotion first, and from there we can head to the Caribbean."

The thought of sea animals and slimy skin made Jamaica recoil. "The Sea World thing, yuck!" Jamaica's head fell to one side and she exhaled forcibly. "Do I have to?"

"Jai, it's for the kids," LaChina told her. "Plus, every time somebody kisses that damn fish their popularity goes up, their record sales bloom, and their bank accounts fatten."

Jamaica released LaChina's arm and shook her head emphatically. "I have to kiss that thing? Uh-un, hell no!" Jamaica turned and started to race away. "There is no way that I'm going to kiss a giant fish!"

LaChina quickly grabbed Jamaica by her arm stopping her. "It's a whale."

Jamaica turned and stared at her friend. "You called it a fish first, not me."

"We're going," LaChina told her.

Jamaica pouted. "It might eat me."

"Jai."

"It's slimy!"

"Jai."

Tony Battles, who had stopped to chat with Jamaica's label representatives, finally closed in. He had the gleam of money in his eyes. Lots of money.

"Hello, ladies," he greeted them.

Jamaica smiled and gave a slight wave. "Hello, Tony."

"Hi, Tony," LaChina replied.

Tony Battles' smile resembled the cat that bought the canary and had it tied up inside of its litter box. He focused in on Jamaica. "Tiera, with you we didn't even need lighting. Your beauty lit up the place."

When Jamaica turned to LaChina she found that her friend was already staring at her. Their eyes locked for several seconds, before Jamaica spoke.

"Girl, I give that a one," she told LaChina.

LaChina nodded. "Yeah, that was kinda weak. I was gonna give it a two, but when I consider the fact that it came from a Morehouse man, who should have come a lot stronger, I'm inclined to agree with you. That's a one."

Together they turned and faced the young director.

"Good-bye, Tony," they said in unison.

Deflated, Tony's mouth remained open, as he watched them walk away.

Jamaica placed her arm inside of LaChina's, as they casually strolled toward the dressing room. In this case, the dressing room was a converted trailer, which had been lavishly outfitted.

"See what I have to put up with?" Jamaica asked her friend. She exhaled loudly and tossed her hair back over her shoulders as they walked. "From dancers, actors, professional athletes, and scores of other people. Either they want to screw me because of the money, or they want to fuck me because of the fame."

"I know, girl." LaChina nodded. "I get it all of the time, and from educated, professional brothers too."

Jamaica rested her head on her friend's shoulder and clasped her hand. "I just want a good man. One without a line, without the number to the tabloids inside of his back pocket, and without dollar signs in his eyes. I want a man for Jamaica, not for Tiera, the Grammy award-winning artist. Not for Tiera, the *Billboard* R&B and Pop Artist of the Year. Not for Tiera, the Soul Train Music Award-winning songstress…"

LaChina poked out her bottom lip and interrupted her friend. "Not for Tiera, the ga-zillion platinum-selling recording artist, and most sought-after actress in Hollywood?"

"You understand?" Jamaica asked her.

LaChina smiled and leaned to the side, wrapping her arm tightly around Jamaica. "Oh, my sister! Looking for Prince Charming to come and rescue you from a life of wealth, stardom, and fame. Poor little rich girl."

"Don't tease me," Jamaica whined.

They stopped just outside of the trailer, where Jamaica reached for the door. She pulled it open still laughing at her friend. Inside at the table sat Jamaica's mother, Beverly Rochelle. She saw them first.

"Oh, Jamaica darling, I'm glad that you are…"

Jamaica closed her eyes and rapidly shut the trailer door, cutting her mother off in mid-sentence. She turned to her friend and leaned her back against the trailer's door.

"China," Jamaica called out to her friend softly.

"What?"

"Girl, get me outta here."